FEARLESS 2

ALSO BY FRANCINE PASCAL

FEARLESS

FEARLESS
2

TWISTED · KISS · PAYBACK

FRANCINE PASCAL

SIMON PULSE

NEW YORK   LONDON   TORONTO   SYDNEY   NEW DELHI

This book is a work of fiction. Any references to historical events, real people, or real places are used fictitiously. Other names, characters, places, and events are products of the author's imagination, and any resemblance to actual events or places or persons, living or dead, is entirely coincidental.

Produced by Alloy Entertainment
151 West 26th Street, New York, NY 10001

SIMON PULSE
An imprint of Simon & Schuster Children's Publishing Division
1230 Avenue of the Americas, New York, NY 10020
This Simon Pulse paperback edition February 2013

For information about special discounts for bulk purchases,
please contact Simon & Schuster Special Sales at 1-866-506-1949
or business@simonandschuster.com.
The Simon & Schuster Speakers Bureau can bring authors to your
live event. For more information or to book an event contact the
Simon & Schuster Speakers Bureau at 1-866-248-3049 or visit
our website at www.simonspeakers.com.
Designed by Angela Goddard
The text of this book was set in Dante MT Std.
Manufactured in the United States of America
10 9 8 7 6 5 4 3 2 1
Library of Congress Control Number 2012938525
ISBN 978-1-4424-6860-3
ISBN 978-1-4424-6861-0 (eBook)
These books were originally published individually.

CONTENTS

TWISTED

To Johnny Stewart Carmen

GAIA

There are circles in Hell.

My father—back when he still cared that I was alive and breathing—used to make me read. Not easy stuff. Even when I was a kid, there was no *Winnie-the-Pooh*, no *Little House on the Prairie*. Not for me.

It was all about the classics. *Hard* classics.

One of the moldy oldies he put under my nose was *The Inferno*, by Dante. This book was seriously tough sledding. The whole thing was written in verse, and it was full of political stuff that didn't always make a lot of sense, and the language was creaky to say the least. But there were good parts.

In this story a guy gets led all around Hell to see how

everybody is punished. A lot of it is kind of like you would expect. Lots of demons with whips. Fire. Snakes. That kind of thing.

But the idea that stuck with me was the way Hell was divided up in circles. The dead guys up in the first circle don't have it so bad. It's just kind of rainy and dull up there. But the really bad people, like murderers (or members of a political party Dante didn't like), they get shoved way down to a circle where they have to run around without feet or burst into flame or get eaten by big lizards or melt like candles.

I remembered this book the other day and started thinking that my life could be sliced up in the same way as hell.

There are the little things. Finding out the deli is out of Krispy Kreme. Losing a chess game against some moron I should have schooled. That's the gloomy, first-circle sort of hell.

Then there's having to live with George and Ella. George knew my father, but I don't really know him. Ella didn't know my father, doesn't know me, and I don't even *want* to know Ella. She's definitely a deeper level of hell.

The next level down is high school. It gets a level of hell all to itself.

Below that comes Sam and Heather. I wouldn't throw Sam in a pit by himself. I mean, Sam's the guy I want to be with. The only guy I've ever wanted to be with. But Sam is with Heather, and together they deserve pitchforks and brimstone.

Then there's my father. My father disappears, doesn't write, doesn't call, and doesn't give me a clue about what's going on. Now we're getting really deep. Snakes and fire. Demons with weird Latin names.

And my mom. The way I feel when I think about her. When I think about her death. Well, that brings us right down to the bottom.

The way Dante tells it, the *very* bottom layer of hell isn't hot. Instead it's a big lake of ice with people frozen inside. They're stuck forever with only their faces sticking out, and every time they cry, it just adds another layer of frost covering their eyes.

Put my whole life together, and that's where I am. Down on the ice. Some days I feel like I have a pair of skates. Other days I wonder if Dante didn't get it wrong. Maybe the ice isn't the lowest level after all.

THE HIGH
SCHOOL
CIRCLE

HER BIG PAL GAVE HER A LITTLE LOVE PAT—
ENOUGH TO BOUNCE HER FROM THE WALL AND
BACK TO HIS BEEFY HAND.

JERKUS
HIGHSCHOOLENSIS

Pretty people do ugly things. It was one of those laws of nature that Gaia had understood for years. If she ever started to forget that rule for a second, there always seemed to be some good-looking asshole ready to remind her.

She stumbled up the steps and pushed her way inside The Village School with five minutes to spare before her first class. Actually early. Of course, her hair was still wet from the shower and her homework wasn't done, but being there—actually physically inside the building before the bell rang—was a new experience. For twelve whole seconds after that, she thought she might have an all right day.

Then she caught a glimpse of one of those things that absolutely defines the high school circle of hell.

Down at the end of the row of lockers, a tall, broad-shouldered guy was smiling a very confident smile, wearing very popular-crowd clothes, and using a very big hand to pin a very much smaller girl up against the wall. There was an amused expression on Mr. Handsome's face.

Only the girl who was stuck between his hand and fifty years' worth of ugly green paint didn't look like she thought it was funny.

Gaia had noticed the big boy in a couple of her classes

but hadn't bothered to file away his name. Tad, she thought, or maybe it was Chip. She knew it was something like that.

From the way girls in class talked, he was supposed to be cute. Gaia could sort of see it. Big blue eyes. Good skin. Six-five even without the air soles in his two-hundred-dollar sneakers. His lips were a little puffy, but then, some people liked that. It was the hair that really eliminated him from Gaia's list of guys worth looking at.

He wore that stuff in his hair. The stuff that looked like a combination of motor oil and maple syrup. The stuff that made it look like he hadn't washed his hair this side of tenth grade. "What's the rush, Darla?" the Chipster said. "I just want to know what he said to you."

The girl, Darla, shook her head. "He didn't . . ."

Her big pal gave her a little love pat—enough to bounce her from the wall and back to his beefy hand.

"Don't give me that," he said, still all smiles. "I saw you two together."

Gaia did a quick survey of the hall. There was a trio of khaki-crowd girls fifty yards down and two leather dudes hanging near the front door. A skinny guy stuck his head out of a classroom, saw who was doing the shoving, and quickly ducked back in. Gaia had to give him some credit. At least he looked. Everybody else in the hallway was Not Noticing so hard, it hurt.

Gaia really didn't need this. She didn't know the girl against the wall. Sure, the guy with the big hands was a prime example of *Jerkus highschoolensis,* but it was absolutely none of Gaia's business. She turned away and headed for class, wondering if she might avoid a tardy slip for the first time in a week.

"Just let me . . . ," the girl begged from behind her.

"In a minute, babe," replied the guy with the hands. "I just need to talk to you a little." There was a thump and a short whimper from the girl.

Gaia stopped. She really, really didn't need this.

She took a deep breath, turned, and headed back toward the couple.

The easiest thing would be to grab the guy by the face and teach him how soft a skull was compared to a concrete wall. But then, smashing someone's head would probably not help Gaia's reputation.

Words were an option. She hadn't used that method much, but there was a first time for everything, right?

She could try talking to the guy or even threatening to tell a teacher. Gaia didn't care if anyone at the school thought she was a wimp or a narc, or whatever they called it in New York City. That was the least of her problems. Besides, they already thought she was a bitch for not warning Heather about the park slasher.

Before long, Gaia was so close that both partners in the

ugly little dance turned to look at her. Tough Guy's smile didn't budge an inch.

"What?" he said.

Gaia struggled for something to say. Something smooth. Something that would defuse this whole thing. She paused for a second, cleared her throat, and said . . .

"Is there . . . uh, some kind of a problem?"

Brilliant.

The guy who might be named Chip took a two-second look at her face, then spent twice as long trying to size up the breasts under Gaia's rumpled football shirt.

"Nothing you gotta worry about," he said, still staring at her chest. He waved the hand that wasn't busy holding a person. "This is a private conversation."

The girl against the wall looked at Gaia with a big-eyed, round-mouthed expression that could have been fear or hope or stupidity. Gaia's instant impression was that it was a little bit of all three. The girl had straight black hair that was turned up in a little flip, tanned-to-a-golden-brown skin, an excess of eye shadow, and a cheerleading uniform. She didn't exactly strike Gaia as a brain trust.

Not that being a cheerleader automatically made somebody stupid. Gaia was certain there were smart cheerleaders. Somewhere there had to be cheerleaders who were working on physics theories every time they put down their pompoms. She hadn't met any, but they were out there. Probably living in the same city with all the nice guys who don't mind if a girl has thunder thighs and doesn't know how to dress.

"Well?" demanded Puffy Lips. "What's wrong with you? Are you deaf or just stupid?"

Gaia tensed. Anger left an acid taste in her throat. Suddenly her fist was crying out for his face. She opened her mouth to say something just as the bell for first period rang. So much for being on time.

She took a step closer to the pair. "Why don't you let her go?"

Chip made a little grunting laugh and shook his head. "Look, babe. Get out of here," he said to Gaia.

Babe. It wasn't necessarily an insult—unless the person saying it added that perfect tone of voice. The tone that says being a babe is on the same evolutionary rung as being a brain-damaged hamster.

Gaia glanced up the hallway. Only a few students were still in the hall, and none were close. If she planned to do anything without everyone in school seeing it, this was the time.

She leaned toward him. "Maybe you'd better get out of here," she said in a low voice. She could feel the cheerleader's short breaths on the back of her neck. "You don't want to be late for class."

The sunny smile slipped from Chip's face, replaced by a go-away-you're-bothering-me frown. "Did you hear me tell you to go?"

Gaia shrugged. It was coming. That weird rush she sometimes felt.

"I heard you. I just didn't listen."

Now the expression on Chip's face was more like an I-guess-I'm-going-to-have-to-teach-you-how-the-world-works sneer. "Get the hell out of my way," he snapped.

"Make me."

He took his hand off Darla and grabbed Gaia by the arm.

Gaia was glad. If she touched him first, there was always the chance he would actually admit he got beat up by a girl and charge her with assault. But since Chip made the first move, all bets were off. Everything that happened from that first touch was self-defense.

Gaia was an expert in just about every martial art with a name. Jujitsu. Tai kwon do. Judo. Kung fu. If it involved hitting, kicking, or tossing people through the air, Gaia knew it. Standing six inches from Mr. Good Skin Bad Attitude, she could have managed a kick that would have taken his oily head right off his thick neck. She could have put a stiff hand through his rib cage or delivered a punch that drove his heart up against his spine.

But she didn't do any of that. She wanted to, but she didn't.

Moving quickly, she turned her arms and twisted out of his grip. Before Chip could react, she reached across with her left hand, took hold of the guy's right thumb, and gave it just a little . . . push.

For a moment Puffy Lips Chip looked surprised. Then Gaia pushed a little harder on his captive digit, and the look of surprise instantly turned to pain.

He tried to pull away, but Gaia held tight. She was working hard to keep from actually breaking his thumb. She could have broken his whole oversized hand like a bundle of big dry sticks. The real trick was hurting someone without really hurting someone. Don't break any bones. Don't leave any scars. Don't do anything permanent. Leave a memory.

"What do you think, Chip?" Gaia asked, still pushing his thumb toward the back of his hand. "Should you be shoving girls around?"

"Let go of me, you little—" He reached for her with his free hand.

Gaia leaned back out of his range and gave an extra shove. Chip wailed.

"Here's the deal," Gaia said quietly. "You keep your hands to yourself, I let you keep your hands. What do you think?"

Chip's knees were starting to shake, and there were beads of sweat breaking out on his forehead. "Who are—"

"Like I really want you to know my name." She pushed harder, and now Gaia could feel the bones in his thumb pulling loose from his hand. Another few seconds and one was sure to snap. "Do we have a deal?"

"Okay," he squeaked in a voice two octaves higher than it had been a few seconds before. "Sure."

Gaia let go. "That's good, Chip." The moment the physical conflict ended, Gaia felt all her uncertainty come rushing back. She glanced up the hallway and was relieved to see that there was no crowd of gawkers. That didn't stop her from feeling dizzy. She was acting like muscle-bound freak girl right in the main hallway at school. This was definitely not the way to remain invisible.

Puffy Lips stepped back and gripped his bruised thumb in his left hand. "Brad."

"What?"

"Brad," he said. "My name isn't Chip. It's Brad."

Gaia rolled her eyes. "Whatever." She lowered her head and shoved past him just as the late bell rang.

Another day, another fight, another tardy.

THINGS GAIA KNOWS:

School sucks.

Ella sucks.

Her father sucks.

Heather Gannis sucks big time.

THINGS GAIA WANTS TO KNOW:

Who kidnapped Sam?

Why did they contact her?

What was with all those stupid tests?

How could she have let the kidnappers get away after everything they'd done to her and Sam?

Why did Mr. Rupert use the words "all right" more often than most people used the word "the"?

Who killed CJ?

Why did she never know she had an uncle who looked exactly like her father?

Was said uncle going to contact her again?

Did she even want him to after he'd been nonexistent for her entire life?

Why did anyone in their right mind choose to drink skim milk?

Was she really expected to pay attention in class when there were things going on that actually mattered?

THE DECISION

Even back when his legs worked, Ed had never been fearless.

He sat in his first-period class and stared at the door. Any moment, the bell would ring. Then he would go out into the hallway and Gaia would appear. Any moment, he would have his chance. In the meantime he was terrified.

People who had seen him on a skateboard or a pair of in-lines might have been surprised to hear it. There had been no stairs too steep to slalom, no handrail Ed wasn't willing to challenge, no traffic too thick to dare. Anyone would tell you, Ed Fargo was a wild man. He took more risks, and took them faster, than any other boarder in the city.

The dark secret was that all through those days, almost every second, Ed had been terrified. Every time his wheels had sent sparks lancing from a metal rail, every time he had gone over a jump and felt gravity tugging down at his stomach, Ed had been sure he was about to die.

And when it didn't happen, when he landed, and lived, and rolled on to skate another day, it had been a thousand times sweeter just because he had been so scared. It seemed to Ed that there was nothing better than that moment after the terror had passed.

Then he lost the use of his legs and grew a wheelchair on his butt, and everything changed. A wheelchair didn't give the sort of thrills you got from a skateboard. There were a few times, especially right after he realized he was never, ever going to get out of the chair, that Ed had thought about taking the contraption out into traffic—just to see how well it played with the taxis and delivery vans. That kind of thinking was scary in a whole different, definitely less fun way.

Legs or no legs, Ed wasn't sure that any stunt he had pulled in the past had terrified him as much as the one he was about to attempt.

He stared at the classroom door, and the blood rushing through his brain sounded as loud as a subway train pulling up to the platform.

He was going to tell Gaia Moore that he loved her.

He was really going to do it. If he didn't faint first.

Ed had been infatuated with Gaia since he first saw her in the school hallway. He was half smitten as soon as they spoke and all the way gone within a couple of days.

Since then, Ed and Gaia had become friends—or at least they had come as close to being friends as Gaia's don't-get-close-to-me force field would allow. To tell Gaia how he really felt would mean risking the relationship they already shared. Ed was horrified by the thought of losing contact with Gaia, but he was determined to take that chance.

For once, he was going to see what it was like to be fearless.

SOUR SEVENTEEN

One idiot an hour. Gaia figured that if they would let her beat up one butthead per class, it would make the day go oh-so-smoothly. She would get the nervous energy out of her system, add a few high points to her dull-as-a-bowling-ball day, and by the time the final bell rang, the world would have eight fewer losers. All good things.

It might also help her keep her mind off Sam Moon. Sam, whose life she had saved more than once. Sam, who was oblivious to her existence. Sam, who had the biggest bitch this side of Fifth Avenue for a girlfriend but didn't seem to notice.

And still Gaia couldn't stop thinking about him. Daydreaming her way through each and every class. If her teachers had tested her on self-torture, she would have gotten an A.

Gaia trudged out of her third-period classroom and shouldered her way through the clogged hallway, her cruise control engaged. Every conscious brain cell was dedicated to the ongoing problem of what to do about her irritating and somewhat embarrassing Sam problem.

It was like a drug problem, only slightly less messy.

It was bad enough that Sam was with Heather. Even worse was Heather getting credit for everything Gaia did.

Gaia had nearly lost her life saving Sam from a kidnapper. She had gone crazy looking for him. And then Heather had stepped in at the last second and looked like the big hero when her total expended effort was equal to drying her fingernails.

Not to mention the fact that the kidnappers had gotten away after they spent an entire day ordering her around as if she were a toy poodle.

Gaia suddenly realized she was biting her lip so badly that it was about to bleed. Whenever she thought about how the nameless, faceless men in black had used her, she got the uncontrollable urge to do serious violence to something. Then, of course, her thoughts turned directly to Heather.

And the fact that Heather had sex with Sam. And the fact that Heather had taken credit for saving Sam. And the fact that Heather got to hold hands with Sam and kiss Sam and talk to Sam and—

Gaia came to a stop in front of her locker and kicked it hard, denting the bottom of the door. A couple of Gap girls turned to stare, so Gaia kicked it again. The Gap girls scurried away.

She snarled at her vague reflection in the battered door. In the dull metal she was only an outline. That's all she was to Sam, too. A vague shadow of nothing much.

For a few delusional days Gaia had thought Sam might

be the one. The one to break her embarrassing record as the only unkissed seventeen-year-old on planet Earth. Maybe even the one to turn sex from hypothesis into reality. But it wasn't going to happen.

There wasn't going to be any sex. There was never going to be any kissing. Not with Sam. Not ever.

Gaia yanked open the door of her locker, tossed in the book she was carrying, and randomly took out another without bothering to look at it. Then she slammed the door just as hard as she had kicked it.

She squeezed her eyes shut for a moment, squeezed hard, as if she could squeeze out her unwanted thoughts.

Even though Gaia knew zilch about love, knew less about relationships, and knew even less about psychology, she knew exactly what her girlfriends, if she had any, would tell her.

Find a new guy. Someone to distract you. Someone who cares about you.

Right. No problem.

Unfortunately, it had only taken her seventeen years to find a guy who didn't care about her.

THE ATTEMPT

Navigation of high school hallways takes on a whole new meaning when you're three feet wide and mounted on wheels.

Ed Fargo skidded around a corner, narrowly avoided a collision with a janitor, then spun right past a knot of students laughing at some private joke. He threw the chair into hard reverse and did a quick 180 to dodge a stream of band students lugging instruments out a doorway, then he powered through a gap, coasted down a ramp, and took the next corner so hard, he went around on one wheel.

Fifty feet away, Gaia Moore was just shutting the door of her locker. Ed let the chair coast to a halt as he watched her. Gaia's football shirt was wrinkled, and her socks didn't match. Most of her yellow hair had slipped free of whatever she had been using to hold it in a ponytail. Loose strands hovered around the sculpted planes of her face, and the remaining hair gathered at the back of her head in a heavy, tumbled mass.

She was the most beautiful thing that Ed had ever seen.

He gave the wheels of his chair a sharp push and darted ahead of some slow walkers. Before Gaia could take two steps, Ed was at her side.

"Looking for your next victim?" he asked.

Gaia glanced down, and for a moment the characteristic frown on her insanely kissable lips was replaced by a smile. "Hey, Ed. What's up?"

Ed almost turned around and left. Why should he push it? He could live on that smile for at least a month.

Fearless, he told himself. Be fearless.

"I guess you don't want us to win at basketball this year," he started, trying to keep the tone light.

Gaia looked puzzled. "What?"

"The guy you went after this morning, Brad Reston," Ed continued. "He's a starting forward."

"How did you hear about it?" The frown was back full force.

"From Darla Rigazzi," Ed answered. "She's talked you up in every class this morning."

"Yeah, well, I wish she wouldn't." She looked away and started up the hallway again, the smooth muscles of her legs stretching under faded jeans.

Ed kept pace for fifty feet. Twice he opened his mouth to say something, but he shut it again before a word escaped. There was a distant, distracted look on Gaia's face now. The moment had passed. He would have to wait.

No, a voice said from the back of his mind. Don't wait. Tell her now. Tell her everything.

"Gaia . . . ," he started.

Something in his tone must have caught Gaia's attention. She stopped in the middle of one long stride and turned to him. Her right eyebrow was raised, and her changing eyes were the blue-gray of the Atlantic fifty miles off the coast. "What's wrong, Ed?"

Ed swallowed. Suddenly he felt like he was back on his skateboard, ready to challenge the bumpy ride down another flight of steps—only the steps in front of him went down, and down, and down forever.

He swallowed hard and shook his head. "It's not important."

I love you.

"Nothing at all, really."

I want to be with you.

"Just . . . nothing in particular."

I want you to be with me.

"I'll talk to you after class."

Gaia stared at him for a moment longer, then nodded. "All right. I'll see you later." She turned around and walked off quickly, her long legs eating up the distance.

"Perfect," Ed whispered to her retreating back.

A perfect pair. She was brave to the point of almost being dangerous, and he was gutless to the point of almost being depressing.

GAIA

Sometimes I wonder what I would say if I were ever asked out on a date.

You'd think that since it's never happened to me, I might have had some time in the past seventeen years to formulate the perfect response. You'd think that with all the movies I've seen, I would have at least picked up some cheesy line. Some doe-eyed, swooning acceptance.

But I pretty much stay away from romantic comedies. There's no relationship advice to be had from a Neil LaBute film.

Besides, you can't formulate the perfect response for a situation you can't remotely imagine.

I figure that if it ever does happen (not probable), I'll end up saying something along the lines of "uh" or slight variations thereof.

"Uh . . . uh," if the guy's a freak.

"Uh . . . huh," if the guy's a nonfreak.

I wonder what Heather said to Sam when he first asked her out. Probably something disgustingly perfect. Something right out of a movie. Something like, "I was wondering when you'd ask." Or maybe Heather asked Sam out. And he said something like, "It would be my honor."

Okay. Stomach now reacting badly. Must think about something else.

What did Heather say when *Ed* asked her out?

Okay. Stomach now severely cramping.

So what happens after the "Uh . . . huh"?

Awkward pauses, I assume. Idiot small talk, sweaty palms (his), dry mouth (also his), bad food. (I imagine dates don't happen at places where they have good food—like Gray's Papaya or Dojo's.)

And I won't even get into what happens after the most likely difficult digestion. What does the nonfreak expect at that point? Hand holding? Kissing? Groping? Heavy groping? Sex?

Stomach no longer wishes to be a component of body.

Must stop here.

Luckily I won't ever have to deal with any of this. Because no nonfreak will ever ask me out. And no freak will ever get more than the initial grunt.

PAINFULLY
BEAUTIFUL

AND WITH THOSE WORDS, GAIA'S SEVENTEEN-YEAR
STREAK OFFICIALLY CAME TO AN END.

THE OFFER

The schedule was a Xerox. Maybe a Xerox of a Xerox. Whatever it was, the print was so faint and muddy that David Twain had to squint hard and hold the sheet of paper up to the light just to make out a few words.

He lowered the folded page and looked around him. People were streaming past on all sides. The students at this school were visibly different. They moved faster. Talked faster. Dressed like they expected a society photographer to show up at any minute. They were, David thought, probably all brain-dead.

Still, nobody else seemed to be having a hard time finding the right room. Of course, the rest of them had spent more than eight minutes in the building.

A bell rang right over his head. The sound of it was so loud that it seemed to jar the fillings in his teeth. David winced and looked up at the clanging bell. That was when he noticed that the number above the door and the room number on the schedule were the same.

A half-dozen students slipped past David as he stood in the doorway. He turned to follow, caught a bare glimpse of movement from the corner of his eye, and the next thing he knew, he was flying through the air.

He landed hard on his butt. All at once he bit his tongue,

dropped his brand-new books, and let out a sound that reminded him of a small dog that had been kicked. The books skidded twenty feet, letting out a spray of loose papers as they went.

The bell stopped ringing. In the space of seconds the remaining students in the hallway dived into classrooms. David found himself alone.

Almost.

"Sorry."

It was a mumbled apology. Not much conviction there.

David looked up to see a tall girl with loose, tangled blond hair standing over him.

"Yeah," he said. There was a warm, salty taste in his mouth. Blood. And his butt ached from the fall. At the moment those things didn't matter.

"You okay?" the girl asked, shoving her hand in her pocket and looking like she'd rather be anywhere but there.

"Yeah," he said again, reaching back to touch his spine. "I'm fine. Great."

The girl shook her head. "If you say so." She offered her hand, even as her face took on an even more sour expression.

Her tousled hair spilled down across her shoulders as she reached to him.

"Thanks." David took her hand and let her help him to his feet. The girl's palm was warm. Her fingers were surprisingly strong. "What did I run into?"

"Me."

David blinked. "You knocked me down?"

The blond girl shrugged and released his hand. "I didn't do it on purpose."

"You must have been moving pretty fast to hit that hard." David resisted an urge to rub his aches. Instead he offered the hand the girl had just released. "Hi, I'm David Twain."

The girl glanced over her shoulder at the classroom, then stared at David's fingers as if she'd never experienced a handshake before.

"Gaia," she said. "Gaia Moore." She took his hand in hers and gave it a single quick shake.

David was the one who had fallen, but for some reason the simple introduction was enough to make this girl, this painfully beautiful girl, seem awkward.

"Great name," he said. "Like the Earth goddess."

"Yeah, well, if you're okay—"

David shook his head. "No," he said.

Gaia blinked. "What?"

"No," David repeated. "I'm not okay." He leaned toward her and lowered his voice to his best thick whisper. "I won't be okay until you agree to go to dinner with me tomorrow night."

THE RESPONSE

"Uh . . . huh."

"What?" David asked, his very clear blue eyes narrowing.

He was a male. He was, apparently, a nonfreak. He was not Sam. He got the affirmative grunt before Gaia could remind herself of the ramifications.

"I said, uh-huh," Gaia said evenly, lifting her chin.

"Good," he said. "There's this place called Cookies & Couscous. It's more like a bakery than a restaurant. You know it?"

Of course she knew it. Any place that had *cookies* in its name and was located within twenty miles of her room automatically went on Gaia's mental map.

"On Thompson," she said.

"Right." He nodded, and a piece of black hair fell over his forehead. "We can eat some baklava, wash it down with espresso, and worry about having a main course after we're full of dessert."

For a moment Gaia just looked at him. He was tall. Gangly. Almost sweet-looking. Very not Sam.

"Baklava," David repeated with a smirk. "Buttery. Flaky. Honey and nuts."

Gaia nearly smiled. Almost.

This could take her mind off Sam. The kidnappers. The uncle. Heather.

"When?" she said.

He smiled. "Tomorrow? Eight o'clock."

Gaia nodded almost imperceptibly.

His smile widened. "It's a date."

And with those words, Gaia's seventeen-year streak officially came to an end.

THE UNSAID

Heather Gannis couldn't believe what she was about to do, but there was no getting around it. There were too many things that had to be said. Things that couldn't go unsaid much longer. Not without Heather going into a paranoid frenzy. And frenzy was not something Heather did well. She liked to be in control. Always.

She looked at her reflection in the scratched bathroom mirror, tossed her glossy brown hair behind her shoulders, took a deep breath, and plunged into the melee that was the post-lunch hall crowd.

Even in the crush of people it only took Heather about

five seconds to spot Gaia Moore. And her perfectly tousled blond hair. And her supermodel-tall body. Before she could remind herself of how stupid it was to do this in public, Heather walked right up to Gaia and grabbed her arm.

Gaia looked completely surprised.

"We have to talk," Heather said.

Even more surprised. Gaia yanked her arm away. "Doubtful," she said.

Heather fixed her with a leveling glare as she noticed a few curious bystanders pausing to check out the latest Gaia-Heather confrontation. "Bio lab," Heather said. Then she turned on her heel and made her way to the designated room.

She almost couldn't believe it when Gaia walked in moments later.

Gaia raised her eyebrows and shrugged, tucking her hands into the front pockets of her pants. "Call me curious," she said.

Wanting to remain in charge, Heather slapped her books down on top of one of the big, black tables and rested one hand on her hip. "Who kidnapped Sam?" she asked evenly.

"I don't know," Gaia said, suddenly standing up straight.

"Right," Heather said, her ire already rising. "Then why did they contact you?"

"I don't know," Gaia repeated.

Heather scoffed and looked up at the ceiling, concentrating on trying to keep the blood from rising to her face. "Is that all you're going to say?" she spat. "You asked for my help, then you tripped me on the stairs, and I spent two hours stuck with the idiot police at NYU trying to convince them I wasn't some crazed stalker, and all you can say is, 'I don't know'?" She was sounding hysterical. She had to stop.

Gaia shrugged. It was all Heather could do to keep from clocking the girl in the head with her physics book. She took a long, deep breath through her nose, and let it out slowly—audibly. Then she picked up her books, hugging them to her chest, and walked right up to Gaia, the toe of her suede boot just touching the battered rubber of Gaia's sneaker. The girl didn't move.

"Stay away from Sam," Heather said, trying to muster a threatening tone. It wasn't the easiest thing in the world. Gaia had threatened her. Gaia had hurt her. Gaia had almost gotten her killed.

The girl was like a statue.

Heather stepped around Gaia and headed for the door. She stopped to look behind her and Gaia was frozen in place, as if someone were still standing before her speaking.

"Freak," Heather muttered. And with that, she was out the door.

Before Gaia could snap out of it and come after her.

TUG-OF-WAR

The pencil snapped. In the silent lecture hall the noise seemed as loud as a gunshot.

Thirty pairs of eyes turned toward Sam Moon, and from the back of the hall came a muffled snicker. Sam closed his eyes for a moment, then slowly raised his hand.

"Yes, Mr. Moon," the physics professor said with a tone of tired amusement. "You can get another."

Sam closed his blue test folder and searched quickly through his book bag for a replacement pencil. All around him he could hear the quiet scratching of lead on paper as the rest of the class hurried to complete the exam. Sam's progress on the test couldn't exactly be called hurrying. There were one hundred and twenty questions on the test and exactly fifty-seven minutes to answer them all. With forty-five of those minutes gone, Sam was on number twelve.

He finally located another pencil and put the bag back on the floor. He looked down at the next question, touched the pencil to the paper. The pencil snapped into four pieces.

This time there was nothing muffled about the laughter.

The physics professor, an older man with a comb-over so complex, it was a science in itself, let loose a heavy sigh.

"Mr. Moon, if this test is causing you so much stress, might I suggest you try a pen?" he said with a sneer. "I would not want to be responsible for chopping down whole forests of precious trees just to keep you supplied with pencils."

Sam would have liked to smack the guy. He would have liked to ask him if he'd ever taken a physics midterm two days after being released by a group of as yet unidentified kidnapping psychos. He would have liked to get up and leave the room.

He didn't. Sam Moon did not shirk responsibility. It wasn't in his blood.

Ignoring the remnants of the last wave of laughter, Sam dug through his book bag a second time, extracted a ballpoint, and went back to work. Even the pen gave out a little squeak in his hand, as if the plastic was that close to breaking.

It wasn't just his recent trauma that was causing his tension, although it had less than nothing to do with the exam—less than nothing to do with frequencies and waveforms and photon behavior.

The real tension came from the tug-of-war that was going on in his brain. On one end of the rope was Heather Gannis. The lovely, the popular, the much-sought-after Heather. The Heather that Sam was dating. Assisting on her end of the rope was a whole army of good reasons for Sam to stay in his current relationship. There was beauty—which Heather certainly had. And there was sex, which Heather was willing to provide. And there was a certain reliability.

Sam knew Heather. He could count on Heather. He might not always like everything about Heather, but he knew her. There were no surprises on that side.

And of course, she had saved his life.

Dragging the rope in the other direction was Gaia Moore. There was no army on Gaia's side. The girl brought nothing but frustration, confusion, mystery, and imminent danger. Technically she was a mess. And from the moment Sam met her, Gaia had seemed to stumble from one disaster to the next. But at least Gaia wasn't boring. She was anything but.

If Sam's head had staged a fair fight, Team Heather would have dragged Gaia right off the field so fast, she would have had grass burns on her face. But something inside Sam wouldn't let that happen. Something in him kept holding on to Gaia's end of the rope, keeping her in the game.

He closed his eyes for a moment and put his hands against his temples. He had to stop thinking about Gaia. Thinking about Gaia when he was already committed to Heather was wrong. More than that, the way he thought about Gaia all the time was getting to be more than a little like an obsession.

"Ten minutes, people," said the professor. "You should be getting near the end."

Sam shook his head, flinging away the rope and all its hangers-on. He studied the next question on the test and scribbled out an answer. Then he tackled the next. And the next. When he managed to concentrate, Sam found that the answers came easily. Sometimes it was nice to have the powers of a good geek brain. He sped through a series of equations without faltering, flew past some short answers, and was within five questions of the end when the professor called, "Time."

Sam gathered up his things and carried his paper to the front of the room, relieved. At least he had cleared the Gaia fog from his brain long enough to get some work done. He hadn't embarrassed himself. Not this time, anyway.

But he wasn't sure how long that would last. The battle in his head was still picking up steam. Soon it was going to be a full-blown war.

MAYBE CONNECTICUT

Gaia stared down at the toes of her battered sneakers and wondered how long it would be before she threw up. Or ran out of the room. Or exploded.

Accepting a date with a guy she had known all of ten seconds seemed like such a desperate thing. A total loser move. Like something a girl who was seventeen and had never been kissed might do.

The whole thing was starting to make her nauseated.

At least it had already served its purpose. She wasn't thinking about . . . all those things she didn't want to think about.

Who knew what this David guy expected out of her? Gaia the undated. Gaia the untouched. Gaia the ultimate virgin.

Maybe knocking David down had spun his brain around backward. Left him with a concussion that led to his asking out the first girl he saw.

Or maybe it was a setup. Maybe Heather and some of the certified Popular Crowd (also known as The Association of People Who Really Hate Gaia Moore) had put this guy in her way just so they could pop up at her so-called date and pull a *Carrie*.

Gaia closed her eyes and moaned. "Stupid. Definitely stupid."

"Uh, you're Gaia Moore, right?"

Gaia looked up from her desk and found a tall blond girl standing in front of her. From the way people were up and moving around the room, class had to be over. Gaia had successfully managed to obsess away the entire period.

"Are you Gaia?"

"Uh, yeah." Gaia was surprised on two counts. The first was that the girl knew her name at all; the second was that she actually pronounced it right on the first try. "Yeah, that's right."

"I'm Cassie," said the girl. "Cassie Greenman."

How wonderful for you, thought Gaia. She had noticed the girl in class before. Although she hadn't seen her running with the core popular-people crowd, Gaia assumed that Cassie was in on the anti-Gaia coalition.

"Aren't you worried?" Cassie asked.

"What am I supposed to be worried about?" Gaia wondered if she had missed the announcement of a history exam or some similar nonevent. Or maybe this girl was talking about Gaia's upcoming date. Maybe Heather and pals really were planning some horrible heap of humiliation. Maybe they were all standing outside the door right now, ready to mock Gaia for thinking someone would actually ask her out.

Not that Gaia cared.

The girl rolled her eyes. "About being next."

"The next what?" Gaia asked.

"You know." Cassie raised a hand to her throat and drew one silver-blue-painted fingernail across the pale skin of her throat. "Being the next one killed."

Killed. That was a word that definitely drew Gaia's attention. She sat up straighter at her desk. "What do you mean, killed?"

"Killed. Like in dead."

"Killed by who?"

The blond girl shook her head. "By the Gentleman."

Gaia began to wonder if everyone had just gone nuts while she wasn't paying attention. "Why would a gentleman want to kill me?"

"Not *a* gentleman," said Cassie, "*the* Gentleman. You know—the serial killer." She didn't add "duh," but it was clear enough in her voice.

Now Gaia was definitely interested. "Tell me about it."

"Haven't you heard?" Cassie pulled her books a little closer to her chest. "Everyone's been talking about it all morning."

"They haven't been talking to me."

Cassie shrugged. "There's this guy killing girls. He killed two over in New Jersey and three more somewhere in . . . I don't know, maybe Connecticut."

"So?" said Gaia. "Why should I be worried about what happens in Connecticut?"

That drew another roll of the eyes from the blond girl. "Don't you ever listen to the news? Last night he killed a girl from NYU right over on the MacDougal side of the park."

Now Gaia wasn't just interested, she was offended. The

park in question was Washington Square Park, and that was Gaia's territory. Her home court.

From the chessboards to the playground, all of it was hers. She used it as a place to relax and as a place to hunt city vermin. Gaia had been in the park herself the night before, just hoping for muggers and dealers to give her trouble. The idea that someone had been killed just a block away . . .

"How do they know it was the same guy?" she asked.

"Because of what he . . . does to them," her informant replied with an overdone shiver. "I don't know about you, but I'm dying my hair jet black till this guy is caught."

"Why?"

Cassie was starting to look a little exasperated. She pulled out a lock of her wavy hair and held it in front of her face. "Hello? Because all the victims had the same color hair, that's why. You need to be careful, too."

"I'm not that blond," said Gaia.

"Are you nuts? Your hair's even lighter than mine." The girl gave a little smile. "It's not too different, though. In fact, ever since you started here, people have been telling me how much we look alike. Like you could be my sister or something."

Gaia stared at the girl. Whoever had said she looked like Gaia needed to get their eyes checked. Cassie Greenman was patently pretty. Very pretty. There was no way Gaia looked anything like her.

"You're nothing like me."

Cassie frowned. "You don't think . . ."

"No."

"I think we would look a lot alike," insisted Cassie, "if you would . . . you know . . . like, clean up . . . and dress better. . . ." She shrugged. "You know."

All Gaia knew was that all the cleaning up and good clothes in the world wouldn't stop her from looking like an overmuscled freak. She wished she was beautiful like her mother had been, but she would settle for being pretty like Cassie. She would settle for being normal. "Thanks for giving me the heads up on this killer."

Cassie wrinkled her nose. "Isn't it creepy? Do you think he's still around here?"

"I wouldn't worry too much." Gaia stood up and grabbed for her books. "If he's still here, he won't be for long."

Not in my park, she thought. If the killer was still there, Gaia intended to find him and stop him.

Suddenly she felt pinpricks of excitement moving over her skin. For the first time all day she felt fully awake. Fully engaged. Fully there. She needed to make a plan. She needed to make sure that if this guy attacked anyone else in the park, it was Gaia.

As terrible as it was, in a weird sort of way the news about the serial killer actually made Gaia feel better. At least she had stopped thinking about her date.

"A serial killer," Ed said slowly. Words he never expected to say unless he was talking about some movie starring Morgan Freeman or Tommy Lee Jones.

Gaia nodded. "That's right."

"And you're excited about this?" Why was he not surprised?

"Not excited. It's more . . ." She tipped back her head and looked up at the bright blue sky, her breath visible for one split second each time she exhaled. "Yeah, well. Kind of."

Ed stopped talking as they moved around a line of people waiting for a hot dog vendor, then took up the conversation again once he was sure no one was close enough to hear. "Don't you think that's a little—"

"Crazy?" finished Gaia.

"That wasn't what I was going to say." Ed stopped in his tracks and looked up into her eyes, rubbing his gloved hands together. Early November in New York City. Almost time to put away the cotton gloves and whip out the leather. "But since you said it—yeah, it seems more than a little Looney Tunes."

Gaia was silent for a moment. She walked a few steps away and stood next to the fence that bordered the playground. Ed followed.

As usual, the equipment was overrun with bundled-up kids. Anytime between dawn and sunset the playground was packed with screaming children. A little thing like someone getting killed in the park wasn't enough to empty any New York jungle gym. They were too few and far between. The sound of laughter and shouting mixed together with traffic around the park until it was only another kind of white noise—the city version of waves and seagulls at the beach.

"This is important," Gaia said at last. "I have to get this guy."

Ed stared at her, trying to read the expression on her beautiful face. Usually that was easy enough. On an average day Gaia's emotions ran from mildly disturbed to insanely angry. But this expression was something new. Something Ed didn't know how to read. "Does this have something to do with Sam's kidnapping?" he asked. "Why exactly do you have to . . . get him?"

Why and *you* being the operative words.

Gaia pushed at her tangled hair to get it out of her face but only succeeded in tangling it further. "Because I do," she said, looking down at him. "And I don't think this has anything to do with Sam. This guy is killing blond girls, not college guys. But this also isn't just some loser snatching purses or some asshole junkie waving a knife to feed a crack habit. This is serious."

"Some of those assholes kill people," Ed pointed out, tucking his hands under his arms. "Stopping them is important, too."

"Yeah, but not like this. This guy, this *Gentleman*, he's killing people because he wants to do it." She stared out at the kids on the swing sets, and Ed saw that her ever-changing eyes had turned a shade of blue that was almost electric. "This guy likes what he's doing."

Ed was chilled to the bone. He blamed it on the sudden, stiff breeze that picked up dead leaves and general city debris all around them. But he knew it was more about Gaia's words.

"What do you know about this guy?" he asked.

Gaia shrugged, hooking her bare fingers around the metal links of the fence. "Nothing, really. He kills blond girls. I'm not sure how many."

"Why is he called the Gentleman?" Ed asked.

"I don't know that, either. I don't really know anything about him . . . yet."

There was one particularly loud playground scream, and Gaia's eyes darted left, searching for possible trouble.

Ed ignored the kids and stared at Gaia's profile. Looking at her was something he always enjoyed, but this time he was looking with a purpose. He hadn't known Gaia for that long, but he had never seen her back away from anything she set out to do. From what he could read of the expression on her face, Gaia was determined to stop this killer. Ed could either get behind her or get out of the way.

"Maybe I could help you," he said.

Gaia shook her head. She didn't even look at him. "I don't want you getting hurt."

Ed tried hard not to be insulted. "Hey, we've been through this before. I'm not going to be out here playing Jackie Chan. That's your job. I just thought I could help you fill in the holes."

"Holes?"

"Holes." He tilted his head in an attempt to catch her eyes. "Like I did with Sam."

She blinked, and her grip on the fence tightened. There. She couldn't deny he'd been indispensable when Sam was kidnapped. He'd figured out where they were holding Sam—not that the information had played a role in rescuing him. But he'd helped Gaia get the key to Sam's room from Heather—not that they'd needed it. But he *had* caused a distraction so that Gaia could sneak into the dorm. Of course, if he hadn't been there, she probably wouldn't have needed a distraction in the first place, but—

"Ed—"

"Let me at least read up on the guy," Ed interrupted before she could shoot him down. "Maybe I can figure out what he's about. What he's got against girls with pigment-challenged hair."

Gaia turned away from the kids and knelt down next to the chair. It was a move that usually made Ed angry—he didn't want people bending down beside him like he was a three-year-old—but anything that brought Gaia Moore's face closer to his own was an okay move in Ed's book.

"Okay," she said. "But you do research. *Only* research. I do the . . . other. Maybe together we can exterminate this guy."

We. Together. Ed liked the sound of that. It wasn't just Gaia going after a killer. It was Gaia and Ed. Batman and Robin. Partners.

"All right," he agreed. "I'll dig into the Net. Maybe stop by the library."

"Good," Gaia said. She smiled. In a strained way.

Forced or not, two smiles in one day from Gaia Moore had to be a record. Still, something about this whole thing had Ed moderately wiggy.

"Want me to call you tonight?" he asked.

"I'll call you," Gaia said. She started walking again, and Ed hurried to keep up. "If you can get some info in the next couple of hours, maybe I can bag this loser before he moves on to a different neighborhood."

She made a sound that might almost have been a laugh and ran the long fingers of her right hand through the heavy mass of her tangled hair. "Besides, I'm busy tomorrow night."

"What's tomorrow?" Ed asked.

"I've got a date." Gaia glanced over at Ed. For a split second she looked small, vulnerable. Like what he was about to say mattered. Unfortunately, Ed's heart was in his mouth, temporarily making speech impossible.

"A date," Ed replied finally. "Wow." Articulate, it was not, but he was pleased to hear that his voice sounded normal. He even managed to keep a smile on his face.

But if the serial killer came for him, Ed wouldn't have to be afraid. He felt dead already.

ED

Girls I have liked:
- Jenn Challener
- Aimee Eastwood
- Raina Korman
- Ms. Reidy
- Jennifer Love Hewitt (Okay, I was fourteen)
- Storm, Rogue, Jubilee, Jean Grey
- The lady behind the counter at Balducci's

Girls I have loved:
- Heather Gannis
- Gaia Moore

Girls who have ripped out my cardiovascular muscle and squashed it under their feet:
Heather Gannis
Gaia Moore

Anyone besides me sensing a pattern around here?

THE GAIA
FLU

ONE GLANCE FROM AFAR WAS ALL HE NEEDED.

BUT HE NEEDED IT LIKE HE NEEDED OXYGEN.

GIVE IN TO INSANITY

The park was just a shortcut. The fastest way from point A to point B.

Besides, cutting through the park would take Sam past the chess tables. Not that he had time for a game, but it never hurt to see who was playing. He had to keep up on the competition. See who was new. Check out who was winning, who was losing. It wasn't like he was looking for anyone in particular. Nope. Not at all.

Except that he was.

Truth? Sam was sneaking through the park, looking for Gaia. Not to meet her, not to talk to her, just to *see* her. One glance from afar was all he needed. But he needed it like he needed oxygen.

Before Sam met Gaia, the park had seemed like the one safe place in his life. Sure, it was a hangout for muggers and junkies, scam artists, aging hippies, and gang members. If you wandered off the path on the wrong day or stayed too long on the wrong night, you could be beat up, maimed, or even killed. Every place had dangerous people, but Washington Square Park had more than its share.

Sam knew about that firsthand.

But none of that stopped him from loving the place. When he was hanging out in the park, he could relax. Nobody at the chess tables cared if he wore the right things, said the right things, or hung with the right people. Playing chess in the park was one situation where Sam could lean back and let his inner geek rise to the surface.

Gaia had ruined that.

From the first time they played, Sam had developed this weird kind of spastic tick. No matter who he was playing, every ten seconds Sam had to look up from the board to see if he might catch a glimpse of blond hair flying loose in the wind or a beautiful face centered around a scowl.

Sam had seen plenty of stories about obsessive-compulsive people. People who can't leave the house without locking the door ten times or who wash their hands a hundred times a day. He just hadn't expected to become one of those people. Glance at the chessboard, look around for Gaia. Move a piece. Check for Gaia. It was more than sick. It was pathetic.

What was worse was that he had no idea how he really felt about Gaia. Sam had good reasons to hate her—had once even told her he hated her—and the kidnapping should have only made him hate her more.

The kidnapping. Something Sam was trying so hard not to think about even though the questions kept flashing through his mind at warp speed.

Why me?

What did they want?

Did they get it?

Who were they?

Why did they let me go?

And, of course, what did Gaia have to do with the whole thing?

He'd been chasing Gaia when it happened. And he had the vague, possibly imagined memory of Gaia's name being mentioned by one of the kidnappers while he was semi-conscious and half dead on a concrete floor. That was the thought that always gave him pause.

Kidnappers mentioning Gaia = kidnappers knowing Gaia = Gaia having something to do with the torture he was put through = Sam should hate Gaia.

But Sam was pretty sure that wasn't how he felt. If it was hate, it was a weird kind. Still, this obsession couldn't be love. It was more like an illness. The Gaia flu. Gaia-itis.

If she had anything to do with what happened to him, she must have been just as much a victim as he was. That had to be it.

Suddenly Sam found himself carefully scanning the park.

He was looking for her now—going out of his way and looking. This wasn't just the possibility of a random encounter anymore. And he was supposed to be on his way to meet his girlfriend.

Sam tucked his chin and kept walking. Eyes down. Hands in pockets. Too bad he didn't have side blinders like the horses that drew carriages through Central Park.

He needed a cure for this disease. Brain surgery. Strong anti-Gaiotics. At the very least, a good psychiatrist.

When he got to the chess tables, Sam found them almost deserted. Only a handful of regulars were playing, taking money from the usual mix of naive college students and overconfident businessmen who strolled through the park. A couple of would-be players were sitting across from empty seats, hoping for fresh victims.

No Gaia.

Sam felt a swirling mixture of disappointment and relief. It was kind of like the feeling he got when someone else took the last scoop of Ben & Jerry's. It was probably good for him to skip that ten zillion additional calories; it just didn't feel good at all.

Zolov was at his table, of course. He was in the middle of a game, so Sam didn't stop to talk. Not that talking would have bothered Zolov. Zolov might be a little crazy, but he knew how to concentrate on chess.

A middle-aged Pakistani looked at Sam with a hopeful expression. "You want a game, Sam?"

He shook his head. "Not today, Mr. Haq. Sorry."

"Oh, sit down and play," the part-time taxi driver, full-time chess hustler said. "It won't take long."

When Sam considered the way he'd been playing lately, that part was probably true. "Sorry, I really don't have time."

Since Sam had become Gaia infected, he had become

Mr. Popularity at the chess tables. Everyone wanted to play him. He had lost money to people he used to put down in ten minutes.

Past the chess tables, Sam picked up the pace. Heather wasn't the kind of girl who took well to waiting.

Sam slipped through the not-so-miniature marble Arc de Triomphe at the center of the park and was almost out of the park. Then he saw her.

Gaia was thirty feet away, talking to a guy in a wheelchair. He recognized the guy. It was Ed Fargo, Heather's ex. But Sam didn't spend any time looking at Ed. That would be a waste of Gaia time.

Her hair was light and golden in the sunlight. Sam couldn't tell what Gaia was saying, but her face was incredibly animated. Even from where he was standing, Sam imagined he could see the deep, shifting blue of Gaia's eyes. A little gray in the center. Streaks that were almost turquoise. It was only imagination, but he had a very good imagination when it came to Gaia.

For just a moment another image of Gaia started to seep into Sam's mind. An image of Gaia in the dark, leaning over him, urgently whispering to him. Sam's heart froze in his chest.

The kidnapping.

He knew that couldn't be right. It was Heather who had come in at the last second to save Sam and give him the insulin he so desperately needed. Not Gaia. Still, there was something about the events that scratched at the insides of his skull.

The path Gaia was walking angled away from Sam. If he stood there for another ten seconds, she would be out of sight. To keep up with her, all he had to do was take ten fast steps. Another ten steps and he would catch her.

All he had to do was forget Heather, forget everything, and follow Gaia. All he had to do was give in to insanity.

Sam took the first step.

TIMES TEN

Heather looked again at the watch on her wrist. Time. Time and then some.

She stretched her neck, looking around for Sam. Heather wished he hadn't asked her to meet him at the entrance of the park. She didn't have to go inside, but even the sidewalk was still way too close.

Heather didn't like the park. She had been cut there,

almost killed by some maniac. Since then she had looked at the clumps of trees and clutter of equipment as hiding places for thieves, murderers, and worse. It didn't surprise Heather that some brainless girl had gotten herself killed there. She was only surprised that it didn't happen more often.

The park held monsters. She was sure of it.

Heather checked her watch again. Ten minutes late. If it had been anyone but Sam, she would have left. She was beginning to wonder if she had the place or time wrong when Sam suddenly stepped into view. Heather put on her best smile and raised her hand in a little wave.

Sam didn't respond. He was walking right toward Heather, but he didn't even seem to see her. There was a distant, distracted look on his face. His curly, ginger-colored hair seemed a little more mussed than usual. Even his normally crisp tweed jacket looked wrinkled. Heather didn't appreciate the change.

Sam had been ill, and of course, there was the whole kidnapping thing, but still. He needed to take better care of himself. After all, appearance was very important. Sam knew that.

Sam took two more steps, stopped, and looked into the park.

For a moment Heather worried that Sam might really be sick again. Or maybe he had been attacked. There was a confused, stunned expression on his face. Maybe some lunatic in the park had hit him on the head. Maybe he was hurt.

Heather started walking toward him quickly. She was almost close enough to touch him when Sam moved again. But he didn't come toward Heather. He stepped off the path and into the grass.

Heather frowned. "Sam?"

Sam jumped. He whipped around and stared at Heather with wide eyes.

"Um. Uh." He stopped and cleared his throat. "Heather."

The way he said it made it seem like he was surprised to see her. Heather couldn't put her finger on it, but something about his expression irritated her. A slight blush tinted her cheeks. She crossed her arms over her chest.

"What's wrong, Sam? Are you okay?" She tried to sound concerned and earnest. It came out as defensive and accusatory. Luckily, Mr. Oblivious didn't seem to notice.

Sam nodded quickly. "Yeah, sure. I just . . ." His face suddenly flushed an incredible bright red. "I just got lost in thought."

Heather's eyebrows scrunched together. She tried to smile again, but it was more difficult this time. "Oookay," she said. "C'mon. Let's get out of here."

Lacing her fingers with Sam's, Heather started to lead him out of the park. He was coming out of the bizarre stupor—

walking like a normal person instead of shuffling like he had moments before. In fact, within seconds he was practically pulling her arm out of its socket.

What was with him? He was acting like something had him spooked. Heather glanced back in the direction Sam had been looking when he'd stopped in place. For a fraction of a second, a moment so short it might have been imagination, Heather thought she saw someone stepping behind a group of trees—someone with pale blond hair.

Heather's blood went cold and hot at the same time. It had only been the barest glimpse, but she knew who that blond hair belonged to. Gaia Moore. And Sam didn't want Heather to see her.

"Sam? What's the rush?" Heather said, just to see if he would tell her the truth.

"Nothing," he said, still pulling.

Heather felt a familiar feeling of humiliation, mixed with anger and tinged with fear, slip through her veins. God, she hated Gaia. Heather hated Gaia more than she had ever hated anyone in her whole life. More than everyone she had ever hated in her life put together. Times ten.

Sam stopped pulling when they reached the far corner, but Heather kept her hand locked together with his as they strolled down the sidewalk. Sam was saying something to her, making suggestions about where they might go, what they might do. Heather gave vague, one-word answers to his questions without really hearing them. It was her turn to be distracted.

Since her first encounter with Gaia, Heather had been burned, humiliated, stabbed, hospitalized, ego bruised, deprived of her boyfriend on various occasions, and detained by the NYU security force.

None of that came close to the reason Heather hated Gaia. It was the way Sam acted around Gaia. Like he couldn't think or breathe. Like he'd never seen anything like her.

And then there was the fact that Gaia was beautiful. She was beautiful without even trying. And that brought Heather to the real heart of it. Not the beauty. Heather hated Gaia because she didn't seem to try, didn't seem to care what others thought of her. Gaia dressed like a refugee. She said whatever she wanted. She never even seemed to notice how guys turned around to watch her when she went by. Gaia acted like she didn't think she was pretty, but Heather knew better than that. Gaia had to know. She just didn't care.

It was driving Heather mad—in every sense of the word.

Sam suddenly stopped walking. His grip on Heather's hand tightened to painful intensity.

Heather came out of her daze and struggled against his tight grip. "Sam? Sam, what's wrong?"

"Nothing," he replied in a harsh whisper. He stopped again and shook his head. "Nothing. Don't worry about it."

Heather stared at him. For a moment she had a terrible premonition that everything between them was over. Ice went down her spine, trickling slowly over every lump in her backbone. *He's going to tell me he's dumping me. Dumping me for Gaia Moore.*

But Sam wasn't even looking at Heather. She followed the direction of his gaze and saw a newspaper stand. Right away Heather spotted the thing that had captured Sam's attention.

Splashed across the front page of the *Post* was a color photo of a young blond girl. Under the picture was the caption KILLER TAKES 6TH VICTIM.

Heather untangled her fingers from Sam's and went in for a closer look. From a distance, the girl in the picture looked a lot like Gaia. A tabloid twin. This had to be the girl that the serial killer had murdered the night before, the one that everyone had been talking about at school.

It wasn't Gaia. Still, Heather felt a little thrill go through her. As sick as she knew the thought was, the idea of Gaia and murder just seemed so right.

FRANCINE PASCAL

New York Post

ANOTHER BLOND BEAUTY DEAD
Gentleman Killer Plants Bloody Knife in Heart of NYC

After a killing spree that has left victims scattered from Connecticut to New Jersey, the serial killer known only as the "Gentleman" has taken his act off Broadway—slicing up an NYU coed just a block from the school's campus.

Carolyn Mosley, 20, a freshman at NYU, was found dead this morning by maintenance workers at Washington Square Park, say city officials. The manner of death points to a connection with the string of killings committed by the infamous serial killer, the Gentleman, according to officials.

Police have been reluctant to share details of the killer's technique, but sources have confirmed that this Gentleman is no gentleman. Death in the Gentleman's victims has been brought about by numerous knife wounds, according to information released by New Jersey police. Victims have received multiple stab wounds and have suffered "extreme violence and extensive damage," according to reports on the previous victims.

"Their throats were cut so badly, they were nearly decapitated," said Stanley G. Norster, a detective who investigated the Gentleman's killings in Connecticut. "There's an incredible amount of anger in these killings. A rage."

Police have admitted to withholding some details of the Gentleman's actions in previous crimes. The FBI has been involved in this investigation for several weeks, and a psychological profile of the killer has been prepared, but this profile has not been made available to the public. Sources inside the coroner's office indicate that the bodies show evidence of torture. The killer apparently administered dozens of cuts and other injuries before the killing blow. The killer didn't stop with death. Other signs

Continued on page 12

New York Times, Morning Edition

NYU STUDENT KILLED IN WASHINGTON SQUARE PARK

NYU—A New York University student was found dead early this morning only two blocks from the university campus, according to police. Carolyn Mosley, 20, a freshman at NYU, died as a direct result of blunt trauma and numerous stab wounds, officials say.

The body was discovered in the southwestern part of Washington Square Park by maintenance workers responding to a report of a gas leak. No leak was found, but Ms. Mosley's body was found at the location of the alleged leak. Police spokesmen refused comment when asked about the possibility that the gas leak was reported by someone involved in the murder.

Mosley was last seen leaving a restaurant on MacDougal Street around 11 P.M., according to officials. The student worked part-time at the restaurant and worked her regular shift there the evening of her death.

No suspects have been named; however, the condition of the body has led to speculation that the case may be related to a series of killings in Connecticut.

Police have scheduled a press conference for 3 P.M. to discuss the case. Case files from the possibly related murders in other states have been requested, according to police.

TO: L

FROM: E

Last night's events confirm Delta presence. High probability of encounter with primary subject and subsequent risk. Advise.

TO: E

FROM: L

Continue to monitor activity. Do not intercede at this time. Will personally visit site within twenty-four hours.

I want to see what happens.

NUMBERING
THE DEAD

THEY HAD NOTHING IN COMMON AT ALL—NOTHING
EXCEPT A GENERAL SIMILARITY OF FEATURES AND
THE FACT THAT THEY WERE ALL DEAD.

PRETTY GIRLS

One after another, the faces and names of the Gentleman's victims appeared on the computer monitor.

Debra Lemasters—more cute than beautiful, with her hair pulled back in a ponytail and wide blue eyes that stared out from a yearbook photo.

Amanda Loring—older, taller. Holding a track trophy aloft while teammates cheered.

Susan Creek—eyes more gray than blue, thinner than the rest. She looked so sad, it was almost as if she knew what was coming.

Clarissa Richardson—very pretty but looking awfully uncomfortable in a tight, off-the-shoulder formal gown and a paper crown that proclaimed her queen of the junior prom.

Paulina Dree—sitting on horseback, her father standing beside her, both smiling. She had a great smile.

And finally, poor Carolyn Mosley, posing in cap and gown, a high school diploma rolled in her hand. Valedictorian of her class. Her family's pride and joy.

The youngest of them was fifteen, the oldest, twenty. They were six young women from three different states. None of them had known one another. Most but not all were good students. Most but not all had participated in some sort of organized athletics. They shared no common hobbies. They didn't read the same books, or like the same music, or share the same dreams.

They had nothing in common at all—nothing except a general similarity of features and the fact that they were all dead. And blond hair.

Gaia's hair, thought Tom Moore. He scrolled through the pictures again.

If he looked closely, he could see a little of Gaia in each of the dead girls. It was far more than the hair. The dead girls weren't identical, but they shared a similar bone structure— wide eyes, strong cheekbones, high forehead. Pretty girls, all of them. Of course, Tom was sure that none of them was as pretty as Gaia. But then again, Tom might be more than a little prejudiced—he thought his daughter was the most beautiful young woman in the world.

Six dead girls who all looked a little like Gaia Moore.

"What have they done?" Tom whispered to the empty room. He leaned back from the monitor and stared into the shadows. "What have *we* done?"

WARM-UP EXERCISES

It never got dark in the city. Not really dark the way it had in other places. Like Connecticut.

He strolled down the sidewalk, careful never to touch anyone he passed. He didn't like to touch people. He didn't like to be touched.

The sun was already going down, but the sky overhead only shifted from blue to a kind of dingy yellow as the lights came on. It wasn't anything close to real darkness. After only three days in the city, he still thought the dirty, nearly starless sky seemed terribly odd.

He craved the darkness.

He moved off the sidewalk and headed down the curving path that led out under the trees. A handful of children were still indulging in a few last minutes of play, but there were parents on hand to watch and a policeman standing at the edge of the playground. A pair of street musicians were putting away their instruments and counting up handfuls of change and folded bills.

They were scared. All of them were scared of the coming night.

He could feel it, almost taste it. For a moment he had a desire to rush into the center of them, screaming and waving his arms, just so he could watch them scatter. He fought down that desire.

No matter how fun it might be to see them run, it wasn't his reason for being in the park. There was important work to be done—a higher purpose. Nothing could be allowed to get in the way of that purpose.

He walked on, passing two more policemen on his way to the chess tables. Like the playground, the boards were almost deserted. Two men still squinted at a game in the failing light. At another table an old man slowly packed away his chess pieces.

The old man looked up as he passed. "You wanting game?" he said. "I will play you."

"No, thanks, Gramps." The idea of playing this guy actually made him smile. The man was ridiculously ancient, with sun-spotted skin and flyaway tufts of white hair. Beating him at chess couldn't possibly be a challenge.

Killing him would be even easier.

It would be a mercy, really. Put the old fool out of his misery. Maybe he would do it. Not as a main course for the evening, but just as a warm-up exercise. Something to keep his fingers busy.

The old man shuffled away, and the moment passed. Pointless, anyway. It was no fun without a real struggle.

He moved away from the tables and down the tree-lined

paths. Even in the middle of the park there was nothing that approached true darkness.

But under the trees and in the shaded places, it was dark enough for his purposes.

CHALK

THE FORM ON THE GROUND DIDN'T EVEN LOOK
LIKE A GIRL. IT BARELY LOOKED LIKE A PERSON.

STALKING A STALKER

Death didn't leave much of a permanent stain. Not on the park, at least.

Gaia reached out and caught a strip of the yellow tape in her hand. Crime Scene—Do Not Cross.

As if yellow tape created some magical force field that could keep everyone away. Gaia wondered if police tape had ever stopped anybody in the history of the world from jumping into the middle of a crime site. The temptation was just too much. Even when you weren't stalking a stalker.

Considering how everyone had been talking up the murder at school and in the papers, Gaia had expected to find the park swarming with cop types. She had thought there would be uniforms keeping back the crowds. Whole squadrons of trench-coat-wearing detectives combing the ground, examining every blade of grass for a clue like a flock of investigating sheep. There should have been technicians spreading fingerprint powder. Flashing lights. Enough doughnuts to soak up a swimming pool of coffee.

Instead there was only this dark patch of grass. If there had been detectives, they were long gone. There wasn't a single cop left to keep people from ignoring the warning on the flimsy yellow tape. No one had even left behind a doughnut.

Losers.

Still, Gaia had a hard time stepping over the line. It wasn't like she was afraid of getting caught. Gaia didn't do afraid.

Maybe it was some new desire to be a law-abiding citizen. She wasn't sure. But the idea of going across the tape, going to the place where the body had been, made Gaia feel weird. Like something way down inside her wasn't quite as solid as it should be. Squishy.

She stood there and took a few deep breaths of evening air before the squishiness started to fade. After all, there was nothing out there but grass.

Gaia ducked under the tape. Inside the magic line the ground was all dented and bumpy—like it had been walked on by a herd of elephants. Maybe there really had been hundreds of detecto-sheep here after all.

The grass in the field was soaked with dew. By the time she'd taken a dozen steps, Gaia's sneakers were soaked through and cold water was making little burping noises between her toes. A lovely way to start a long evening.

Almost dead center in the field she saw the rough outline of a body marked in white. Just like in the movies. Only this line wasn't made from tape. It was powdered, chalky stuff, like they use to mark the baselines at a ball game.

Somewhere in the back of Gaia's head, random associations started to fire.

Strike three. You're out. Game over.

When she considered where she was standing, this seemed more than a little sick. But Gaia had never claimed to be in complete control of what went on in her head.

She stood with the toes of her wet sneaks almost touching the crumbling chalk line. The form on the ground didn't even look like a girl. It barely looked like a person. It was just a rough outline with something like a hand pointing one way and two blocky leg things shooting off the other end.

Despite all the violence Gaia had seen in her life—despite all the violence she had caused—there was something about this scene that gave her pause. She wasn't scared; she just felt ill. Ill and numb and . . . responsible. And sad. Where there had been a girl with warmth and memories and a smile, there was now just chalk and dew. It was almost too much for her.

Gaia turned away, wanting to block out the images of premature dying, but her eyes were drawn back as if some unseen thing were pulling her.

Gaia was no big believer. She didn't go in for ghosts, or voodoo, or little leprechauns with colored marshmallow cereal. If people wanted to call themselves witches, that was cool with Gaia as long as they didn't expect her to believe in witchcraft. She might be an overmuscled, fear-deprived, jump-kicking freak girl, but Gaia didn't skim the tabloids for predictions or use a Ouija board to communicate with the dead. For all the weirdness in her life, she knew where to draw the line between what was real and what was not. Or at least, she thought she did.

But the area inside the police tape gave Gaia a bad feeling. Something worse than a mugging or robbery had happened there. And Gaia could still feel it.

She looked up from the line on the ground and did a quick check of the trees around her—just in case any werewolves or zombies were approaching. Then she laughed at herself.

Still, he could be out there. Right there.

There was that whole bad film noir/cheesy paperback theory that criminals return to the scene of the crime.

It sounded like an idea dreamed up by a lazy detective or by some writer who didn't know where to go with the plot. Just sit on your ass, and the killer will come to you. In Gaia's book that was way too easy to be true.

There was no real reason to think the killer might come back to this place. None at all. Gaia had the whole park to patrol. She couldn't stand here all night, staring at an empty field. Glaring at the trees made about as much sense as her Sam obsession.

But when she looked again, something was out there. Right at the bottom of a bunch of little ash trees, stuck in a chunk of shadow was—something. Maybe someone.

The all-over sickness she had been feeling started to turn

into the more familiar let's-go-kick-some-ass buzz. Gaia took a slow step toward the shape in the shadows. She squinted until her eyes watered. Was someone really there? She couldn't be sure. She took another step. It was so hard to see. The shape in the shadows could be a crouching person, or it could be a shrub or a trash can.

Then the shape moved.

NO KILLING TONIGHT

He was up and running before she had a chance to blink. There was no reason to run, really. He could just kill her now.

He wasn't afraid of her.

But he was in the mood for a challenge. He wanted to run. Run until it hurt. Until the air coming in and out of his lungs burned the delicate flesh of his throat.

He wanted her to feel the same thing.

And so he ran. There was no way she would catch up to him. Which meant no killing tonight. But that was okay.

He wanted to see what she could do.

GAIA VS. BAD GUY

Gaia's legs were pumping even before her brain had finished realizing that it really was a person out there. Someone had been there in the shadows, watching her. Now the person was running. So was Gaia.

She made it out of the chewed-up field and jumped the police tape on the far side. For a moment she stood there, frustration tightening her throat. It was a terrible thing to be ready for a fight and not find anyone to punch.

Then she saw the shadow guy again. He was a hundred feet away, cutting across the grass by the side of the path. Gaia started after him.

Then something strange happened.

The average Gaia-versus-bad-guy race lasted all of five seconds. It wasn't that she was Ms. Olympic Runner, but the same thing that made Gaia strong also made her pretty damn fast in a sprint. Her father said it was part of being fearless. That little regulator that keeps people from pushing their muscles to the absolute limit was absent without leave in Gaia. She could push her legs a hundred percent. Maybe further. Gaia could even push her muscles so hard that she broke her own bones.

Disgusting but true.

There was a price to pay for beating herself up like that,

but the upside was irresistible—before Gaia began to fade, most losers were on the pavement.

Not this guy. Shadow Man was fast. More than fast. A real speed demon.

Gaia and the shadow whipped along the path through the heart of the park, jumped a hedge, and skirted a gnarled old oak. Gaia didn't gain a step. She could never get close enough to see more than a hazy form in the distance. Several times she almost convinced herself that nothing was out there but shadows—no man at all. But she didn't stop.

By now Gaia was solidly in the zone. Nothing mattered in the world but catching the guy in the shadows. The chessboards came and went in a blur. The playground. The sprinklers. Then they were out of the park, powering north on Fifth Avenue.

In the back of her mind nagged the vague thought that she had no clear reason to pursue him except for the fact that he was running away from her. But the chase was on, and her instincts pushed her hard to catch him.

She zipped past knots of people and saw startled faces turning her way. A woman jumped back as Gaia thundered past. A guy dropped a bag of groceries, and apples went bouncing along the sidewalk.

Gaia didn't slow. They had been running now for a solid minute at a speed that would have been impressive for a ten-second sprint. Her chest heaved in and out as she tried to draw in all the air in New York.

Then she realized she was gaining on the shadow. Not much, but the gap was definitely closing.

Another hundred yards and she had gotten close enough to see that he was wearing some kind of long, floppy black coat. Not a trench coat, but something from a cowboy movie. A duster.

How could he run this fast in that thing?

Gaia followed as the duster flapped past the trendy crowd waiting outside Clementine's, past the glowing signs at Starbucks, and on across Fourteenth Street without even looking at the streams of passing traffic. Her heartbeat seemed to move up through her body with every step. One moment it was pounding against Gaia's ribs. The next it was beating in her throat. The next it was throbbing in her skull.

Shadow Man took a hard right onto a side street, then ducked down an alley. Gaia was right behind him. The gap between the two runners had closed to no more than fifty feet. Forty.

A mesh fence blocked one end of the alley. Gaia slowed a step, getting ready to fight, but the guy in the black coat didn't hesitate. He jumped up, landed one foot on a Dumpster, and sprang from there to the top of the fence. Two steps and he was over the ten-foot barrier. He hit the other side running.

"What?" Gaia gasped.

She might not get scared, but she was still quite capable of being amazed.

Gaia ran up to the fence, looped her hands in the mesh, and flung herself upward. She flipped head over heels and her feet came down on the top of the gate. A very slick move.

Then the top of the gate sagged, and she fell.

The pavement wasn't friendly to Gaia's knee. She hit with a force that sent jolts of fire running up her thigh and set off flares of white light in her head.

Gaia stayed there for the space of two breaths. Then she got on her feet and ran again.

Black Coat had widened his lead on Gaia to a good hundred feet, but she soon had it back to fifty. He cut right again, this time along University Place. Gaia followed.

The pair sprinted past a series of nightclubs. The door of each one spilled out different music, but Gaia went past them so fast, they blended like notes in some insane song. Disco high C. Jazz G. Bass blues.

Thirty feet.

Shadow Man was wearing running shoes. Gaia could see them now. The off-white soles flashed at her under the flapping hem of his long coat. She found something comforting about the shoes. At least it was nice to know he wasn't running so fast in penny loafers.

Twenty feet.

A policewoman shouted at Gaia as she dashed across Fourteenth Street and headed south. She didn't bother to stop. If the policewoman wanted Gaia, she had better start running.

Now Gaia realized the man had brought her right back to Washington Square Park, and they ran through shadows cast by huge oaks and ghost white birch.

Ten feet.

Gaia could almost reach out and touch the flapping coat. Almost. The air in her throat tasted like fire, and there were little sparks of white light dancing in her eyes. In another ten seconds this psycho was hers.

Then somebody screamed.

Gaia thought for a second it was her. She was hurting badly enough to scream.

Then the sound came again from somewhere off to her right.

Five feet.

All Gaia had to do was keep running and she could catch the black coat. But what if she caught him and he turned out to be innocent? Really fast, but innocent.

What if the Gentleman was killing someone else in the park right that second? Gaia tried to get her oxygen-starved brain to make a decision. Another scream.

"Oh, shit," she wheezed through her breathing.

Gaia turned right, leaving Black Coat to run on into the night, and dashed toward the commotion.

It didn't take her ten seconds to find who was doing

the screaming. Standing under a pool of light was a young girl in blue jeans and a black sweater. Tugging on her purse strap was a potbellied, long-haired guy with a tangled brown-and-gray beard that went halfway down his chest. The girl had both hands clamped to her purse and her feet well planted. She was putting everything she had into it. The guy might outweigh her by a good fifty pounds, but she was giving him a fight.

"Let go!" the girl cried.

The guy laughed. "Come on, baby. I need it worse than you."

Gaia didn't think either one of them saw her coming. By then she was running at roughly the speed of a 747 pulling out of JFK. Gaia didn't slow a bit as she tucked in her head, lowered a shoulder, and smashed into Brown Beard.

The impact was enough to make Gaia fall to her bruised knee and send fresh neon bolts of pain ripping through her body. The bearded guy was knocked at least ten feet. He lay facedown on the grass with one hand stretched out over his head and the other trapped under his body. For just a second Gaia flashed back to the chalk outline on the ground. Hand up, legs spread.

She shook her aching head to clear away some of the fog and climbed to her feet. It seemed like a long way up.

"Y-You . . . ," Gaia started, then took a breath and tried again. "You okay?" she asked the girl.

The girl nodded. Gaia couldn't see her clearly, but she was very tall and very slim. Delicate-looking. And she was definitely young. Way too young to be walking around the park alone at night. Of course, who was Gaia to talk?

"Who are you?" the girl asked.

"I—" Gaia couldn't think of a good answer. If she even had a name, she had misplaced it somewhere. Somewhere back along the long minutes and longer miles of her run. Gaia turned around and staggered back the way she had come.

"Where are you going?" the girl called.

Gaia didn't bother to answer. There wasn't enough air to talk and run.

She put up her arms, drew in a deep breath, and started back to the spot where she had last seen the shadow man.

Gaia made maybe three whole steps before the ground jumped up and gave her a hard slap in the face.

SAM

You'd think that I wouldn't have a very vivid imagination. I'm a science geek, right? I play chess. It's all analytical. It's all about numbers, proofs, strategies.

Solid definitions.

There's no room for imagination.

But sometimes I don't even believe what my mind can come up with. There are things living in my head I'm sure any shrink worth his cheap spiral notepad would kill to delve into.

My imagination is especially vivid when it comes to Gaia Moore.

And not in the way you think. I'm not a total pervert.

Although . . . Well, yes, the brain does travel in those circles, but I'm a guy. You have to forgive it.

I'm talking about the sick side of my mind. The dark side. The side a lot of people probably have but don't talk about. And ever since this afternoon, that side has been transmitting Gaia pictures. Not pleasant Gaia pictures.

Pictures of Gaia dead. Pictures of Gaia cut. Pictures of Gaia bleeding and crying and gasping and sputtering. They only last for seconds at a time before I drive them away. But in those seconds they scare me to death. They arrest every functioning part of my body and take the breath out of me.

Why?

Because they could become reality.

THE
CONNECTION

ED STARED AT THE HANDSET IN CONFUSION.

"WHO IS THIS?"

"SAM MOON," SAID THE VOICE.

"I'M TRYING TO REACH ED."

Ed hit the keys on his computer so hard, the whole desk started shaking. The words on the computer screen glowed back at him.

LOSER. LOSER. LOSER. BIG LOSER. ALL THOUGHT AND NO ACTION MAKES ED ONE GIANT LOSER. LOSER. LOSER.

Somewhere, three screens' worth of LOSERs away, there was a letter that started with "Dear Gaia." It was a letter that explained everything. It was a letter that put into words all the things Ed wished he could have said that morning.

LOSER, Ed typed one last time, moving his fingers slowly across the keys and striking each one as if he meant to knock a letter from the keyboard.

L. O. S. E. R.

He closed his eyes for a moment and rubbed at his temples. It turned out that losing, or at least not getting the woman you loved, caused a massive headache. Three aspirins had gone down his throat and Ed still felt like his skull was going to bust wide open. He almost wished it would.

With a sigh he moved the mouse up to the corner of his document and clicked the close button.

Save changes? the machine asked.

Ed clicked on the No button and watched as both his letter to Gaia and his three-page tribute to self-pity blinked into nothing.

He took in a deep breath, turned his back to the computer, and rolled over to the heap of books lying on his bed.

He had braved the snarling stone lions and endless wheelchair ramps at the main public library to come up with this stack. Six books, all of them about serial killers and murderers. Ed wondered if the librarians would add his name to some list they kept behind the counter. Serial killer junkies. Murder geeks. Or maybe Hannibal Lecter wannabes.

It was possible they even suspected that he was the Gentleman. But Ed doubted that. Sometimes being in a wheelchair was a weird kind of being invisible—no one ever looked at the wheelchair guy as a threat.

Ed grabbed the first book off the stack and flipped open the pages to the introduction. Staring back at him was a wild face framed by wilder hair. It was a woodcut picture of a killer from the Middle Ages—a man who had killed dozens of children near a small village in France. In the picture the man held a child in one hand. Not all of a child. Part of the body had already been eaten.

A quick flip of the page and Ed was facing newspaper

sketches of a shadowy Jack the Ripper stalking the streets of Whitechapel in a cape and top hat. Across from the sketch was a diagram of a woman who had been dissected more completely than Ed's frog in freshman biology.

Another page and there was a black-and-white photo from the 1930s. This time the killer was a calm-looking man from Germany who had ground some of his neighbors into sausages. Flip.

He was looking into the fantastically mad eyes of Charles Manson.

On the next was the dumpy face of John Wayne Gacy.

Flip. Jeffrey Dahmer.

Flip. A middle-aged Russian guy with thick-framed glasses. Maybe he had killed fifty. Maybe it was a hundred. No one knew for sure.

Ed tried to read more of the text around the pictures, but he was having a hard time concentrating. And for an admittedly frivolous reason, when he considered the subject matter in front of him.

Gaia had a date. Ed's chance had been there. All he'd had to do was roll up to Gaia, open his mouth, and tell her how he felt. She had been right there. Right there.

Of course, she could have shot him down. Absolutely *would* have shot him down in flames. A girl like Gaia. Ed had to be crazy to think he could ever be more than friends with Gaia. He should be glad she even noticed him.

Ed looked down at his book and stared into the face of the Russian killer. A world that could put Ed in a wheelchair and have Gaia making a date exactly at the wrong moment seemed like just the kind of world that could produce a serial killer. They were probably as common as cockroaches.

The phone rang.

Ed stared at it with mixed emotions. It was a little early, but he had no doubt that it was Gaia on the other end. Usually, he called her, but since she was going to be out patrolling, and he was going to be fact-finding, she'd said she'd call him when she got in.

On most nights Ed looked forward to the late-night Gaia call. She was never exactly a blabbermouth, but compared to the way she was at school, Gaia was far more open on the phone. The phone calls were the only times when she really spilled her thoughts. Ed loved it. He just wasn't sure he could take it right now. Not after everything that had happened. He didn't think he could sit there and make happy noises while Gaia talked about her upcoming date. The thought made his blood curdle.

Who was this date-worthy guy, anyway? Where had he come from? And what gave him the right to ask out Perfection Personified?

The phone rang again. If Ed didn't answer, he wouldn't have to hear about the mystery guy. He wouldn't have to kick himself for being such a gutless wonder.

Of course, if he stopped answering, Gaia might never call again.

Ed scrambled for the phone.

"Hey," he said as he lifted the receiver, "I know why they call him the Gentleman."

"Is this Ed Fargo?" said a voice on the other end of the line. A guy's voice.

Ed stared at the handset in confusion. "Who is this?"

"Sam Moon," said the voice. "I'm trying to reach Ed."

Sam Moon.

Ed knew who Sam was. They had even spoken a time or two, but that certainly didn't make them friends. Back in the days when Ed had traveled sans wheelchair, Heather had been his girlfriend. Now she was Sam's.

"What do you want?" Ed's voice came out a little rougher than he had intended.

"It's about Gaia Moore," said Sam.

Wonderful. Did Sam have a date with her, too? Maybe she'd lined up the football team for the weekend. Open wound. Salt at the ready. "What about Gaia?"

"It's just that . . . well—"

Ed wasn't breathing. "Well, what?"

"You're her friend, right? I've seen you together."

"I'm her friend," Ed agreed. And that was probably all he was ever going to be. Once again tiredness and anger got the better of him. Still, it was nice that Sam had noticed. Maybe he was even jealous. "If you're looking for tips on asking her out, you better talk to someone else because—"

"I'm not calling about anything like that," Sam said quickly.

"Then what do you want?"

Sam took a deep breath.

"I want you to help me save Gaia's life."

QUITE CONTRARY

"Are you awake?"

Gaia looked up. Or tried to look up. All she could see was dark and slightly less dark. Neither one of them seemed to form any shape that made sense.

"Don't worry," said a voice from the not so dark. A girl's voice. "I'm going to go call an ambulance."

"Uhh," Gaia grunted. She struggled to move her rigid jaw muscles. "Nuhhh."

No. Don't do that.

"Do you want me to stay with you?"

What Gaia wanted was for this disembodied voice to go away and leave her alone so that she could recover.

It was the most irritating thing—the real price of stressing her body in ways that no human being was built to take. For a few seconds, at most a few minutes, Gaia could push herself way past the limits of normal human strength and endurance, but when that time limit was up, Gaia's body went on strike. Her muscles stopped talking to her brain, and her body stopped moving. It would pass soon enough, but until it did, Gaia was absolutely helpless.

It was a feeling she didn't cherish.

"Look," said the voice. "I don't know what's wrong with you, but I don't think you're dying."

Great diagnosis, Doc.

"So I'm going to sit here with you and make sure you're okay." Gaia felt a warm body next to her arm. It didn't feel all bad, but she didn't want it there. "If you're not, I guess I better call an ambulance."

"Gooo way," Gaia managed to whisper. Gradually her muscles were waking up again, but she was still embarrassingly weak. She could probably get up; she just didn't want to try it in front of this girl.

Just how long had she chased the man in the black coat? Had they run two miles? Three miles? More than that? Every second of the run had been at a dead sprint. Add in a badly bruised knee and a shoulder that just might be dislocated, and Gaia felt like crap. Tired, abused crap.

Finally Gaia pushed her scraped hands onto the pavement and stood up shakily. She'd only been out for seconds, but it felt like an eternity to her.

"I think you really are going to live," said the girl.

Gaia licked her lips. "You sound surprised," she said in a harsh voice.

The girl shrugged. "Well, I've seen a lot of things, but I've never seen anybody kick ass one second and go into a coma the next. What are you on, anyway?"

Gaia started to laugh at the absurdity of the question, but it turned into a cough. A harsh, racking cough.

"You sure you don't want to go to the hospital?" the girl asked, reaching for Gaia's arm. "St. Vincent's is right down the street."

"No." Gaia shook her head. "I'll be all right. Really."

"Whatever you say," the girl said, eyeing her with disbelief.

Gaia turned her head and had to fight down a fresh wave of dizziness. "Where is he?"

"The guy who was after my purse?"

Gaia nodded.

"Don't know," said the girl. "He ran off. The way you hit him, I'd be surprised if he's not on his way to the nearest emergency room with a half-dozen cracked ribs."

All the systems in Gaia's body were coming back into

action like a computer being booted up after a long sleep. Unfortunately, her nerves were waking up along with her muscles. There was pain everywhere.

Gaia thought she heard something behind her and turned quickly. Nothing was there, but the head rush that overtook her was so overpowering, she momentarily stumbled. The red-haired girl reached out for her.

"I've got . . . oof!" The slim girl stood in close and held Gaia with both arms. "Damn, girl. You're solid."

Solid. That was a nice way to say she weighed as much as a water buffalo.

"I'll be okay," she said. "Just go on. Let me sit here a little longer, and I'll be fine."

"Nope. If you're not going to let me take you to the hospital, you at least have to let me buy you a cup of coffee," the girl said. "Not that you need to add caffeine to whatever weird substance you've got running through your veins."

Gaia closed her eyes. "I don't think—"

The girl shook her head. "Come on. A double latte is the next best thing to surgery."

Gaia started to laugh, but it was still a bad idea. It made too many things hurt too much. Maybe sitting and sipping would be the best things for her right now. Besides, if Shadow Man came back, she couldn't be sure she could defend herself.

"All right," Gaia agreed. "Coffee."

PERFECTLY PATHETIC

He watched from the best darkness he could find. Sweat poured down from his temples. His back. His underarms. His lungs felt like they'd been roasted over an open flame. Bent at the waist, holding his hands above his knees, he fought for breath. She was good. He had to give her that. But the scene in front of him made his pulse race faster than any sprint ever could.

She was also down. And she wasn't getting up. Couldn't, apparently. Not without help.

It was all he could do to keep from laughing through his gasps. How pathetic. How perfectly pathetic.

A skinny girl with tangly red hair was aiding the one. The target. The ultimate trophy.

His eyes narrowed into slits as his breath started to slow.

He could take them both. Two for the price of one. He could practically smell them from here. The fear would smell even better. He licked his lips. He could almost taste it.

As the girls shuffled off, he straightened his back. There would be no satisfaction in taking her now. Not when she couldn't even walk on her own. The side dish wasn't enough to sweeten the deal.

He wanted a fight.

He would have what he wanted.

But there were too many cops around. Too many pissants. There would be no more girls in the park tonight.

Unless, of course, he dragged one there.

TOM
MOORE

Once, when Gaia was a baby, she was playing in a sand-box in Central Park. It was a sunny day in early spring. I remember because Katia was picking buttercups and tickling Gaia's chin with them.

We turned our backs on Gaia for one moment. Just to clean up our picnic before retrieving her and heading for home.

Suddenly, out of nowhere, a crazed pit bull came charging at Gaia. She was two. Only two. Sweet. Small. Seemingly helpless.

Before I could blink, the pit bull was bearing down on Gaia and her playmate. With the attack instinct of an animal, my lovely daughter leaped at the wild dog and sank her baby teeth into the dog's hind leg.

That was when we knew we had a very special girl on our hands.

MARY

THERE WAS A DISTINCT POSSIBILITY
SHE COULD LIKE THIS GIRL.

SHARING STORIES

Gaia's arm was flung around the red-haired girl's shoulders as they stumbled their way across the winding pathways. The muscles in Gaia's knee felt like they had been stomped flat, stripped raw, and rubbed in coarse salt.

They neared the entrance of the park and found a young policeman with an unlikely handlebar mustache standing guard over the end of the pathway. Gaia made an effort to stand up straighter, putting less of her weight on her smaller companion. The last thing she wanted was for the cop to think she was drunk or on some kind of drugs.

"What do you two think you're doing in there?" the policeman called as they approached.

"Just taking a walk," the red-haired girl said.

The cop gave a snort. "You picked a bad place for a walk. Didn't you hear what happened in the park last night?"

"They're only slicing up blonds," the girl replied. "It's in all the papers."

"I wouldn't be too sure about that." He paused and looked them over. "Besides, your . . . *friend* is about as blond as they come."

There was something about the way he said *friend* that caught Gaia's ear. Maybe it was because she was so tired, but it took her a moment to put the idea together.

Two girls. Walking alone. Arms around each other.

This guy thought they were lesbians.

Gaia leaned harder on her companion and smiled. Might as well give him a show. His already ruddy face darkened, and there was a spark of interest in his eyes.

Men. So predictable. He quickly glanced away.

"We're leaving the park now," Gaia said. "So we'll be okay."

When the policeman looked at them again, he seemed a little irritated. "Be careful," he said. "If you have to come back this way, go around the outside of the park."

"Sure," said the girl. "Thanks for the profound advice."

They moved away and turned down Sullivan Street toward a row of cafes. Tired as she was, Gaia watched the stream of people moving in and out of the buildings with interest. Living in the city that never slept certainly had its high points. Getting coffee and doughnuts at any hour of the day or night was civilization at its peak.

Now that there were other people around, Gaia thought again about her weakness. She pulled her arm away from the red-haired girl's shoulders. "I can make it on my own now."

"You sure?" The girl kept her arm at Gaia's waist for a few steps, as if measuring her steadiness, then let her go. "For someone who was unconscious five minutes ago, you've made a miraculous recovery."

"I heal fast," said Gaia.

"Let's hope so." The girl stopped by a narrow building with a red door and a long list of coffees displayed in the window. "Come on—I'm buying."

Inside, the place showed signs of being in the middle of a theme change. There was a blackboard over the counter that read Coffee Cannes and a big-screen TV stood in a corner playing some film with subtitles, but the framed movie posters had all been taken down and stacked in a corner. In the front half of the shop the tables had been removed along both walls, and even though it was after eleven at night, workmen were busily installing computers and workstations in their place.

The red-haired girl found a table as far from the chaos as possible—which wasn't very far—and dropped her slim body into a cane-bottomed chair.

"I'm going to stop coming to this place when they're finished with the remodeling," she said. "It was cool to get my coffee with a Bergman flick. Caffeine and data is not my mix."

Gaia carefully bent her swollen, tender knee and eased herself into a chair across from the girl. "You don't have to buy," she said. "I've got cash."

"Save it." The girl slid her purse from her shoulder and dropped it in the center of the table. "If it weren't for you, I wouldn't have any money to pay for this, anyway. The least I can do is buy you a cup."

Gaia looked up at the board above the counter. Coffee and milk appeared in every possible combination. "Coffee," she said. "Just coffee. Nothing fancy."

The red-haired girl grinned. "I know exactly what you need." She twisted in her seat and shouted to the man behind the counter. "Hey, Bill, bring two cups over here. And none of that weak-assed Colombian. Bring the *stuff*."

The man behind the counter gave a tired nod and turned to a row of gleaming steel machines. A few moments later he dropped two huge mugs on the table, then turned without a word and went back to his post.

The coffee in the mugs produced tall plumes of steam, but that didn't stop the red-haired girl from lifting her mug and taking a long gulp. She shivered as she lowered her coffee. "Ahhh, as long as there's coffee, life goes on."

Gaia took a tentative sip. It was strong, bitter, and blazingly hot. It also seemed to carry a caffeine kick that rivaled espresso. Gaia could almost feel the coffee circulating in her veins. Perfect.

The girl reached a small hand across the table. "I'm Mary," she said.

Gaia took the hand. "Gaia."

"Gaia." The girl squeezed her fingers for a moment before releasing them. "Cool. Like the goddess."

Gaia blinked. Was it just her, or were people around here getting smarter? "Hardly a goddess."

"Well, you were certainly a powerful force of nature tonight," said Mary. She lifted her cup and took another slug of hot coffee, then she planted her elbows on the table and looked at Gaia. "Wait a minute—I know you."

Gaia's shoulders tensed.

"You do?"

Mary nodded. "I saw you at a party. You were there with Ed Fargo." She stopped and grinned. "Heather Gannis went nuclear on your ass."

Gaia rolled her eyes. It figured. "Yeah, that was me."

"Cool," said Mary. "So, you know Ed?"

Gaia nodded. She suddenly felt even more self-conscious. Ed was one of the few people who had seen her in the middle of a postfight collapse. Pretty soon the two of them would be sharing stories.

"Uh," Gaia mumbled. "Can I ask a favor?"

"You don't have to ask," said Mary. She made a dramatic sweep of her hand. "As an ass-kicking goddess, anything you want is yours."

"Cool. I mean, okay." She took a breath. "Could you please not talk about what happened tonight?"

"Not even with Ed?"

"Especially not with Ed," said Gaia.

Mary looked disappointed. "Well, all right." A mischievous smile crossed her face. "It would make a hell of a good story, though. The way you hit that guy, I thought—" She shook her head. "I don't know what I thought."

Gaia took another careful sip of the hot brew and studied the girl across the table. She was tall, at least as tall as Gaia, ridiculously thin. But her features weren't "elegant." Mary had a short, narrow nose set above full lips. Her eyes seemed almost too large for her head and were colored an intense green, with hardly any traces or flecks of other colors. Her skin was pale and freckled, yet there was something exotic about the angle of her big eyes. But the feature that really caught the attention was the hair. Surrounding Mary's face and tumbling down her back was a tangled mass of curls, curls, and more curls. She kept pushing them out of her face, and they would bounce right back.

She was oddly beautiful.

"Where did you come from, anyway?" Mary asked. "What were you doing in the park?"

Chasing a supersonic serial killer.

"I was just out for a run," Gaia lied. "I heard you yell and thought maybe I could help."

Mary nodded, a smile on her lips. "You definitely helped. You probably saved my life."

"I didn't save your life."

"How do you know?"

Gaia shook her head. "That guy you were fighting was just an ancient hippie. He probably wanted some money for drugs."

"That guy was an ancient hippie with a *gun*," Mary said.

"Gun?" Gaia frowned and tried to think back. "I didn't see any gun."

"It was there," said Mary. "He had it in one hand and pulled on my purse with the other. I thought he was going to kill me."

"Why didn't you let go of the purse?" asked Gaia. She hated the question as soon as it was out of her mouth. People were always saying that. Sit still. Don't fight. Give the bad man your purse like a good victim.

"No one gets my purse," said Mary. "All my shit's in there." She stopped for a second, then lowered her voice. "Actually, I guess there's nothing in there that's worth dying for, but I was just pissed off. I hate not being able to walk across the park without someone bothering me."

Now that was a sentiment Gaia could fully agree with. "You really think that guy had broken ribs?"

Mary grinned broadly. "I sure hope so."

Gaia half smiled. There was a distinct possibility she could like this girl.

But she wasn't making any promises.

PILE OF CATTLE

The black Mercedes pulled up behind a long line of police cars, the early morning sunlight glinting against their windshields. A few of the officers standing by gave it a glance, but no one moved to order the car away. Slowly the rear window rolled down.

Loki looked out. It was ridiculous. Absolutely ridiculous. There had to be at least fifty policemen in the park. They were everywhere, from uniforms standing guard by the gate to technicians literally up in the trees.

Loki couldn't stop himself from laughing. It was all so silly. If there ever had been any clues in this place, this herd of cattle had destroyed them. Not that he expected the police to catch the killer. Not this killer.

Loki raised his window and pushed open the door. "I'm going to go over and take a closer look."

"Do you want me to come with you?" asked the woman in the front seat.

"No. Wait here. This shouldn't take long."

"Yes, sir," said the woman.

Loki climbed out and started toward the park.

A tall, African American officer blocked his way. "I'm sorry, sir. No one is admitted to the park this morning."

"Official business." Loki reached into the pocket of his

overcoat and pulled out a badge case. He flipped open the case and held an FBI identification card up for the policeman to see. It was a fake, of course, but it was a very good fake. It came from the same machines that produced badges for actual FBI agents.

The officer looked from the card to Loki and back again. "Maybe I should get my lieutenant," he said uncertainly.

"There's no reason to do that," said Loki. "Just move out of my way."

The policeman stepped aside.

Loki moved on up the path. The day had started out overcast, and low clouds still blocked the rising sun, but as he approached the actual crime scene, Loki put on a pair of dark sunglasses. There were still a few men left in the NYPD who had once worked with him as a young government agent. It was many years in the past, and even that identity had been false, but in case any of those men happened to be on the murder investigation team, Loki didn't want to be part of an uncomfortable reunion.

The crime scene was in a grassy field near the corner of the park. A pleasant enough place, with benches, trees, and gray squirrels that dodged around the policemen's feet. Pleasant, but utterly boring.

Loki ignored several other policemen who tried to talk to him and walked straight to where the body lay crumpled on the ground. It was a young girl, as expected, with long blond hair splayed out in a fan around her head. There was blood matted into the hair. More blood on the ground.

"Can I help you?"

Loki looked around and saw a plainclothes officer. From the man's cheap coat and old-fashioned hat, he had to be a homicide detective.

"I'm Frank Lancino, Connecticut state police," Loki said. He reached into his coat and produced another identification card. Just as fake. Just as good. "I've been called in to consult on this one."

The detective nodded. "I heard they were talking to your guys." He jerked his head toward the body. "What do you think? Same asshole you had up your way?"

Loki knelt next to the body. The girl had been killed with a knife, but not with a single wound. There were cuts on the arms. Cuts on the legs. Puncture wounds that went all the way through the body and a long slice that cut half-way around her neck. "Yes," he said. "Yes, this certainly looks like the work of our boy."

The detective sighed. He jammed his hands into his tweed overcoat. "What are we going to do about this? Any ideas?"

Loki straightened. "First you need to talk to your technicians." He pointed at the ground. "If they can't do a better job outlining a body than that, who knows what else they missed."

"That outline's not from this body."

"It's not?" Loki looked at the detective curiously.

"That's from the previous victim," said the detective. "It looks like the killer did this one on the same spot as the one from the night before."

Loki had to fight back a smile. It was a nice touch. A very nice touch. He squinted at the trees around them. What were the odds that the subject of this investigation was out there right now, watching them? Loki thought it was very likely. Every artist wants to see the reaction to his work.

"Can I ask you some questions about the cases you've seen?" asked the detective.

"Later," said Loki. "I need to get to the station house. I'm sure I'll see you there."

Loki quickly retraced his steps and retreated to the car. The woman hustled around to open his door for him, then jumped back behind the wheel to steer the big sedan away from the curb.

"It's going to be interesting," said Loki.

The woman's green eyes were reflected as she glanced at him in the rearview mirror. "When do you think they'll meet?"

"Soon." He glanced out the window at the passing scenery. Rushing pedestrians. Colorful awnings. A man hosing down the sidewalk. It was another world. "Even now they could be moving toward a meeting."

"And when they meet?"

Loki gave a quiet laugh. "It will be one unbelievable fight."

"What if she dies?" the woman asked, her voice tight.

"Well, then, she's failed," Loki said. If she couldn't handle this, she was of no use to him, anyway.

"She has more training," the woman said. "You've seen how she can fight."

"Yes," Loki agreed. "But he has another advantage. He knows what he is. He knows what he's capable of."

"What is he capable of?" asked the woman.

"Anything."

DRESS FOR DISTRESS

Gaia woke up, then wished she hadn't.

She rolled over and sat up in the bed with a groan. Even before she peeled back the covers, she had a good idea of what she was going to find, and the real thing didn't disappoint. Her right leg was bruised from thigh to ankle. Her knee was one big scab, and every color of the bruised-and-abused rainbow decorated her leg—all the way from battered purple-blue to super-sickening yellow-green.

There was still a lingering whole-body soreness from her adventures the night before, but it wasn't as bad as she had predicted. Gaia was relieved to find that despite how awful her leg might look, it wasn't too stiff. She could walk without a problem, but it was going to be a while before she was up for another run like last night's.

She grabbed a pair of scuffed jeans from the back of a chair and carefully worked them up her injured leg. Then she pulled a hooded sweatshirt out of the closet and slipped it on. One glance in the mirror told the story. Gaia Moore, girl geek.

Why should today be any different from every other day?

She started toward the bedroom door, then had a startling thought. Today was different from every other day. Today she had a date.

Gaia groaned, limped back to the mirror, and took a longer look. She wasn't encouraged by what she saw.

Would there be time to change after school? Maybe. But what if David saw her in school? If he saw her like this, he would want to cancel.

Which would probably be a good thing. She shouldn't have said she'd go out with him in the first place.

But that thought hadn't even made it across her brain before another one chased it.

What was wrong with going out with a guy? Couldn't she just allow herself to be normal for five seconds?

Gaia shook her head. It was too early in the morning to start arguing with herself. It was *always* too early to argue with herself. She half expected a little devil and angel to pop up on her arms and start debating.

"I'm going," she said aloud. "I'm going, and that's it."

"If you're talking about school," said a voice in the doorway, "then it's about time."

Gaia spun around and saw Ella standing in the doorway. As usual, Ella looked like she was dressed for an evening at the clubs. Even at eight in the morning the *über*-bitch looked ready for dancing. Or an affair. Probably whichever option presented itself first.

This morning her ensemble was a short, glossy leather skirt topped off by a green blouse with a neckline that showed the top of her breasts. Her scarlet hair was swept back from her face, worked into an elaborate coif that Gaia couldn't have reproduced given an entire week.

"Ever heard of knocking?" Gaia asked.

Ella arched one perfectly plucked eyebrow. "Not in my own house, I haven't." She waved a lacquered nail at Gaia. "What are you doing up here talking to yourself? School starts in ten minutes."

"Then I'm not late yet."

Ella gave a sigh that held all the exasperation in the

world. "Just don't expect me to give you a ride. I have a business appointment this morning."

Gaia nodded. "Getting started a little early today, aren't we?"

The comment brought a frown to Ella's cherry red lips. "And what is that supposed to mean?"

"Nothing," said Gaia. "It's only that I noticed that you had a . . . business appointment last night, too. One that kept you out pretty late. Seems like you've had one every night since George went out of town."

Now Ella's lips pressed together so hard that Gaia was sure she'd have to reapply her lipstick. "Careful, Gaia." For a moment Ella looked almost dangerous. "George has done a lot for you. Your father meant the world to him. It would be ungrateful to insult his wife."

Gaia was about to make a reply to that when she noticed something odd about Ella's choice of words. "'Meant'?"

"Pardon?" Ella replied.

Gaia took a step toward her. "You said my father *meant* something to George." Did Ella know something about him? Had something happened?

"Did I?" The sarcasm in Ella's voice was so acid, it could have eaten through steel.

Gaia was amazed to find that her throat was getting tight. She had trouble speaking. "Yes, you did." She was angry at herself. She'd shown Ella too much vulnerability.

Ella gave a sly smile that would do any cat proud. "Just a slip of the tongue, I'm sure." She turned away. A few seconds later, Gaia could hear the tapping of Ella's pointed heels down the stairway.

For several long moments after that, Gaia could only stand there, trying to catch her breath and get her thoughts under control. Her father had left her. He didn't care anything about her, so why should she care about him? Still, the tightness in her throat didn't want to leave.

"He's not dead," she told herself.

Ella was just trying to screw with her. That was all. Superbitch in action.

Gaia looked again at the girl in the mirror. Now she saw not only a beast with tree trunk legs and lumberjack shoulders, with tangled hair, dressed in tasteless clothes. Now the beast had bloodshot eyes, too.

There wasn't much Gaia could do about the legs or shoulders, at least not in ten minutes, but she could try to do something about the clothes. She stripped off the worn jeans as fast as she could without descabbing her knee and tossed them on the bed. The sweatshirt followed. Then she confronted the dreaded closet.

The trouble with Gaia's wardrobe was that nothing inside the closet looked much better than the things she'd been wearing. Gaia had a pair of capri pants, but they did nothing but accentuate her she-hulk hips and legs. There were a few dresses wrapped up in dry-cleaner plastic. Gaia hadn't worn them in years.

Besides, any sort of skirt was out. Unless she wore it with jet black hose, the Technicolor glory of Gaia's bruised leg was bound to show. Even with black tights there was the possibility of blood and ooze and . . . nope. No skirt.

Gaia finally settled on a pair of drab olive drawstring pants. They weren't too attractive, but at least they were clean—and they hid her legs. Gaia fumbled through crumpled sweaters and sweatshirts before settling on a slightly less baggy black sweater.

She studied the results in the mirror. Lumberjack shoulders. Tree trunk legs. Tangled hair.

Unless the grunge look came back before first period, Gaia was as fashion-free as ever.

GENUINE
MONSTERS

BUT SERIAL KILLERS WERE DIFFERENT.
THEY WEREN'T RUN-OF-THE-MILL KILLERS
WHO HAPPENED TO GET AWAY WITH IT
MORE THAN ONCE.

ODD COUPLE

Ed had done stupider things in his life—most of them on a skateboard, surfboard, or other so-called extreme-sport implement, but this was high on his list of "I can't believe I'm doing this" moments.

He was skipping first period—cutting school—to see a guy who had stolen his old girlfriend. Worse than that, he was cooperating with a guy who obviously loved Gaia. Ed wasn't an idiot. Sam could spout that "oh I only want to help her" bullshit all day and into the next, but the truth was that Sam was seriously into Gaia. Worst of all, Ed knew that Gaia was seriously into Sam. The whole situation tied his intestines in knots. Big ones.

The assigned meeting place for their little get-together was the chess tables in the park—neutral ground. But the police still had the park closed off, so that spot was out. Instead Ed was patrolling the sidewalk along the north border, hoping to intercept Sam. And if he missed him, that was just too bad.

"Ed?"

Ed turned and saw Sam walking toward him. "What's wrong? Don't they have clocks in college? I was about to give up on you."

Instead of answering the question, Sam hooked his

thumb toward the park. "What's going on? Why the big crowd this morning?"

"Haven't you heard?" Ed asked, glancing at the organized mayhem. "The Gentleman made another call last night."

Sam's eyes flicked toward the trees at the edge of the park, and the tan went out of his square-jawed face. "You don't think . . . I mean, it couldn't have been . . ."

Ed seriously considered letting him stew for a moment, but his conscience got the better of him. "It wasn't Gaia."

"You're sure?"

"Yep," Ed said with a nod. "The TV guys say this one happened before eleven last night. I talked to Gaia after that."

Sam still looked concerned, but the concern was tainted by obvious envy. Score one for the Ed-man.

"Was she okay?" Sam asked.

"She was fine." Actually, the conversation had been disappointingly short. Gaia had said she was tired, and she hadn't wanted to talk about the murders. But Ed liked the idea that he knew more about Gaia than Sam did. Sam might be on Gaia's short list for sex, but Ed was the one Gaia talked to every night.

Sam fiddled with the collar of his oxford shirt. "Are the police any closer to catching this guy?"

Ed shrugged. "If they have any suspects, the papers aren't mentioning it. Except the *Post*—I think they've pinned it on Elvis, or aliens, or a coalition of brunettes jealous of all that fun blonds are supposed to have."

Sam only nodded. "I'm worried about Gaia."

That was the heart of the matter. That was what had convinced Ed to cut school and meet with a guy who he barely knew—but who he hated on general principle.

Sam was afraid because of how closely Gaia resembled the first girl killed in the park. For Sam it was about protecting a girl he feared was in danger.

For Ed it was a different story. Ed knew the big secret, and from the way Sam talked, he was pretty sure that Sam didn't. Sam apparently loved Gaia, but he didn't know that Gaia was Wonder Girl. He didn't know she could slice and dice Bruce Lee without breaking a sweat.

Ed was proud to be in on it. But it gave him more reason to be scared for her. Gaia wasn't just the killer's ideal victim; she was actively seeking the killer's attention. She was all set to find this demon, shove his teeth down his throat and his arms up his nether regions, then put in a call to the police. Case over. City saved.

It had seemed like a good idea. There wasn't much Gaia couldn't handle.

But Ed was no longer so sure. Between the phone call from Sam and his stack of serial killer bios, Ed worried that maybe Gaia was in over her head. Sure, she could land a roundhouse kick with the best of them. He had seen her take out three thugs in one go. But serial killers were different. They weren't run-of-the-mill killers who happened to get away with it more than once. These guys were strange, creepy. They were genuine monsters.

Ed was pretty sure that Gaia wasn't experienced in taking on monsters. When it came to these guys, she needed just as much help as the next person. Problem was, Gaia would never recognize the fact that she might need help— let alone admit it.

"What have you found out?" asked Sam.

Ed nodded toward a bench along the perimeter of the park. "Let's go over there where you can sit down," he said. "I'm tired of looking up at you."

Sam followed instructions. He went to the bench, sat, and waited for the Ed report.

"You know the basics, right?" Ed asked.

"Six victims," Sam started, then he turned his head and looked over his shoulder. "Seven now, I guess. Connecticut, New Jersey, and here. All of them stabbed, all of them blond, all of them around Gaia's age and size." He stopped and ran one hand through his ginger-colored hair. "That's about all I know. I don't even know why they call him the Gentleman."

"I do," said Ed. "It's from an old movie, *Gentlemen Prefer Blondes*."

Sam nodded slowly. "I've seen it. Marilyn Monroe, right?"

"Bingo."

Sam looked down at the ground and shook his head.

"That's not much help. How are we going to catch this guy before he has a chance at Gaia?"

"We're not," Ed replied.

Sam's head jerked up sharply. "What do you mean?"

Ed rolled slowly back and forth in front of the bench. Wheelchair pacing. "You're the college guy. Isn't it obvious that if three states' worth of cops can't catch this guy, we're not going to do it?"

Sam's frown grew deeper. "Then why are we even talking?"

"Because," said Ed. "We don't have to find the killer." He raised one hand and pointed in the direction of the school. "We only have to stick to Gaia."

EMPTY CHAIRS

Gaia was thirty minutes late to first period. Even compared to some of her previous arrival times, it was a new achievement in nonpunctuality. Even so, her teacher decided to ignore her.

Gaia had barely started at this school, and already she had been the butt of so many jokes, people were getting tired of it.

It was a good plan. Give them so much to laugh about that it wears them out. Too bad she hadn't actually *planned* to do it.

Gaia settled into her seat and the public address speakers crackled to life.

"May I have your attention, please?" said the voice of an unseen school office worker. "This is a schoolwide announcement."

The last event deemed worthy of a schoolwide announcement had turned out to be a pep rally. Earth-shattering stuff.

"Due to recent events, the school will be closing early today. The last period will end at one P.M. Additional counselors will be on hand in the lunchroom for any students who feel they would benefit from a counseling session. School hours will return to normal tomorrow. Thank you." The voice ended with another squirt of static.

The announcement of an early end to the school day drew a few muted cheers but didn't get nearly the reaction that Gaia had expected. She leaned toward a skinny, red-haired guy at a nearby desk.

"What events are they talking about?" she asked. "Why let us out early?"

The redhead nodded his pointy chin toward a desk at the front of the room. An empty desk.

Gaia stared at the desk, trying to remember whose body normally filled it. It wasn't Hateful Heather. Heather was in her usual place of power at the center of the room. It wasn't Ed. Ed wasn't in this class. Gaia frowned as she tried to remember. It was . . . It was . . .

Cassie Greenman. The girl who had told Gaia about the killing the day before. The girl who had said they looked alike.

Gaia turned to the red-haired guy again. "What happened to Cassie?"

Redhead moved his lips to form a single word. Gaia didn't have to be much of a lip-reader to make it out. Gentleman.

The headache that had only threatened in Gaia's bedroom suddenly came on with full force. "Where?" she asked.

The guy looked toward the teacher and tried to avoid Gaia's attention.

"Where?" she said again, more than a little louder. "Where did it happen?"

"In the park at eleven o'clock," the redhead shot back. He picked up his book and opened it, angling the pages so they formed a screen to ward off Gaia.

It didn't matter. Gaia had asked all the questions that mattered. She closed her eyes and tried to fight back waves of nausea and confusion. It was too coincidental, too weird. Cassie knew about the murderer. Why in the world would she be anywhere near the park at eleven o'clock at night?

How could Gaia have failed a second time? It almost felt like this killer was taunting her. Once again he had struck right under her nose. And this time it had been someone Gaia knew.

Gaia had thought she could catch this guy before he did any more damage. She had maybe hoped there was something good in being fearless. Maybe even something good in being a muscle-bound freak. Something that made her life worthwhile.

Obviously she was wrong.

MARY

I make friends pretty easily. I'm fun. I'm loud. I know how to have a good time.

People are drawn to me.

But I'm not always drawn to them.

But this Gaia person? I genuinely like her. She intrigues me. That's why I gave her my number and told her to call if she ever felt like hanging out.

It's obvious she never will, but it's a gesture. And when you make a gesture, sometimes people feel they owe you something. And when people feel they owe you something . . . Well, that can come in handy from time to time.

A SIMPLE JOB

THE SOONER THE INFORMATION REACHED SAM,
THE BETTER THE CHANCE OF SAVING GAIA.

MURPHY'S LAW

Tom Moore tugged down on his brown cap and did his best to shade his face. He had no reason to suspect that anyone would recognize him on the campus of NYU, especially dressed as he was in the brown uniform of a package deliveryman, but it didn't pay to take chances.

Years of experience had taught Tom that Murphy's Law was always in full operation when you were undercover. If anything could go wrong, it would. Even when nothing could go wrong, it went wrong, anyway.

Today's expedition into the city seemed like a simple thing—drop off a package, run, and hope that the person getting the package knew what to do with the information it contained. That only made Tom more cautious. It was the simple jobs that turned into nightmares.

He felt a little odd, walking between the square buildings along Washington Place. Part of it was the feeling that any older person gets visiting a college or high school. An out-of-place feeling. Only Tom didn't need to be surrounded by kids to feel out of place. He was out of place just being alive.

He reached the gray concrete steps of the dorm and hurried inside. Put on the right uniform, and you can get anywhere. Show a little paperwork, and people will even point out the right door.

Three minutes later, Tom had walked through a disheveled common room and was rapping his knuckles against a dented oak panel marked B4. He'd hand the boy the box and go.

A feeling of guilt added to Tom's uneasiness. This boy's relationship to Gaia had already led him into serious trouble. Involving him further might well get the boy killed.

Tom shoved away the guilt. He had to do what he could to protect Gaia. It would be impossible to get the information directly to her—Gaia was under almost constant observation. If Tom tried to get close, he would only get himself killed. And more to the point, Gaia as well.

There was no response to his knock. He tried again, rapping a little harder this time.

"Package," he called through the closed door. "Package for Sam Moon."

One of the doors on the other side of the common room opened, and an overweight young man, his hair shaved down to a dark stubble, stuck out his head.

"He's not here," he said, a strong southern accent in his voice. "I saw him leave about half an hour ago."

Tom frowned. "Do you know where he could be?"

The stubble-haired neighbor shook his head. "He usually comes back here between classes. You want me to hold on to that for him?"

Tom's fingers instinctively tightened around the package. He ran through the possibilities. He could try to find

Sam elsewhere. He had pulled the boy's class schedule off the Internet, and he could always wait for Sam outside a classroom. Unfortunately, package delivery companies didn't usually ambush people in hallways.

He could try coming back later, but that had its own set of risks. The sooner the information reached Sam, the better the chance of saving Gaia.

Tom looked at the boy with the shaved head. There was no reason to think he couldn't be trusted. No reason except that he appeared to have about as many brain cells as a ceiling beam.

"If I give it to you, will you be able to give it to him today?" Tom asked.

"As soon as he shows up," the boy promised.

Tom hesitated a moment longer, then nodded. "Sign here," he said. He passed a clipboard over, watched the boy sign it, and then—reluctantly—handed him the box.

The boy stepped back and started to close the door.

Tom grabbed the edge of the door and held it open. "This is an important package," he said. "You need to see that he gets it right away."

"Yeah," the boy replied, obviously perplexed. "Sure." He pulled on the door, and Tom let it go.

"Tell him it's from Gaia," Tom said to the closing door. "An important package from Gaia."

The door closed with a click, and a moment after, Tom heard the sound of one, two, three locks being set. He stared at the old, scratched wood door for a moment, then turned and started out of the building.

He was aware that he hadn't acted like a deliveryman. It didn't matter. Sam's neighbor could think anything he liked.

As long as he delivered the package.

SCREAMING DESK

Gaia never knew a piece of furniture could scream.

It was there in every class she had shared with Cassie Greenman. A desk. An empty desk.

It was just a plain desk, scratched up and written on by so many students, it was hard to even make out where one set of initials stopped and the next one started. A couple of pieces of plastic, some plywood, and twisted-up metal. But every time Gaia looked at it, she heard this weird kind of wailing down deep in her brain.

She wondered if she was going crazy—even more crazy than usual. But Gaia didn't think she was the only one who heard the screaming.

All day, other people kept glancing over at the desk. The Empty Desk. And every time they looked that way, they'd get this expression on their faces. Instantly zoned. Even the teachers seemed to be looking at it as if they expected the desk to answer a question or make a comment on the class.

It was profoundly weird.

Gaia knew they cut a couple of hours off the day, but by the time the last bell rang, she would have sworn that she had been in school for at least three weeks.

If anybody had asked her what had been covered in her classes that day, Gaia couldn't have repeated a word. Not that she was ever Ms. Perfect Attention. But ever since the morning announcement the only sound track in Gaia's head was the screaming desk and a running loop of her conversation with Cassie.

As far as Gaia knew, it was the first time she had ever talked to Cassie. And the last.

The thing that really bugged Gaia, the thing she just could not get around, was this:

What in hell was Cassie Greenman doing in Washington Square Park at night? It didn't make any sense. Cassie had seemed genuinely scared of the killer. She had even talked about dyeing her hair to take her off the victim list. Cassie Greenman might not have been a rocket scientist, but anyone smart enough not to play on subway tracks would have known better than to go into the park.

Except Gaia, of course, but that was different.

Gaia took a last look at the screaming desk as she staggered out of class. It had eyeball magnetism, that desk. It was like a tooth missing right in the middle of someone's smile. You couldn't stop looking at it. Gaia wondered how long it would be before someone else sat there and filled in the gap. She was willing to bet that desk was going to be empty for a long time.

Gaia made it down the hall, pounded her locker into submission, and shoved her stuff inside.

Why hadn't she seen Cassie in the park? It wasn't exactly teeming with people. How could Gaia have missed her?

Thoughts of Cassie grew so thick, it was like walking around in a literal fog. Gaia trudged slowly along the hallway, lost to the world. Then she started around the corner by the school office and ran smack into what felt like a concrete wall.

She gave a mumbled "sorry" and started to move on.

"It's all right. At least this time you didn't knock me down."

Gaia looked up at the voice. "Huh?"

"Hi," said David. "Remember me? David Twain, boy obstacle."

Gaia blinked away the tangle of twisted thoughts. David hadn't felt like a wall yesterday. Last night must have taken more out of her than she thought. "What are you doing here?" she asked.

David grinned. "It's school. They make you go."

"I mean . . ." Except Gaia didn't know what she meant. Her brain was still deep in the Cassie zone, and she was having a hard time getting it back in the real-world dimension.

"I'm going to have to start wearing football pads," David said, rubbing at the back of his neck. Gaia watched his forearm where he'd rolled up his sleeve. He was better-looking today. Somehow the thought pissed her off.

"Sorry," Gaia said again, stepping around. "I'm not all here at the moment."

"Yeah, I've seen the studies," David said, shoving his hands in his pockets. His binder was tucked under his arm with one book. There was no backpack. Gaia brought her hand to her forehead, confused by her inadvertent observations. Since when was she interested in this kind of thing?

"What studies?" she asked, focusing in on the little space of skin between his dark eyebrows.

"About you," David replied. "Four out of five doctors warn that you're a major source of bruises."

Gaia shook away the last of the Cassie fog and tried to concentrate on what David was saying. Some part of her brain told her that she had just missed a joke, but she was in no mood to go back and figure it out.

"Whatever." Another brilliant response from Ms. Gaia Moore, ladies and gentlemen.

David smiled. Dimples. Annoying.

"Well, *whatever* you are or aren't, I *was* looking for you," he said. "In fact, looking for you was my number-one objective for the afternoon."

"Why?" The fog was rolling back in.

"The date, remember?"

Gaia blinked. Date. For a moment the words belonged to a foreign language. Something they might say in the jungles of Borneo or maybe on the far side of the moon. Then she remembered. Coffee. Baklava. Her first ever genuine date. It was amazing what a little thing like murder could make you forget.

"Look, David," she said. "Maybe we shouldn't. You know, because of . . . Cassie and all."

His face was quickly overtaken by an expression of concern. "I'm sorry. Were you two close?"

"No. It's not that. It's . . ." Gaia wondered how David would react if she explained to him that she was the ugly sister of Xena, Warrior Princess, and Cassie was one of the helpless peasants Gaia was supposed to protect from the rampaging hordes. "It bothers me."

David nodded. "It bothers me, too." He gave a quick look around the hallway. "I just moved here last week. Everybody keeps saying that New York is this really safe place, that there's not nearly as much crime as people say. They act like it's all in the movies. But I get here and there's this big murder thing going on."

Gaia shrugged. "They're only killing blond girls. You shouldn't have to worry."

That off-center smile crept back onto his face. "Yeah, but I kind of like blond girls," he said in a low voice. "I want to keep them around."

It wasn't the smoothest response in the world. On the Skippy scale, Gaia marked it closer to regular than extra creamy. But he was trying.

"Okay," she said. "Maybe we could go somewhere. Just for a little while."

"Anywhere you want," he replied. "If you don't feel like dessert, maybe we could just go over to Googie's and grab a burger."

Googie's. Yet another spot on Gaia's Guide to the Village. It was a place so tacky, it was . . . really tacky. "For a guy who's only been here a couple of days, you sure have homed in on prime sources of empty calories."

David patted his disgustingly flat stomach. "I have a list of priorities whenever I move." He raised his hand and started ticking off the points. "First, locate an immediate source of sugar. Two, find a good greasy burger. Three, pin down a decent pizza." He lowered his hand. "Once all that's done, you're ready to move on to number four."

Gaia raised an eyebrow. "What's number four?"

The dimples retreated, and David looked at her for the first time with a completely serious expression. "Find the right girl to share it with."

Gaia had to give him credit. He was Not Sam, but he was good. She did a quick top-to-bottom survey. Chinos: pressed, but not too neat. Khaki shirt over black T-shirt: again, looking a little less than perfect. Just an average guy. And average was okay with her.

Gaia did a little mental arithmetic. If what she had heard was right, then both victims had died in the park in the middle part of the evening, somewhere before midnight. If Gaia was in place by nine-thirty, ten at the latest, she should be ready to tackle the killer if he came back for thirds—not that she would be the only person looking for him there tonight. She'd still have time for a quick dinner, a change of clothes, and working her way past Ella.

Not that the last part was hard. Ella had been off doing Ella things every night for a week.

"You're sure you want to go out with me?" Gaia asked. She knew it was tempting fate, but she felt like she had to give him a final chance to back out.

David nodded. "Absolutely."

"Then here's the deal. Meet me at Third and Thompson at six, and we'll eat."

"What's at Third and Thompson?"

"Jimmy's Burrito." Gaia gave him her best excuse for a smile. "Even greasier than Googie's."

A SIMPLE PLAN

Sam leaned against the cool stone of the Washington Square Park arch. He looked around to make sure that no one was watching, then pulled a small yellow radio from his pocket and squeezed the trigger on its side. Even alone, he still felt like an idiot.

"Do you see her?" he asked. He let go of the trigger, then quickly pressed it again. "Over."

There was a moment of silence before Ed's voice came back. "Yes, I see her. I'm in a wheelchair. I'm not blind. Over."

"Which way is she going? Is she heading toward the park?"

Static.

"Ed? Is she going toward the park?"

Static.

"Ed?"

"You're supposed to say 'over' when you're done."

"Over, for God's sake. Is she going toward the park? Over," Sam snapped.

Static.

"Ed? I said over."

"I heard you. I was just moving to keep up with Gaia. Have you ever tried to roll and use a walkie-talkie at the same time?" he hissed. "Next time you decide to steal radios, I suggest you get one with a headset. Over."

Sam pushed the trigger again. "I didn't steal these. I paid for them."

It was at least temporarily true. They were good radios, guaranteed to have at least a two-mile range and fourteen channels, and they had fancy built-in scrambling so no one else could listen in on the conversation. Very nice radios. Also very expensive.

There was no way Sam could afford to keep them. So he had paid for them at an electronics store with a thirty-day return policy. As soon as Operation Protect Gaia was over, the radios were going back. At the moment they were paid for.

"Which way is Gaia going?" Sam asked again. "Over," he added quickly.

"It looks like she's going home," Ed's voice replied. "Probably to get ready for her date. Over."

Sam stared at the radio in his hand. He had to have heard that wrong. "Say again."

Static.

"Ed?"

"You didn't say 'over.' Over."

Sam squeezed the radio, envisioning Ed's neck between his fingers. "Can you forget the stupid 'over' and just repeat whatever it was you said?"

"I said, she's going home." There was a hint of laughter in Ed's radio voice.

Sam gripped the radio. "Not that part."

"Then what . . ." Static. "Oh, you mean the date."

"What date are you talking about?" It took all his effort to release the talk button so he could listen for a response he was sure he didn't really want to hear.

"Don't you know about the date?" More glee. Obvious this time.

Sam was glad there was at least a mile of space between them. If Ed had been close enough to reach, the Gentleman wouldn't be the only one in the park committing murder.

"Obviously I don't know about the date," Sam said slowly. "If I knew about the date, would I be asking about the date?"

"Gaia has a date tonight," Ed's voice replied. His voice had changed. There was resignation in it now. "She warned me about it yesterday."

No one had warned Sam. Of course, Gaia and Sam weren't on the best of terms. They had basically no reason to speak at all. But Sam still felt blindsided by the enormity of Ed's announcement.

Gaia had a date. *She's not yours,* he reminded himself. *She was never yours.* Somehow he still felt betrayed.

"Who is she going out with?" Sam asked.

"A new guy," Ed replied flatly. "David something." Sam was about to ask another question, but before he could, Ed's voice came again. "I need to move again if I'm going to keep her in sight."

Sam pushed himself away from the cold marble of the arch. "All right. Call me if she comes back out. We'll work out positions."

"Roger," said Ed. "Over and out. Ten-four. Copy tha—"

Sam switched off the radio. He flicked a switch that would make it ring like a telephone if Ed called, then dropped it into his jacket pocket.

Sam went through a mental list of questions about the date, but he couldn't think of how to ask them without sounding jealous. Was he jealous? He thought about it for a moment and decided the answer was yes. He might not be able to define his own feelings about Gaia, but he was sure about one thing—he didn't want her going out with anyone else.

With Gaia gone back to her brownstone to prepare for the unthinkable date, Sam wasn't sure what to do. He could hang around the park for the afternoon, maybe get in a game. But losing a game of chess didn't seem very appealing without at least the chance of seeing Gaia.

After a few moments of indecision he turned to go back to his dorm. This was probably the only chance he was going to get to shower, eat something, maybe even grab a quick catnap. He would be back on duty soon enough.

Sam strolled across Washington Square North and headed uptown. The plan he and Ed had worked out was a simple one—until the Gentleman was caught, killed, or had moved on to another state, they would keep Gaia under close observation. Close observation defined as spying on her night and day.

There were two upsides to this plan. First, it would keep Sam occupied, thus keeping his mind off the obsessive kidnapping questions. Second, the plan involved seeing Gaia. A lot.

For today both Sam and Ed would both be on duty. If Gaia appeared, they would stay close. If Gaia got in trouble, they would help her. If they made it through the first day, they would switch over to working in shifts. Ed would watch Gaia during the school day; Sam would take over in the afternoons. It seemed like a simple plan.

Sam only hoped the killer was caught before Sam died from exhaustion.

A group of skateboarders went past, headed for the park, followed closely by a knot of laughing kids. The police had kept Washington Square locked up for most of the morning, but now that the barriers were down, the usual park population was rushing in to fill the void.

Sam cast a sideways glance as a barrel-chested man in a Greek fisherman's hat strolled past, a newspaper tucked under his arm. The man didn't seem familiar. He definitely wasn't a regular. Maybe he was the killer.

Another man went past. This one had a narrow, hatchet-shaped face and wild, bushy eyebrows. Killer material for sure.

There was a middle-aged Asian woman wearing a long, dark coat—an awfully heavy coat for a day that was pretty warm. She could have hidden anything under that coat. After all, even if the press called the killer the Gentleman, there had been no witnesses to the killings. Who was to say this Gentleman wasn't a Gentlewoman?

Sam was looking at another man when he realized how crazy this was. Of course these pedestrians didn't look familiar. Fifty thousand people must walk down Fifth Avenue to Washington Square on any day of the week. Maybe more like a hundred thousand. Sam couldn't possibly recognize them all.

It was time for Sam Moon to stop playing Sam Spade. A blast of sugar laced with caffeine, some sack time, and an icy shower were all required. Any order would do.

He managed to make it back to his dorm without spotting

any more serial killer wannabes on the streets. But that didn't mean there wasn't still one out there. Maybe Sam could just have the caffeine and the shower. The nap would take too long. He couldn't leave Gaia out there alone while he snoozed. So no nap.

That decision made, Sam actually felt a tiny bit better. He walked through the common room and was about to open the door to his bedroom when he heard another door open.

"Hey, Sam," said a voice at his elbow. "Think fast."

Someone who had gone through high school playing basketball would have had an instant response to those words. Sam played chess. He turned around just in time to take a cardboard box between the eyes.

"Ouch," he said as the small package bounced off his forehead and thumped to the floor.

"You got bad hands, Moon." Sam's suite mate, Mike Suarez, leaned back against his door frame, grinning.

Sam reached for the package. "My hands are okay; it's my head that's slow." He picked up the box and turned it over in his hands. "What's this?"

"Delivery guy brought it for you this morning," Mike replied. "That's all I know." He shrugged and winked. "You better work on those hands."

"Right." Sam returned the smile, although he felt more like smacking Mike's head right back.

Sam turned to the door and pushed it open, reminding himself for the umpteenth time that he really had to get that lock fixed. As soon as he was inside, he looked at the package again, wondering who might have sent it. It was a small box, little bigger than a stack of index cards, and the label had no return address.

There was only one way to find out. He grabbed the paper at the edge of the box and started to tug.

"Sam?"

This time the voice came from inside his room. Sam looked up in surprise and saw Heather sitting on the edge of his bed. "Heather! Jesus, you scared me."

Heather smiled at him. "We didn't have the best night last night," she said. "I thought I would try to make it up to you."

Sam opened his mouth to say something else, but the subject slipped away before it could get to his tongue. Heather's long, rich brown hair had been set loose to spill around her shoulders. She was wearing a short, black skirt that ended well above her knees and a white shirt. A big white shirt.

"That's my shirt," he said.

Heather nodded. "I borrowed it." Her lips pursed into a pout. "I'm sorry. You want me to take it off?"

"No, I—"

The pout on Heather's lips was replaced by a sly smile. "I was hoping you would say yes." She raised her fingers to the top button and slowly slipped it open. Then she moved down to the next. "I think we should try again, Sam," she said. "The last time didn't end so well, did it?"

Her tone was inviting, but her eyes conveyed a whole other message. She was giving him a chance to make it up to her. Make up for chasing after Gaia and leaving her naked. Alone. Unsatisfied. One chance.

There was no way Sam was stupid enough to disappoint her. He didn't want to.

He quickly shoved the little package into his coat pocket next to the yellow plastic radio and closed the door.

Apparently there would be no nap, no shower, and no caffeine.

STRANGER

"SOON I'LL BE THROUGH THE MAIN COURSE."

HE LOOKED AT LOKI OVER HIS SHOULDER.

"I THINK I'LL TAKE UP BRUNETTES FOR DESSERT."

THE THING

"You might as well come out," Loki said calmly. "I know that you're following me."

The boy stepped out from the trees and stood in the dry grass at the edge of the sidewalk. "Well, if it isn't my dear uncle Loki," he said in a cheerful tone. "Whatever brings you here?"

Loki kept his hand in his pocket and closed his fingers around the comforting bulk of his 9-mm pistol. "You couldn't resist, could you?" he said. "You had to come and watch."

The boy shrugged. "I admit, there is a certain pleasure in watching all the little bugs scurry around." He waved his hands extravagantly. "The police run here. The FBI runs there. And you run in between."

"Do you think this is funny?"

"Oh, very," the boy said. "But that's not why I'm here."

"Then why are you here?" Loki took a half step back. He tried to judge the odds. His skills with a firearm weren't as polished as they had been ten years before, but he was still quite fast. He could pull his semiautomatic pistol and get off ten rounds before most men even realized he had moved. But against this boy . . . Loki thought his chances of surviving were no better than fifty-fifty.

The boy turned and looked back through the screen of trees at the people passing through the park.

"Actually," he said, "I was only taking in the menu. Picking out a little something for tonight." He gestured at a group of girls laughing near the fountain. "There are so many possibilities here."

Loki studied the boy as if he were a stranger. It was almost true. A year before, the boy had been just that—a boy. A boy with an unusual predilection. Then he'd been unsure of himself. Awkward. Looking to Loki and others for guidance.

A year could change everything. The man—the thing—that Loki faced had as little relation to that uncertain boy as a kitten did to a tiger. In every way that counted, he was a stranger.

"I didn't think any of that group would be to your taste," Loki replied, glancing at the gaggle of young women.

"No?"

"I thought you were only after blonds."

The stranger with a familiar face laughed. "So true," he said. "But that was only the appetizer. Soon I'll be through the main course." He looked at Loki over his shoulder. "I think I'll take up brunettes for dessert."

Loki frowned. He wasn't squeamish. He never had been. One life lost, a hundred lives lost, what did it matter? But there were things he cared about: years of work, research, effort. Those things should never be wasted.

Against his better judgment he took a step forward.

"Come back," he said. He thought about touching the stranger's shoulder but decided against it. "Come home."

"Home?" The boy made a noise that might have been the start of laughter but quickly turned into something more like a growl. "Home," he said again. His face twisted into a sudden sneer, and he began to pace back and forth between the trees and the edge of the concrete path, his black coat billowing in the wind. "Couldn't you find a better word than *home?*"

"It was your home," Loki said in his most reassuring tone. "For most of your life you were—"

The boy whirled. His eyes were sharp. "Oh, don't say happy," he snapped. "It was an experiment. A rat cage. A prison. Not a home. And I was never, ever happy in that box." He raised his arm and pointed an accusing finger at Loki. "That place is the reason I'm here. The reason for everything."

Loki sighed. It was a sad, tired sound, the sound of an old man who was past his prime and weary of the world. It was a sound Loki had practiced.

"All right," he said. "I don't suppose there's anything I can say to make it better now." Hidden in the pocket of his coat, his hand tightened on the grip of the pistol. He began to raise the barrel.

The boy blinked, and as quickly as it had come, his rage seemed to evaporate. A broad smile returned to his face.

"Don't tell me you're going to shoot me," he said. "Not

after you've come so far to ask your poor prodigal son to come back to the farm."

For ten seconds they stood in silence. Loki had no idea what the boy was thinking, but his own mind was playing over scenarios as fast as a chess computer trying out moves. In this game there were only two opening moves: Leave the boy alone or kill him. Each of those moves had its possibilities and its dangers. Loki made a quick glance around and judged his distance from the other people in the park. There were no police nearby, and the risk of auxiliary damage was low. Now was the time.

"I was wrong to let you out," said Loki. "You're undisciplined. Unready. You have to come back with me."

"Or you'll kill me," said the boy.

Loki nodded. "Yes."

The boy was fast. Incredibly fast. One moment he was ten feet away. The next Loki's hand was hit by a rock-hard blow that sent the automatic pistol spinning away. Before he could react to that first attack, a fist cracked against his chin. He reeled backward, red fog swirling in his brain.

Strong hands caught Loki by the shoulders and spun him around.

"You made me the way I am for a purpose," the boy hissed in a low whisper, "but I've got my own objectives now. The first one is to kill your golden child." The fingers tightened. "And then I'm coming for you."

The boy released his grip, stepped back, and smiled. It was almost serene. He touched one finger to his forehead in a mock salute, then turned and strolled casually across the park.

Loki watched him go. In a way, he was greatly relieved that he hadn't managed to kill the boy. He couldn't be certain if it was the right decision.

But he would know soon enough.

A HAPPY GAIA

The best thing about having a date at Jimmy's was that it had all the ambiance of a shoe box. Maybe less.

That didn't mean Gaia didn't like it. Ambiance came way, way down on the list of her requirements in a restaurant. Way below sour cream and globs of melty cheese.

Besides, no ambiance equaled no need to dress up. No need to dress up equaled no need to worry about changing clothes. No need to worry about changing clothes equaled a happy Gaia.

That was the theory. In the real world she decided to make a change.

What she really needed was something dark. Something nice. Cool. Something sort of *Matrix*-like. Something that would hide stains.

Fat chance of finding it in her closet. This was depressing. For a split second Gaia thought of the red-haired girl. Mary. The smudged number on the crumpled coffeehouse napkin in the pocket of last night's jeans. Had Mary meant it when she said to call her? Was that what girls did? Call for advice before dates?

Right. Like that was going to happen.

Gaia went back to the black jeans she had looked at in the morning and decided to give them another try. They fit a little snug—snugger than she would have liked across her bulging butt. Still, they didn't look too bad.

She stared a few minutes longer, then closed her eyes, reached in, and selected a hanger at random. Gaia opened her eyes to peek. A big denim shirt. Not an inspired choice, but at least a choice.

She gave her hair a few strokes, pulled it back, and slipped it through her one and only scrunchie. There. She was dressed, and the whole thing had taken less than half an hour. It had to be a new record.

Gaia checked the clock. Plenty of time to cruise by the park, lose a game to Zolov, and still be early for her date.

Date.

Gaia felt a shimmery feeling in her legs. Not a major quake, but at least a 3.5 on the do-I-really-want-to-go-through-with-this scale. The date was only a couple of hours away, and she still couldn't get a good handle on the idea. Gaia was going to a restaurant. With a guy.

It wasn't a completely unknown situation. She had been out on social occasions before. Of course, the last time was probably when she was twelve. It wasn't completely unheard of. Except this time the guy was actually coming because of Gaia. He would look at Gaia. And talk to Gaia. Worse, he would expect Gaia to talk back and be interesting for minutes on end.

She wondered if she could just keep her mouth full of burrito and let him talk. Guys liked to talk. That's what she had heard, anyway.

With this stellar plan in place Gaia started downstairs, sure that she was on her way to end her status as the world's oldest undated girl. It was possible that she would even break the great kiss curse.

But a new obstacle was waiting for Gaia before she reached the ground floor. She closed her eyes and sighed.

She'd forgotten about the Wicked Witch of the Wonderbra.

Ella looked at Gaia over the rims of her purple-tinted sunglasses. "Where are you going?"

"Nowhere," Gaia replied.

Ella smirked. "Then maybe you shouldn't go. It's getting late."

"Late?" Gaia pointed at the window beside the staircase. "It's barely after four. It's broad daylight out there."

Ella pursed her glossy lips. "I know, but with all those murders going on, I really think you need to stay in. It's just too dangerous."

The person on the stairs looked like Ella. The perfume drifting toward Gaia in invisible clouds certainly smelled like Ella. But her mind had clearly been replaced by the mind of someone else—someone who cared if Gaia kept breathing.

Or at least bothered to pretend to care.

What the hell was she supposed to say? Part of her just wanted to walk out like she normally would, but some morbid part of her was tempted to play along.

"I . . . uh . . . won't stay late." That was at least partially true. Gaia could circle back by the brownstone after her early date with David. Then she could slip out again as soon as Ella got over this caring fit.

Ella waited a few seconds, then nodded. "All right," she said, "but whatever you do, stay out of the park. And try to get home before eight. It's a school night."

Gaia stared. Body snatchers were definitely at work. This whole conversation could not be occurring. Not with Ella.

She tried to answer but could only manage a nod. Ella's behavior had baffled Gaia beyond the ability for rational speech.

TIMING IS EVERYTHING

Sam wondered if you could drown in hair. Heather's hair was long and lush and altogether beautiful to look at. Breathing through it was a different story. No matter how Sam turned in the narrow bed, he seemed to end up with a suffocating curtain of brown spilling over his face.

Heather murmured something and snuggled against him. Her soft skin felt extraordinarily warm against his legs and chest.

Like Heather, Sam was nearly unconscious in a postsex daze. It was amazing. Sex was like the greatest sleeping aid in history. One minute he was more charged up than he had ever been in his life, the next minute his arms and legs seemed to weigh a thousand tons. Each.

Sam pushed open a gap in Heather's hair wide enough

to permit a breath of air. He couldn't allow himself to actually sleep. With the serial killer working the neighborhood, Heather's parents would panic if she was out late. And Sam had something to do. Something important. But for the moment he couldn't remember exactly what it was. He settled himself against Heather's warm softness and began to slide toward sleep.

This wasn't so bad. He could live with this. Having a beautiful girl naked in your bed was about as close to perfect as life could get.

For the moment, at least, Sam's obsession with Gaia seemed distant. Silly. There was nothing wrong with Heather. So what if she didn't know what a rook was? So what if she had a small cruel streak? It would be okay. It would work out. He was sure that he could love Heather.

Except, as his drowsiness pulled him down the slope toward true sleep, he brushed his lips against Heather's brown hair and imagined it was gold.

A buzzing alarm began to sound. Sam groaned and flapped his arm at the clock on the bedside table. He smacked the button over and over, but the noise kept coming.

"Mmmm." Heather rolled over and brushed her lips against his face. "Turn that off," she whispered.

"I'm trying." Sam propped himself up on one elbow and picked up the clock. He pressed the button again. He slid the alarm switch to off, but the noise didn't stop. He stared at the clock blankly for a few seconds longer, then realized what was wrong.

The sound wasn't coming from the clock.

Sam scanned the room, searching for the source of the noise. It wasn't the phone. It wasn't the stereo. It was . . . a coat.

Across the room Sam's jacket was lying folded across the back of a chair—not the neatest fold in the world, but then, he had been in sort of a hurry to get undressed. For some reason, the coat was buzzing.

"Sam," Heather called. "Please. That's so annoying."

"Sure. Right." Still more than half asleep, Sam carefully eased himself away from Heather and rolled off the side of the bed. He stumbled over discarded clothing, banged his knee against his desk, knocked over a stack of books, and made it to the coat without generating any more noise than a rogue elephant in a bell factory. He fumbled in the pocket of the coat and grabbed something. What he pulled out was a bright yellow plastic radio.

Sam's heartbeat slammed to a stop.

Oh, yeah. The radio.

Free of the coat, the buzzing noise was louder than ever. Sam flipped the radio over and over in his hands, searching for the switch. At last he located the trigger on the side and pressed it. The buzzing stopped.

Sam breathed a low sigh of relief. He would call Ed back

as soon as he could, but in the meantime at least the radio was quiet. The last thing he wanted to do was explain to Heather what he—

"Sam?" said a loud voice from the radio. "Sam, are you there?"

Panic shot through Sam. All remains of the after-sex sleepiness were blown away in an instant. He looked at the bed, trying to ascertain whether Heather was waking up, then he squeezed the trigger on the radio.

"I'm here," he said as softly as he could.

"Took you long enough," Ed's voice replied. "I've been sitting here buzzing you for the last five minutes. I was about to give up."

Sam wished he had.

Heather rolled over on the bed and stretched her hands above her head. "Sam," she said in a voice that was half a yawn. "Who's on the phone?"

"Nobody important," Sam replied with forced cheerfulness. "Go back to sleep." He lowered his voice and spoke into the radio. "Look, can you call me back later?"

"Hey, this thing was your idea." The quality of the radio was plenty good enough to pick up the irritation in Ed's voice. "Are you going to help me or not?"

"What's happening?"

"She's in the park," Ed answered. "She's been playing chess against that old guy. The Russian."

"Zolov," said Sam. "He's Ukrainian."

"Whatever. The game's over, and she's leaving."

Heather raised her head and rubbed at her eyes. "Sam . . ."

"Just a minute." Sam walked across the small room and stood as far from Heather as he could. "Look, can't you follow her?" he whispered to the radio.

"I'm too obvious," Ed replied through a crackle of static. "If I leave the park, she's going to see me."

Sam sighed and closed his eyes. They should just let her go. This whole business was seriously screwed up.

Sam squeezed the trigger, ready to tell Ed to pack it in.

For a full five seconds Sam held down the little button, but the words wouldn't come. If he gave up and something happened to Gaia, Sam would never be able to live with himself. That much he knew.

"All right," he said in a low tone. "Watch her as long as you can. I'll be right there."

"Hurry."

Suddenly Sam noticed a small plastic switch at the top of the radio. He flicked it, and the speaker inside went dead.

He'd found the off switch. Great timing.

Heather sat up and held the white sheets against her chest. "What's wrong?" she asked.

"Um, nothing," Sam said. He moved across the darkened room and found his clothes lying on the floor. Still trying to be as quiet as he could, he picked up his pants and began to slide them on.

"Where are you going?" asked Heather. There was a lingering fog of sleep in her voice, but it didn't hide an edge of irritation. "Aren't you going to stay with me?"

Sam ran a hundred excuses through his mind, but all of them seemed too lame to speak.

He could always tell her the truth. On the other hand, he wasn't ready to die.

"I have a class," he said.

"Now?" Heather pushed her hair back from her face and frowned at him. "I thought you had a short day on Tuesdays."

"It's a lab," Sam replied. He dragged out his shirt and began to put it on as fast as he could. "A . . . um, makeup lab from one I missed earlier."

"How long will it take?"

That depends on Gaia.

"A couple of hours," he said. "Three at the most." He finished with his shirt, dropped into a chair, and started putting on his shoes.

Heather stretched her long, bare legs but didn't get up. "Then I guess I better get dressed, too. I have to get home."

"Okay," said Sam. He stood up. "I've got to run, or I'll be late."

Heather pulled the pillows together and leaned back

against them. "All right," she said. "Mind if I use your shower before I go?"

Sam smiled. "No problem. I wish I could stay."

He did wish he could stay. Although the decision to watch over Gaia was already made, Sam felt a fresh wave of indecision.

After all, the last time he'd left Heather to chase Gaia, he'd ended up kidnapped and half dead.

It would be nice if he could stay here. It would be nice if he could think of nothing but Heather.

It would probably be a lot safer, too.

But the undefined feelings he had for Gaia Moore were too hard to ignore.

Sam picked up his jacket and put it on. As he did, he noticed the small package still nestled in the right-hand pocket. He took out the box and held it up to the light. Small box. Brown paper. Nothing special. He started to leave the package behind, then he changed his mind and dropped it back into the pocket. If he ended up on a nightlong Gaia stakeout, he would at least have something to look at.

"Well, I guess I'm going," he said as he moved toward the door. "Are you going to be all right going home by yourself?"

"I'll be fine."

There was a new tension in Heather's voice that caught Sam's attention. He turned back to her and looked at her lovely face. "Are you sure?"

"I'm sure," said Heather.

Sam wanted to ask her more, but Ed was waiting and Gaia was moving. If he was going to catch up to them, he needed to get outside. "Okay, then, bye."

He turned and grabbed the doorknob. He was halfway into the hall when Heather called again.

"Sam?"

"Yes?" he replied without turning.

"Does this have anything to do with her?"

Heather named no names, but Sam didn't bother to ask for a definition of "her."

"No," he said in a hoarse voice. He cleared his throat and tried again. "No, it's just class."

He waited a few seconds more, but Heather said nothing else. Sam stepped through the open door and left.

DAVID

"I FEAR NOTHING," DAVID SAID.
"THAT'S ANOTHER OF MY SPECIAL POWERS."

THE WILD BURRITO

At first Gaia was feeling fairly pleased with herself. She was handling this date thing okay. No pressure. She had even kept it together in her game against Zolov. She'd lost, of course, but she always lost to Zolov. At least this time she had come close.

She tugged at the scrunchie in her hair as she walked. There was absolutely no reason to get tense about this dinner. They were only going to grab fast food from a cheap restaurant. Nothing fancy.

She was fine—right up until she turned the corner onto Thompson. The closer Gaia got to Jimmy's, the more she could feel a pressure pushing her backward. It was as if there were this weird wind coming from the restaurant. It blew harder as Gaia got closer until every step toward the restaurant was like pushing into a gale. Other people walked down the sidewalk with no trouble, but Gaia felt like any moment the wind might grab her and send her flying back across the park.

Gaia slowed. Jimmy's Burrito was only a dozen steps away, but they were hard steps to take. She steeled herself, squared her shoulders, and walked to the door.

Lightning didn't strike. No earthquakes shook the ground.

Gaia took a deep breath. She glanced inside, scanned the tables and booths. No sign of David.

Maybe he wasn't coming.

David had probably wised up at the last moment. Maybe he had talked to someone else at school. Maybe he had finally come to his senses. Whatever the case, it was clear he had realized that dating Gaia was a big mistake.

Disappointment settled into Gaia's empty stomach like lead, but there was an equal amount of relief. No David. No date. There was still some chance of potential irritation if the story "How Gaia Got Stood Up" became part of the next day's grind of boring school gossip. But Gaia doubted that would happen. The story was too dull, considering what was going on.

"So what do you recommend?" a voice asked.

Gaia turned to find herself face-to-face with David. She struggled for something witty to say, but her well of wit was experiencing a drought. "I, um . . . I see you found the place."

David tapped a finger against the tip of his nose. "Able to detect taco sauce at a hundred paces." He held up his arms and pretended to flex huge muscles. "It's one of my secret powers."

Gaia forced a smile. She actually *wanted* to smile, but her face wasn't responding to her brain, so she had to force it. "You have others?"

"Too many to number," David said. He crowded in close

to Gaia and leaned forward to look at the menu taped up against the window. "What's good here?"

"Depends on what you think is good." He was very much in her personal space. Gaia stepped aside, hoping it wasn't the wrong thing to do. He didn't even blink.

"Anything," he said. "As long as it's hot."

"They have plenty of hot," Gaia said. Another smile. This one didn't take as much effort.

"I am the terror of hot peppers everywhere." David stepped past Gaia and pulled open the front door. "Jalapeño parents tell stories of me to frighten their children."

This time Gaia actually laughed. Suddenly all the tension she had felt about this date seemed completely stupid. David was just a person. A funny person who, for some reason, seemed to like her. None of those things was bad. Not everything she did had to turn into a disaster movie. Did it?

She stepped through the open door and waited for David to follow. "I'm not talking about wimpy peppers like a jalapeño," she said as he entered.

"Jalapeños are wimpy?"

"Extremely," she said. She was bantering. This was banter. Who knew?

They walked past the newsstands inside the door. Gaia picked out a booth off to the side of the restaurant and slid her butt across the red vinyl seat.

"They serve serious peppers here," she said. "They don't mess around."

David dropped into the seat across from her and pulled a plastic-coated menu from between two bottles of hot sauce.

"So what makes a serious pepper?" he asked. "I'm ready to do battle with any vegetable in the place."

"Good." Gaia reached across the table and plucked the menu from his hand. "Then I'll order for us."

"Go ahead," said David. "I'm not afraid."

Gaia looked at his blue eyes. Something weird was going on. She actually felt, well, almost comfortable. This was not her. This was some other girl who actually knew how to talk to other human beings.

A waitress approached, and Gaia delivered the order. David picked up the menu again after the waitress left. "What's the special burrito?" he asked.

Gaia snatched the menu a second time. "Just a burrito."

David's eyes sparkled. "But what's so special about it?"

"You'll see," said Gaia.

Much to her own surprise, Gaia was actually enjoying herself. So far, at least, she hadn't suffered from a brain fart causing her to say something inexcusably stupid. It was only a matter of time, of course, before she was revealed as a hopeless social outcast, but at least she was enjoying a few moments of normal life.

"So . . . ," David said.

Gaia stared at him. "So . . ."

They lapsed into silence. Uh-oh. This was getting less good. Gaia pressed her hands against the sticky vinyl. Was she supposed to say something? Was *he* supposed to say something?

That was when the emergency cop out system flipped into action. Gaia stood up, nicking the edge of the table with her bad knee.

Ow.

"Where are you going?" David asked.

Gaia took a deep breath. "Bathroom."

NOT QUITE NORMAL

"So you've proved you're an idiot with nothing to say," Gaia told her dripping reflection. The cold-water-in-the-face splash had done nothing for her spirits. It had only served to form huge blotches on her shirt and soak the hair around her face. Lovely.

9445678901234567890123456789

She might as well go back out there and seal the deal. Send him running for the hills. If the city had any.

Gaia opened the door and was headed back down the dark, grimy hall past the kitchen when she heard a huge crash, followed by a bloodcurdling scream. She stopped in front of the open kitchen door.

There was a fire. A big one.

This could really put a damper on her already dampered date.

Without hesitation Gaia strolled into the kitchen, took the phone out of the hand of a trembling fry cook, and hung it up before he could dial 911. She grabbed the fire extinguisher and yanked it off the wall, walked over to the searing, leaping flames, and doused them with one good squirt.

The sprinkler system didn't even have time to kick in.

Gaia turned and looked at the three white-clad, grease-stained kitchen workers who were huddled in the corner, looking like they'd fallen there out of shock. From the way they were gaping at her, she could have been an angel plunked in the middle of their crusty linoleum floor directly by the hand of God.

Gaia flushed. Sometimes she forgot her reactions to danger weren't quite normal.

She took a deep breath and tried to smile. "Uh . . . you can still make the burritos, right?"

"Everything okay back there?" David's face wore a worried expression as Gaia returned to her seat.

"Fine," she said, averting her eyes. She cleared her throat noisily. "And dinner is on the house."

He glanced past her toward the kitchen, a question obviously forming. "Why did they—"

"So how do you like New York?" she interrupted, placing her hands flat on the table. Lame question. Better than trying to deal with his.

He narrowed his eyes at her, obviously mulling his options. Which line of questioning was better/safer/more intriguing? Finally he leaned back into his bench, resting one arm across the top.

"I'm not sure yet if I like it," he said.

Gaia smiled, glad he'd made the right choice.

He looked toward the windows at the front of the restaurant. "It's great to get a burger anytime you want," he continued, "and to find an open bookstore at three A.M., but I think it's just too crowded for me."

"I like crowds," Gaia said, watching a group of people standing in line to pay their bill. "It's easy to get lost in them. Go unnoticed."

She felt her skin flush. She stared at the chipped tabletop. She hadn't just said that, had she?

"I can't imagine you'd go unnoticed anywhere," David said.

Gaia blushed more deeply. He hadn't just said that, had he?

"Anyway, I don't know if I'll be here long enough to adapt," David said.

Gaia glanced up. "You just got here. Why would you be moving?" Why wouldn't he be moving? She'd waited seventeen years for a first date. She'd probably be waiting another seventeen for a second.

"You know." David shrugged. "Family stuff." For the first time he looked a little uncomfortable.

"Following your parents' jobs?"

Now David looked down at the table. "My parents are . . . I'm not with my parents."

Gaia felt a nearly irresistible urge to touch him. "That's something we have in common," she said. "My parents are gone, too."

David raised his head. "That's weird, isn't it?"

For a moment they just looked at each other. This silence wasn't nearly as uncomfortable as the first.

"What is this?" David asked.

"What?" Gaia asked back.

David pointed up. "This music," he said.

A song played from invisible speakers. Gaia hadn't noticed it until that moment. She strained to hear.

> *Her waiting dark heart,*
> *The violence in her eyes,*
> *The hunger in my body,*
> *The things she denies.*

"It's this band called Fearless," Gaia replied, shaking her head slightly. "They play around here."

"Fearless?" David repeated, raising his eyebrows.

Gaia confirmed with a nod. At one point when she'd first moved to New York, it had seemed like this random band with this ironically appropriate name was following her around. It was almost too bizarre. But now it didn't even affect her. She was used to it.

The waitress came back, with two oval platters loaded with burritos, corn flour tacos, and heaps of seasoned rice and beans. Gaia took her plate and dug in quickly, sweeping together a blob of sour cream, rice, and a chunk of steaming burritos. The combination of flavors was almost too good.

David eyed his plate. "What are all these little brown peppers?"

"Ever heard of *habañeros*?" Gaia asked through a mouthful of food.

His eyebrows scrunched together. "I don't think so."

Gaia grinned at him. "Good luck."

David picked up one of the peppers between his fingers, examined it for a moment, then tossed it into his mouth. Gaia heard it crunch between his teeth. A moment later David's blue eyes opened so wide, they looked like they might fall out of their sockets.

"Wow," he whispered.

"Pretty hot?" asked Gaia.

He nodded. "I don't think I'm really tasting it. It sort of made my ears ring."

Gaia took another bite of her own meal and watched as David chewed his way through a second pepper. "Most people are scared to death of those things."

David took a third pepper and crunched it. A red flush spread over his face, and he trembled.

"I fear nothing," David said. "That's another of my special powers."

Gaia looked at him. Maybe they had more in common than she thought.

THE OTHER GUY

Sam Moon was an idiot.

Nope. Even *idiot* didn't sound bad enough. It was an insult to idiots everywhere.

He had started out in situation A. In situation A he was lying in bed with a beautiful girl. A beautiful naked girl. A beautiful naked girl who wanted nothing more than to be with him. A girl with whom he had just had sex.

But from there Sam had proceeded straight to situation B. In this case he was up, out of bed, and running off to chase a different girl. Only this girl didn't want him. Probably hated him. Definitely didn't want to have sex with him.

Oh, yeah, and she was on a date with someone else.

As Sam crossed the street and stopped in the middle of the crowded sidewalk, he hoped his parents would someday have another son. He would be wrong ever to pass these pitiful genes along to the next generation.

Sam stood across from Jimmy's Burrito and watched Gaia eat her dinner with the guy she was dating. The back of the guy's head was nothing special. From what Sam could see, the pair were eating, talking, and even laughing.

Gaia was laughing.

Sam's heart squeezed. He tried to think of all the times he had been with her—which weren't many. Now that he thought about it, Sam wasn't sure he had ever gotten her to smile, much less laugh.

Gaia was having a good time. Meanwhile Sam was miserable in every way possible. He felt guilty. Tired. Jealous. Foolish. You name it. If it was bad, he felt it.

Sam leaned back against a brick wall and tried to keep his head down. He didn't have a hat, or a big trench coat, or even sunglasses to make him harder to recognize. If Gaia looked out the window and saw Sam looking back, it would be the perfect end to a perfect day.

The radio buzzed in his pocket. Sam hated the sound. First thing in the morning these suckers were going back to the store. He dragged out the radio and squeezed the trigger.

"What do you want? *Over.*"

"A report," Ed replied. "You haven't even told me if you found her."

Sam said nothing.

"Sam?"

He smirked. "You didn't say *'over.'*" He sounded like a child. He didn't care.

"Over," Ed said.

"I found her," Sam replied. "She's okay. They're eating."

"Where?"

"Jimmy's Burrito."

Gaia laughed again. Another slice to the heart.

"Jimmy's?" Ed laughed. "Man, he got off cheap."

Sam glanced across the street and saw that Gaia was washing down a bite of something with her drink. He also saw that at least two people were giving him odd looks.

Sam turned his back to them. "Ed, I have to get off," he said.

"I need more details," Ed replied. "Booth or table?"

"Booth," Sam said through clenched teeth. He braced his free hand against the wall. "I'll talk to you later."

"Same side or across from each other?"

Sam rolled his eyes. "Across from each other."

"What are they eating?"

"Ed!" Sam shouted into the radio. "I can't tell what they're eating, and I don't read lips, so don't bother to ask what they're talking about. I'll call you if anything happens."

He snapped off the radio before Ed had a chance to reply and shoved it back into his coat pocket. His fingers brushed against the little box. Sam took it out. It didn't look like much.

Sam took a glance at Gaia, then tore at the paper on the outside of the box. Whoever had wrapped it had used plenty of tape. It took him a lot of tugging and tearing to get the paper unraveled. Once the paper was crumpled in his pocket, he was left with a featureless box of gray cardboard. He snapped a couple more pieces of tape and lifted off the lid.

The first thing Sam saw inside was a piece of folded paper. At the top of it was written *Sam Moon*. He picked it up, unfolded it, and started to read.

Sam—

I know that you have some connection with Gaia Moore. I hope that you continue to feel affection for her and that you will take the concerns expressed in this letter seriously.

Gaia is in danger. If I could take direct action to save her, I would, but circumstances prevent my appearance.

Instead I am passing this information along to you in hopes that you will know what to do with it. Watch out for Gaia. She is stronger than she appears to be, but she is not as strong as she believes. She can be hurt.

She needs you, Sam. Don't let her down.

Don't reveal the existence of this package or note to Gaia. For her own safety there are things she cannot know.

By the time he was done reading, Sam's heart was pounding in his ears. He read through the note again, clutching the page. There was no signature, no clue as to who had sent the package.

This little scrap of typing paper was about the weirdest

thing Sam had ever run into in his life. Sure, he had been standing on the street playing undercover cop, but this note was straight out of some spy novel.

His immediate suspicion was that Ed had sent the package. Who else could have known that he was involved in any way with Gaia? It had to be a joke. If he called Ed on the radio, Sam could probably get Ed to confess.

But the longer he stood there, the less Sam believed in his own theory. Certain words in the note kept drumming against his brain.

Gaia is in danger.

She can be hurt.

She needs you, Sam.

He folded the note and shoved it back into his jacket pocket. Then Sam looked inside the little box again. There was another folded sheet of paper. With shaking hands Sam pulled it out and found that it was some kind of information form. Name. Age. That sort of thing.

Only this form had been attacked by someone with a big, fat black marker. Whole lines of the form were completely blacked out, but Sam could still read a few things.

Eyes: Blue

Several lines below that was another clear line.

IQ: 146

So whoever this sheet belonged to, they had blue eyes and they were smart. Sam wondered for a second if the sheet was about Gaia, but then he spotted another piece of uncovered info.

Height: 6'2"

Gaia was tall for a girl, but not anywhere close to that tall.

The biggest area of readable type was a box of text marked Evaluation.

```
    Subject demonstrates almost complete
lack of empathetic response. Does not
act under social constraints. Does not
operate in a frame of behavioral mores.
It is our opinion that this subject
should be considered deeply sociopathic.
Extreme caution is recommended.
```

Sam glanced back up at the glowing windows of the restaurant. What did any of this have to do with Gaia?

Sam put away the sheet. All that remained in the box was a small black-and-white photo. Sam pulled it out and raised it closer to his eyes.

Sunset was coming on fast, and the streetlights were just beginning to flicker. In the gloom Sam had to squint to make out the grainy, low-quality photo.

The guy in the photo was young. He had short, wavy black hair and a squared-off chin. There was a flat, angry expression on his face. He seemed a little familiar. Sam knew that he had seen the guy in the photo before.

Then he remembered where.

Sam let the box fall out of his fingers and ran right through the traffic on Thompson. He drew a chorus of horn blasts as he darted between the cars, and a couple of people had to slam on their brakes. Sam didn't care. He charged up the steps into Jimmy's, shoving people out of the way as he went.

But when Sam got inside, the booth at the side of the restaurant was empty. Gaia was gone.

DOUBLE DARE

HIS EYES NARROWED, AND HIS TEETH CLENCHED
TOGETHER SO HARD, GAIA COULD SEE THE
MUSCLES BULGE AT THE CORNER OF HIS JAW.

DAVID

"What time are they closing the park?" David asked.

"I heard they were closing it at seven," Gaia responded. "Both the killings happened sometime around eleven or twelve. They probably want to make sure they get everybody out well ahead of that."

She took a deep breath and watched the fog it caused disappear into the night sky.

"Let's go," David said.

Gaia looked at him. There was no way to know what he was thinking. His expression conveyed nothing.

"It's almost seven," Gaia said. "The police probably won't let us in." Not that that mattered to her.

"Are you scared?" David asked.

A challenge. Interesting. Gaia felt the skin around her eyes draw tight.

"I'm not scared," she said.

"Then let's go." David pointed. "If they have the gates blocked, we can always sneak over the fence."

Gaia stopped, hands in pockets. She looked him directly in the eyes, giving him a chance to back out. "If we go into the park, we'll probably get caught."

"So?" He kept walking. She followed.

"So, they'll put us in jail," she said. "Aren't you scared of that?"

"No." He turned to look at her, walking backward. "I guess I'm just naturally fearless."

TWO DAVIDS

"What did you say?"

Gaia stumbled to a stop on the sidewalk and leaned against the iron fence that guarded the park's south side.

David shrugged. "I said I was naturally fearless." He struck a dramatic pose, chin lifted, chest out, eyebrows lowered. "Intrepid explorer David Twain, ready and able to penetrate the deepest mysteries of unexplored regions."

Coincidence. That's all it was. It wasn't like *fearless* was a word reserved just for her. "You really aren't scared to go in the park?"

"Not me," he said. He folded his arms over his still puffed-out chest and raised an eyebrow. "What about you, little lady?" he said with a Hollywood cowboy accent.

"You a-feared to go in that thar patch of woods?"

There was something odd going on here. Something had shifted.

This seemed like the same funny, talkative guy Gaia had shared burritos with back at Jimmy's. Obviously it was the same David. Only now it seemed like there was somebody else there, too. Like there were two completely different people looking at her with those dark blue eyes.

"All right," Gaia said, refusing to tear her gaze from his. "Let's go."

"Cool," David said. He stood up on the tips of his toes and looked over her head. "But there's already a cop down by the entrance. You're probably right that they won't let us by."

Gaia looked up at the fence. "So I guess we'll have to go in this way."

She braced herself, bent low, and jumped. Gaia's beat-up right knee protested, but she still managed to grab the top of the fence. A few seconds later she was over and in the bushes on the other side.

David clapped in rapid applause. "I think you're doing the wrong thing by staying in school," he said through the fence. "You should definitely run off and join the circus."

"I'll think about it," Gaia replied. "Are you coming over here, or are you too much of a chicken?"

There was nothing funny about David's reply this time. His eyes narrowed, and his teeth clenched together so hard,

Gaia could see the muscles bulge at the corner of his jaw. He wasn't happy.

He jumped for the fence. With his longer arms he had no trouble grabbing the iron crossbar at the top. It took him a little longer to pull himself up, and he wasn't nearly as smooth working his way over the top, but less than thirty seconds later he dropped to the ground beside Gaia.

"I told you," he said. "I'm fearless."

Gaia started to wonder if maybe he was telling the truth.

ABSOLUTELY FEARLESS

"Where's the spot?"

"This way," Gaia replied. She circled a small fountain and pushed south past the makeshift stage where bands sometimes played on the weekends. She was moving fast. She wanted to get there and get it over with. "Why do you want to see it, anyway? You're not some kind of murder groupie, are you?"

David laughed. A normal laugh. "No. Absolutely not. I just wanted you to know I wasn't afraid."

"You keep saying that." She looked toward him, then back at the path, her ponytail of golden hair flipping back and forth as she moved. "Why are you so worried about not being afraid?"

David took a couple of quick steps and moved up to walk beside her. "I just think it would be cool, that's all. Not to be afraid of anything."

"Why?"

"Because then you'd really be free, wouldn't you?"

Gaia blinked. Interesting theory.

They passed under a group of oaks, and the shadows thickened around them. "Being fearless wouldn't make a person happy."

David reached up and snapped off a small dead limb. "Why not?" he said. "It's being afraid of things that makes people sad."

Gaia shook her head. "That's not true. Even without fear you still get lonely, or angry, or depressed."

"There's nothing wrong with angry," David said. "Sometimes you have to be angry. Sometimes it's what you need."

Gaia couldn't argue with that. "And what about the others?"

"What? Sad and lonely?" David shrugged. "I don't really feel those things."

Gaia reached the edge of a concrete path and stopped. "It doesn't sound like you feel much."

"All I need."

For a moment the two of them stood in silence, then Gaia turned her back on him, raised a hand, and pointed at the open space on the other side of the path.

"This is it," she said. "This is where they found the bodies." She turned back to look at David. She met his gaze dead-on. "But I think you already knew that."

PAINLESS

David reached behind his back and pulled out a long knife. The blue-steel blade was almost black in the dim light, but the sharp edge caught the glow from distant streetlamps and threw off glittering sparks.

Damn, he loved that.

"You're smarter than I anticipated," he said. "I like it." He stretched out a hand to Gaia. "Come on, I'll make it painless."

"No, you won't," Gaia said.

David grinned. "You're right. This is going to hurt like hell."

THE
GENTLEMAN

THERE WAS A WILDNESS IN HIS EYES.
HOW HAD SHE NOT NOTICED IT BEFORE?

THE RESCUE PARTY

"I'm not the one who let her get away," Ed's voice crackled through the radio.

Sam glared at the little yellow transistor. "I was distracted," he said. "Besides, it doesn't matter now. We've got to find a way into the park."

"I'm with you on that," Ed replied. "So, what's the plan?"

Sam looked across the street. There were now two policemen standing by the nearest entrance to the park, and he didn't think for a moment that the officers were just going to step aside and let them in. "I'm going to have to go over the fence," he said after a few seconds' thought. "I don't see any other way."

"What about me?" asked Ed. "I don't know if you've noticed, but I'm not very good at going over things."

The thought had already occurred to Sam, but he didn't have a solution. "I need your help so I can get in. You come down here and distract the police."

Ed sighed. "That's me. Ed Fargo, distraction specialist."

"What?" Sam asked, confused.

"Forget it," Ed answered. "Distract them how?"

Sam glanced around and winced. Every second counted. There was no time to argue. "I don't know. Ask directions. Fake a heart attack. Just get them looking the wrong way long enough for me to climb the fence."

He didn't wait for Ed's reply. Instead he switched off the radio and dropped it into his pocket. He darted across the intersection, took a last longing look at the gate, then walked quickly toward the corner where the police would be far away and nearly out of sight.

Sam was only halfway to the corner when he got a break. The sounds of yelling and of running feet came from the direction of the entrance. Sam turned and saw the policemen wrestling a man with a potbelly and a stiff, graying beard.

It was the best chance Sam was going to get. There was no point in waiting for Ed when there was already a perfect distraction. He hurried across the sidewalk, bent low, then jumped for the top of the fence. His fingers managed to catch the square bar at the top, but the metal bit painfully into his palms. He started to bleed. Gritting his teeth, he slowly pulled, kicked, and scrambled his way to the top.

He stopped there for a second to catch his breath. Down at the entrance the police were busy putting handcuffs on the bearded man. No one was looking.

Sam smiled. He had made it. Now he only had to find Gaia before it was too late.

He started to jump, but his foot slipped and his jump turned into a fall. The cuff of his pants caught on a point at the top of the fence. Sam pendulumed back and smashed against the fence with bone-jarring force. He kicked his feet, but the thin strip of fabric held him in place as firmly as a rope. He grabbed at the bars and tried to pull himself back up.

A hand grabbed Sam by the collar and jerked him away from the fence. Upside down, he found himself staring into a stern face topped with iron gray hair and an NYPD cap.

"What do you think you're doing, son?"

"I've got to get into the park," said Sam. "There's this girl, and she's in danger."

"Really?" The policeman grabbed Sam's arms and pulled them roughly behind his back. A moment later Sam felt hard, cold steel close around his wrists.

"What are you doing?" Sam shouted.

"My job," said the policeman. "What's your name?"

"Sam . . . Sam Moon."

"Well, Sam Moon, you're under arrest."

YOU DIE

Gaia almost laughed.

She'd always thought she had perfect bad-guy radar. How wrong she was.

"What are we going to do now?" she said. There was a wildness in his eyes. How had she not noticed it before?

He looked at Gaia as if she were completely brain-dead. "Oh, please!" He pointed his nose up in the air and put on a thick British accent. "That should be immediately obvious to the most casual observer." Then he looked her directly in the eyes. "You die."

He was about to lunge. But Gaia wasn't going to take on a knife. "What's the matter? Scared to fight me hand to hand?"

David paused. He looked at the knife. His knuckles turned white. "I fear nothing from you," he said. He placed his weapon on the ground.

Gaia had to struggle to watch him and not look at the knife. Watch the opponent's every move. Every twitch. It was a basic rule of fighting, something her father had told her a thousand times.

But she couldn't stop herself. She checked the position of the knife. And that's when David hit her.

Gaia had been hit before. You didn't make it through the belts in any martial art without having your ass handed to you a hundred times. Gaia's nose had been bloodied by the best. But she was sure she had never been hit harder than that first blow from David.

He hit her with a straight left that knocked Gaia all the way across the path. She snapped through the stupid plastic police tape at the edge of the field, slipped on the grass, and fell.

Judo saved her life. To the naked eye, judo seems to be all about grabbing people by the arm and flipping them in the air. That wasn't it at all. Judo was about falling.

Gaia was falling backward. If she fought against that kind of fall, she would only spin her arms in the air and still end up sitting on the grass. Instead Gaia went with it. She pushed off hard, threw back her hands, and took the fall, using her arms as shock absorbers. Another quick push and Gaia was back on her feet.

David was almost on top of her. He swung again, but this time Gaia caught his wrist and pulled it past her.

For a moment they were almost face-to-face—so close, all Gaia had to do was move her lips to end her long kissing drought. The thought turned her stomach.

David pulled left, then quickly back to the right. It was an elementary move, and Gaia was braced for it, but David was very strong. Gaia was great at keeping her balance, but not even she could keep her balance when both of her feet were off the ground. That wasn't a rule of judo—that was a rule of gravity.

She didn't go down, but it was close. Before Gaia could recover, David drove a pile-driver fist into her side so hard, Gaia imagined she could hear her ribs crack. Maybe it wasn't imagination.

David grabbed at Gaia. He took her arm, jerked her back toward him, and threw another punch. Gaia blocked with a forearm and drove a knee into his gut at the same time.

David released his grip on her and fell back a step. Gaia didn't let him.

She took a quick step forward and delivered a kick that took David across the hip. Another that struck him in the thigh. He staggered and stepped back again.

This was more like it. Gaia spun, trying to deliver a solid kick to the body.

David blocked it easily. He took the blow against the flat of one palm, pushed sharply to throw Gaia off balance, then followed the push with a straight left that took her right between the eyes.

This punch was even harder than the first. The sound of his knuckles hitting her skull was amazing. It was like somebody had broken a rock with a sledgehammer. Like an ax biting into a tree.

Sparks of red light swarmed through Gaia's eyes. Her ears started to ring. All at once her arms and legs gained fifty pounds each.

She tried to get her hands up to block, but they didn't listen to orders. Another punch whistled in and hit her on the temple. This one was a right hook. That was another thing Gaia had learned early about fighting: If you're going to get hit in the face, get hit by a straight punch. Straight punches hurt, but if you get hit from the side, hurt doesn't even come close.

The night flashed into bright shades of yellow and blue. There was a sound in Gaia's ears like the roar from a hundred seashells.

She backpedaled fast and managed to avoid the next shot. Another punch came. Blocked. Another. Dodged. Another. It glanced off the top of her head without shooting any fireworks through her skull, but this time she felt the warm flow of blood across her forehead.

Gaia kicked out wildly and was lucky to hit David in the side. She didn't think it really hurt him, but at least it made him back off.

"Getting scared yet?" David taunted.

Somehow David knew about her, but this wasn't the time to figure out how.

Gaia didn't waste breath on talking. Her head was starting to clear, but the blood from her forehead was dripping into her eyes. Gaia's ribs ached, and the knee she had messed up the night before was starting to get in on the complaints. If she was going to end this on her feet, Gaia had to end it soon.

David launched another punch, but it was a long overhand right, and Gaia had time to get out of the way. She feinted a punch with her left, ducked his response, and stepped back. Did the same thing with the right and took another backward step.

There was a rhythm to David's fighting. If Gaia could work it out, she could time her shots and plaster him without taking blows of her own. All she needed was time.

Suddenly David lunged forward and grabbed Gaia with both his arms. Grabbing like that was a really stupid move—unless you were as strong as a gorilla. David could have made gorillas beg for mercy.

He squeezed the breath out of Gaia in a painful rush, and this time she knew the cracking sound had to be at least one of her ribs turning into a two-piece. She kicked her feet along David's shins, but he didn't let her free. So Gaia lowered her head and butted him in the face.

David howled. His nose exploded in blood. He lost his hold on Gaia and clamped a hand over his face.

Gaia drew a painful breath and jumped forward. She got off a kick to the chest, and David was staggering. Then a kick to his side, and he groaned. His hand came away from his face. Blood spilled over his lips and dripped from the point of his chin. In seconds his shirt was stained by a spreading pool of darkness.

He punched. Gaia blocked and counterpunched. It wasn't a perfect hit on his solar plexus, but it was good enough to make David gasp for air. She hit him again, driving her fist into his gut so deep, Gaia wouldn't have been surprised to feel his backbone.

David made a wild, flailing punch. Gaia blocked it easily.

He threw another, and she turned it aside. He stepped back. He was breathing hard, and Gaia could hear air whistling through his smashed nose.

"What about you?" she said. "Still fearless?"

"I . . . don't . . . have . . . anything to fear from you," he said.

It was time to end this thing. Gaia started forward, planning to put her foot where David's face was, but something grabbed her by the ankles. She glanced down. Tape. Stupid yellow police tape. Somehow yards of it had become tangled around her legs. It snapped easily enough, but it distracted Gaia for a second.

A second was too much to give up in the middle of a fight.

When she looked up, David's fist was six inches from her face and coming in fast. Gaia tried to dodge, but the blow still caught her on her right jawbone.

This time Gaia didn't just see sparks. This time she went someplace. Someplace where squirrels played banjos and the trees were cotton-candy pink. The seashells were roaring again, and this time they were joined by a brass band. Gaia tried to put out her hands and catch herself, but for a second there she couldn't even tell if she had hands. Gaia didn't know if she was standing or lying on the ground.

She wasn't even sure if she was still alive.

It took a few seconds for the furry-tailed rats to put away their instruments and the night to go back to something like normal. When it did, Gaia figured out that she was on the ground. There was something under her hands. Grass, but something else, too. Something gritty and crumbly. It took her a moment to realize that it was chalk—the chalk that had marked the body lines of the dead girls.

From somewhere behind her Gaia heard David laugh. "That's great," he said. "That's perfect. I'll go get the knife. You just stay put." His smashed nose turned "that's" into "dat's" and "great" into "gweat." It would have been funny if he wasn't about to kill her.

Gaia struggled to sit up, but the best she could manage was to roll onto one knee. The banjos might be packed away, but her head was still spinning. Everything hurt.

David didn't seem to be in much better shape. He limped as he crossed the field and stopped near the path for a moment to lean against a tree. He was banged up pretty good, but he was still going to kill Gaia. He knelt down beside the path and reached for the knife.

Gaia saw salvation coming from twenty feet away. David saw it, too, but he was slow. He barely managed to turn his head before Ed Fargo hit him like a freight train.

A TIME
TO DIE

DAVID WAS COMING. HE WAS CLIMBING
ALONG GAIA'S BODY, AND HE STILL HAD HIS KNIFE.

Gaia would have screamed for Ed to stop if she'd had the time. The collision happened with such speed that it looked more like a car accident than a wheelchair ramming.

One of David's hands, the one reaching for the knife, was trapped under a wheel. Instantly every finger on that hand had snapped, one after another, like twigs. The metal frame of the chair caught him under the arm, rolled him over, and left him sprawling on the ground. His head hit the asphalt with a sickening crack, and Gaia saw every limb of his body go slack.

David was down for the count.

At the moment of impact Ed was thrown up and out. He flew almost twenty feet in a low arc before he thumped to the ground between a pair of pines. Freed of his weight, the chair rolled on another few paces, curved, then toppled on its side.

That was when Gaia hit the ground. The paralyzation had set in.

For the space of five seconds everything was still and quiet. Then the broken bodies started to move.

David was up first. Gaia couldn't believe her eyes. She'd thought he was done. Unconscious. Useless. Yet he climbed to his feet, clutching his broken, bleeding hand against his chest. Who *was* this guy?

"Gonna . . . kill . . . you both," he grunted. He looked in the grass, located the knife, and lifted it in his good hand.

Gaia struggled to rise. She had to stop him.

She couldn't move. Gaia's muscles twitched and squirmed like bags full of snakes, and she was barely able to raise her head from the ground.

David looked at her, then looked at Ed. Slowly his split lips widened into a horrible, bloody grin.

"Which one first?" he said.

Me, thought Gaia. Come for me. But even her mouth had shut down. She could do nothing but watch as David decided who would die.

A HUNDRED FEET AWAY

Every branch grabbed at his coat. Every stone seemed to be out to trip his feet.

Tom Moore ran desperately through the woods. Loki wasn't the only one with fake identification, but it had taken Tom much longer than he expected to convince the police guarding the park that he should be allowed inside.

He pulled the gun from his coat pocket as he ran and thumbed off the safety. He only hoped it wasn't too late.

THE LAST RESERVES

Gaia opened her hand and closed it again. It wasn't much, but it was something. Her body was returning to her.

A dozen yards away, David limped toward the pilot of the overturned wheelchair. Ed had his hands under him and was dragging himself back as fast as he could. It wasn't fast enough. David would be on him in seconds.

Ed was about to die.

Gaia reached down and pulled at her reserves of strength. The tank was almost empty. She absently thought of what her father used to say when he had driven the family car long past the point the needle dropped to *E*.

Vapors. I'm running on vapors.

Slowly she rolled over onto her trembling arms.

Painfully she pushed her aching legs under her and climbed to her feet.

David glanced at her, then continued after Ed.

Gaia tried to go toward them, but she could barely manage a step. Her head swam, and her knees were weak. She wasn't going to be fast enough. There was only ten feet between David and Ed. There was at least thirty feet between Gaia and David. There was no way for Gaia to get to Ed in time.

"Hey," she called in a hoarse whisper.

David kept after Ed.

"Wasn't I the one you wanted?" Gaia's voice was a little stronger this time.

The gap between David and Ed was down to five feet. David raised his knife to strike.

"Hey, chicken!" Gaia screamed.

David froze.

"Are you afraid to fight me?"

David pivoted like a rusty screen door and looked at Gaia. "I'm not afraid of you."

"Then show me."

Gaia had trained herself to hold back. Even when she was fighting a mugger or a thief, she was careful to stop, not injure. She threw those rules away.

David staggered toward her with the knife held high. He pointed the glittering blade toward Gaia's face and swung the edge from side to side.

David was strong. David was fast. But by now Gaia knew one thing for sure—David wasn't well trained. She leaned back her arm as if she were going to throw a punch.

That was all it took to draw David's attention. He leaped at her with surprising speed.

Gaia fell back. Her balance was gone. She was going to hit the ground—there was no stopping that—but there was enough strength in her legs for one last good kick. She pivoted on her left foot, kicking and falling at the same time.

David's right leg broke with a noise like a gunshot. A thin, high whine escaped his blood-smeared mouth as both he and Gaia toppled to the ground.

SEEING STARS

Gaia lay on her back in the grass, biding her time. She knew David thought she was spent. Done. Gone. But she was just waiting. Overhead, the gloomy clouds that had covered the sky all day finally parted. Stars peeked through.

She'd never seen stars in the city. But they were up there now, sparkling down at Gaia as if they had come out just to watch the bitter end.

From somewhere nearby she could hear sounds of breathing. They weren't pleasant sounds. The breathing was kind of wet, as if the person making the noise was pulling as much blood as air into his lungs with every breath.

A hand grasped Gaia's ankle. Another closed on her knee. Something hard and cold pressed against the skin of her leg.

David was coming. He was climbing along Gaia's body, and he still had his knife.

Patience. Patience.

One of David's hands came down in the middle of Gaia's stomach with painful force. The other hand, the hand with the knife, slid along her arm.

It was strange. After a lifetime of feeling alone, or embarrassed, or just plain angry, what Gaia felt now was calm. She had done everything she could. Somewhere, way down in her brain, a voice was calling for her to get up. Get up and fight. But that voice was faint and far away.

Gaia was tired. Very, very tired. But maybe, just maybe, if she waited until just the right moment, she could finish this thing. And maybe she could live through it.

Tangled black hair came into view. Even from this close, Gaia could barely recognize the face as David's. His nose flattened like a pancake. His face painted over in blood. His lips pulled back in a snarl of rage.

Slowly David dragged himself beside Gaia. Then he raised the knife and held it above her chest.

"See?" he croaked through bloody lips. "See, I'm the best after all. I can beat you. I'm the best."

Gaia had no idea what he was talking about. David sat up straighter, raised the knife high, and plunged it down at Gaia. She raised her arms. Watched his eyes widen in surprise. And then it happened.

POPPED

The sound came three times, all very close together. Hiss. Hiss. Hiss. It was like the noise of air being let out of a bicycle tire. Like water falling on a hot skillet.

SPLATTER

David's shoulder erupted. His body twitched around to the left, and blood poured out across his chest. There was a cracking, and for a moment Gaia saw something white exposed in the core of his wounds.

Bone.

"I . . . ," said David. "You . . ." A bloody foam spilled from his lips, it hit her face with a sickening splatter. David toppled off of Gaia and fell still at her side.

For several seconds Gaia lay there, trying to understand what had happened. Something had hurt David. Something had stopped him.

She wasn't going to die. Not now. It seemed like an impossible thought.

Someone stepped into view at the edge of the clearing. Gaia turned her head for a better look.

She saw a tall figure in a trench coat. She saw the gun in his hand. She knew the face. Her uncle. Apparently he couldn't call or write, but he had an uncanny ability to materialize when she was in danger.

The figure at the edge of the clearing only stood there for a few moments. Then he turned and stepped back into the shadows of the trees.

Gaia closed her eyes.

EXIT, STAGE LEFT

It took Ed nearly ten minutes to get his wheelchair upright, get his battered self into it, and roll across the damp ground to Gaia's side. For every one of those ten minutes he harbored the unthinkable thought that she was dead.

And yet when he actually reached the center of the clearing, he was amazed to see Gaia sit up and push her ratty hair away from her face.

Total, utter, complete, euphoric relief.

Ed calmed his heaving chest before he let himself open his mouth. "Hey, Gaia," he called. "Your new boyfriend's the killer."

Gaia made a tired, gasping noise that might have been laughter on the planet Exhaustion. She stood slowly, swayed on her feet for a few seconds, then staggered over to lean against Ed's chair.

"Thanks for the update," she said. "How did you get in here?"

"Easy." Ed rapped his knuckles against the armrest of the wheelchair. "I got in while Sam was getting arrested."

Gaia blinked. "Sam got arrested?"

"Worked out great as a distraction," Ed said with a grin.

"Okay," said Gaia. She shook her head and swayed so badly that she almost lost her grip on the chair.

"What happened?" asked Ed. "I couldn't see what was going on. I was so afraid . . . I mean, I was afraid he was going to . . ."

"Kill me?" Gaia nodded slowly. "He almost did. We'll leave him for the police."

David suddenly moaned. His broken, bleeding hand scrabbled at the grass.

Gaia pulled back her foot and kicked him again. The moaning stopped.

Ed looked at her and shook his head. "You know, sometimes I can't tell if you're really brave or just perpetually pissed off."

BROKEN

Tom knew he had to get moving. Once Loki and his operatives had figured out that Tom Moore was here, they wouldn't pass up the chance to bag him when they had it.

He turned to leave and heard movement behind him. Quickly he pressed against the dark trunk of an elm and waited.

A man was coming across the field. It was a tall man, a man Tom had no trouble recognizing.

Loki walked straight across the trampled field. He paused a moment beside the broken form on the ground. Then he knelt, grabbed the boy by the hair, and delivered a sharp slap across the face.

David groaned.

"Wake up," said Loki. Another slap. "Open your eyes."

The eyelids fluttered.

"She shot you?" Loki said. "She used a gun?"

The boy on the ground said something. From his place by the trees, Tom couldn't hear the words, but he could hear Loki's reply.

"Home?" Loki shook his head. "I'm afraid that boat has already sailed. You're worthless to me now."

The boy spoke again, and this time Tom could make out his words.

"I'll tell," he said. His voice was high and raw, like a child who had been crying. "I'll tell them everything."

"Yes." Loki released his grip on the boy's blood-soaked hair and stood. "Yes, I'm sure you would."

Tom knew what was coming next. He turned away from the scene and started to make his way through the woods. He had gone no more than a dozen steps before he heard the gunshot.

GAIA

There have always been horror stories about first dates, blind dates, setups, hookups, and probably a bunch of scenarios I've never even heard of.

But this has to be one for the record books.

This is the type of thing that could only happen to someone as undateable as me.

At least I didn't kiss him.

KISS

To Nicole Pascal Johansson

GAIA

I'll probably never have kids. I'm not just saying that. There are a few really good reasons to think so:

1. I can't even manage to get a guy to kiss me, let alone . . . all that;

2. I seem to have very, very bad family karma (if you believe in karma, which I don't, but it's kind of a fun word to say);

3. Somebody tries to kill me at least once a week.

If you knew me at all, you'd know I'm not being a wiseass when I say that. Let me give you a quick example: I went on the first real date of my life recently, and the guy tried to murder me—literally—before the night was over. So, really, what are the chances I'm going to stick around on this earth long enough to find a guy to love me so much that I'd actually want to have kids with him in the far distant future?

But if by some miracle I ever did have kids, I would never, never, never have just one.

I remember this old neighbor of mine telling me how great it was to be an only child, how you got so much more support, love, attention, blah, blah, blah, blah. How you didn't have to share your clothes or fight over the bathroom.

I would die to have a sister or brother to share my clothes with. (Although to be honest, what self-respecting sibling would want any of my junk?) I fight over the bathroom with *myself* when I'm feeling really lonely.

The summer I was thirteen, the year after my mom . . . and everything, it was over a hundred degrees practically the entire month of August, so I used to go to this public swimming pool. All the lifeguards, and lifeguards-in-training, and lifeguards-in-training-in-training, and swim team members chattered and gossiped and giggled while I sat on the other side of the pool. I never made a single friend. One day I overheard my foster creature at the time say, "Doesn't it seem like all the other kids at this pool arrived in the same car?"

That, right there, is the story of my life. I feel like the whole rest of the world, with all their brothers and sisters and parents and grandparents and uncles and aunts, arrived in one big car.

I walked.

The neighbor I mentioned earlier, the one who was so psyched about only children? I think he neglected to consider how the whole scenario would look if you didn't have parents.

THE COLOR
OF FEAR

GAIA SUCKED IN A FEW SHALLOW GASPS OF AIR,

RAISED A PAIR OF WIDE, HAUNTED EYES TO HIS,

AND WHISPERED, "I SEE DEAD PEOPLE. . . ."

FLESH CRAWLER

"Mrs. Travesura?"

At first Ella Niven didn't realize the voice was speaking to her. Then she remembered. *Travesura* was the Spanish word for "mischief." It was the name she'd given when she'd first made the appointment.

She looked up from her magazine. The stunning Asian receptionist was smiling down at her. "The doctor will see you now."

Ella nodded. Setting down the magazine, she grabbed her purse and the shopping bag resting beside her chair and followed the woman.

There were several other women in the posh waiting room. All were reading magazines. All were the indeterminate age of the extremely wealthy—somewhere between thirty-five and death. Clearly most of them had consulted the plastic surgeon many times before this.

Ella noticed that most of the women also had shopping bags with them. She recognized the familiar logos of Chanel, Saks Fifth Avenue, Bergdorf Goodman, and a couple of other Fifth Avenue boutiques, all glimmering like badges of honor.

Ella's own shopping bag was from Tiffany. As she crossed the room, she was acutely aware of each of the other women taking note of the robin's egg blue bag in her hand.

The receptionist led her out of the waiting room and into a long, gray corridor. At first Ella thought the walls were made of slabs of marble—but was shocked to realize they were actually enlarged, black-and-white close-ups of human flesh. A gigantic palm here. A colossal kneecap there. She'd never considered how the wrinkles and creases of one's skin could look like striations in rock.

Up ahead, the corridor ended in a pair of brushed-aluminum doors. The receptionist indicated that Ella could continue on alone. When Ella was within a yard of the metal doors, they glided open soundlessly.

The office was large and spare. Floor-to-ceiling windows wrapped around two sides of the square chamber, giving a panoramic, sixty-story view stretching from Central Park to the East River.

As Ella entered, the doctor was standing behind a large, black desk that gleamed like highly polished onyx. Oddly, it was bare except for a light blue folder that seemed to float—weightlessly—above the slick surface. It must have been an optical trick.

The doctor was tall, and pale, and bald. He wasn't dressed in a physician's white coat, as Ella had expected. He wore a black suit over a black turtleneck.

Drawing closer, Ella discovered that her initial impression was wrong again. The man *wasn't* bald. His hair was white, but cropped exceptionally close to his skull. His skin was the same ghostly color. That's what had created the illusion of baldness.

Still, the doctor's eyes were his most remarkable feature. They were deep set and a light shade of yellowish green. They gleamed like cat's eyes beneath his brow. In all her life she had never seen eyes that color.

Not on a human, anyway.

"'Mrs. Travesura,' I presume?"

His tone of voice made it clear he knew it wasn't her real name.

She nodded cordially. "How do you do."

The doctor didn't answer but gestured to the chair opposite him—an artsy contrivance of chrome bars and black leather straps.

The doctor sat down. "I understand, from our initial conversation, that there is a certain . . . procedure . . . that you wish me to perform."

"That is correct."

"Now. If I am not mistaken, you are . . . shall we say, *employed* by a certain L—

"Exactly," Ella interrupted. She needed to shut off this particular line of inquiry as quickly as possible. "I am. He, however, is not to be contacted under any circumstances. I must shield him from this undertaking. It is of utmost importance."

The doctor nodded, but he looked skeptical.

Ella knew he had past connections to Loki. That's how she had found him. But if he were to contact Loki directly, Ella knew her plan would be derailed instantly. Loki would accuse her of deep, twisted jealousy. But the fact was, when Ella succeeded with this plan, and Tom Moore arrived at the bedside of his poor, disfigured, comatose daughter, Loki would be forced to give Ella the credit she was due.

For now, she needed to change the course of the conversation. She cast her gaze at the mysterious blue folder and gestured toward it.

It worked. "Ah . . . the portfolio," he explained, placing his hand lightly on the folder. "It represents my . . . *side business,* if you will. 'Before' and 'after' photographs of some of my more *interesting* accomplishments." He slid it across the desk toward her. "Care to take a look?"

Ella stared down at the ice-blue folder in front of her, but she didn't touch it. She didn't need to see what was inside.

"Oh, c'mon . . . go ahead." He pushed the folder a few inches closer to her. "Aren't you in the least bit curious?" His tone was friendly. Flippant, almost. But—glancing back up at him—she saw that the man's eyes had locked on her with the cold, intense scrutiny of a snake. It was as if he were mentally willing her to look at the pictures. Daring her, even.

When she didn't respond, he reached forward and started lifting the cover. "Just take one little—"

"*I'm familiar with your work,*" she interrupted.

The doctor instantly snapped his hand away. The folder whispered shut.

He shrugged. "Suit yourself."

Ella had the feeling she'd just failed some kind of test. She tried to regain ground.

Sitting up taller, she leaned forward slightly, bowing her shoulders so that her cleavage was displayed at its most alluring angle. "Believe me, Doctor," she began in a persuasive voice, "I wouldn't be here if I weren't already *highly* confident about your . . . skills."

If the doctor noticed her breasts, he made no show of it. His eyes remained locked on her own.

"And yet," she went on—leaning forward a little more— "regardless of your expertise, I think you may find this particular . . . patient . . . to be an *extremely* unwilling subject."

"Many such patients *are* reluctant," the doctor agreed. "At first." His eyes seemed to sparkle at some dark, private memories.

"This one is different," Ella stated firmly. She was growing annoyed. Why wasn't he looking at her chest? She leaned forward even more. "You might as well know, Doctor: You're not the first . . . professional . . . I've contacted in this matter. Others have tried to treat this patient. They failed."

"My success rate is impeccable," the doctor assured her. "And as I informed you at the outset, Mrs. *Travesura*, one gets what one pays for." He stressed this last phrase meaningfully.

Ella took the hint. Reaching down, she picked up the Tiffany shopping bag that was lying at her feet. She placed it on the desktop, sliding it toward the doctor across the slick surface. As she did so, her hand accidentally brushed up against the folder.

Despite herself, she flinched.

The doctor noticed this, and his lips curled in mild amusement. He took the Tiffany bag, glancing inside.

Ella watched him and waited. She didn't expect him to react at the sight of the money; he was no doubt used to seeing such large sums of cash. She was waiting for him to notice what *else* was in the light blue bag.

The doctor's smile faded. Reaching into the bag, he removed a small, rectangular device. It might have been a cellular phone, except that it had a tiny LCD monitor where the earpiece should be. He held it up, a question forming in his bile-green eyes.

"It's a tracking device," she explained before he could ask. "Satellite technology. Effective within a fifty-mile radius. It allows you to pinpoint the precise location of a radio transmitter." Opening her purse, she withdrew a tiny metallic chip about the size of an aspirin. "*This* transmitter, which will be planted on the subject tonight."

She paused to gauge the doctor's reaction. It was crucial that he go along with the plan.

"Interesting," was all he said. He placed the tracking

device down on his desk and sat back in his chair, steepling his fingers together on his chest.

Keeping her voice steady, Ella continued: "You will use the device to track the subject. There is a telephone number on the back. Once you have completed the job, you are to go to the nearest pay phone and call this number. Is that understood?"

The doctor stared at her over his fingertips. "Perfectly."

Was he mocking her? She couldn't tell. But she didn't care now. This transaction was drawing to a close.

"Good," she said. "Well—uh, *Doctor*—I believe that about covers it."

She stood up. So did he. She would not let him try to shake her hand. The thought of being touched by those long, bloodless fingers made her flesh crawl.

There was only one more matter to square away before she could leave.

She placed her hands on his desk. "I have to make sure we're perfectly clear on one point," she informed him, trying to make her voice as threatening as possible. "You may be as . . . *thorough* . . . as you desire. In fact, I encourage you. But it is of the *utmost importance* that the subject makes it through the procedure. *Alive*."

The doctor stepped around his desk, smiling widely and warmly. "Your concern, Mrs. Travesura, is quite touching," he said, his voice dripping with sarcasm. "But it's unnecessary."

He suddenly dropped his smile—and with it, his act. "The subject will live. I can assure you of that." His voice was much colder now. Deader. As devoid of life as his skin. "There's no challenge in it for me otherwise."

He nodded at the folder, still sitting on his desk. "*They all lived*," he informed her, his voice ringing with chilling pride.

SHORTCOMINGS

Gaia Moore moved quickly along West Fourth Street in the direction of Washington Square Park, not bothering to slow her pace for her friend, Ed Fargo, who wheeled along a yard or two behind her.

As she walked, Gaia switched the strap of her beat-up canvas messenger bag from her left shoulder to the right. It was a smooth, fluid movement—one she made often over the course of her day. If she was doomed to have the overdeveloped deltoids of a Russian gymnast, at least she'd make sure they were *equally* overdeveloped. Being a super-muscular freak was bad enough. Being a lopsided one was too much to bear.

Gaia was painfully self-conscious about her body. Even now she was aware of her muscular arms and shoulders, although they were safely camouflaged beneath the bulky yellow-green Polartec parka she'd started wearing since the weather turned cold.

Long ago she'd given up trying to fight it. No amount of doughnut scarfing could erase the six-pack definition of her abdominals. Her genetics were simply stacked against her. Her muscles were as much a part of her as her blue eyes and her light hair and her extreme devotion to chocolate.

"Jesus, Gaia, could you slow down? The speed limit is thirty miles an hour, last I checked."

Gaia cast a glance back at Ed. "Why don't you speed up? You've got *wheels,* for God's sake."

It was a game they played. If she'd actually slowed down for his benefit, Ed probably would have clocked her. He appreciated pity exactly as much as she did.

The chess tables were coming into view. Gaia hoped there would be a new face today so she could earn some money for lunch.

Over the past three months she'd developed a reputation among the chess players. When she'd first arrived on the scene, it had been fairly easy to score a twenty-dollar game. That was in late August. Now the only regular who would play her for cash was old man Zolov, an international master. Since Gaia had helped save Zolov's life back in September, the "undefeated chess champ" of Washington Square suddenly began losing to her at regular intervals. A little *too* regular. It seemed as if they'd traded the same twenty dollars back and forth ten times in the past week.

And then there was Sam Moon. Sam could also get a game off her, but he was a different story entirely. They had played only once. They played to a deadlock until she'd freaked out and forfeited her king. Sam wouldn't take her money, but he had walked off with her heart that day.

Impatiently Gaia gathered her long hair from where it blew in her eyes and mouth and threw it behind her back. She'd forgotten to bring a hair band.

Maybe if she were lucky, Zolov would let her win today.

If she were really lucky, Sam Moon wouldn't show up at all.

Ed had caught up and started badgering her the way he'd been doing all day. "Gaia. Do the line from the movie. *Pleeeease?*"

And maybe—if she were really, *really* lucky—a certain someone would get his wheelchair caught in a sewer grate any moment now.

She glanced in annoyance at her self-appointed best friend. What had she done to deserve him?

"I'm not going to do it, Ed. So you can stop asking."

"Please, Gaia? I'm going to Pennsylvania tonight, so I won't get to see you for a whole four days. Besides, I promise I won't laugh this time. I promise."

"That's what you said the last time. *And* the time before that." God, why had she ever attempted that stupid imitation? She was just fooling around in the cafeteria at school, and Ed acted like it was the most hilarious thing he'd ever seen in his life. He wouldn't shut up about it.

"That was the old me. I've changed since then. I swear."

"The only thing you've changed is your underwear— and that's debatable."

"Guy-uhhhhhhhhh . . ."

"Oh, sure, whine my name. That'll convince me."

"I'll pay you."

"You don't have enough money."

"Oh, you might be surprised."

"I doubt it. Seeing as you can't even afford socks that match." She gestured at his feet.

Ed shot her a confused look. "What are you talking about?"

"Your socks. Are you celebrating Christmas a month early? Or did you get dressed in the dark this morning?"

Gaia had walked a good ten paces before she realized Ed was no longer at her side. She spun around.

He'd stopped in the middle of the sidewalk and was bent over in his seat, staring down at his feet with a strange, aggravated expression on his face. "Aw, man. You're kidding me, right?"

Gaia put her hands on her hips. "Kidding you? You put them on, elf boy, not me."

Ed squinted up at her. "Great. Thanks. Make fun of the color-blind guy. Go ahead."

Gaia cocked her head. "You're not color-blind," she pronounced.

Ed frowned, crossing his arms. "I think I would be the one to know."

Gaia stared at him. Her hands slipped from her waist, flopping at her sides. "Seriously? You're color-blind?"

"Hey—don't worry. You can't catch it." Ed slapped his wheels, gliding toward her once more.

"It's just that you never told me."

"Hmmm, that's funny. It's usually one of the first things I say to people: 'Hi, I'm Ed. I'm color-blind.' I think it's good to get one's physical shortcomings out of the way, y'know, *up front.*" He rolled to a stop in front of her feet, then peered furtively around the park. "Now, uh, Gaia, don't let this next bit of info freak you out, *but . . .*" He leaned in toward her, shielding his mouth with one hand conspiratorially. ". . . I'm *also* in a wheelchair."

Gaia was too busy looking at Ed's feet to think of a good comeback. One green sock, one red. Could he really not tell them apart? Not at all? She raised her gaze to his eyes, studying them, not sure what she was looking for. They were a dark brown with gold lights. Eyes the color of a double espresso, she found herself thinking. Inwardly she groaned. *Guess you don't need those refrigerator magnets to write crappy poetry.* The point was, Ed's eyes didn't *look* color-blind. They looked . . . well . . . like regular, everyday eyes.

Regular, everyday, *annoyed* eyes.

"Please, by all means, Gaia. Keep staring at me like that. It does wonders for my self-esteem."

"Sorry—" Gaia barely had time to scoot out of the way as Ed blew past her. "It's just that you're the first . . . I mean, I never knew a person who was color-blind. What's it like for you?"

God, I must sound ridiculous, Gaia thought, stepping after him. *Why don't I just say, Hey, Ed, you can't see colors, and I can't feel fear. Let's start a club!*

Once she was beside him again, Ed looked up at her, amused. "Are you feeling okay, Gai?"

"Yeah. Why?"

"Because you asked me a question."

"And?"

"*And* . . . didn't you sort of stipulate way back when that we wouldn't ask each other questions because if *you* ask *me* something, that would mean *I* get to ask *you* something in return?"

This time it was Gaia who stopped in her tracks. "Right. You're right, Ed. Forget that I asked."

"No, no, no, no, no," Ed said, swiveling around to face her with a mischievous grin. "Not so fast. You can't back out now. A deal's a deal." He rubbed his hands together gleefully. "So—I believe the category is color blindness. What's the question gonna be?"

"Does it make you jealous?" She was startled to hear her own voice saying those words. She hadn't meant to say them out loud.

Ed blinked a couple of times. "Jealous?" he repeated, sounding confused. "What do you mean?"

Gaia chose her next words carefully. "Do you ever feel . . . upset . . . that other people can . . . experience something that you . . . can't?"

"Upset? Not really." He shrugged. "After all, it's not like being color-blind means everything looks black and white to me. I mean, I still see things in color. For example, I can tell that jacket of yours is the color of mucus. It's just that certain colors look alike to me. Mostly I have difficulty telling reds from greens." He pointed down at his feet. "Obviously."

Gaia self-consciously eyed her jacket. "Do you ever wish you *could* tell the difference?"

Ed nodded. "Well, sure. There was a pretty ugly incident involving hot sauce a few years back." He grimaced at the memory. "But most of those taste buds grew back. Eventually." He scratched the back of his neck. "Traffic lights pose a theoretical problem, but I figured out at a young age that red is on top, and green is on the bottom. Aside from that, I don't really think about it too much . . . except when I commit the very occasional fashion faux pas and some heartless person goes and points it out to me." He shot her a fake-hostile glance but quickly leavened it with another shrug. "But—honestly?—I can't say I'm jealous of people who aren't color-blind."

"Why's that?" Gaia prompted.

Ed bit his lip, thinking. "Hmmm . . . I can't explain it all that well, but it's sorta like this: I can't imagine a world with more colors than I see it in already. I just can't. And . . . well . . . I don't think you can truly be jealous of something if you can't imagine having it in the first place. Besides"—he ran a finger across the arm of his wheelchair, adding casually, almost to himself—"there are better things to be jealous of."

Gaia gave him a rare smile. What *had* she done to deserve him?

After a moment he looked away self-consciously. "Uh . . . did any of that make sense?"

She nodded. "Yeah. It did."

"Good." Ed sat up a little taller in his seat. "So, I believe now it's *my* turn to *ask you* something."

Gaia took a deep breath, then let it out slowly. "Shoot away." Part of her almost wished he *would* ask her one of her secrets. Considering all he'd witnessed over the past three months, she supposed it was a wonder he hadn't guessed them all already.

Ed stroked his chin thoughtfully, gazing skyward. "Let's see now. . . . I get to ask the mysterious Gaia Moore a question." He was clearly savoring the moment. "Anything I want. . . . Anything at—"

"You got five seconds, Ed."

"Okay, okay!" Ed scowled at her. Then he snapped his fingers. "Here's one: Where'd you learn how to—no, no, scratch that." He waved his hand in the air as if erasing an imaginary chalk mark. "I got a better one: Why don't you ever talk about your—" He stopped himself short again, reconsidering. "No, not that one, either. How about—"

Gaia let out a low grumble.

Ed looked up at her, as if he were just struck by an idea. "Say. Can I ask you to *do* something instead?"

Gaia cocked a wary eyebrow. This actually represented an easy way out, but she didn't want him to know it. "I suppose. . . ."

Ed grinned evilly. "Do the line from the movie."

"Except that."

Ed pointed at her with both hands. "Oh, no! You can't back out of it now. A deal's a deal."

Gaia glanced at her watch. "Wow, what do you know? It's already the end of lunch period."

"Gaia!"

She sighed, resigned. "Fine. But you better not laugh this time."

Ed pantomimed zippering his lip.

Gaia held up a warning finger. "I'm not kidding, Ed."

Now he crossed his heart, holding up three fingers in the Scout salute.

"All right." She moved a couple of steps to a nearby bench, plopping down on the hard, cold slats. Gearing her throat, she cast a wary eye around the immediate area. Aside from a cluster of sooty-looking pigeons pecking at the ground nearby, this particular section of the park was empty. Thank God.

Ed repositioned his wheelchair in front of her for a better view.

Gaia sucked in a few shallow gasps of air, gripped the neckline of her coat with two white-knuckled fists, raised a pair of wide, haunted eyes to his, and whispered, over a trembling lower lip: *"I see dead people. . . ."*

Ed the Expressionless Eagle Scout managed to maintain his deadpan for an entire second and a half. Then he let out a guffaw so loud, it echoed clear across the park, sending the pigeons exploding skyward in a frenzied, flapping cloud. It was a wonder he didn't flip himself over backward.

Gaia slapped her hands down on the bench, standing up in annoyance. "What's so funny? I thought I was pretty good that time."

"Good?" Ed was doubled over now, his face bright pink. *"Good?"* He could barely choke out the word through his laughter.

"Okay, that's it." Gaia kicked the side of his wheel with her boot and huffed off. "I'm outta here."

A few seconds later she could hear him behind her, struggling to catch her. "Gaia—wait—please—" All the laughing had left him panting for air. Good. She purposely picked up her pace. "Please—Gaia—wait up—I'm sorry—I'm sorry, but—it's just that—if you could see what you—"

She turned around. "Spit it out, Ed."

Ed placed a hand on his chest, taking a moment to catch his breath. "You have got to do the most terrible impression of being scared I have ever seen in my life."

He cracked up again.

Gaia hoped the sudden flush in her cheeks appeared to be a reaction to the cold.

Ed, my color-blind friend, you have no idea. . . .

S A M

I used to think you could pretty much divide people into two categories: those who believe in love at first sight and those who don't.

I was a proud member of the second category. I used to think you fell in love with your brain. . . . Um, that came out wrong. Let me rephrase. I used to think your brain was in use when you fell in love. You sort of decided it over time, like I did with Heather. I saw her, I thought, man, that girl is beautiful. I talked to her, I thought, yeah, and she's smart and funny, too. I spent some time with her and thought, hey, we actually like a lot of the same stuff. I kissed her and thought, yo, this is fun. After that, as far as my brain and I were concerned, we were in love.

Then I met Gaia Moore. Every time I've ever had anything to do with Gaia, my brain has said, shit, this girl is nothing but pain, misery, and trouble. And in this case my brain was totally right. But in spite of my brain's lack of cooperation, I've fallen in love with her. It happened the first time I ever saw her. It was like a clap of thunder, a bolt of lightning, a monsoon, all those cheesy metaphors I never believed before (although there actually was a monsoon going on at the time). There is no good reason for me to love Gaia. There are only good reasons against it. Every day I struggle to release myself from it. Every day I try to convince myself that it will go away.

So anyway, I guess you could say my brain is sticking with the second category, claiming that no, there is no such thing as love at first sight. My heart has betrayed it in favor of the first category, arguing, yes, absolutely, it's the only kind of love there is. And now my brain and my heart aren't even on speaking terms, anymore. When I said "divide people," that wasn't exactly what I had in mind.

I told my friend Danny about this theory, and he told me he also had a theory for how to divide people: those who divide people into two and those who don't.

HELL HATH NO FURY . . .

HER ARMS WERE AROUND HIM,
HER HEARTBREAKING SCAR PRESSED AGAINST
HIS CHEST, HER LIPS AGAINST HIS EAR . . .

A GOOD IDEA

". . . and Medea, so consumed was she by her bitter jealousy, so desperate was she to take vengeance on her unfaithful husband, Jason, that she murdered her rival with a gift of a poisoned cloak and then went on to kill her own children. . . ."

Heather Gannis glanced up at the animated face of her literature teacher, Mr. MacGregor, who was talking much louder than necessary and brandishing a paperback edition of Euripides. Jesus, why were parents so up in arms about violence on television? The seriously grisly stuff was happening in these Greek plays.

She heard a snort of laughter from the back of the room. She turned quickly, recognizing the laugh before seeing its owner. Ed Fargo, her former true love, was laughing at something Gaia Moore had written on the corner of his notebook. The sound of it was corrosive in her ears.

Gaia could make Ed laugh. It was a rare ability and another affront to add to the long list.

Heather wasn't superstitious. Unlike the ancient Greeks, she didn't believe in fate. She wasn't religious and had little tolerance for the wu-wu astrology and Ouija board crap many of her friends were into.

But for Gaia, she made an exception. Gaia, with her fairy-tale yellow hair and her long, graceful limbs, was too terrible to accept at face value. How could one girl captivate Heather's boyfriend, enslave her ex-boyfriend, humiliate her, nearly get her killed, and completely destroy her self-confidence in less than three months? Gaia was a clear message from Somebody Up There that Heather deserved punishment.

Since Gaia had arrived in September, her evil had radiated. First there were the slashings, culminating in Heather's own near death. Then there was the stuff that happened to Sam. Then Cassie Greenman. Heather, like the rest of the school, was haunted by her murder.

All these tragedies weren't a coincidence. They just weren't.

". . . So for Monday, I'd like you all to read *Oedipus Rex*." Mr. MacGregor wrapped up his lecture just as the bell rang, signaling the end of a very long day at Central Village High. "Have a great Thanksgiving holiday, folks."

The classroom burst into cusp-of-vacation activity. Heather sighed as she jotted the assignment in her notebook. She had a feeling that play was going to be another doozy.

"Hey, chick."

Heather glanced up as two of her friends, Carrie Longman and Melanie Young, materialized at her desk. "Hey," she said, digging around to find a smile. "Whatsup?"

"You feel like Ozzie's?" Melanie asked.

Heather carefully piled her books and zipped them into her backpack. Her eyes landed momentarily on her empty wallet. A large mochaccino at Ozzie's cost over three bucks.

Her friends thought nothing of buying two of them a day. Heather couldn't keep up, and she refused to let anybody else buy one for her. The old Gannis pride kicked in triple strength when it came to shallow displays of fortune. Or lack thereof.

Besides, she had something important to do this afternoon. Something she'd put off for too long.

Heather stood and smoothed her long, slim, blood-colored skirt. She strode out of the classroom, and her friends followed close behind. "Can't make it. Sorry," she said breezily.

"Oh." Carrie hovered at Heather's locker, taking a moment to regroup. "How about Dean & Deluca? They have those excellent caramel brownies. We can go to Union Square after and get started on Christmas shopping."

"You all go. Maybe I'll catch up later," Heather said noncommittally. "I've got something I need to take care of this afternoon."

Melanie and Carrie stared at her in silence, obviously hoping she would elaborate. She didn't feel like it. She slammed her locker shut. She pulled on her black nylon jacket and slung her backpack over her shoulder. "See ya. Leave your cell on, Carrie."

Once Heather was rid of them, she slipped into the bathroom. She got weirdly obsessive about her appearance every time she was about to see Sam, although she knew her boyfriend was even more oblivious to her subtle efforts than most guys.

She studied her face and her hair. She applied a coat of lip gloss and ran a brush through her long, smooth hair. No perceivable difference. Staring at the high neck of her white T-shirt under her soft, black V-necked sweater, she suddenly had an idea. Ever since "the incident"—the slashing that had put her in the hospital late in September—she'd worn a scarf or a shirt or sweater with a high neck every time she left her apartment. Now she discarded her jacket, dropped her backpack on the floor, and pulled both the sweater and the T-shirt over her head at the same time. She pulled the two garments apart, folded the T-shirt neatly into her backpack, and put the sweater back on.

She spent another minute gazing at her reflection. Yes, that was a good idea.

CHOOSE

Sam tipped back his head and rested it on the top of the park bench. He closed his eyes and soaked up the low, late autumn sun. For the end of November, the air was sweet and warm. Probably almost sixty degrees.

Wednesdays were his favorite days. His classes ended early, so he allowed himself to hang out at the chess tables. That was one of the great things about college—those one or two class days that left you lots of time to waste. He'd already hustled twenty bucks off an unwitting stranger, then given it right back to Zolov in a rout. It was a weird form of charity, but whatever. Hustle from the stupid and lose to the smart. 'Twas the season.

"Hey, handsome."

He lifted his head and blinked open his eyes. Heather was bearing down at twenty feet, beautiful as ever in her red skirt and whispery black jacket. He heard the dry acorns cracking under the heels of her boots.

"Hi," he said, rubbing his eyes. "How's your day?"

"Okay," she said. "The usual high school plundering of spirits. How 'bout you?"

He laughed. Heather was so cool, so together. Never awkward or at a loss for words. "Oh, you know. Wasting some more of my youth at the chess tables." He paused. "Looking forward to tomorrow."

Instantly he felt annoyed at himself for having gilded the truth like that. He was looking forward to the gauntlet of the Gannis family Thanksgiving in the very plain sense of the phrase—observing that it would take place in the near future. He wasn't looking forward as in eagerly antici-pating it.

"Oh, yeah?" She angled her head coyly, causing a curtain of shiny chestnut hair to fall forward over her shoulder. It reminded him of sex, which started that tingly feeling spreading through his body, which in turn made him feel guilty about what had happened the last time they had sex. And the first time they had sex.

"Looking forward to my dad's dry, stringy turkey? My mom's sickly turnip-brown sugar thing?" she challenged. "Looking forward to Phoebe eating nothing and complaining about Binghamton? Lauren talking on her cell phone straight through dinner? Hmmm." She appraised him with one lifted eyebrow. "Are you telling me the truth?"

Sam laughed again, wishing his heart would listen to reason once in a while. "Well. *You'll* be there."

Heather awarded him a little smile. She pointed to the spot on the bench next to him. "Is this seat taken? Do you mind if I sit?" Her tone was light, but he registered that her eyes were serious.

He scooted over fast, feeling ungentlemanly. "Of course. Definitely. Sit."

She sat and dropped her backpack on the other side of her. She wasn't so close that any part of her was touching him, but neither was she so far that he couldn't feel her warmth. "Listen. There's something I need to talk to you about." She turned to face him, nailing him with her odd-colored eyes. They weren't blue, but they weren't not blue, either.

"Sure, of course." He was getting nervous now. He was saying "of course" too much. "Talk away."

"It's kind of serious. Just to give you fair warning. It's something we've been needing to talk about for a while now."

"Of c—" He clamped his mouth shut. He felt like strangling himself. "Okay. I'm warned."

Heather took a deep breath. "I know that you have some kind of . . . *relationship* with Gaia Moore."

Sam could tell it was painful to her to say the name, and he felt awful.

"I know that you know her somehow, and I need you to tell me what's going on between you."

Sam swallowed. Jesus, Heather had a knack for getting right to the point. He hoped his face didn't betray his dire discomfort. He needed to choose his words carefully. He cleared his throat. "There's nothing going on."

Liar. You think about her every hour of every day.

"I barely know her. I've hardly ever spoken with her. There's never been anything . . . romantic between us."

But you wish there were. You dream about her at night.

Sam glanced up, reminding himself that he was having a conversation with Heather and not with himself.

"So what *is* there between you?" Heather pressed. "Why was she there the night we . . . " She trailed off and then started again. "How did she know you'd been kidnapped?

Why did you need to leave in such a hurry the last time we were together in your room?"

All the saliva in Sam's mouth had dried up, and from what he could tell, it was never coming back. He tried swallowing again. "Honestly, Heather, I don't know. The last couple of months have been so strange. I really don't know anything about her." That last bit, finally, was a sincere answer.

"Have you ever . . . *been* with her?" Heather stopped and tried again. Here was a girl who accepted no cowardice, particularly not in herself. "Have you kissed her? Hooked up with her? Had sex with her?"

"No," Sam answered firmly. *But God, how I've wanted to.*

Heather looked relieved but no less serious. "Okay, here's the really important thing I need to say to you." She pulled one sleeve of her sweater up over the palm of her hand. "I don't like Gaia Moore. I hate her. I think she's dangerous, and I wish she'd stay away from you." Heather caught her breath for a second before she rushed on. She was nervous, but admirably determined. "I need you to tell me now that whatever there is between you is over. That you won't have anything to do with her anymore." She fixed him with her eyes again. "Because if you can't, it's got to be over between you and me. You have to choose."

Whoa. Sam looked down at his jeans, pressing his hands into his thighs, raising his shoulders up around his ears.

This was hard-core. This was much more than he'd ever expected. He had to think.

Heather was not only offering him a choice; she was offering him a way out. He could be free of the guilt and the craziness. He could be free to figure out what the hell *was* going on between him and Gaia.

"So is it over?" Heather asked, her voice quiet and wobbly.

Sam turned to her. The answer he'd been contemplating withered in his throat. Her eyes were round and glazed with tears. Her jacket had fallen open, and the low V neck of her sweater revealed a long, jagged rent in the delicate white skin along her collarbone. The cut through which she'd lost so much blood and nearly her life. It was still angry red in color. Still unhealed.

His mind flashed back to that night. Finding Heather in the park, lying in a puddle of her own blood. The strange, dissonant whirlpool of hospital sounds and smells and colors, then the unsettling piece of information that a girl from Heather's class, a girl named Gaia Moore, had seen the gang member with the knife in the park and she'd passed up an easy opportunity to warn Heather.

Sam's gaze was riveted on the wound. He couldn't seem to look away. All the while Heather kept her head up, seemingly unaware of what he was seeing and feeling.

"Sam?"

He dragged his eyes back up to her face. He was miserable.

He was filled with shame. He was torn in two. "Heather, it's not only over. It never began."

Her arms were around him, her heartbreaking scar pressed against his chest, her lips against his ear by the time he realized that he hadn't said which girl he was talking about.

MARY MOSS

"Why are you like this?"

That is a question I've heard from a lot of adults in my life. Some of them related to me, some not. If they don't ask it outright, I see the question in their eyes. And I'm not being paranoid. Trust me.

"Like this" in my case means loud, impulsive, messed up, combative, undisciplined, annoying. Other stuff, too.

The reason the question gets asked so often, with such impatience, is because there's no easy explaining when it comes to me.

I come from a nice family. Two parents, not one. We're rich, not poor. We're well educated. Or I should say, they're well educated. They pay lots of attention to me. They read me books when I was little. They made me drink my milk. It's really not their fault.

I have two nice brothers. They both go to good colleges now. Growing up, they only teased me and beat me up the normal amount.

Why am I like this?

I don't know. Some people have a lot of space between thinking and saying or thinking and doing. I don't have any. Some people look at themselves from the outside and try really hard to make what they see look good. I stay on the inside. I'd rather feel good than seem it.

Sometimes I love that about myself. Sometimes I hate it.

Why am I like this?

I don't know. I have a couple of theories, though.

. . . LIKE A WOMAN SCORNED

IT WAS NOT OF "UTMOST IMPORTANCE"
THAT THE "SUBJECT" BE KEPT ALIVE. THAT HAD
BEEN THEIR MISTAKE FROM DAY ONE.

WORSE THAN STUPID

Gaia rested her head in her hand, staring at what remained of her frozen pizza, trying to fight off a terrible wave of loneliness. It seemed mean-spirited of biology to have left fear out of her DNA but to have made her feel loneliness so acutely.

The Nivens' brownstone was empty and quiet except for the odd siren or car alarm blasting from Bleecker Street. Those were sounds you stopped hearing when you lived in New York City. Like a buzzing refrigerator or the hum of an air conditioner. You incorporated them into your ears.

The kitchen was sparse and orderly as usual. There was no sign, other than her plate on the faux-country wooden table, that a seventeen-year-old girl had just prepared and eaten her dinner there. Gaia was camping at the Nivens' more than actually *living* there. Low-impact camping. After five years in foster homes she'd learned never to settle in too much, never to get comfortable.

George had been called away on business just before the Thanksgiving holiday. She liked George. He was awkward with her, but sweet and well meaning. He had known her father. She would even feel disappointed by his absence, but like the sirens on Bleecker Street, disappointment was something so customary, Gaia hardly felt it anymore.

On the plus side, when George was gone, Ella was usually

gone, too. And Ella was most nearly likable when she was gone.

Gaia washed her plate, dried it, and returned it to the cabinet. No trace.

Thanksgiving wasn't Gaia's favorite holiday. The day was designed around warm family get-togethers, parents, grandparents, uncles, aunts, cousins. Blitzing yourself on great food. Thinking about all the wonderful things your life had brought you and feeling grateful for it.

Gaia had no family anymore (save one recently discovered man claiming to be her uncle, whose name she didn't even know). On account of that she had trouble feeling grateful. Instead it brought to mind the wonderful things that life had taken away from her, which sent her down the spiral of thanklessness. And that didn't require a special day. That was every day.

Gaia peered into the fridge. She was still hungry, craving something sweet.

Apparently George had done the shopping for Thanksgiving before he'd been called away. The refrigerator was crammed with food, including a massive raw turkey on the bottom shelf.

It was a little depressing, seeing all the food that George had bought and now wouldn't get to cook. Depressing but not exactly tragic. Although George could find his way through a tuna casserole, Gaia suspected his culinary talents fell a few drumsticks short of turkey with all the trimmings.

Ella certainly wasn't going to do it. Gaia doubted George's dumb wife could figure out the recipe for ice. The only way Ella would put her hands in a turkey was if her iPod had been shoved inside.

It was revolting how tightly Ella had George wrapped around her finger. For a person who made a living in the intelligence community, George Niven was pretty moronic when it came to matters in his own home. You didn't have to be in the CIA to see that Ella was playing him.

No, the only way that bird was getting cooked was if Gaia did it herself.

Without warning, Gaia's mind was flooded with a rush of overlapping images. Memories of another time, another place.

Chestnut stuffing . . . cranberry relish . . . a fire in a stone hearth . . . an ivory chess set, the pieces carved to look like Norse gods: Odin, Frigg, Thor, Loki . . . a man's sudden, shocked laughter: "My God, she just beat me, Kat!" . . . a gravy boat shaped like a swan and a woman's accented voice, saying: "It's lovely, isn't it? It was my grandmother's. Her name was Gaia, too. . . ."

The mental pictures evaporated at the sound of the front door being unlocked, followed by the sharp, staccato click of high heels on the marble entranceway. The hall light snapped on.

Gaia glanced over at the wall clock. 9:51.

Great. Apparently Ella's coven decided to wrap things up early tonight.

Quickly Gaia reached across the counter and flicked off the light. She closed the refrigerator, not hungry anymore.

It was uncanny: No matter how hungry Gaia was, whenever Ella approached, appetite retreated. Maybe it was an allergic reaction to Ella's unique combination of silicone, hair spray, suffocating perfume, and spandex microminis.

With the refrigerator door closed, the kitchen was swallowed up in shadow. The only light now came from the hallway and the faint red glow cast by the microwave's digital display.

Gaia stood silently in the reddish gloom, mentally urging Ella to stay away from the kitchen. She was hoping to hit the park this evening, maybe see if she could lure a mugger or two. A run-in with Ella would put a damper on that plan. Ella would pull the Carol Brady routine, and Gaia was in no mood to answer stupid, pointless questions at ten o'clock at night. "How was school?" "Great! I purposely blew my history exam and scammed sixty bucks at the chess tables before dinner, and now I'm gonna go to the park to kick some punk ass clear into tomorrow. Thanks for asking!"

She had the sneaking feeling Ella would *not* be amused.

Gaia listened closely for signs of life, but all she could hear was the loud ticking of the grandfather clock in the hall. When Ella still hadn't appeared after sixty more ticks, Gaia stepped cautiously into the corridor.

Maybe this was her lucky night. Maybe Ella had gone upstairs already, sparing Gaia the scary sight of a grown woman who still looked to Barbie for fashion cues.

No such luck.

Ella was standing smack-dab in the middle of the foyer. True to form, she was sporting a metallic turquoise miniskirt with matching pumps, topped off with a fuzzy pink angora sweater that had probably been too tight on the baby she stole it off of.

Gaia's luck hadn't completely abandoned her: Ella was faced away from her and hadn't heard her approaching. Gaia could still avoid detection. In fact, she was all set to scurry back into the kitchen—until she saw what Ella was holding.

Avoiding detection suddenly stopped being important.

"What do you think you're doing?"

Ella spun around, one hand still buried deep in the pocket of Gaia's electric yellow-green Polartec coat. For a second she just stood there—frozen, guilty—then she narrowed her eyes, jutting out her chin in defiance. "What does it look like? I'm searching for drugs." She started rifling through the pockets once again, as if daring Gaia to stop her.

Gaia was across the foyer in three swift strides. "Let me save you some trouble, Ella. There aren't any." Grabbing hold of her coat, she yanked it hard out of Ella's manicured clutches.

Ella reacted as if she'd been slapped, her hands recoiling like two wounded pink spiders.

Gaia stared her flatly in the eyes. "And for future reference? I don't do drugs." Then, just in case Ella still didn't understand, she added: "Leave my stuff alone."

Ella's nostrils flared. "You think I don't know what you do?" she accused. "You think I don't see you sneaking out of here at night, heading to the park? I know what goes on out there." She jabbed her finger at the front door, tossing her copper-colored hair indignantly.

Gaia rolled her eyes. *"Please."* To Ella's blow-dried mind, the only reason Gaia might possibly want to go to Washington Square Park was to do drugs. Well, if that's what she wanted to believe, let her. There was no way Ella would buy the truth, even if Gaia had the patience to tell it to her. Which she didn't.

Besides, how did you explain that your hobbies included luring out and beating up would-be felons for sport?

Hell, even someone with a measurable IQ would have a hard time believing that one.

Gaia turned to leave, but Ella suddenly seized her sharply by the arm, spinning her around.

"I know what you are."

Ella's press-on nails felt like five plastic knives gouging through the flannel of Gaia's sleeve.

Gaia jerked out of the woman's grasp. "Trust me, Ella. You don't know the first thing about me."

Ella was physically shorter than Gaia, but her stiletto pumps put them at roughly the same eye level. Idly Gaia found herself wondering just what color Ella's eyes would appear to the color-blind Ed Fargo. To her they were the ugly, radioactive green of mint jelly. Did that mean they would look *red* to him? Or would Ella's *hair* look *green?* Somehow the mental image of a red-eyed, green-haired Ella wasn't too hard to conjure.

Ella's lips curled into a sneer. "I knew you'd be trouble the minute you set foot in this house. George wouldn't listen to me, of course. 'Poor little Gaia, she's had such a hard life. She needs our help.'"

Gaia was impressed. For a bimbo with no discernible skill as a photographer, Ella could do a pretty mean impression of her husband's voice. She'd obviously missed her calling in life.

Ella continued tauntingly: "Well, I got news for you. Maybe that wounded-bird routine works on George, but it never fooled me. Not for *one minute.*" She punctuated the last two words with two sharp pokes to Gaia's shoulder.

Gaia glanced down at the spot where Ella had touched her. "Are you through?"

"Not quite. I also know you're doing everything in your power to flunk out of school."

Gaia raised an eyebrow. "Really?" *And what was your first clue, Nancy Drew? The string of F's, maybe?*

"That's right. Your principal called to say that you're

officially on academic probation." Ella smiled smugly. "Congratulations, Gaia. And after only three months. I hear at your last school, it took you a whole semester."

Whoa. This was definitely *not* the Carol Brady moment Gaia had anticipated five minutes ago. Gaia didn't know *what* role Ella thought she was playing tonight, but if the woman was hoping to get some kind of reaction from her, she'd have to keep on hoping. Gaia wasn't going to give her any satisfaction.

Ella crossed her arms and shook her head in mock pity. "Poor George. He still has some misguided notion that you're intelligent—that we'll actually get rid of you in a couple of years when you go to college. Ha!" She made an ugly snorting sound. "*That's* a joke. Do you think colleges would even *touch* a person with your grades? Do you?" Ella leaned forward, lowering her voice to a whisper. "Or do you think colleges simply let in little blond girls who can beat old drunks at chess and are friends with cripples?"

Gaia's hands involuntarily curled into fists. Her heartbeat accelerated. But she kept her voice remarkably cool and collected as she warned: "You should watch what you're saying, Ella."

"*This is my house!*"

Ella's voice exploded with such raw, unbridled rage that Gaia found herself backing away defensively. "In *my* house *I* say what *I* want *and you listen!*" Her breath was hot on Gaia's face.

My God, Gaia thought, who *is* this person? This wasn't

the old Ella who Gaia knew and disliked. She had seen that Ella angry before, and it had never been anything even remotely close to this. *This* person . . . this was someone different. Someone wholly unfamiliar.

The woman's face was contorted in a mask of fury. Her pupils were mere pinpricks in two poisonous green irises. Her lips were curled away from her teeth.

"Things are going to change around here, *starting now!* From now on, you come straight home from school. No stops in the park, no chess games. *Understand?* You're going to go to your room and you're going to do your homework. No phone, no TV. And at night you're going to stay in this house if I have to nail every damn window shut myself. You're going to stay in this house if I have to nail your *goddamn feet to the floor!*"

Whoever this person was—Ella or her more evil twin—Gaia had finally had enough.

"I don't have to take this from you," she informed the crazy woman standing before her. "You're not my mother."

"I'm *not?*" Ella reared back, slapping her left breast in a truly third-rate imitation of shocked dismay. "No, I suppose I'm not," she continued, leaning forward again, green eyes narrowing into slits. *"My* heart's still *beating."*

Gaia watched her fist smash into Ella's face before her brain even knew she was throwing the punch. It was that automatic. That impulsive. As uncontrollable as a sneeze and (good thing for Ella) about as sloppy as one, too. Unlike her more thought-out punches, this one barely connected with its mark, catching the underside of the woman's jaw.

Not that it made a big difference.

Ella spun, crumpling to the marble floor like a sack of bricks, landing on her hands and knees.

Everything was suddenly deathly quiet.

For the next fifteen seconds there was nothing but the sound of Ella's steady, heavy breathing and the slow, rhythmic ticking of the grandfather clock in the hall: *Ticktock. Ticktock. Ticktock.*

Gaia felt like she should do something—*say* something—but she didn't know what. "Sorry" didn't seem right. For one thing, she wasn't sorry. Not yet, anyway. Maybe later she would be.

Instead she just stood there, frozen in place, absently rubbing the knuckles of her right hand, watching Ella's shoulders rise and fall, rise and fall, inside the tight angora sweater.

Ticktock. Ticktock. Ticktock.

After another fifteen seconds Ella slowly crawled away from Gaia toward the foot of the stairs. Once there, she reached up and grabbed hold of the banister, then hoisted herself to her feet. Her spandex skirt had bunched up around her waist, and she took a moment to pull it back down. She smoothed down her sweater. Then, squaring her shoulders, she started slowly up the stairs.

She was halfway to the second floor when Gaia found her voice.

"Ella . . ."

Above her, Ella paused but didn't turn around. Tilting her head slightly, like a sleepwalker hearing her name being called, she said softly: "Wait there." Her voice sounded strange. Thick.

She continued up the stairs.

Gaia watched as Ella's legs disappeared from view. Listened as the click of Ella's heels faded away, drowned out by the clock in the hall.

Ticktock. Ticktock. Ticktock.

It sounded remarkably like a time bomb.

DISSOLVING

Blood. She was tasting her own goddamn blood.

Once she was out of Gaia's sight, Ella moved more quickly. Around to the next flight of stairs. Eighteen steps to the third floor. Right foot, left foot, right foot. Up, up, up.

Her tongue felt too large for her mouth. It was too wide, too thick. As she mounted the stairs, she explored her tongue's surface with her teeth, wincing as her incisors sank into the gash she'd bitten into it when the little bitch had punched her.

When the little bitch had punched her.

The cut felt deep.

The little bitch had punched her.

Despite the pain she bit down harder now, feeling oddly energized as more blood welled into her mouth. It tasted sharp and bitter, like acid.

Punched her. Her.

It *was* acid, she decided, stepping swiftly onto the third floor. Acid, pumping through her heart, coursing through her veins. She could feel it—couldn't she?—burning in her cheeks, raging in her ears. It would dissolve her. It *was* dissolving her. Eating her from the inside out. She had to hurry. There was no time to lose.

Ten feet down the hall to her dressing room.

Her gun was in the dressing room.

She didn't care what Loki would say. Didn't care what he would do.

She was tasting her own goddamn blood!

Besides, she knew what had to be done now. It was obvious. Loki had been wrong. Loki *was* wrong.

It was *not* of "utmost importance" that the "subject" be

kept alive. That had been their mistake from day one.

As long as his daughter was alive, Tom Moore wasn't going to risk her life by showing his face anywhere near her.

But the bastard *might* come to her funeral.

GO

Ticktock. Ticktock. Ticktock.

Gaia stood in the foyer. Watching the stairs. Waiting for Ella to return.

Should she stay? Try to fix this gaping rupture? Was there any point? Could she make herself apologize for George's sake?

Stay or go?

Ella was insane. This night was insane.

Stay or go?

She could hear Ella's footsteps again. She was coming back down the stairs now, rounding the landing one floor above.

Without realizing she'd made a decision, Gaia let her long strides carry her down the hallway. Numbly she pulled on her coat and threw her bag over her shoulder. The cold doorknob filled her hand, and she turned it with a click.

"Good-bye, house. Good-bye, George," she whispered. "Sorry about this."

She had a feeling as she stepped out the door that she wouldn't be coming back.

GAIA

I remember the summer I started carrying pennies.

I was five years old, and we were living in our Manhattan apartment. My mom's dad got sick late that spring. He was dying, it turns out. Every weekend when we'd drive my mother to visit him in his hospital in New Jersey, my dad would take me to the Jersey shore.

You see, when you're driving back into Manhattan from the Jersey side, you have to go through a toll booth. Nowadays things are pretty high-tech, with laser scanners and special stickers you can get for your car, but back then my dad would pay using tokens.

Of course, to a five-year-old, a coin's a coin. And to me, those tokens looked just like pennies.

Somehow, in my little-kid brain, I concluded that in order to get back home, you needed pennies for the tolls. From that moment on, I started carrying extra pennies with me. Just in case.

For some reason, I had this silly notion that my parents could somehow lose me. You know—just take their eyes off me around a corner or something and not be able to find me again. Maybe all kids think like that when they're small. Anyway, I wanted to make sure that if I ever got separated from my folks, I'd have enough money to pay the toll and get back home on my own.

Later on, when I was older and knew better, I still carried pennies. By then it had just become this sort of superstitious habit of mine. My talisman. My good luck charm.

It wasn't until I was in sixth grade that my father finally noticed and asked me about it. When I explained the whole toll booth story to him, he laughed. Told me I always worried about the wrong things.

A year later my mother was killed and my father took off, leaving me behind.

So I guess it wasn't such a silly notion after all.

I don't carry pennies for good luck anymore. They don't work all that well, as it turns out.

A REASON TO STAY

MARY ATTACHED HERSELF TO GAIA BY THE HAND,
AND GAIA LET HERSELF BE PULLED TOWARD A
WAITING GROUP THAT, FOR THE MOMENT
AT LEAST, COULD PASS AS FRIENDS.

RED LIGHT, GREEN LIGHT

There were times when a four-dollar vanilla latte with an extra dollop of foam seemed like the answer to every single one of life's problems.

Tonight it just seemed like an overpriced cup of coffee.

Sitting at one of the window seats at the Starbucks on Astor Place, Gaia forced herself to take another slug of the sickly sweet concoction. It wasn't easy. Ten minutes ago it had been lukewarm. Now it was closer to cold. It reminded her of the milk left over from a bowl of sugar cereal.

Outside, across Fourth Avenue, the giant clock face on the side of the Carl Fischer building showed that it was almost eleven.

God, what a night. Living with George and Ella had never been great, but it was a place to be. A place to keep what little stuff she had. And her tenuous toehold in their house had made her a New Yorker. She liked that.

Now it was gone, and she had that slightly metallic, nauseating taste in her throat that came with running away. Or drinking syrup-sweet coffee soup. Or the combination.

She knew the taste because she'd run away before. Never successfully, though. She always ended up back where she started or in a different foster home, facing even greater doubt and suspicion from her newest "family."

This time would be different. Packed into the various zippered compartments of her messenger bag and parka were bills totaling over eight hundred dollars—three months of chess winnings. She carried it on her all the time. It was ironic. She used to carry pennies for luck. Now she kept twenties for when her luck turned sour.

It was a lot of money, but it wouldn't last long in New York City. She would be smart to leave town.

With that thought, a picture bloomed in her mind. The face of Sam Moon, sitting across the chess table from her, drenched by rain, staring directly into her heart as no one, man or woman, ever had.

It would be hard to leave him. It would be crazy to stay for him.

Then there was Ed. Her first real friend since . . . forever. She was addicted to Ed.

And to the park. And the action. The density of criminals. The number of places where you could buy doughnuts at 2 A.M. The sirens.

But tonight Ed had taken off with his family to drive to Pennsylvania for a classic Thanksgiving with bickering parents and adoring grandparents. He wouldn't be back until Sunday. It just pointed out how different they really were. How different they would always be.

Sam belonged to somebody else (whom she incidentally

hated). Ed was a decent, good person with a family who loved him. Far too decent for her.

There was nothing for her here.

She tipped her head and rested it against the cold glass window. The pale, late November color of her hands picked up a green glow from the traffic light at the intersection just beyond the window. Go.

Predictably, a minute later, her hands were bathed in red. Stop.

For minutes at a time she watched hypnotically as her hands changed from green to red.

Go. Stop.

Walk. Don't walk.

She'd let the traffic light decide her fate.

Behind her, there was a complaint of hinges and an inrush of street noise as someone pushed into the Starbucks through the side entrance. A second later Gaia was assaulted by a blast of arctic air. She felt its icy fingers snake around her neck and trickle down her spine and watched in morbid fascination as the skin of her arms pebbled into gooseflesh.

The sight transfixed her. It always did.

She traced a fingertip along the surface of her forearm— slowly, exploringly—from the crook of her elbow to her wrist. Every tiny, raised bump gave her a tiny, perverse thrill.

Gooseflesh. A symptom of fear.

Of course, in Gaia's case, it was just hair follicles reacting to an extreme change of temperature. That's all it would *ever* be with her. Still, she liked to believe that in some small, weird way, getting goose bumps was like getting a tiny glimpse into what fear felt like. The simple fact that she could experience one of fear's physical manifestations made her feel less . . . different, somehow. Less freakish. More . . . human.

The goose bumps were beginning to fade.

Gaia sighed. Who was she trying to kid? She would *never* know what fear was like. No more than Ed could know what it was like to tell red from green.

Red and green. Gaia suddenly remembered her appointment with Destiny. Would she stay or would she go? Taking a breath, she raised her eyes and looked out the window.

The light was yellow.

Gee, thanks, Destiny. You sure know how to toy with a girl's emo—

Gaia's thoughts were interrupted by something reflected in the plate glass window. Someone was rushing up behind her. Someone with red hair.

Before she could turn around, something cold and metallic was pressed against the back of her neck. "Don't make a move," a female voice warned.

Gaia didn't move. She just sat there, staring down at her arms.

There wasn't a single damn goose bump in sight.

Mary Moss was expecting the girl's shoulders to jump or at least her muscles to tense. They didn't, although Gaia did turn her head quickly. "Your money or your life," Mary growled, pressing the metal tube of lipstick into Gaia's back.

Mary snarled menacingly, waiting for a reaction.

Gaia didn't look scared, but she didn't look quite tuned in, either. She was glowing red from a traffic light outside, and her eyes were wide and confused.

Mary softened her expression and produced the tube of lipstick for Gaia to see. "Gaia, it's me. Mary. Are you okay?"

Gaia seemed to pull her eyes into focus. She took the lipstick and examined it.

"It's called Bruise," Mary offered. "Great color, poor firearm."

Now Gaia was green. She handed the lipstick back.

"How's it going?" Mary asked, taking the seat across the little table from Gaia and tucking the lipstick tube in the outside pocket of her backpack.

Gaia looked pretty out of it. Her light hair was gathered in a messy wad at the back of her head. Her acid green jacket was half inside out, hanging untidily over the back of the chair, and her messenger bag was clamped between her feet on the floor. On the table before her was the better part of a once frothy coffee substance.

Gaia rubbed her eyes. "Sorry. You surprised me. I'm— I'm . . . all right. How 'bout you?" she answered vaguely.

Mary studied the girl's face, wondering what was really up, knowing she'd probably never know. That was part of what made Gaia fascinating to her.

"Great. I'm not going to sleep tonight," Mary announced.

Gaia was paying attention now. "Oh, yeah?"

"Yeah. The night before Thanksgiving is one of the great nights in New York. It's a night for locals."

Gaia looked puzzled. "As opposed to . . ."

"Tourists. Gawkers. The bridge-and-tunnel crowd. Hardly anything that New York is famous for is actually happening for the locals. Broadway shows. Carriage rides through Central Park. Those dumb theme restaurants. The stores on Columbus Avenue."

"Um. Okay," Gaia said, not caring enough to argue if she did happen to disagree.

"Obviously the parade tomorrow is a major gawk fest. But tonight, right outside the park, they blow up the floats for the parade. That part is still fun. It doesn't really get good until after midnight, so I'm going to a club first to hear this very cool neighborhood band. You want to go?"

Gaia just looked at her, waiting for her to finish, clearly not feeling a big need to act friendly. That was another thing Mary liked about her. "Well. Thanks and all," Gaia said distractedly, tapping her fingers against the table. "But—"

"You have other plans," Mary finished for her.

Gaia cocked her head. "It's not that. It's—"

"So come," Mary said.

Still there was hesitation in Gaia's face.

"You've got a curfew?" Mary tried.

Gaia shook her head.

"Your folks wouldn't be into it?" Mary suggested.

Gaia shook her head. "No folks."

"No folks?"

"I don't have any," Gaia said. Just a statement of fact.

"Jesus. I wasn't expecting that answer. God. Sorry."

Gaia's eyebrows collided over her nose. She was angry. "Sorry for asking me a perfectly normal question? Why do people say that? Why do they always flip out and apologize for no reason?" Her eyes were intense, challenging.

Mary's own anger reared up instantly. "I'm not sorry I asked you the question, you idiot," she snapped. "I'm sorry your parents are dead."

Gaia's eyes widened, then her face got calm. "Oh."

"Fine," Mary said. She got up to order a triple espresso from the lone counter person. Starbucks sucked, but her favorite café had just changed management and installed computers every five feet. She turned back to Gaia, pleased to see the girl had gotten over her anger just as quickly as Mary had. "So, you coming?"

Gaia looked somewhat bamboozled. "I guess. Sure."

JUST LIKE SAM

"*. . . I'm blind. I'm empty. I'm stupid. I'm wrong. . . .*"

Gaia wasn't quite sure how this had happened.

She'd gone from being a bleak New York casualty, a teenage runaway, to being a frivolous club kid. Here she was, sitting in a round, red velvet booth at a downtown club surrounded by New York's young indulgents, listening to a band, Fearless, whose name and lyrics dogged her life in the creepiest way.

"*. . . I need you to tell me I'm not what I am. . . .*"

The singer was ranting. Gaia stared into her vodka and tonic and tried not to think about it too much.

Most of the people at the table, including Mary, were on their third drinks before Gaia had drunk a third of her first. She didn't like alcohol very much. For one thing, it didn't taste good. Maybe that was babyish of her, but it was true. Besides, from what she could tell, the real reason people drank was to dull their fear. Not what Gaia needed. What if alcohol consumption pushed her from zero fear into negative fear? Gaia slid the sweaty glass a few inches toward the center of the table. That didn't seem like a good idea.

She turned her head as Mary tugged on a piece of her hair and then glided toward the dance floor. "You're having fun," Mary shouted over the din. It was more command than question. "Want to dance with us?"

"No," Gaia mouthed. It did actually look like fun, but somehow it didn't seem right, punching Ella out cold and hitting the dance floor in the same two-hour period. She felt obligated to remain dysfunctional and sullen for at least another hour.

Still, she couldn't help smiling at Mary, who was whirling like a dervish through the crowds. Mary was a wild dancer, not surprisingly, and her hair paid no attention to gravity. Gaia couldn't help admiring her. Mary had none of the self-consciousness that sometimes made it embarrassing to watch a person dance.

Gaia glanced at her watch. If she was leaving town, she needed to get going. Traveling on Thanksgiving was notoriously bad. It would be smarter to catch a train or a bus tonight. That way she could sleep in transit and not have to pay for a place to stay.

All of Mary's friends were dancing now. Gaia was alone in the booth. The place was packed, and she felt a bit self-conscious taking up this seating area for eight. She realized a guy standing by the bar was looking at her. No, make that staring. He appeared to be at least thirty. Ick.

Oh, shit, he was coming toward her. She directed an intensely unfriendly expression at him. *Go away now. I do not like you.*

He turned back to the bar. Ahhh. Good. Gaia had to hand it to herself. She could give a mean look like nobody.

Gaia gazed around the club. She'd never been to a place like this before. It was loud. It was dark. People were having fun. It seemed like a great place to go if you were a bored New York City kid looking to hook up. It was a weird place to go shortly after you'd decked your so-called foster mother, on a night you were running away for good.

But what if she *were* just a regular kid, stressed out and angst ridden in a contained, urbane, happy kind of way, looking to hook up? It was a fun game to play sometimes.

She scanned the bar. There was a guy near the front windows who was sort of cute. He had hair the same color as Sam's. His nose and chin couldn't compare, though. And he appeared to be at least five inches shorter than Sam.

Another guy in a booth two away from hers had a good smile. Nice teeth. A little crooked. His eyes were nice, too. Not like Sam's, of course. Not turn-your-world-over nice.

Besides, he was wearing one of those big, fancy metal watches. She hated those.

She slid her drink around in its little puddle on the glass table. The volume in the place notched up even higher. She turned to the entrance and saw another cluster of people packing themselves in. Her eyes froze. Oh, wow. There. That guy was beautiful, Gaia thought distantly. Tall, perfectly built. He had gorgeous red-brown-blond hair, neither wavy nor curly but somewhere in between. Just like Sam, her mind informed her dreamily.

Holy shit. Gaia sat up very straight. He wasn't *like* Sam. He *was* Sam. Her mind raced. Her heartbeat quickened. Goose bumps sprouted on her arms. *Almost like fear.* But not fear. Something else.

Gaia's eyes darted to the faces of Sam's nearest companions.

Clunk. Down slid her hopes.

Yes, indeed. The good-news, bad-news duo. Hateful Heather was in her usual spot right there beside him. Why *shouldn't* Sam and Heather make an appearance on this night from hell? How could it be otherwise?

Gaia averted her gaze. She pointed her face at the tabletop. She really didn't want them to see her. A word from Heather might just throw her over the edge.

Suddenly she felt terribly conspicuous in the booth by herself. Where were Mary and all her friends? Why couldn't they park their damn butts in the booth for five minutes and stop having so much fun? Grrrr.

Gaia rested her face in her hand, using her fingers to cover up almost the entire part of her face that Sam and Heather could feasibly see from their angle. She would just stay like that until they got busy dancing or went to the back, and then she'd leave. She'd head for the bus station. Fine.

Oh, no. She couldn't actually look up to confirm her suspicion, but she had a terrible feeling that the group, which included her favorite couple, was heading straight toward her booth. There was definitely a shadow moving in. No. Go! Go!

"Excuse me? Would you mind if we shared your booth?" It wasn't a voice she recognized. Could she get away with not looking up?

"Excuse me!"

Go away, she urged silently.

"Excuse me!"

All right, that was annoying. She snapped her head up just as Heather and Sam registered the reality of whom they were about to share a booth with.

Who looked least happy? Sam? Heather? Gaia?

Hard to say.

Gaia thought she gave a mean look, but Heather's was better.

Gaia shot to her feet. "All yours. I was just going."

Six pairs of eyes stuck on Gaia as she fumbled to put on her parka. It seemed to take two hours. First it was inside out. Then she couldn't get her hand through the sleeve. As she grabbed for her bag, she knocked over her drink and spritzed the group with watery vodka and dead tonic. Why couldn't she keep her beverages to herself?

She couldn't bring herself to look at Sam. This wasn't happening.

"Gaia, wait." It was Mary, suddenly positioning herself as a bulwark between Gaia and the booth stealers. "Where are you going?"

"I—I gotta go. Now."

Mary looked around. She took in the presence of Heather. A light dawned in her eyes. "Hey, if it isn't the charming Ms. Gannis. Gosh, I remember the last time we were all at a party together. You were riding quite the welcome wagon that night."

Heather was silent.

Mary gave Gaia a confident smile and spoke loudly enough for Heather's benefit. "Don't worry, Gaia. If Heather treats you like that again, I'll smack her."

Heather looked stunned. A couple of Heather's friends seemed to think Mary was kidding around. Gaia didn't look at Sam to gauge his reaction.

Mary attached herself to Gaia by the hand, and Gaia

let herself be pulled toward a waiting group that, for the moment at least, could pass as friends.

"Bitch," Mary mumbled to Gaia, not letting go of her hand. "Let's get out of here."

Gaia felt like crying as she bobbed along after Mary. Nobody ever took care of her like that. Gaia was so taken aback, she didn't know how to feel.

Following the electrified red hair, she experienced a rush of real warmth in spite of the stiff, late-autumn breeze.

Maybe there *was* a reason to stay in New York for a while longer.

POISON

Heather felt like she was chewing on a lemon. She couldn't seem to get the sour taste out of her mouth or remove the pinched expression from her face.

Sam sat down next to her, stiff as a two-by-four, saying nothing.

That was the best strategy. They would just let this pass

and get on with their night. No need to talk about it.

"Who is that girl?" Sam's friend Christian Pavel wanted to know.

"You mean Mary Moss? The redhead?" Heather heard her friend Jonathan Singer respond.

"No, the blond one."

Heather waited numbly for the conversation to be over. She tried to think of some effective way to change tracks.

"That's Gaia Moore," Jonathan said flatly.

"She's unbelievable," Christian said.

Every person at the table waited in uncomfortable suspense to hear the precise way in which Christian Pavel found Gaia Moore unbelievable.

"She's gorgeous. A total goddess. Do you know her? Can you introduce me?"

No one said a word. Heather's mouth was drawn up like a twist tie. She felt like crushing all ten of Christian's toes under the table.

Sam cleared his throat. "H-H-Have you all seen this band before?" he asked the group gallantly, putting a wooden arm around Heather's shoulders.

Conversation resumed. Heather watched Gaia's back disappear through the door. She wished she could give Gaia a poisonous cloak. Then again, Gaia's phlegm-colored jacket was pretty poisonous as it was.

LUSTFUL LOOKS

Sam sat in the booth, as cross and sullen as a sleep-deprived toddler. Too sullen to drink. Or dance. Or make small talk.

He was annoyed at Heather for being his girlfriend. He was annoyed at Christian for looking lustfully at Gaia. (That was *his* department.) He was annoyed at Gaia for a whole list of things:

1. Not being his girlfriend;
2. Looking so spectacularly beautiful;
3. Ruining his life;
4. Ruining his relationship;
5. Not meeting his eyes for a single second tonight;
6. Not being his girlfriend.

Mostly he was annoyed at himself. For blundering deeper into the thing with Heather. For being so goddamned stiff and awkward tonight. For not talking honestly with Heather about what was really going on. For having blown a perfectly good chance to do so.

For still staring at the door fully forty-five minutes after Gaia had walked through it.

My Dear Gaia,

Having seen you so recently (though you did not see me), my pain at being apart from you is only stronger. You have grown into a formidable woman, Gaia, as your mother and I knew you would. Your strength and intensity still astound me. I see now that you have the spirit to fight fiercely for your life, and that is a great comfort to me.

My other comfort is the knowledge that at last you have a good home with my kind old friend George. It's a safe place. I trust George will do his very best by you. I'm glad to know you'll have Thanksgiving there, with someone who truly cares for you.

Each year at Thanksgiving, I write to tell you that you are my reason for thanks, my reason for living. Each year, with my heart full of hope, I pray that next year we'll spend this holiday together. And though realism chips away at my hope, I'm still praying.

Know that I love you, Gaia. That you are always in my heart.

Tom Moore signed the letter and thought about Katia. Twice a year he allowed himself to cry for her, and this was one of those times.

When he was done, he walked to the file cabinet. The top drawer was stuffed full of letters like this one. He found the manila folder labeled Thanksgiving Letters and dropped it in.

He dug his hand in the pocket of his corduroy trousers and felt the penny that lay in the bottom. Perhaps, with luck, this would be the last time he would need to write to Gaia on Thanksgiving.

FUN FOR A CHANGE

GAIA CLUTCHED THE STRETCHY PLASTIC
IN HER FIST AS THEY ROSE UNDER A CLOUD
OF HELIUM, HIGHER AND HIGHER.

THE GOOD UNCLE

"What *the devil* went on there tonight?" Loki's voice thundered.

Ella stood before him, heavy with a strange mixture of shame, pride, and frustration. Her jaw throbbed, and her tongue felt like it belonged to somebody else. "We fought. She punched me. She left." Ella didn't bother to mention the part where she got out her gun and went after Gaia, fully intending to blow her brains out. Luckily that part didn't appear on the surveillance tape.

"Stupid woman, have you lost your mind?"

Ella cupped her jaw tenderly. There would be no sympathy from him. That was certain. "The girl hit me."

"I would have hit you, too, the way you carried on," Loki said sharply.

Ella held her painful tongue. It was as expected.

"Absurd self-indulgence," he spat, pacing across the soft, honey-colored herringbone floorboards. Last month he had a vast loft above the Hudson River. Tonight she'd been ordered to meet him in a starkly modern apartment building on Central Park South. He'd only be there so long as he kept perfect anonymity. Then he'd relocate again. "Why I put up with you, I do not know."

Ella remained quiet. He'd get bored of the tirade eventually. The greatest mistake would be to attempt to defend herself. That would only inject a surge of energy into the project. Where Loki was concerned, what the world gained in a terrorist, it had lost in a lawyer.

His angry voice faded into a dull roar. Ella stared out the large picture windows, waiting for him to be done. Three-quarters of a mile uptown, the enormous helium balloons for the Thanksgiving Day parade were rising to life from the lawns of the Museum of Natural History on Seventy-seventh Street. Long ago, in her other life, she'd gone with friends to watch.

That was before Ella had been "discovered." Well before Gaia had come into their lives, a much more perfect fulfillment of Ella's early promise. Ella felt a wave of nausea climbing her chest.

"Ella!"

She turned to him. Oh. He was finished, then. He'd asked her a question of the nonrhetorical variety. "I'm sorry?"

"You are sorry. A truly sorry creature. I asked you why you were caught with your arm in Gaia's coat."

"I was planting the tracking device," Ella replied.

"And were you able to complete that *onerous* task?" His voice was laced with sarcasm.

"I was."

"Fine. And I gather you've chosen someone to perform the job?"

"Yes." Ella fiercely hoped he would not ask who that was.

"Well, then. With any luck we'll be done with Tom shortly." He smiled the least cheerful smile Ella had ever witnessed. "That should be fun. And then the real plans begin."

A BIG, RED M&M

"So who do you like?" Mary asked. "Clifford, the big red dog? Kermit? Snoopy?"

The night was misty. The stones around the beautiful, castlelike Museum of Natural History were slick with yellow and brown leaves. Gaia and Mary were still clutching hands like kindergarten friends, running through the crowds, watching the enormous balloons come to life.

"Spiderman is cool," Gaia observed, gazing at the balloon reaching four stories into the sky. A net above them kept the balloons on good behavior until the parade began in the morning.

"Spiderman is already up, up, and away," Mary said

somewhat breathlessly, pulling Gaia along. "We need to pick one that's only partway blown up."

"We do?" Gaia asked.

Mary raised her eyebrows mischievously. "We do."

Gaia caught up even with her. "What exactly are you planning?"

"Something fun. You'll see." She glanced over at Gaia. "You scared?"

"Uh-uh," Gaia replied.

"Here." Mary yanked her to a stop. "These ones are good. Shhh. Stay still a minute."

The ones Mary was referring to were huge ponds of half-inflated plastic, one red, the other green. Gaia couldn't tell what they were.

Mary looked around. "Okay, follow me. Move quickly, before anybody sees us."

Gaia nodded, intensely curious.

Mary paused in thought. "Hang on. Which one? Red or green?"

"I don't care," Gaia said.

"Pick!" Mary ordered.

Gaia rolled her eyes. "They're the same. It doesn't matter. I don't even know what we're doing."

Mary was still glaring at her expectantly.

"All right, fine. Red," Gaia said.

"Go," Mary hissed.

She darted around the growing balloon to the side that was closest to the museum fence and used the fence for a boost. She transferred her weight from the fence to the balloon, clamored up the soft, loose plastic, then rolled down into the sagging middle. Gaia followed close behind. When they settled in the middle, they had to cling to the plastic to keep from rolling on top of each other.

"This is cozy," Mary said, laughter in her voice.

"I still don't know what we're doing," Gaia said.

"Shhh. Stay still. We have to keep quiet."

Mary's excitement was contagious. "Why?" Gaia asked.

"'Cause the last time I did this, I got arrested," Mary explained happily.

"Oh," Gaia said.

"Scared yet?" Mary asked.

"Not yet," Gaia replied.

Gaia heard the rush of helium into the balloon get louder.

"Cool," Mary whispered. "They're turning it up."

"They?"

"The inflators," Mary said.

"Is that a word?" Gaia asked.

Mary's giggle came out like a snort. "I think so."

Gaia felt the helium filling the space under them. They were rising appreciably. "Now what?" she whispered.

"We wait," Mary said. She reached for Gaia's hand and

held it again. Gaia was so unaccustomed to physical contact (apart from punching people) that it felt weird to her. Weird, but nice, too.

As the minutes passed, the plastic began to fill and grow around them. Soon the thin, rubbery plastic was puffing up all around them, becoming more and more taut.

"What is this balloon, anyway?" Gaia asked.

Mary lifted her head and looked behind her. "Judging from the green one next door, I think it's an M&M."

"An M&M?"

"Yeah, look." Mary rolled partly onto her side and pointed at the green twin.

"We're on a giant red M&M?" Gaia realized she was getting punchy because for some reason, this seemed hilarious.

"Okay. This is where it starts to get fun." Mary's face was flushed with anticipation. "Hold on tight, okay? I think we've got a facial feature of some kind here."

It was thrilling. Gaia clutched the stretchy plastic in her fist as they rose under a cloud of helium, higher and higher. She was amazed nobody had seen them yet. She twisted her head and saw the buildings above. The ritzy apartment buildings on one side, the museum on the other. They were rising faster now, above the streetlights, nearing the tops of the trees. Closer and closer to the gauzy, dark purple night sky. She looked ahead to the ever improving view of Central

KISS

Park with its dark carpet of trees and the twinkly lights along Fifth Avenue.

Gaia felt her own breath swelling inside her chest. It was magical. "Beautiful," she whispered to Mary.

Mary squeezed her hand.

Gaia tried to stamp this feeling, these sights, into her brain so she could remember them later, when she needed to convince herself there was happiness in the world.

"Oh, shit!" Mary suddenly cried, puncturing Gaia's reverie. Mary yanked her hand from Gaia's, pinching wildly at the plastic of the balloon to steady herself. "I'm losing it, Gaia!"

The plastic had grown so taut under their hands, it was hard to keep holding. Mary's grip was slipping fast.

Gaia turned to her new friend, expecting to see fear in the girl's eyes. Instead she saw wide-eyed thrill.

"Gaiaaaa!" Mary was yelling. "Eeeeeee! This is where it gets *really* fun! When I say go, let go!"

A laugh erupted from Gaia's throat. This was crazy. It *was* fun.

"Go!" Mary screamed.

"Ahhhhhhhhh!" The two girls' voices mingled in a scream as they slid on their stomachs all the way down the growing mountain of balloon and landed hard on the ground.

They lay there for a moment in a tangled clump.

"Are you okay?" Mary asked, pushing her hair out of her face, trying to organize her limbs.

"Okay? That was awesome!" Gaia jumped to her feet and pulled her friend beside her. "Let's do it again."

Mary laughed and swatted Gaia on the shoulder. "I *knew* we were gonna get along."

EXTRA LOVE

Two hours later Gaia lay beside Mary on the grassy part of Strawberry Fields and watched the first light of sun spread across the sky. The air felt damp and surprisingly mild.

Gaia fell in love with the place on first sight. She loved the curving pathways and the odd accumulation of humanity gathered on the handsome benches. She loved the white-and-black mosaic that said "Imagine" in the middle.

"This is my favorite place," Mary said, grabbing the sentiment right from Gaia's mind.

"I see why." Gaia turned her head to see Mary's face.

Mary yawned and raised her arms, stretching long

fingers toward the sky. Gaia caught the yawn from her.

"Hey, Mary?"

"Yeah."

"Thanks for inviting me along on this night. It's been great."

Mary turned to her and smiled. "It wouldn't have been great without you."

Gaia must have been very tired because she was saying things she would never normally say. She was forgetting to censor her feelings and words, forgetting what the consequences could be. "And thanks a lot for looking after me at that bar."

"No prob," Mary said to the sky. "I always take care of my friends."

Gaia thought for a few moments. "Why is that?" she asked. Her voice was so quiet, she wasn't sure it would carry to Mary, two feet away.

Mary yawned again. She put her fingers into her fiery hair. "Because I can afford to."

Gaia squinted at her. "What do you mean?"

"I get a lot of love. From my folks, my brothers. I have extra."

In the pale morning light, that seemed to Gaia both a totally unexpected and beautiful thing to say. She tried to imagine what kind of parents would love Mary so well *and* let her stay out all night, doing whatever she pleased. "Why not keep it for yourself?" Gaia heard herself asking. It was unusual for her brain to connect to her mouth so directly. "That's what most people would do."

Mary considered this. "I have trouble holding on to it."

Silence enveloped them again.

After a long time Mary turned on her side and propped herself up on her elbow. "So, what are you doing for Thanksgiving dinner?"

Gaia hesitated. She couldn't say she was doing nothing. It was too pathetic. It was begging for sympathy and an invitation. But she couldn't lie, either. She had a feeling Mary wouldn't buy a lie very easily. "Oh. Well. I was thinking I might—"

"Wait a minute," Mary broke in. "Why am I asking? I know what you're doing."

Gaia furrowed her brow. "You do?"

"Yeah."

"Okay. So?"

"You're eating with my family."

"I am?"

"You are. You definitely are."

"Are you sure?"

"Completely, one hundred percent sure."

Gaia couldn't help but let a smile out. "Great. I'll let myself know."

The doctor tied the belt of his nondescript and greatly despised tan trench coat. In recent years he'd become attached to very fine clothes. But this coat continued to be useful to him when he was conducting his "side business." It was not only too boring to warrant notice, but of such an inferior material that it was machine washable. That part was important.

Pausing briefly at the corner of Fifty-fifth Street and Fifth Avenue, he studied the information stored in the tracking device. Now, this was a very busy girl. First the West Village, then Astor Place. Then the remote East Village, then West Seventy-seventh Street, Central Park, and what appeared to be a high floor of an apartment building on Central Park West and Sixty-fifth Street. Did teenagers no longer find sleep necessary at all?

He would need to follow her carefully. He wanted this job done by midnight, and her current location—no doubt in a private home—was far less than ideal. That whorish woman—what was her less than amusing alias? Travesura?—had assured him this girl spent a lot of time on the streets and in public places. It had better be so.

He touched his trusted knives, tied up in felt casing in his roomy pocket. This girl was reported to be quite beautiful and exceptionally strong. That was enticing to him. That's why he'd taken on the job.

"Excuse me!" he snapped, nearly colliding with a shabby-looking woman pushing a stroller containing a shabby-looking infant.

He tried to remember why there were so many people—so many children—milling around the streets of New York City on a Thursday morning at nine o'clock.

ED

For me, Thanksgiving is a mixed bag. On the one hand, there's turkey with stuffing and my grandfather's apple pie. I love that. On the other hand, there are turnips and pumpkin pie. I'd like to know: Who really likes pumpkin pie? Let's all be honest.

On the one hand, there are people like me, hanging out with my grandparents. I love them. On the other hand, there are people like Gaia, who have nobody. That's heart-breaking.

If you think about it, even the first Thanksgiving was in no way a cause for bilateral cheer. I mean, sure, the Native Americans had shown the Pilgrims how to farm the land,

and they were psyched about their first harvest. But what did the Native Americans have to celebrate? Alcoholism, VD, and blankets infected with smallpox.

TOO NICE

ONE ARM. TWO ARMS. THE FABRIC SETTLED
WITH UNEXPECTED EASE OVER HER STOMACH
AND BUTT, THE SKIRT GRAZING A FEW
INCHES ABOVE HER KNEES.

THE RED DRESS

"This is too nice." Gaia said it out loud to the Victorian-colored glass chandelier that hung over the vast, pillow-laden guest bed in Mary's family's apartment.

Being friends with Mary was too nice. Mary's unbelievably huge and fantastic apartment on Central Park West was way too nice. The smell of roasting turkey and buttery stuffing was too nice. The thought of spending Thanksgiving with a real family for the first time in five years . . . too nice to think about.

Gaia tried to remind herself to keep her suspicions close around her, but Mary, this place . . . it was dazzling. Can't you just enjoy something? she asked herself impatiently. Accept that some places, some people are purely nice?

She didn't have time to answer herself. There was a knock on the door, and seconds later, Mary opened it partially and poked her head in. "Hi."

"Hi."

"Did you sleep?"

"Like a vegetable."

"Me too. Guess what time it is?"

Gaia shrugged. She wasn't used to having someone talk to her while she was lying in bed. She wasn't a slumber-party kind of girl. She sat up and hugged a pillow on her lap.

"One o'clock. P.M. Big meal is in one hour."

Gaia cleared her throat. What exactly had she gotten herself into here? "Is it a dressed-up sort of thing?" Her voice came out squeaky. She didn't want to bring up the fact that she had no home, no possessions, and certainly no Central Park West party clothes at the moment.

Mary had a knack for coming to Gaia's rescue without Gaia even having to ask. "Just a little. I've been laying out stuff in my room. I have the most fabulous dress for you. Come on."

Gaia sat on the edge of the bed. She was wearing a big gray T-shirt she'd worn under her flannel shirt last night. Her legs were bare, her feet covered by white cotton socks. "Like this?" she asked.

"Sure," Mary said. "It's just down the hall. No brothers in sight. I mean, in case you care."

Mary was under the mistaken impression that Gaia was a normal human being who did things like this. The easiest thing would be to play along, to pretend she had comfy pals whose clothes she borrowed, in whose homes she felt perfectly fine wandering around in a T-shirt and socks.

Gaia was a terrible actress. She skulked down the hall and darted into Mary's room like an escapee from Attica.

Once the door was shut, she made herself relax. Mary wasn't kidding about laying out clothes. If there was a carpet in the spacious room, it would have taken an archaeologist to find it. Only the rough shapes of the various pieces of furniture were apparent under thick piles of clothes.

Mary was unapologetic about her colossal slobbiness. Gaia liked that in a person.

"Okay, you ready for the perfect dress?" Mary asked.

Gaia nodded.

"Tra la." Mary held up a tiny, red, crushed velvet dress with a plunging neckline.

Gaia stared. "Are you kidding? I couldn't fit my left foot into that dress."

Mary frowned. "Have you tried it? No. Shut up until you try it."

Gaia held out her hand for it. It weighed about three ounces. "Yes, ma'am. I've never been dressed by a fascist before." Feeling large and self-conscious, Gaia pulled the T-shirt over her head and quickly yanked the dress over her head and shoulders. One arm. Two arms. The fabric settled with unexpected ease over her stomach and butt, the skirt grazing a few inches above her knees.

Mary was surveying the progress with her hands on her hips. When Gaia turned around, her frown blossomed into a smile. "Wow! See?" She took Gaia's hand and pulled her in front of the full-length mirror on the back of her closet.

Gaia gazed at herself in genuine surprise. The dress actually fit. Granted, it was made of stretchy stuff. And it did cling to her gigantic muscles in an unforgiving manner.

"I look like Arnold Schwarzenegger in a dress," Gaia mumbled.

"*What?*" Mary demanded. "I'm going to smack you, girl. You look incredible."

Gaia turned around to examine her backside. "I have incredibly huge muscles."

Mary blew out her breath in frustration. "Guy-aaaaa," she scolded. "You have the body every woman would die to have. You have the long, defined muscles that keep the rest of us slogging it out in overpriced gyms around the country. You have to see that."

"I see Mr. Universe."

"Shut *up!*" Mary roared. Now she was mad. She held out her hand. "So give it back. Seriously. I mean it. If you can't appreciate that it looks beautiful, you don't deserve to borrow my goddamned dress."

Gaia cast her a pleading gaze. "Look, I'm trying. I really am." She studied herself in the mirror for another minute, trying to see herself through other eyes.

The dress really was extraordinary. Gaia loved the too long sleeves and the way they flared at the wrist. "Please let me borrow it?" Gaia asked, weirded out by hearing those words in her voice. "I'll say anything, true or untrue. I am a waif. I can't do a single push-up."

Mary laughed. "Fine. It's yours. In fact, you can have it

for keeps. After seeing you in it, I won't be able to stand the sight of me."

Now it was Gaia's turn to glare. "Hang on. *You're* allowed the exaggeratedly negative body image, but not me? Who made these rules?"

Mary waved a hand in the air. "Point taken. Never mind. But keep the stupid dress." She gestured at the snowstorm of clothes. "I have others, as you may have noticed." She rooted around the bottom of her closet and threw Gaia a pair of black cotton tights.

"Thanks," Gaia said.

"Oh, and here."

"Ouch." A dark red, forties-style pump flew out of the closet and hit Gaia on the shin. Thankfully, she dodged its mate.

"Sorry," Mary murmured. Now she was gathering jewelry for Gaia.

"What size are your feet?" Gaia asked, staring suspiciously at the shoe.

"Eight."

"I wear eight and a half," Gaia said

Mary was busy untangling a dump of necklaces. "So? Close enough."

Apparently Mary didn't get hung up on little matters like housing all five toes.

Again, though, Mary was right. The shoe was close

enough to fitting. Gaia put on the second one and stomped around the room, trying to get used to the heels.

Mary spent the next twenty minutes coaxing Gaia into the makeup chair, and the twenty minutes after that brushing Gaia's hair, spangling her with jewelry, and hunting down the exact right shade of lip gloss. At last she was done. "Oh my God, my brothers are going to be drooling," she announced, nodding at her finished work.

Gaia did feel prettier, but she also felt like someone else.

"Are you ready to meet the clan?"

If Gaia had the potential to feel nervous, now would have been an obvious time. "I guess so." She looked at Mary. Mary was still wearing blue nylon warm-up pants and a wife-beater tank top. Light freckles stood out on her thin shoulders and arms. Her hair was possibly the craziest mess Gaia had ever seen.

"Oh, I'm fine," Mary claimed. Her eyes darted around the room, and she picked up the first thing in her path, a blue chenille sweater, and stuck her head through. "All set," she confirmed.

Gaia was speechless as she followed Mary out of the room. She remembered what Mary had said about not holding on to love very well.

POTATO PHYSICS

"How are the potatoes coming, Sam?" Mrs. Gannis's voice floated into the kitchen.

Sam looked up from the huge aluminum pot. He felt like a wolf with its leg caught in a trap. He finally understood the wolf's perverse temptation to chew off its own leg.

Why had he insisted, in that breezy, thoughtless way, that he would take care of the mashed potatoes? At the time, mashed potatoes seemed like the simplest thing on earth. You get potatoes; you mash them.

Besides, he'd figured this important job in the kitchen would keep him out of the fray of tense Gannis-family relations. It would give him a little breathing room from Heather, too, which they both needed. It had gotten to the point where every single thing brought them right back into the danger zone. A casual question from Heather's mother about what they'd done the previous night, an innocent reference to chess, a song on the radio about a girl with blond hair. Not being in the same room with Heather or talking about anything at all seemed the safest bet.

But Sam now understood that making mashed potatoes belonged in a category with particle physics, only harder. Before you mashed them, you had to cook them to make them soft, it turned out. How were you supposed to do that?

First he'd thrown the whole pile in the oven, but what was the right temperature, and how long would it take? Then he took a cue from the one meal he'd ever made successfully—spaghetti. You made hard noodles soft by boiling them. So he boiled up the potatoes. It seemed to take hours before they were soft.

Now he was beating the crap out of those poor, boiled potatoes, working up a sweat. On the table was a whole tool kit of discarded instruments. The dinner fork was too small, obviously. The plastic whisk was wimpy. The metal slotted spoon made a tremendous racket. At last Mr. Gannis had acquainted him with a tool called a masher. A masher! A holiday miracle. Who could have guessed there'd be an implement built for this exact purpose?

Now he was madly mashing. Only the potatoes still didn't look right. Mashed potatoes were supposed to be smooth and pale yellow in color. These were lumpy and riddled with brown skin. Oh. Something occurred to him. You were supposed to take the skin off first, weren't you? He tried to fish out the bigger pieces of skin. It was hopeless.

Well, maybe they tasted good. He took a taste.

They tasted slightly more flavorful than air. All right, well, that's what salt was for. He shook in a small blizzard of salt.

He cast an eye at the fridge. Hmmm. He took out a box of butter. He remembered his mom once saying that her motto for cooking was, When in doubt, add butter. He threw in a stick. He threw in another stick. He was still in doubt. He threw in a third.

He stirred, hoping his mother hadn't just been being witty.

DISAPPOINTMENT

"So, Gaia, how long have you lived in New York?"

Now Gaia remembered the problem with meeting strangers, particularly the parents-of-friends variety of strangers. They asked you things.

Gaia chewed a piece of turkey breast and tried to look agreeably at Mary's mother. She swallowed it with effort. "Well, I guess I—"

"No questions," Mary interrupted, coming to Gaia's rescue yet again. "No interrogating Mary's new friend, Mom."

Mary's mom laughed, which Gaia thought was pretty sporting of her. She gave Gaia a conspiratorial look. "My daughter is very bossy. You may have noticed this."

Gaia liked Mary's mom so far. She had dark red hair, sort of like Mary's but far better behaved. She wore cropped black wool pants and a bright orange velvet button-down shirt that clashed mightily with her hair. It wasn't standard middle-aged mom apparel, but it wasn't a grown-up person trying too hard to be cool, either.

The family's cook, Olga, appeared at Gaia's elbow with a steaming silver serving dish of baby vegetables. They were tidy and beautiful, not the creamed, vegetable slop that usually showed up on Thanksgiving. Gaia guessed from Olga's accent that she was Russian and that she hadn't been speaking English for long. "Thank you," she murmured, trying to serve herself without bouncing baby potatoes into her lap. Or Mary's dress's lap.

"The food's fantastic," Mary's brother said to Olga.

Was he Paul or Brendan? Gaia couldn't remember. He was the cuter one, though, with light blue eyes and a quarter-inch of stubble on his chin.

"Absolutely," Mary's father agreed. He raised his glass for at least the fourth time in the meal. "Let's give thanks for Olga, a godsend." They all clinked glasses and agreed yet again. Gaia noted that there was sparkling water in his glass and not wine.

Olga seemed pleased with the attention. "Stop eet, Meester Moss," she ordered coyly.

Out of the corner of her eye, Gaia saw Mary stand up.

"I gotta pee. I'll be back in a minute," Mary announced to the table at large.

Mary's mom smiled in her forbearing way, and Gaia saw an emotion she wasn't sure how to analyze. There was something in the woman's face that struck Gaia as both worried and apologetic at the same time.

Suddenly Olga was back at Gaia's elbow, this time holding a basket of corn bread. It smelled like happiness. "Would you like some?" Olga asked.

Remotely, without really thinking about it, Gaia registered that Olga's words came out clear and crisp, without an accent.

"Of course. It smells delicious. Did you make this, too?" Gaia asked politely.

She served herself a fat piece of corn bread, and when she looked up, the entire Moss family, minus Mary, was staring at her. Olga was staring, too.

Gaia glanced from face to face. Oh, shit. What had she done now? These stares were too extreme to signify she'd used the wrong fork. She felt her mouth to see if she was wearing a mustache of cranberry sauce or anything.

"You speak Russian," Mr. Moss declared.

"I do?" Gaia found herself asking dumbly. She looked back at Olga and realized what must have happened. Olga must have murmured to her in Russian, and she must have answered in Russian without thinking. "I—I guess I do. Some, anyway," Gaia said, her fingers pinching and pulling at the napkin under the table.

Gaia felt badly thrown by this. Her mother spoke Russian to her from the time she was a baby, and Gaia grew accustomed to switching back and forth between languages hundreds of times a day. But those words gave her a feeling on her tongue that she associated purely with her mother. She hadn't spoken Russian in five years.

The table was still silent. Gaia felt her vision blurring. She stood up, keeping her gaze down. "Excuse me for just a moment," she mumbled.

"Of course," Mrs. Moss said.

Gaia walked blindly from the dining room and down the hallway. She hadn't meant to go to Mary's room, exactly. She just wasn't thinking.

The moment she opened the door to Mary's room, Mary froze. Gaia took two steps forward and froze, too.

Mary was bent far over her dressing table. Her eyes, turned now to Gaia, were large. In her hand was a rolled-up tube of paper. On the tabletop was a mirror, and on the mirror were several skinny rows of white powder cut from a tiny white hill. A razor blade winked at her in the light.

Gaia was naive and inexperienced, but she wasn't stupid. She knew what Mary was doing, and it made her feel sick.

She stared at Mary for another moment before she turned and left the room. She strode to the guest room and gathered her bag and coat.

She forced herself to take a detour on the way to the elevator.

"Mr. and Mrs. Moss," she announced from the entrance to the dining room. "I'm so sorry, but I have to go. Thank you very sincerely for letting me come."

She made her way to the elevator vestibule without a backward glance. She shrugged on her coat as the car descended. Yellow-green jacket. Red dress. She thought of Ed.

Outside on the street a siren blared, surprising her with its jarring unpleasantness.

BUTTER

"My God, Sam, these are the best potatoes I've ever eaten," Mr. Gannis said heartily, serving up his fourth helping. Sam hoped he wasn't going to be responsible for putting the man in the hospital with a heart attack.

He looked at the other plates around the table. Each of the four underfed Gannis women still had on her plate an untouched pile of potatoes so calorie packed, they were bleeding butter. Heather met his eyes apologetically. "They're awfully, um . . . rich."

Dear Ed,

 I'm sorry not to be saying this to you in person, but good-bye. I have to leave New York for a while. Things got out of hand with Ella, and, well . . . hopefully I'll get the chance to tell you about it someday.

 It's time for me to set up a new life. I'm almost of legal age to be on my own now. And with all of my useful skills and abilities—not to mention my sunny temperament—I should have all kinds of great job possibilities:

 Waitress

 Counter-person at 7-Eleven

 Tollbooth attendant

 Dishwasher

 So before I go, I just wanted to tell you this one thing, and I hope you'll forgive me for being sappy. But as I wracked my brains to think of stuff to be thankful for, the only thing I felt sure of is you. You are a much better friend than I've ever deserved.

I will never ever forget you for as long (or short) as I live.

Gaia

PENNSYLVANIA STATION

HE WHEELED BACK AND OPENED THE DOOR JUST
WIDE ENOUGH SO THAT HE COULD TOSS THE
BLOODY SCALPEL INTO THE TRASH CAN.

ONE WAY

Gaia looked up at the big destination board that hung above the expansive waiting area of Penn Station. The board operated like the tote board on *Family Feud*—its tiles turning to reveal all the destinations. "Survey says . . . Trenton—Northeast Corridor—track 12—5:09." "Survey says . . . Boston—New England Express—track 9—5:42."

The place was ugly and crowded, and it smelled bad. And by the way, she wondered sourly, whose brilliant idea was it to call the train station smack-dab in the middle of New York City Pennsylvania Station? Hello? Ever take a geography class?

She felt tired and sad and cranky, no longer riding the powerful surge of anger and indignation that made it much more satisfying to run away.

She eyed the different cities, having absolutely no idea where she wanted to go. If she could go anywhere, she'd choose Paris. The Latin Quarter. She'd sit at the terrace of a quaint café across from the Notre Dame cathedral. Sip a double espresso as she read some poems from Baudelaire's *Fleurs du mal*. But that wasn't going to happen. Not today, anyway. She didn't have a passport, let alone money for the flight.

Hmmm. Maybe Chicago. She'd always wanted to visit

the museum there. If she couldn't go to Paris, she could at least sit for an hour in front of Gustave Caillebotte's wall-sized painting, *Paris Street, Rainy Day.* She first saw it in an art magazine she was flipping through while waiting to have a wisdom tooth pulled. The dreary scene spoke to her. Ambling along a cobblestone street on a gray, rainy day. That was her.

Engine, engine, number 9, going down the Chicago line. If the train falls off the track, do you want your money back? Yes. Y-e-s spells yes, you dirty, dirty dishrag—you.

She waited in the Amtrak ticket line behind a twenty-something couple from Jersey who—Gaia gathered from overhearing—had met the night before in an East Village club. They couldn't keep their hands off each other. Pinching, groping, giggling. It took everything Gaia had not to gag before she finally reached the window, where she came face-to-face with Ned, the ticket vendor.

She leaned forward to speak into the round voice amplifier.

"Chicago. One way." He visibly perked up at the sight of her. His eyes leered at her from behind the thick Plexiglas.

"Going all by yourself?"

"Yeah. Is that a problem?"

"No . . . I just thought . . ." He raised his eyebrows suggestively.

"Thought what?"

"I don't know, a girl as pretty as yourself. Just seems like you'd have a . . . companion."

She sighed. "Well, I'm alone. Is there a sleeping car on that train going to Chicago?"

He swiveled on his seat and clacked a succession of keys at his computer. "Not until nine-thirty tonight."

"How about another train, then? Is there any train with a sleeping car leaving soon? Doesn't matter where it's going."

He looked at her. Then back at his screen. Ten more seconds of clacking. "There's a train to Orlando leaving in about an hour."

Gaia took a moment to ponder Orlando. It was a light-year away from this rainy day. It was an artificial city populated by tourists and the people who served the tourists. It was the land of water slides and theme parks, of Mickey Mouse and The Simpsons Ride.

"There's definitely a sleeper car?" Gaia wanted to confirm.

"There is a sleeping compartment, yes," Ned replied.

"I'll take it."

What the hell. She needed a vacation. And a little sun never hurt anybody. If it was warm enough, maybe she'd even buy a bikini. Hit the beach.

But she still had a whole hour to kill. After Ned slid her ticket under the window, she leaned a final time into the voice amplifier.

"Is there someplace that sells stamps around here?"

GETTING ACQUAINTED

The doctor quickened his steps as he approached the escalator that would carry him down into the bowels of Penn Station, unquestionably the most hideous train station in the country. But he was pleased to be here. He was downright overjoyed that his target had abandoned her safe perch up on Central Park West and come down here.

The ugly, subterranean corridors were hardly fit for any human pursuit, but the place fit his needs quite perfectly.

According to his device, she was less than two hundred feet away. He scanned the crowds in the hope of identifying her, acquainting himself with her face before he went to work.

OUT OF ORDER

Gaia reread her letter to Ed. She was seated at the counter of a small coffee-and-muffin place in the train station's row of shops and eateries. What a stupid letter.

She went to crumple the letter, then stopped herself. She needed to say something to him. She thought of him calling her on Friday night at eleven o'clock, expecting another of their ricocheting, sleepy, oddly intimate conversations. He'd call her and find out she wasn't there. Really, really wasn't there.

Gaia sighed. She propped her chin in her hand. This was harder than leaving had ever been before. None of the other places had Ed.

Or Sam.

She folded her letter carefully and put it in the envelope. She wrote out Ed's address and placed the stamp in the corner so it wasn't crooked.

She felt the eyes of a man slumped at the next table over, hovering on her legs. She turned to him.

"Letter to Mom and Dad, sweetheart?" he asked. The smell of stale alcohol on his breath made Gaia wince.

Okay, she thought. That's it. She was sick of being leered at. Time to lose the dress. First the smarmy ticket vendor, now this loser.

"That's right. *Honey*," she said. Turning her attention back to the envelope, she licked the inside edge of the flap and sealed it.

"I like to watch you do that."

Gaia narrowed her eyes at the old pervert. Blech. As she got up, she knocked over her half-filled paper cup of coffee so that it spilled into the man's lap.

"Oh, I'm sorry," she lied. Then she swung her bag over her shoulder and took off.

A minute later she arrived at the women's rest room. A hand-scrawled sign taped to the door read Out of Order.

Perfect. She didn't need to pee. She could change her clothes in peace. But pushing open the door, she was immediately struck by the most powerful stench this side of the Hudson. She wanted to bolt, get out of there, but the room was empty—it would take her only a minute. Slip off the dress; pull on the jeans and sweatshirt. Off. On. Go. Like a pit stop at the Indy 500.

Just as long as no one lit a match.

She hurried to a stall. Holding her breath, she quickly slipped off Mary's shoes. She was peeling off the tights when all of a sudden she heard the door fly open.

"Let go of me!" a young female voice demanded.

Gaia looked through the crack of her stall: Two thugs had just entered, dragging behind them a teenage girl, dressed in a Nike sports bra, a leopard-print skirt, and just one stiletto heel. The other one must've been out there somewhere, floating among the sea of arrivals and departures. Quickly Gaia pulled the tights back up over her waist.

"Let's have it, bitch," ordered the shorter of the two, the one with the New Jersey Devils baseball cap.

"I don't got it. I swear," the girl cried.

The girl's hair was blond and tangled. She looked no older

than Gaia—maybe sixteen or seventeen. Like Gaia, she'd probably done the rounds in foster care. Like Gaia, she'd probably run away at least once. Gaia suspected she was a prostitute and that the bigger guy was her pimp.

Each of the men grabbed one of the girl's pale arms, and together they shoved her into the dirty, white-tiled wall. She cried out in pain but managed to protect her head.

Gaia watched from the stall, letting her anger grow inside her chest. She hadn't had any real release in days. The anger was right there, so easy to call upon. There was her rage at Ella. Her fury at crazy, misguided Mary who had everything in the world and chose to screw it up.

"We're not playing games this time, sunshine," said the big, bearlike thug, whose belly hung out from a black T-shirt that asked, Got Milk?

Gaia saw his big, paw hands fumbling, then heard a noise. Flick. The Bear underlined his threat by holding up a fierce-looking switchblade that gleamed under the fluorescent light. "Now, let's see it or you'll have a brand-new face to look at in the mirror." He held the knife against her cheek.

Gaia threw open the door of her stall.

The two men turned to stare at her.

Gaia forgot until she read the particular looks in their eyes that she was still wearing Mary's clingy, short red dress.

"Check you out," the man in the Devils hat said, studying her appreciatively. "We've got a regular party happening in here."

"Get off her," Gaia said.

"Pardon?" the big one asked, curiosity and amusement flashing in his eyes.

Gaia came closer. She spoke loudly and enunciated her words clearly. "Get off the girl. Let her go."

The Bear shook his head. "Is this your business? I don't think so. Why don't you stand aside, sweetheart? It'll be your turn next."

Gaia liked to protect her conscience by being absolutely clear about her intentions before she did harm. "I'm warning you. I'll kick your ass if you don't lay off her."

They both guffawed at her. "Len, grab her," the big one instructed the smaller guy. "This is gonna be fun."

Len did as he was told. When he reached for Gaia's arm, she backhanded him hard against the side of his neck. She caught him by surprise. He staggered sideways. Gaia kicked him hard in the chest and watched him slam into the hand-drying machine and slide to the floor. Len was disappointingly easy.

"Holy shit."

Gaia turned her head to see the Bear staring at her with astonishment. She'd talked enough. She went after him.

The Bear was holding that blade, which made her approach trickier. She didn't hesitate, though. He stood to confront her, as she gambled he would, and she grabbed the knife-wielding arm by the wrist and bent it sharply behind him. She wrenched the other arm back to join the first and pulled him down so she could lodge her knee in his back.

The Bear groaned in pain. The blade clattered to the ground. The girl backed off into the corner, shivering.

Gaia let his arms go. Now that the blade was out of the way, she could give him some room.

He literally growled as he turned on her. He raised his arm to punch her in the jaw, but she caught it long before it landed and took the force of his own sloppy effort to flip him onto the linoleum. It was kind of a trademark move of hers. Effortless. Fairly graceful. Totally satisfying.

She backed up a few steps and let him get up. She hated herself for enjoying it, but she did. The Bear deserved anything she gave him and much more. He'd obviously spent too long believing that women could be intimidated. Let him remember this.

It was all he could do to get himself back on his feet. He staggered toward Gaia, swinging at her. His lack of skill was pitiful. There wasn't much point in trying to make it a real contest. She clipped his jaw with her right fist. She very likely broke his nose with her left. She wanted to leave him a memento.

His eyes displayed real fear now. Although Gaia couldn't feel fear, she was astute at recognizing its signs. Wild, darting eyes, rapid, shallow breaths. Gaia took that as her cue to finish him. She landed a hard, fast blow to a calculated spot under his ear. As expected, he crumpled to the floor, unconscious. Gaia knew he'd feel like shit when he came to. But he *would* come to and not much worse for the wear, either.

Suddenly the girl was shrieking. Gaia heard movement behind her. Much closer than she was expecting. Before she could regroup, the smaller guy appeared in the corner of her eye and shoved her hard in the back, sending her sprawling across the floor. Gaia got up fast, but he was barreling toward her.

Gaia turned, smashing his face with a roundhouse kick so powerful, she was sure she'd knocked him out. But she rushed the kick and threw herself badly off balance. She lost her footing, and her head came down hard against the corner of the porcelain sink.

Gaia groaned, holding the side of her head. She put both of her hands on the side of the sink for support and swayed back up to her feet.

At last the wretched-smelling room was quiet. The girl was backed against the tiled wall, gazing at Gaia with a stunned expression. "Are you okay?"

Gaia nodded. "I think so."

The girl put her hands up to her cheeks. "God, I don't know what to say. Thank you. I never had anyone stick up for me before. Is there anything I can do for you? Buy you a coffee?"

Gaia shook her head, then leaned herself up against the wall for support. Her eyes closed. Her head was pounding ferociously. She'd hit it hard.

"Hey," the girl said, reaching out to her.

"I'll be fine," Gaia tried to assure her. "Just give me a minute." She shielded her eyes with her hand. Her pupils were reacting sluggishly to the bright, fluorescent light above.

Gaia started to slide down along the wall until she ended sitting up on the floor. Right next to the girl.

"I'm gonna call 911."

"No!" Gaia ordered. "I just need to rest." She started to drift, to give in. "Rest," she murmured again. And then she blacked out.

UNHOLY MOMENT

"All aboard for the Southern Star, now boarding on track 12. All aboard!"

A large segment of the Penn Station crowd shuffled in unison toward the steps that led down to the waiting train.

He shuffled right along with them, his yellow-green eyes darting wildly. Searching for his target. His tracking device told him he was at point-blank range.

He reached the platform and caught a glimpse of her—a blond in a yellow-green Polartec jacket, carrying a black messenger bag. She was just stepping into one of the train's sleeper cars. He calmly made his way through the frantic human herd and boarded the same car, but at the other end. He walked with haste and purpose through the car, noticing the blond up ahead. She was scanning the compartment numbers as she advanced, finally entering one near the middle—on his left. Number 33A.

He arrived there not more than ten seconds later, pausing a moment to close his trench coat over his tie—a Salvatore Ferragamo yellow silk, dotted with little teddy bears. A client had given it to him a few years back to thank him for the perfect cheekbones he had given her. And they were perfect. He had truly outdone himself. So in the name of mastery and precision, he always wore the tie for these unholy moments. It had become part of the ceremony. Priests wear their robes; he wore his Ferragamo teddy bear tie under his cheap, washable trench coat.

He slowly, silently turned the brass handle of the compartment door and entered.

"Hey!" the blond snarled. "This one's taken."

"Is that right?" he replied with zero inflection in his

voice. Then he grinned like a used car salesman as he stepped inside.

"Hey!" she repeated. "What do you think you're doing?"

He just kept smiling and closed the door behind him, pulling down the shade to cover the small window.

DONE DEAL

Five minutes later, he stepped off the train. One of the conductors, doing some final work on the platform, gave him a curious look.

"Wrong train." The doctor tossed him a shrug, pretending to be embarrassed. "I must be blind."

He made his way back up the steps, back to the vast waiting room with the giant destination board. On the way he couldn't help thinking that the redheaded woman was a little off in her assessment. The girl was hardly "tough." Annoying, maybe, but tough? And her face wasn't so pretty, either. He imagined a little sculpting work on that nose would make for a significant improvement. . . . Perhaps a little Gore-Tex in those thin lips. An injection for those premature lines in her forehead. Under different circumstances he would have certainly left his card.

Oh, well . . .

He stopped at the rest room, whose door had a crude Out of Order sign taped to it. A perfect place to get rid of the instrument. But when he opened the door, the stench that hit him was so overwhelming, he had to quickly close it. He started off, then changed his mind. He wheeled back and opened the door just wide enough so that he could toss the bloody scalpel into the trash can.

A few feet to the left of the trash can he saw the prostrate body of a teenage girl. She was graceful, blond, quite pretty, in fact. Probably strung out on drugs. From the bruise on her face it looked like somebody had beaten her up. Her pimp, no doubt. It was pitiful, really.

He tossed the scalpel and watched it sink cleanly to the bottom of the trash can.

Too bad, he thought as he was making his exit. It had been such a trusty tool. Why, he had used it just that morning on Mrs. Gardner. Carved her the best-looking chin money could buy.

GAIA

After I hit my head in the train station, I saw red and green sparklers bursting in front of my eyes. I must have passed out after that because I had this weird, dream-like reverie about Ed and his being color-blind. Don't ask me why.

In my dream I was color-blind, too. I couldn't see green, which my whacked-out mind was convinced was the color of fear. Green looked the same as red, but red wasn't the color of fear, according to my dream self. What was red the color of?

It became this desperate, urgent thing I needed to figure out. What was red the color of? Green was fear; what was red?

What was red?

Well, red is the color of tomatoes, you might say sensibly, and shut up already. But you know how dreams are.

Anyway, I guess it was around then that I came to.

NOT A PENNY

HEATHER WAS TOO HURT TO FEEL IT.

HER HEART WAS ON AUTOPILOT ONCE MORE.

"YOU'VE FALLEN FOR HER, HAVEN'T YOU?"

A FREAKING MESS

Her vision and awareness came back slowly. She blinked open her eyes and then closed them again. Then came the smell.

What the hell was that? Where was she?

Gaia forced open her eyes. Oh God. The bathroom. The awful bathroom in the train station.

She sat up and looked around her. The thugs she'd fought were still passed out on the other side of the room. One of them was breathing loudly, fitfully. The other was clutching his jaw and moaning. They'd be up and at it soon enough.

And the girl. Where had the girl gone? Suddenly Gaia froze. She clambered to her feet, ignoring the searing pain in her temple. She checked the floor around her. She checked the stall where she'd begun to change. Mary's shoes were just where she'd kicked them off, but her bag was gone. Her bag with her wallet and her money and her clothes and shoes. Oh Christ, and where was her coat? Her coat with the train ticket to Orlando inside the pocket.

It was gone. All of it. Shit.

Well, that was gratitude for you. Save somebody's ass, and they'll rob you blind. Give a lot and they'll take a lot more.

Shit!

She moved to the sink, splashed cold water on her badly bruised face. When she looked in the mirror, she got a shock. The left side of her face, her cheekbone all the way up to her temple, was already covered by an ugly purple bruise. The corner of her lip was bleeding, not to mention her mascara. Mary's velvet dress was ripped in two places. She was a freaking mess.

She retrieved the shoes and squeezed them on her sore feet, trying not to let herself cry. Now what? She'd arrived at the station full of cash and ready to start a new life.

She'd be leaving it broke and broken.

HUNTED PREY

"Where is Gaia? I thought she'd be joining us."

Ella took a protracted sip of her third glass of merlot, letting the velvety nectar wash over her tongue. Then she made a whole show of sliding back the sleeve of her blouse to glance at her watch.

"Oh, my, it is getting late, isn't it?" she said, wondering

just how Gaia was doing. Although the obnoxious girl had run, she had certainly not gotten away. It was helpful that Gaia had taken off *after* Ella had slipped the tracking device into her coat pocket.

Ella sat with two of George's old agency friends and their wives. They were gathered at a table for six in the opulent dining room of La Bijou, an haute-cuisine restaurant on West Sixty-fourth Street, off Broadway. Most of the patrons here were silver-haired, silver-spooned socialites who just an hour earlier had been watching the new opera across the street at Lincoln Center. The waiters were French to a fault.

And then there was the menu. A menagerie of hunted prey, ranging from roasted duck to wild Scottish hare to rock Cornish hen with the word of caution to be careful of possible bird shot.

This was George's consolation prize to Ella for his being called away on Thanksgiving. The restaurant was fine with her; the company, a bore.

"I would so like to see Gaia, that poor thing," Mrs. Bessemer agreed. "Her parents were such lovely people."

Ella stifled a yawn. She shrugged daintily. "Gaia is a teenager, as you know. Her appearances are difficult to predict. I told her of course how much you'd all like to see her, but . . . Gaia has a mind and a schedule of her own." Ella lied effortlessly, without even needing to listen to herself.

Besides, she has an appointment with a doctor, Ella added silently. She tapped her menu. "Listen, why don't we just go ahead and order? I'll order a little something extra for Gaia so when—if—she comes, she can join right in. I'm sure she won't mind."

That said, her iPhone went off. She opened her purse, extracted the iPhone, and looked at the number. "That's probably her now. If you'll excuse me, I'll be back in a moment."

INSULT AND INJURY

The doctor stood inside the phone booth just outside Penn Station's southwest entrance, annoyed at this particular aspect of his written instructions. Who used a phone booth anymore? It was rather galling. He'd punched in the phone number as instructed, and now he waited for the ring. There it was.

"Mrs. Travesura, I presume?"

"Yes, Doctor. Is it done?"

"Of course."

"Excellent. And in what condition is our patient?" The woman could barely contain the pleasure in her voice.

"Alive, as promised," the doctor responded. "Though not likely to recount her experiences anytime soon." He wouldn't reward her with the graphic details.

"No one saw you?"

The doctor sighed impatiently. "Absolutely not."

"I'm sure. Now, did you remove the bug from the pocket of her coat?"

This had grown annoying, verging on insulting. "Mrs. Travesura. I am a professional. You need not grill me on these absurd details."

"I apologize . . . *Doctor*. If you'll permit me one last question?"

He sighed again. "Yes."

"Are you holding the tracking device in your hand?"

"I am."

"Good. Good-bye, then, you disgusting, evil bastard."

The doctor was blinking in fury, barely able to process the childish affront, when the device began beeping in his hand. He held the readout close to his face, trying to discern the message in the darkness of the booth.

He could make out numbers scrolling across the screen. 5 . . . 4 . . . 3 . . . 2 . . . 1 . . .

The explosion ripped the tiny booth apart.

NO REFUNDS

Gaia turned at the sound of the explosion. Virtually every-one in the station jumped at the noise. Within a minute she heard a symphony of sirens.

She glanced ahead of her in frustration at the single open ticket booth. She glanced behind her at the ten or so people who continued the line, all of whom looked as cranky as she felt. She didn't care if her own feet exploded. There was no way she was losing her place in this line.

Scores of policemen were zipping in and out the south doors of the station. Many civilians were running around, too, wanting a piece of the action.

"There was a bomb!" she heard somebody shouting. "Right out front. Blew up a phone booth!"

There were lots of oohs and ahs and murmurs through-out the station, but Gaia was morbidly amused to see that not a single person left her line.

Just wait until the camera crews from the local news get here—then it will really be a circus, Gaia found herself thinking.

Another ticket salesperson opened a second window. That would speed things up. Minutes later, Gaia was waved forward. Before she reached the window, she realized she was being reunited with her old friend Ned.

"How can I help you?" His eyes showed not a flicker of recognition. Apparently she was a lot less attractive battered and bruised.

"Remember me? I bought a ticket to Orlando from you about an hour and a half ago. The sleeper car?"

His face was blank.

"Well, listen, my ticket got stolen. I need to get a refund."

Ned shrugged. "Sorry. Train 404 to Orlando is long gone. Unless you can produce the ticket, I can't give you a refund."

Gaia rolled her eyes. "How can I produce a ticket if it got stolen?"

Ned's face was devoid of interest or sympathy. "No ticket, no refund."

Gaia was starting to feel desperate. If she couldn't get a refund, she'd have no money. Not a cent. Nothing. How long could she last on the streets of New York flat broke? Even the flophouses cost a few dollars. "Ned, please. We're . . . *friends,* practically. Can't you help me out here? I really, really need the cash."

Ned shook his head. He wouldn't look anywhere near her eyes. A pretty, confident, sexily clad girl with a wallet full of cash was interesting to Ned. A bruised, desperate, penniless girl was not. He focused his gaze over her head. "Next?" he called to the person at the front of the line.

Suddenly Gaia felt overcome by a wave of dizziness

so powerful, it almost made her sick to her stomach. She grabbed the edge of the high counter to steady herself. "Ned! Ned. Please. Don't be an asshole. Just listen to me for a minute, okay?" Gaia could hear her voice rising in her ears. "Ned! *Ned!*" God, if he weren't enclosed in the bullet-proof booth, she'd love to belt him. "Ned!"

The next thing Gaia knew, there was a police officer, a young Hispanic man with a crew cut, grabbing her by the arm. "Come on, miss," he said. "There's a long line here, okay? Gotta keep it moving."

"But I—" Gaia grabbed her arm back. "My ticket got stolen. And all my money. And I really need—"

Gaia stopped. He wasn't listening. It was hopeless. She could tell the policeman was looking her over, and she could tell exactly what he was thinking, too. Gaia was wearing a shredded, clingy minidress, high heels, and a big bruise on her head.

"Come on, miss," he said again. His voice was patient, tired, pitying. "Do you want to step out of the way, or do you want me to arrest you? I'd think a girl like you would have good reason to stay out of the way if you can help it."

A girl like you. It was obvious he thought she was a hooker. A hooker addicted to drugs who'd just been shaken up by her pimp. It was ironic, but that was exactly what she looked like. While the *actual* drug-addicted hooker who'd been shaken up by her pimp was zipping off to Orlando in a pair of jeans and a fluorescent yellow-green Polartec jacket, carrying almost 450 bucks in her pockets.

Gaia wondered if her luck could be any worse.

THE (OTHER) MAGIC WORD

Heather lay back on the couch and rested her head on Sam's lap as he flipped channels with the remote control. Without looking at her, he rested his hand on her stomach. She felt her iridescent pink silk blouse riding up over her belly button. She studied his face above her. It was so unbelievably handsome. His strong jaw was smooth and clean shaven for this event. His brownish gold hair had gotten long and was curling around the collar of his cobalt blue oxford shirt. His complicated hazel eyes were framed by long black lashes. She wanted those eyes on her. On her face, her hair, her breasts, the bare swath of skin above her skirt.

But at the moment his eyes were riveted on the television

screen as he burned through almost a hundred channels' worth of programming. It was hopeless sitting in a room with a boy, a television, and a remote control. You never got any attention or even the pleasure of watching any one show for longer than three minutes.

She smiled up at him. She didn't mind. This was the kind of relationship problem she enjoyed having.

She heard clinking sounds from the kitchen. Her parents cleaning up the last of the dishes. She heard the faint sound of laughter—Lauren talking on the phone. From her and Phoebe's room she heard the inevitable hum of the stair-climbing machine, Phoebe's most prized possession. God forbid an ounce of turkey should stick to her hips.

"Having a nice Thanksgiving?" she asked Sam.

"Hmmm," he said, his eyes not flickering from the screen.

"My dad loved your potatoes."

"Mmmm."

Sam wasn't going to talk, obviously. But he did move the remote control to the hand that rested on her stomach. He used his free hand to caress her forehead, softly pushing her hair back from her face. She breathed in deeply and let out a sigh of pleasure. It felt so nice, she wished they could just stay like that forever.

For the first time in weeks she felt truly relaxed. The dinner had gone fairly well. No hysterics or anything.

She was relieved to have finally confronted Sam with the Gaia issue and gotten the answer she wanted.

"Hey, wait, hold it there a minute," she ordered. The local news was showing footage of the Thanksgiving parade. She used to love that when she was a kid. The camera zoomed in on one enormous balloon after another: Barney, some pig or other, Kermit, two gigantic M&M's. She remembered sitting on her dad's shoulders for hours—so long that both her feet would fall asleep—and watching the floats and marching bands go by.

The report on the parade ended abruptly, and the picture changed to show a gloomy-looking Penn Station lit up by dozens of red flashing lights.

"God, what happened there?" Heather mumbled.

"Shhh," Sam ordered, leaning in to listen.

". . . Two mysterious tragedies here in one evening," the telegenic special reporter was saying into the camera. "Are they related, and if so, how? That is what detectives are asking tonight as they start a two-pronged investigation here in Penn Station."

The camera moved to show a phone booth that had been blown to bits. Twisted metal and glass were everywhere. "A bomb was detonated here, outside of New York City's busy Penn Station, less than an hour ago. . . . One person dead, not yet identified . . ."

The camera moved to show a stretcher carrying a girl.

"... And in a second calamity, a young girl, not yet identified, was brutally slashed and disfigured in her sleeping compartment in a train pulling out of Penn Station at 6:47 P.M. She remains in a coma at Roosevelt Hospital . . ."

Beneath her, Heather felt Sam's legs go rigid. "Oh my God," he whispered. "Jesus."

Suddenly Sam was on his feet, dumping Heather's head rudely onto the couch. She sat herself upright quickly. "Sam, what's your problem?"

Sam was stammering, pointing at the TV. "Th-That's— could that be? I think that might be Gaia's coat! That green coat? Oh my God."

Sam was pacing, holding his head, unable to watch the screen and then watching it again. "Her hair. Do you see her hair? It's blond. Is that Gaia? Could that be her?"

Heather glared at him in disbelief. He was *freaking*. Absolutely freaking. She'd never seen him anything like this. She wanted to slap him.

She went closer to the TV and studied the picture. Yes, she recognized that hideous jacket. She squinted and tried to get a look at the face, a crazy mixture of emotions swarming around her heart.

Just before the camera switched back to a shot of the shattered phone booth, Heather caught a glimpse of the girl's face. It was heavily bandaged, but she could see enough to know it wasn't Gaia.

Sam paced. His face was the color of skim milk.

Heather angrily snatched the remote control from his hand and used it to switch off the TV.

"What are you doing?" Sam demanded fiercely. He tried to take the remote back. His eyes were wild.

"Calm down!" she shouted at him.

"Heather! Please!" He made another grab.

"Calm down, you idiot! It *wasn't her!*" she screamed at him.

Those were the magic words. Sam stopped moving finally. In his beautiful hazel eyes Heather saw so much hope and relief, she thought she might throw up.

Sam took a breath. "What did you say?"

Heather didn't try to hide the disgust in her face. And Sam was so far away, he didn't seem to see it or care. "I said, it wasn't her. It wasn't Gaia," Heather repeated flatly.

"Are you sure?" Sam asked, his eyes too vulnerable for words.

Heather couldn't help wondering, in a profoundly awful way, whether anybody, *anybody* would ever care about her as much as Sam seemed to care for Gaia right now.

Real rage began smoldering in her stomach. Couldn't he at least *pretend* he didn't adore Gaia so deeply? Couldn't he consider Heather for *one single second* and attempt to spare her feelings? "I'm sure," she spat out bitterly.

"Oh," he said.

Finally he brought his eyes back to Heather. He seemed to remember she was in the room with him. He took another few breaths. He looked tentative. He was ashamed. But more than that, more than anything, he was relieved that cut-up girl wasn't his beloved Gaia.

In one quiet moment everything was dear. They'd both known the truth long before this. Sam was obsessed with Gaia.

Heather was too hurt to feel it. Her heart was on autopilot once more. "You've fallen for her, haven't you?" Her voice was empty.

Sam ran a hand through his hair, leaving most of it standing straight up. He looked down at the floor, then back to Heather's eyes. "I guess I have." His voice was so quiet, he mouthed the words as much as said them.

At least he didn't lie or try to bullshit her, she told herself. His honesty made for cold comfort, though.

"I don't know why. I'm so sorry," he finished earnestly.

She hated him.

"Don't apologize," she snapped icily. "Just . . . get out of here. I don't want to see you right now. We'll talk about it some other time." Anger was accessible to her right now. Pain was not.

Numbly she strode to the coat closet and grabbed his corduroy jacket. She practically threw it at him. "Please go!"

He looked sorry, all right. Sorry and regretful, but also

relieved. So relieved, he was ashamed of himself. He was happy to be getting out of there and away from her.

She hated him.

"I'm sorry, Heather," he said again as he walked out of the apartment. "I'm really sorry."

She hardly waited until he was clear of the door before she slammed it with all her might.

She wheeled around. "I hate you!" she shouted at the empty living room.

For some reason the story of Medea invaded her head again. The bitter, scorned, miserable woman.

Heather went back to the couch and threw all the pillows on the floor. It was lucky for Sam that they didn't have any children.

GRANDPA FARGO'S FAMOUS APPLE PIE

Ingredients:

8 red Rome apples

½ cup sugar

½ teaspoon cinnamon

2 tablespoons flour

pinch of nutmeg

pinch of salt

1 recipe pie crust

1 tablespoon butter

1 well-beaten egg

Filling:

Peel and core apples and slice into ½-inch wedges. Place in large mixing bowl. Add sugar, cinnamon, flour, nutmeg, and salt. Toss until thoroughly blended.

Roll ½ pie crust dough to ⅛-inch thickness. Line 9-inch pie plate with dough, allowing ½ inch to extend over edge. Add filling. Dot with 1 tablespoon butter. Roll out rest of dough and lay over pie plate, tucking excess dough along pie-plate edge. Crimp along edge with knife handle to create a wavy pattern. Use fork to puncture a few holes into top of crust in pattern of your choice. Brush top of pie with 1 well-beaten egg.

Bake at 425 degrees for 15 minutes. Turn down heat to 350 degrees and bake for ½ hour.

FREEDOM/ NOTHINGNESS

WITHOUT THINKING, SHE THREW HERSELF ON
HIS BED. IT WAS SICK, BUT SO DELICIOUS.

WOBBLY

Green. Red. Green. Red. Out the front window of the diner on University Place, Gaia watched the traffic light run its cycle again and again. She thought of Ed.

She'd meant to go, she really had. But here she was again.

She realized she was still shivering. She put her hand to her throbbing head. God, what she would do for a dollar to buy a hot cup of coffee.

"Excuse me, sweetheart, but if you're not going to order anything, I'm going to have to ask you to leave." The waitress wasn't mean. She was old and tired. She had turned a blind eye to Gaia for the last forty-five minutes. Now she was doing her job.

"But it's so cold out," Gaia said, mostly to herself.

"What's that, hon?" The waitress leaned in.

"Nothing, I'm going." It took all of Gaia's strength to climb out of the booth and balance herself on her feet. The room spun around her. She closed her eyes, trying not to be sick.

"Are you okay?" the woman asked.

Gaia opened her eyes. She steadied herself against the top of the vinyl seats. "Yes, I'll be fine," she said. She walked as steadily as she could to the door and steeled herself for the cold blast of wind.

Back out on the street she hugged herself for warmth. She wished she had her coat. She wished she had a blanket. She wished she had anything heavier than this skimpy red dress. And Mary was wrong. These shoes *were* too small. Her feet ached.

She made herself walk. What now? Where could she go? The light to cross Thirteenth Street was red. To cross to the west side of University was green. She crossed.

She kept walking west. Her teeth chattered uncontrollably. When she got to Fifth Avenue, the light to cross was red. The light to cross Thirteenth to the south was green. She crossed.

The wind that whipped up Fifth Avenue seemed to find its way into her skin—into every muscle and nerve and tendon. It chilled her blood in her veins, and her veins circulated that chilled blood all through her body and into her heart.

The light to cross Twelfth Street was red. The light to cross to the west side of Fifth was green. She crossed. Without instructions her feet were taking her to her home in New York City—Washington Square Park. She crossed Twelfth Street and got another green signal to cross Eleventh. The miniature Arc de Triomphe that marked the northern entrance to the park was in full view now.

She glanced up and stopped. The building to her right was familiar. Familiar mostly in a painful way. It was Sam's dormitory, the place where she'd walked in on Sam and

Heather having sex. She started walking and stopped again. Another image appeared in her mind. The broken doorknob. Too well she remembered the wobbly brass sphere almost falling off in her hand, giving her access to one of the worst sights a person could see. But right now, from where she stood, the broken doorknob held a certain appeal.

NOW WHAT?

Sam felt disgustingly light on his feet as he walked down Third Avenue. He should have been miserable or at least heavyhearted. But he wasn't. His muscles were buzzing with life. The world looked new to him. Clean and fresh and in excellent focus.

He looked at the shops on either side of the avenue, closed up for the holiday, with their iron safety gates pulled down and locked. It was the kind of sight that had depressed him when he'd first moved to New York. Tonight he liked it.

He was sorry about Heather. He was sorry *for* Heather. He genuinely was. She didn't deserve to be treated the way she'd been treated. But nor did she deserve to have a boy-friend who thought so constantly of someone else.

And now, for the first time in months, he felt free. Free for the moment, anyway.

Free to be with Gaia, a voice in his mind added.

Hold up, he ordered that voice. He wasn't sure about any-thing yet. He wasn't sure what the real status was between him and Heather. He wasn't sure whether Gaia had ever looked at him the way he looked at her.

Most importantly, Gaia was a major proposition. For him, he knew, she represented a love-of-his-life possibility. He had to be slow. He had to be careful. He had to make sure he didn't somehow get killed in the process.

He stopped at a red light. His happy legs had covered a lot of ground without him even knowing it. Now where?

He imagined his dorm room. It would be so lonely tonight. The place would be absolutely deserted. But where else could he go? All his friends were back home or visit-ing relatives. He imagined his family back in Maryland. His older brother was bringing his new girlfriend home to meet the folks. His parents were sorry that he wasn't there, and now, the way things had turned out, so was he.

His mind turned to Gaia, as it often did. Where was she spending Thanksgiving? She didn't have parents; that was one of the few things he knew about her. A very sad circumstance on a day like this. Did she like the Nivens, those people she lived with? Was she in their house on Perry Street right now? Was she happy? On some level he knew she wasn't, and that gave him a deep, achy feeling he didn't often feel for another person.

Why did he care for her like this? How had it happened?

He saw the lights of an all-night diner burning up ahead. It was one of the few establishments open along the whole avenue. Maybe he'd duck in there. Find himself a copy of *The New York Times* and while away the evening with a couple of cups of coffee.

THE KEY

There is no way Sam could be here, Gaia told herself for the tenth time. She was certain of it. Sam was the kind of guy who had a loving family and scores of other good backup options for Thanksgiving in case the family thing wasn't happening. In fact, he was probably sharing warm food and feelings with the she-wolf.

Still, Gaia felt self-conscious as she stepped into the

entrance of the NYU dorm. She was tired of looking like a prostitute in this awful dress. The place was nearly deserted but for the omnipresent security guard at a table a few yards into the lobby. Shit, she'd forgotten about him. He was absorbed in a noisy hockey game playing on the tiny TV perched on the table less than a foot from his eyes.

The warm air felt so good. If she could just manage to stay in here for a few minutes, maybe she'd be okay. Now that she'd finally slowed her pace, the dizziness was coming back.

The guard and his TV were in their own little world. Maybe she could just . . .

"Excuse me? Uh, miss? Can I help you?" Damn. There must have been a time-out in the game or something. The security guard was now staring at her with his full attention.

"H-Hi. I j-just. Um. My f-f-friend lives here, and he inv-v-vited me over," Gaia said. She was shivering so hard, it was difficult to talk.

The security guard got a knowing look in his eyes. "Hey, I'm sorry, sweetheart, but we can't have none of that here." He took in her slinky, ripped dress, her heels, what was left of her makeup. "This is a college building, you know? You oughtta get out of here." He kept jingling his keys in one hand. It seemed like a nervous habit. She noticed that the key ring said Mustang and showed the black silhouette of a horse bucking against a blue background.

"B-B-But I—" Gaia knew there was really no point in

arguing. There was no way he was letting her past his table unless she clobbered him, and she simply didn't have the strength. She just wanted to use up a little more time inside. She couldn't face the cold again. What could she talk about with him? The New York Rangers? Cars? Guns?

"Look, kid, I'm sorry. I really am. You look like hell"—he shook his head with a mix of sympathy and disgust—"but you can't stay here."

MOVING RIGHT ALONG

Sam took out his wallet soon after he'd sat down at a table to see how much cash he had. He rifled through every compartment. Unfortunately, he had none. He checked the pockets of his jacket. He had no money. Not one red cent.

He remembered now that he'd given Heather two twenties to buy pies for dessert from an overpriced Upper East Side gourmet shop.

He flagged down a waiter. "Excuse me, do you take credit cards?"

The surly waiter fixed him with a look that clearly meant no.

"Do you know if there's a bank or an ATM around here?" he asked.

The waiter looked like Sam had burned his house down. "Twenty-theerd," the man replied in a clipped, Eastern European accent.

"But this is Thirty-first Street," Sam said, wondering why he bothered.

"Twenty-theerd," the waiter said, louder.

Sam blew out his breath. "Okay, thanks." He headed toward the door. It looked like he was going to end up in his dorm room after all.

MOONY

As she left the dormitory, the cold practically knocked Gaia senseless. She was covered head to toe in goose bumps, only they didn't seem the least bit compelling.

Suddenly, a few yards from the building, she stopped.

Her eye caught on a logo on the hood of a car parked directly outside the dorm's entrance.

So she wasn't totally senseless. She walked slowly around the car, studying it for another moment. Then she saw the vanity license plate. RANGERFAN, it read. Oh God. Could it be? Could there actually be a small piece of good luck in all of this blackness?

Gaia put her hands to her head. She needed to expel the dizziness, to gather her wits and her physical capabilities if she had any left.

Okay, now. She raised her foot to the side of the hood and shoved it hard. The car rocked violently, and a car alarm blasted through the silent night air. Perfect.

She ran to the side of the building and backed herself up against the wall, a few feet beyond the front awning.

Exactly as she'd hoped, the security guard dashed out of the building to check on his precious vehicle. Thank God.

Gaia found enough speed left in her legs to carry her into the building, undetected. With excitement fizzing in her veins she sprinted into the stairwell and up four flights to the door of Sam's suite.

She slowed down. Okay, this was starting to bring back some bad memories. Still, it was warm. There was a bed. She had to put her emotions on ice for a while.

Slowly she opened the door to the common room of the suite, blanking out her mind. Good, it was empty. The door to room B5, with its infamous doorknob, was just ahead.

Please be broken still, she begged of the doorknob. She closed her eyes and closed her hand around it at the same time.

Yes. She let out a breath. It jiggled brokenly in its socket, and she was able to push open the door.

Icy as her emotions—and the rest of her—were, she wasn't prepared for the effect of the smell. The tiny dorm room smelled like Sam. In a good way. In an aching, moony, grab-you-by-the-heart way. The smell intoxicated her. It gave her shivers. Why was it that a smell could evoke a person more powerfully than a million pictures could?

This, she realized, was what people meant when they talked about chemistry.

Without thinking, she threw herself on his bed. It was sick, but so delicious. His bed. Where he slept. She imagined him in his boxers, tangled in the sheets. His shoulders, his torso, his stomach, his . . . God, what heady torture.

She sat up. She had to pull herself together. She was semidemented from bashing her head and from cold and exhaustion. Time to act like a sane person.

First thing was to get out of this dress. She pulled it over her head in one swift move. She pulled the shoes off her miserable feet and stripped off the tights. She wound up the dress, the shoes, and the tights in a ball and sank them into the wastebasket next to Sam's nightstand.

Shower. She needed a shower. She wanted a boiling hot shower so bad, she could feel it.

Aha. There was a towel hanging over the door of Sam's closet. On his bureau were a bar of soap and a bottle of shampoo. Eureka. She had to hope that this dorm really was as empty as it appeared.

She cast off her bra and panties, feeling an unfamiliar and lustful pleasure at seeing them strewn about on Sam's bed. She wrapped herself in the towel and set off in search of the bathroom.

She listened for the sound of the germs, and they led her to a totally filthy and wonderful bathroom off the common room. What could you ask from a bathroom shared by four college students? She didn't care. She loved every microbe.

She blasted the shower as hot and strong as it would go and climbed in.

She gathered sex felt pretty good, but she couldn't imagine it felt much better than hot jets of water pounding against her frozen flesh. Ahhhhhhh.

Suddenly the tiles were starting a slow spin around her. She pressed her palms into her eyeballs. It didn't help. She sat right down on the floor of the shower and let the water beat down on her head. She would wait for the dizziness to pass.

When her body finally felt warm from the outside in, she got back to her feet and scrubbed her hair and face and body and rinsed for ages. She had to force herself to turn off the water.

She wrapped herself in Sam's towel and crept back into his room. Now what? Should she sleep naked or should she . . . hmmm. She went over to Sam's bureau and opened the top drawer. Waiting for her there were a soft, clean, ribbed white tank top undershirt and a pair of well-worn cotton boxers in a faded plaid of blues and greens. Yum.

This night had turned from sheer torment to the most sensual and thrilling experience of her life. She felt a bit like a stalker, but she wasn't doing any harm, was she? She'd put everything back in order before Sam returned. He'd never even guess she was there.

On the floor at the foot of his bed she suddenly spied his shoes, the scuffed leather, lace-up shoes he'd been wearing the day they played chess. For some reason, the sight of them stole her breath. Though empty, the shoes sat in a pose that was strongly suggestive of Sam—of exactly how he stood and walked. It was crazy that a pair of uninhabited shoes could carry so much subtle information about him. But they did. They brought him right into the room with her.

The aching feeling was back in force. She shivered again. An army of goose bumps invaded her arms and legs and back. *Almost like fear.*

It was like fear, but it wasn't fear.

Maybe it was . . . love.

Dear Gaia,

 *I made a decision today, a few hours after you left.
I'm going straight—I'm giving up drugs. Not "one day
at a time" or any of that crap. I'm giving it up for good.
Right now. When you saw me snorting coke today, I saw
myself through your eyes, and I hated what I saw. If I keep
going like this, I'm going to die. Yeah, it's that bad. And I
don't want to die yet.*

 *You probably wish I'd just leave you alone. You're
wondering why I'm dragging you into my problems. I'm
not sure, exactly. I'm not a very reflective person. But for
some reason, I really do want to be friends with you. I
want to be close. (Don't worry. Not in that way. I'm not
a lesbian.) I've made a specialty out of not caring what
other people think. But I do care what you think. I want
you to think I'm a good person.*

 *I have this idea about you and me. I have everything—
parents, money, friends, a lot of love. You have nothing. I
get so much, and the thing that sucks is, my heart is like a
sieve. I want you to have some of what I have. You deserve
it, not me.*

 That's weird, right? Sorry, it's just how I am.

 *So, anyway, I'm kicking the drugs whether I ever see
you again or not.*

 *But I just wanted you to know that wherever you are,
however you feel, you always have a friend out there in*

the world. Not a perfect friend or anything, but one who's
trying to do better.
    Mary

Mary finished the letter and stuck it in an envelope. She'd get a stamp from her mom later. Then she got an idea. She went to her desk drawer, where she'd had a one-pound bag of M&M's ever since Halloween. She dumped the entire contents on her floor and picked out every last one of the red ones. She transferred the letter into a bigger, sturdier envelope and threw in all of the red M&M's to keep it company. She threw in a few green ones, too.

Now she'd need a whole bunch of stamps.

THE COLOR
OF LOVE

HE WAS LEANING FORWARD, LEANING OVER HER.
SO CLOSE NOW. SO REAL. "CAN I?" HE WHISPERED.

SOMETHING SUBLIME

"Hey, Bauman. What's up?" Sam said to the security guard. "How're the Rangers?"

Bauman grimaced. "Down by two in the third. How's your holiday, Moon?"

Sam actually thought about his answer. "Good," he said. "Surprisingly good." Except for the fact that all twenty digits had lost feeling about a mile ago. He rubbed his hands together. "Quiet here tonight, huh?"

"Yes, it is," Bauman answered vaguely, his attention back on the game.

"Later. Happy Thanksgiving," Sam called over his shoulder as he entered the stairwell. Not that he expected his bland sign-off to compete with the Rangers. He was pathologically polite. He couldn't help himself.

He took the stairs slowly. Was he the only student in the entire building? It felt almost eerie.

None of his suite mates were around, that much he knew. He swung open the door of the common room. The place was exactly the pigsty he'd left it. He didn't even bother to turn on a light. He'd so completely frozen himself, walking almost seventy blocks, he was eager to strip down and climb under his down comforter.

He took out his key and had started to fit it in the lock

when the doorknob fell off in his hand. "Shit. Gotta get that fixed," he cursed under his breath, as he did two out of three times he entered his room.

A warm, reddish light from the street was filtering through the small window, lighting the bed. . . .

Oh. Jesus. Sam stepped backward. He was suddenly transported to a Three Little Bears moment. There was someone sleeping in his bed.

He stepped forward and froze. His heart stopped beating. He stopped breathing. Brain function shut down.

Could that someone be . . . ?

He turned his eyes to the door and then back to the bed again, sure that the mirage would be gone. It wasn't. There was still a sublimely beautiful blond girl in his bed who looked very much like Gaia.

He'd heard that people hallucinated in the happiest way just before they died of exposure. He hadn't chilled himself that badly, had he?

Now. Time to breathe, lungs. Time to beat, heart. His vital organs appeared to need a little coaching. There. Better. Okay, deep breaths. Yes.

He would just calm down, slow down, and think a minute.

He crept a little closer, terrified that this magnificent vision would disappear if he disturbed the air the slightest bit.

Still there. Please stay, he begged it. If this was a figment of his imagination, then he prayed his imagination would keep it up.

He would just look at her. That would be okay, wouldn't it? Even if it was an imagined version of her, he still wanted to look. The few interactions he and Gaia'd had were so charged or awkward or plain antagonistic that he never got to study her, to see how her face looked in repose.

Her head was turned to the side, and her silken yellow hair—hair he'd fantasized about more times than was good for him—was splayed out on the pillow, leaving a shadow of dampness on the white cotton. Her bewitching eyes were closed in sleep. Her face was serene and lovely beyond description—light freckles over her cheeks. He drew closer. Palest, finest down along her jawline. Her eyelids flickered. He drew back.

She was still again. He came closer. His eyes moved down her neck.

Oh Christ! She was wearing his T-shirt. He felt the blood churning in his ears, gathering in other parts of his body. His T-shirt, which had spent its long, dutiful life covering large, rough stretches of masculine skin, now had the exquisite experience of gracing skin so delicate and fine, it was almost transparent. He envied it.

He saw that the too large shirt had gotten pulled around under her, revealing the sloping side and top of her breast.

He had to look away. Partly because it was too much to

take and partly because he felt wrong seeing her like this, without her knowing he was seeing her. Without her wanting him to.

He made himself take a few steps backward and put his hands over his face to regain his composure.

He knew now, more than ever before, that he loved her. He loved her deeply and urgently, with a fierceness that made him know he'd never grasped, even grazed, the concept of love before. But he couldn't go on like this, without knowing how she really felt.

And what if she wasn't real at all but a figment of his fevered, lustful mind?

Well, then she'd be more likely to tell him what he dreamed of hearing.

A REAL KISS

Gaia was dreaming a blissful dream. Surrounded as she was by the smell and feel of Sam, by his place and his things, it was natural that she should dream of him vividly.

In the dream he was there beside her, sitting on the edge of the bed. He was so close, she could feel his warmth and smell his smell more intensely. An alive smell now. He took her hand so gently and held it. Just held it. Making her safe.

Consciousness was tickling her eyelids, summoning her. *Please, sleep, stay with me. Don't make me go back yet.*

But it was happening. She couldn't help it. She was waking up in spite of every effort to fight it. She flicked open her eyes.

No.

She closed them again.

How could it be?

She opened them again. Was the dream still with her? . . . Or was it . . .

"Sam?" she whispered, her heart filled with awe.

He was still holding her hand. In the dream and . . . here. He was still holding it, one of his hands cupping her fingers, the other holding her wrist. His beautiful hands with the wide nails and fraying cuticles. The ones he'd used to stomp all over her chess pieces that day in the park when this had started.

"Gaia," he said. She'd never heard her name sound just that way before.

He was leaning forward, leaning over her. So close now. So real. "Can I?" he whispered.

"Please," she said.

He took his hand from her wrist and touched his first two fingers to her elbow, then drew them in an air-light caress up to her shoulder. "Mmmm," she sighed.

As his head hovered over her she looked up at his neck and chin, touching her finger to the place where his whiskers started, moving them up over his jaw, feeling the slight hollow of his cheek, the strong bones that came together at the corner of his eye. He gazed down at her, his eyes voracious and questioning. She turned her head to face him straight on.

"Oh," he said, drawing in his breath. He touched his fingers to the ugly bruise along the side of her cheek and forehead. His face showed real worry. "Are you okay?"

She felt like crying just then. She'd forgotten about everything that had happened. Now she remembered, and she felt ashamed of it and of all the ugliness and violence she represented in Sam's good, peaceful life. "I'm sorry," she said randomly, her eyes filling with tears.

"No, Gaia," he whispered. "Don't. Just . . . be with me."

The feelings inside her were too round and full. She couldn't hold them. Her chest was bursting, and her head was spinning.

He pulled her up so she was sitting beside him and gently held her face in his hands. He put his lips, gentle as sunlight, to the wound on her forehead, then dotted her cheekbone with kisses.

Please, please, please, she begged silently. Wishing.

Oh God. And then he found it, and her wish happened. His lips found her mouth, and the gentleness gave way to intensity. A kiss. A real kiss more perfect than any imagined. She was kissing him back, hungrily, pressing herself against him.

A thought came to her as his lips melted into hers. *This,* she thought, *is the mouth that I was meant to kiss. This is the mouth I will always kiss, and no other.* And blending into that thought was another thought. More a feeling than a thought, because there were no words to it at all. But the feeling was that her lips and her hands had found a home. The one safe, healing place on earth. And that maybe, maybe . . . who could ever say? But maybe she really would have kids someday. (Not just one.) Because there was somebody in the world for her. She knew that now, from this kiss, and nobody could take that away.

His hands held the back of her head now; they were buried in her hair. His lips explored hers. She tasted him and felt him and smelled him all at once. Her senses mixed and blurred. Her blood roared in her ears.

He stood up and pulled her with him. He pressed the entire length of his body against her. She tilted back her head, not wanting to break the kiss. She let her hands explore his graceful, muscular back, his wide, sturdy shoulders. She touched his neck and felt the way his hair curled sweetly around his ears. Digging her fingers into his hair, she pushed him deeper, harder into the kiss.

He moaned. His arms were around her now, gathering her up, holding her as tight and close against him as she could be and still remain a separate person. His lips left hers, landing under her jaw, down her neck, her collarbone.

"Aaaaaah." A breathy sound escaped her lips. The dizziness was overpowering; it was shutting her in. These feelings were too fragile and beautiful to be held, the love too big to fit into her scarred, shrunken heart.

"I love you." Did she think it, or did she say it? Or did he say it? Or did she imagine he said it? Were the words in the air or just in her mind?

Before she could be sure, the darkness engulfed her, and she released herself to the sureness of Sam's arms.

SIREN SONG

"I love you," Sam whispered against her neck. "I love you."

He'd always wondered what it would take to say those words, how much he'd have to push and prompt and coach himself to utter them. He didn't realize it wouldn't require any intention at all—that the words could come without thought or plan, as naturally and passionately and irreversibly as a kiss, without waiting for his consent.

Suddenly he felt her weight sink into his arms.

"Gaia." He pulled her up to him, finding her face with his lips, kissing her eyelids. They were closed. "Gaia?"

Her eyes didn't open. She breathed a sigh. Her head fell forward, resting against his chest. "Gaia?"

He cradled her head in the crook of his elbow and tipped her back gently. "Gaia? Are you all right? Gaia?"

She had fainted. She was motionless in his arms. All the feelings whirring in his chest changed directions, from pure exultation to surprise and fear.

He picked her up in his arms, cradling her against him. "Gaia. Gaia!" He jostled her, hoping to rouse her. Her head fell back, exposing her delicate throat.

"Gaia, please? What happened? Are you okay?" Panic was building. His eyes found the terrible bruise on the side of her head. Could it be . . . ? What if . . . ?

"Gaia, come on. Stay with me here, would you? Please, Gaia." The fear was talking. He was listening only distractedly.

He managed to support her weight with one arm and with the other plucked the phone from his nightstand. He dialed 911.

"Thirty-two Fifth!" he blared into the phone as soon as he heard a voice pick up. "Fourth floor. Send an ambulance."

"Sir, can you tell me what has happened?" the voice urged calmly.

"M-My . . . girlfriend." (Girlfriend?) "She's fainted. I can't rouse her. She hurt her head. Maybe—"

"All right, sir, we'll send the ambulance immediately."

Sam's heart was slamming in his rib cage. Thoughts were careening around his brain like a million errant Ping-Pong balls. "Oh, Gaia, please be okay," he begged her still body.

He laid her down as gingerly as he could on his bed. It was cold out. He needed to cover her. Did she have clothes or . . . ? No time.

He grabbed his thick, terry cloth robe from his closet and wrapped her in it. It was a strange set of circumstances that would force him to willingly cover her magnificent body, not to let his eyes linger over her exquisite stomach and hips and legs.

He found a wool blanket on the shelf and bundled her in that, too. Then he scooped her lifeless body up and strode out into the hallway. He punched the button for the elevator, his ears pricked for the sound of a siren. It was the one time he invited that sound, desperately wanted to hear it.

The elevator came. Sam stabbed at the lobby button.

There it was! The siren! Thank the Lord for a quick response. He raced past a stunned-looking Bauman and met the ambulance just as it was pulling up outside.

Fear blended with appreciation as Sam watched the emergency medical team burst into action, their limbs and instruments a blur of confidence and precision. He loved them in that moment as much as he loved his parents and friends.

Before a minute had passed, Gaia was bound in a stretcher, hooked up to various medical gadgets, tucked into the back of the vehicle with Sam beside her. The engine roared, the siren kicked in again, and they were off to St. Vincent's, just a few blocks away. Sam held her hand tight, never wanting to let it go.

"I love you," he whispered to her again, pleading with his crazed heart to stay in his chest for a while longer.

He considered it for a moment, his newly awakened heart. He remembered the puzzling conflict between heart and mind. Well, it was settled now.

In case there was any mystery, he now knew who was in charge.

HEAVEN

Gaia was floating. Sam was there, holding her hand. There were unfamiliar people, sounds, words, things she couldn't make sense of, but there was always Sam. He held her. He gave her his warmth.

"I love you." The words came to her in Sam's voice. She wanted very much to open her eyes and see if it really was Sam, and if so, to see if he was talking to her when he said them, as she fervently hoped he was. And if he was saying those words to her, and maybe even if he wasn't, she wanted to say the same words to him.

But she couldn't. She couldn't open her eyes or make words.

Was she alive anymore? Was Sam real? Was he really there with her?

Maybe it was him. More likely it was heaven.

But if this was heaven, if this was what death felt like, then it was okay with her.

HEATHER

I've been trying to figure out why I don't have any tears for Sam tonight.

I do hate him at the moment; that's true.

But I thought I loved him.

All this time I figured I haven't been able to cry over him because I'm too numb. I'm too bottled up and confused to feel things very well.

I never imagined the possibility that I didn't love him.

Because I do love him. I mean, I'm pretty sure I do.

I mean, I do. Don't I?

You know what's really retarded? An hour after Sam left, I called Ed Fargo.

Then I remembered he was in Pennsylvania. He was there for Thanksgiving with his weird, obese grandmother who called me Feather.

HUNGER

THEN THE MEMORIES FELL INTO FRAGMENTS AND
SHARDS THAT DIDN'T MAKE ANY SENSE AT ALL.

MORE DISAPPOINTMENT

Ella rolled her eyes at the emergency-room doctor in St. Vincent's Hospital. This was a night of highs and lows, currently stuck on low.

The doctor was talking about Gaia, bleating words like *concussion* and *subdural* something and *hematoma* something else. But he wasn't saying anything about "slashed to ribbons," which was what Ella really wanted to hear.

She was jubilant when she'd first gotten the call from the hospital, sure that her plans had gone off without a hitch. Then she entered a period of confusion after she arrived at the hospital, during which it appeared that Gaia *hadn't* been slashed at Penn Station. Gaia, she was told, had spent several semidelirious hours before a doting Sam Moon brought her to the hospital, unconscious, from his NYU dormitory. The girl who'd been slashed (Ella had followed the story excitedly on the eleven o'clock news) was *not* Gaia, and yet Gaia had found her way to the hospital with some grave problem nonetheless.

Ella perked up when she heard the doctor use the word *coma,* hoping that her goal might be achieved even without the extra bonus of disfigurement. But wretched, impossible Gaia had miraculously managed to sidestep the coma, in spite of a serious head injury.

"Mrs. Niven, I'm sorry to bother you with all of this information. I'm sure you'd like to see her," Dr. Somethingorother was saying. He was Indian or maybe Pakistani and spoke precise, melodious English.

Ella sighed. She couldn't very well say no, could she? "Of course," she said.

"You'll be pleased to know she's already been moved out of ICU. Her condition is stable."

Whoopee.

Ella followed the white coat up an elevator and down a hallway, through a set of swinging doors, past a waiting room and a nurses' station.

Dr. Whatever turned around to talk some more. "She's not yet fully conscious. Still a bit bleary. Try not to be alarmed. We do expect her to make a quick recovery, but it's never as quick as all of us would like."

If Gaia woke up before she was thirty, it would be too quick. Ella nodded blandly. She hated doctors. Particularly the one she'd blown up earlier in the evening.

The doctor stopped in front of room 448. The door was partially open. He gestured for her to enter first. She started into the room and quickly stepped backward. She backed out into the hallway.

"Excuse me, Doctor," she said. "But there's somebody else in the room."

The doctor's eyes lit up. "Yes, that's her friend who

brought her here. His name is Sam, I think? He hasn't left her side in hours. He is quite devoted to her, no? He is the one who gave us the information to find you."

"Fine," she said. "Very nice. But would you mind asking him to leave? I really need some time alone with my . . . foster daughter." Sob, sob. "Besides," she added in a confidential tone, "if I can speak frankly, I don't like that young man. I wouldn't be surprised if he were part of the reason that Gaia is here in the first place. . . ." She let her voice float off enigmatically.

The doctor hesitated. Clearly he didn't know what to think, and yet he was too polite to question her. "Yes. As you wish," he said.

"I'll just use the bathroom and collect myself for a moment," Ella said, stepping down the hall. "I'll come back when I can see Gaia alone."

A strong instinct was telling Ella she didn't want to be introduced to Sam Moon. A somewhat twisted instinct, but those were the ones she'd learned to listen to.

ONE WITNESS

Sam watched Gaia's eyelids for signs of her waking. Just in the last five minutes she'd opened and closed her eyes three times, once almost focusing on his face. His heart soared. Dr. Sengupta said she was going to be okay, and he was starting to believe it.

Sam ran his thumb from the tip of her index finger up her hand and wrist to the soft underside of her forearm. Her eyes flickered.

He leaned over her and buried a gentle kiss on her neck. That was more for him than her. He hoped she didn't mind. The hint of a smile seemed to pull at the side of her mouth. Or did he just imagine that?

What he really wanted to do was to climb into the narrow bed and press her close to him, to hold her with his whole body until she woke up. And after she woke up, too. But you weren't really supposed to do that in a hospital, were you?

Most people hated hospitals, and in theory, Sam did, too. But this hospital, on two separate occasions, had brought him closer to Gaia. It was the site of some of his worst experiences and yet some of the happiest feelings he'd ever had.

"Sam?"

He glanced up. He saw Gaia's doctor and felt slightly abashed. "Yes?"

"I'm sorry to ask you because I can see how much you wish to stay with Gaia, but her guardian, Mrs. Niven, has asked for time alone with her."

Sam knew it was a reasonable request, but his heart was breaking nonetheless. "Maybe I'll just wait in the waiting room for a few minutes till she's done."

Dr. Sengupta took in the state of Sam's hair and clothing with kind eyes. "Why don't you get yourself home and have a rest? Perhaps you could come again tomorrow? Visiting hours, as you might imagine, are long over."

Visiting hours? Sam was no visitor! He was . . . what? Nothing. He was nothing. But Gaia was his life. Did that count for anything?

"But I—" He really, really didn't want to go yet. He wanted to help usher Gaia back into the land of consciousness, to be with her when she crossed over. He needed to make sure they both knew that what happened between them was real. "Please, could I just—"

"I'm sorry. I have to respect Mrs. Niven's request." The doctor did look truly sorry.

Sam turned back to Gaia. He took both of her hands and brought them to his heart. He leaned over and pressed his cheek against her good one. "I love you, Gaia," he whispered in her ear. "I can't help it anymore." It might not have been a classically romantic thing to say, but it was true. She'd understand, he knew. He kissed her ear, then straightened up.

Her eyelids were fluttering again. He saw her hands moving against the sheet as soon as he'd released them. Were her hands looking for his? Did he just hope so?

"Thank you, Doctor, for everything," he said, trying not to look as unhappy as he felt. "She's really going to be okay, right?"

"Yes, I believe she is."

Sam trudged out of the room and down the hallway.

"Good luck to you, Sam," the doctor called after him, and the words somehow sounded ominous.

Every cell in Sam's heart was telling him not to leave her now. He was afraid that once he was gone, their magical, frightening night together would be gone, too, with him left as its only witness. And not the most reliable witness, either.

DISAPPOINTMENT
X 1,000,000,000

It was hard and cruel. It downright sucked. In her dream, hovering someplace beyond the living, Gaia had Sam. He held her and told her he loved her.

Here, in reality, she had Ella.

She wished she could go back to being dead.

". . . You have quite a track record, Gaia. Twice in the hospital in two months," Ella was blathering. "You're going to send George's insurance premiums into the stratosphere."

Gaia exerted all her strength propping herself up in the hospital bed. It made her uncomfortable for Ella to see her lying down.

". . . And insurance only covers eighty percent of the bill, you know," Ella continued pettily.

Gaia looked down at her hands. They felt cold and lonely. "Thanks a lot, Ella," she said numbly. "That makes me feel a lot better. If the photography thing doesn't work out, maybe you could get a job with Hallmark in the get-well-card department."

Ella exhaled in annoyance. "And you're a rude ingrate as well."

Gaia closed her eyes, wrapping her misery around her like a blanket. She was right back where she started. She'd thought she'd made a new friend. She hadn't. She'd thought she'd run away. She hadn't.

She'd gotten nowhere, changed nothing.

Her mind summoned an image of Sam. She was kissing him, touching him, wrapping her body around his in his bed. The image brought a deep flush to her cheeks.

But that hadn't really . . . They hadn't actually . . . had they?

She glanced at Ella.

What exactly *had* happened to her? How had she gotten here? She tried to piece together the endless, surreal day. She remembered being at Mary's house, of course. She remembered hitting her head on the sink in the bathroom at Penn Station. She remembered passing out—if you could call that remembering.

Things got fuzzier after that. She didn't remember coming to, but she did remember trying to get a refund for her stolen ticket. She vaguely remembered an explosion. She remembered walking outside and being cold.

Then the memories fell into fragments and shards that didn't make any sense at all.

She glanced at Ella again. She could hardly stomach the notion of needing information from the bitch goddess, but how else was she going to know?

Gaia took a breath. She needed to sound as disinterested as possible. "So, anyway, Ella. What happened to me? How did I get here? How did you get here?"

Ella opened her eyes wide in fake surprise. "Wait a minute. You are asking *me* questions about *your* life?"

Gaia shrugged. "You know, severe head wound and all." She touched her hand to her bruise. "I just wondered if the doctors told you anything about how I ended up here."

Ella studied her for a moment. "Actually, yes. Do you really not remember anything at all?"

Gaia shook her head. "Not much."

Ella nodded slowly. "Well, you made quite a little scene. The cops found you outside an NYU dormitory. You were delirious, totally out of it, raving endlessly about somebody named Sam."

Gaia felt her heart clench. The flush returned to her cheeks and deepened by one hundred times. If she'd really believed she'd made her heart tough enough to withstand disappointment, she'd been badly, profoundly mistaken.

"I was alone?" Gaia asked in a small voice, even though she knew she'd regret it. "I came here alone?" She was so far gone, she was giving evil Ella a straight shot at her vulnerability.

"Except for some freaked-out cops, yeah," Ella informed her.

So Gaia's fragments of memory weren't memory at all. They were fantasy. Sam hadn't kissed her, held her, told her he loved her. Those were the crazed delusions of her bashed-in head and her pitiful, hungry heart.

She was tempted to bash her head again, to return to the place where she'd had those feelings. Of course they didn't happen in reality. Not in her reality, anyway. It was too nice, too purely good to have happened in her life.

Gaia lay back again. Ella didn't matter. Nothing mattered.

Her misery wasn't a blanket. It was a strait-jacket fastened way too tight, threatening to squeeze out her last bit of hope.

SAM

I had a terrible thought when I woke up this morning in the bed that Gaia and I had shared, briefly, last night.

I had the thought that I dreamed the whole thing.

I would have stuck with the thought, but I smelled Gaia's faint, sweet smell in my bed. I found more than one long blond hair on my pillow. I found a somewhat tattered red dress and shoes balled up in my garbage can. I confirmed that my undershirt and boxers were, in fact, missing.

Then I had a fear that was worse than the thought. I was afraid that it had actually happened, but that Gaia wasn't there. I mean, her body was there. But she was so badly hurt and delirious, and practically comatose, that everything I imagined between us happened to me. Only to me.

This fear makes me physically sick because I hate the thought of having taken advantage of her in some way.

Selfishly, that's not even the very worst part. Even worse, I fear I've opened my stubborn, tyrannical heart to an event—a girl—so stunning and miraculous, I've even gotten my brain to join in on the thrill of it. Only to discover that it never actually happened.

Which could make a man feel like a creep and a big, pathetic fool.

My brain, not surprisingly, is threatening a very sour "I told you so."

That's the fear, anyway. I'm not sure it's the truth.

But I can say this. I never understood loneliness until I woke up in my bed without her this morning.

GAIA

Maybe Ella was telling me the truth. Maybe I was discovered by the cops, raving outside of Sam's dormitory, and taken to the hospital alone.

But when I stepped out of the hospital bed after my night of observation and walked my bleary self into the bathroom, I discovered something peculiar. Under my hospital robe, I was wearing a man's undershirt and a man's boxers. These are things I know I do not own. I don't care how hard I banged my head.

At the back of the boxers, just under the waistband, scrawled in permanent black marker are two wonderful words. Can you guess them?

1. Sam

2. Moon

These pieces of physical evidence happen to fit with some memory shards I have—fuzzy, I'll admit. I have bits of memories of being in Sam's dorm room, and putting those things on.

I'm not saying Sam definitely kissed me. I'm not saying he told me he loved me or anything like that.

I'm just saying, maybe Ella was wrong. Maybe she lied. Maybe.

In all honesty, I don't even want to find out for sure. I want to hold on to these pieces of memory—hopes, if you want to be a killjoy. I can't bear to discover these things didn't happen. I need to cling to the possibility that they did.

Because even the *possibility* of something so beautiful could sustain a heart as desolate as mine for a long, long time.

PAYBACK

To Alice Elizabeth Wenk

GAIA

When I was five, my babysitter, Claire, took me to see my first movie. It was already dark when we came out of the theater, so we started walking toward this big intersection two blocks down where we were sure we could catch a cab.

I was still feeling dazzled by the memory of the music and the big colorful screen when a huge, heavyset man stepped out of a doorway and yanked Claire into the hallway of a nearby brownstone. At that moment I remember being startled and feeling worried about Claire, but I never—not even for a minute—felt scared.

I watched silently as the man shoved a rag into Claire's mouth and began dragging her up the stairs. And instead of running for help like any other kid would have done, I followed the attacker as he dragged Claire, kicking and clawing, up four flights. The guy never even looked around to see where I'd gone.

When we got to the roof, he started tearing off Claire's clothes and fumbling with his belt. Of course, I didn't know what that meant at the time, but I knew fear when I saw it, and it was written all over Claire's face. At that moment I started executing my plan, even though I didn't know I *had* a plan yet.

The guy didn't know what hit him when a spray of gravel pounded his shoulder. And when he turned around to see where it came from, there I stood—my body planted firmly not ten feet from him at the edge of the roof— utterly calm. I swung back my arm and let go another missile shower of biting gravel pellets into his face.

Cursing, he leaped to his feet and charged at me, but just as he lunged, I ducked and rolled out of his way. A nanosecond later all two hundred pounds of him was pitching over the edge of the roof.

He fell four flights to his death.

I can't stand bullies. I can't stand men who think they can push women around. When I can kick some guy's ass for picking on a girl who's usually half his size, it's one of the few times I'm thankful for this strange fearlessness that I've had since birth. It's one of the few times when

I forget to feel like a freak, when I forget to want to be normal—something I can never be. Because no matter how little control I have over my own life and how little courage I have when it comes to Sam, or friendship, or letting people in, I *can* do something for the weak one. The loser.

That is when I feel really alive. Because no matter how strong I think I am, the loser always seems to be a lot like me.

THINK ABOUT SAM

WHAT IF THE MEMORY SUDDENLY SNAPPED
INTO VIVID TECHNICOLOR SURROUND SOUND AND
IT WAS NOTHING BUT A BIG FAT . . . NOTHING?

WEIRD WEEKEND

"You can't possibly imagine how psyched I am that you called," Ed Fargo told Gaia Moore as she stepped out onto the sidewalk in front of her apartment. "I escaped just when my dad was about to retell the retelling of Uncle Alan's story about how he and my mom mooned the nuns on her wedding day. It's like a fish story. Every time someone tells it, Sister Rose suffers a different fate. This time I think she would have had a stroke, and I don't think I could have handled it."

Gaia winced at the sunlight, taking in a deep breath and letting it out slowly. "Right."

Ed sighed. "You're going to have to bring your level of excitement down a notch, G.," he said, a hint of irritation in his voice. "I know you haven't seen me in three days, but your enthusiasm over my presence is making me blush."

"Sorry," Gaia said, stuffing one bare hand into her pocket as she started to walk. The other was clutching a small paper bag she'd picked up off the kitchen counter. "Weird weekend," she mumbled, not sure what, exactly, she should tell him. It had been hard enough when she'd admitted to Ed that she had feelings of, yes, a sexual nature for Sam Moon. Gaia wasn't exactly the heart-to-heart type, and letting anyone in on her secrets went against every fiber in her being. But this had now become more than just a crush. It was bordering on insanity. And Gaia wasn't sure whether telling Ed would help take the weight off her shoulders or merely confirm that she was a first-rate lunatic. Gaia didn't have that many friends to spare. In fact, she only had this one now that Mary was out of the picture. So how much was too much to tell?

It was Sunday morning, and ever since she'd left the hospital on Friday, all Gaia had done was mainline sugar and obsess. Obsess about Sam, think about Sam, dream about Sam. The dream involved kisses that had never really happened. Words that had never really been spoken. They couldn't have been real, no matter how much her muddled, confused brain kept trying to make her believe that they were. Her mind had been sifting random, incongruent images nonstop. Images Gaia couldn't possibly make sense of.

Part of her didn't want to try. What if the memory suddenly snapped into vivid Technicolor surround sound and it was nothing but a big fat . . . nothing? What if nothing at all had happened between her and Sam? Gaia was sure her heart couldn't handle it. As pathetic as it was, she'd rather hold on to the possibility of something perfect than be hit with the reality of nothing much.

Gaia sighed and pushed forward at her usual breakneck pace, forgetting for a moment that Ed was navigating his wheelchair through the crowd of babbling women surrounding them. She turned around long enough to notice one of the women inadvertently whack his arm with a J. Crew bag. The Christmas shopping rush had officially begun.

The hustle and bustle failed to draw Gaia out of her own confused thoughts as Ed struggled to keep up with her. There were only two things she knew for sure. First, she had been in Sam's room on Thanksgiving. She knew this only because when she was leaving the hospital, a bleary-eyed intern had handed her back her clothes. A T-shirt, a pair of boxers, and a robe. All men's. All with the distinct, musky Sam smell nestled within their folds.

All of which were stashed in a plastic bag, inside a backpack, which was zippered shut and locked with a minilock under her bed. Ella-proof packaging.

The second thing Gaia was completely sure of was that Ella knew something she wasn't telling. That was the part about this whole thing that ate at Gaia like acid through a tin can. Ella knowing more than her. It was just cosmically wrong.

"So what's up?" Ed huffed, catching up to her just before she stepped onto the street, ignoring a solid Don't Walk signal.

"Park," Gaia grunted, holding up the little white bag. "Doughnuts."

"Articulate," Ed commented. "You're quite the cave woman today."

Gaia ignored the comment and kept walking, leading the way into Washington Square Park and dropping onto the first bench she saw. Scowling, she immediately shoved three-quarters of a glazed chocolate doughnut into her mouth. The sticky dough gathered in a lump and lodged halfway down her throat. Where to start?

"Didn't you get enough turkey this weekend?" Ed asked, removing one of the doughnuts from the bag on her lap.

"No turkey," Gaia said while chewing.

"You have to be kidding." Ed picked off a piece of dough-nut and popped it into his mouth. "Turkey is the only thing that makes the whole family-gathering debacle bearable."

Gaia shrugged. "I think I might have kissed Sam."

Ed suddenly let out a strangled, choking sound. Gaia turned to him in time to see his eyes fill with water before he doubled over.

That was when the convulsions started.

Ed began to cough like she'd never seen him cough before. He sat gasping, doubled over in his chair, clutching the remaining piece of doughnut so hard, it crumbled into sad little bits and toppled to the ground.

"Ed?"

Gaia started to slap him on the back.

"Ed?"

"I'm okay. I'm okay," Ed said, sitting up and pounding on his chest with his fist. "It just went down the wrong pipe."

Gaia pulled away her arm. Yes, she knew Sam had a girl-friend. And she knew that girlfriend was probably pure evil and her archnemesis to boot. But did that really make the news choke worthy? She hadn't even told Ed the part she'd *really* been worried about. The part about not remember-ing. The part about not knowing whether she'd really kissed Sam or whether she'd just raved outside his dorm like a semi-concussive psychopath, like Ella had told her she had.

Glancing back at Ed, Gaia noticed he'd finally recovered and was gathering himself to ask her something. By the look on his face, it was probably something she didn't want to answer.

"Okay, okay, spit it out," she snapped. Patience wasn't one of her strengths.

Ed blushed and looked at his feet. "So, uh, did you and Sam . . . do—do anything else?" he stammered.

Gaia could feel herself turning bright red.

"Um. Um. Well, maybe . . . I don't know," she blurted out.

"You don't know," Ed repeated.

"It's a long story," Gaia said, sucking the sticky sugar off her index finger. "I'd had a fight earlier. A bad one. And I kind of passed out, and I don't remember much. Ella's trying to make me think nothing happened."

"Oh."

Gaia looked down at her whiter-than-white hands and picked at her nonexistent fingernails.

"I haven't heard from him, though," she said, fiddling with a cuticle. "So I guess . . . I guess that means that maybe he doesn't . . . want me."

The look of sadness on Ed's face made her angry. She wasn't telling him this stuff so he could throw her a pity party. She just needed to tell someone she could trust. And she needed to let out the anger. The anger that she couldn't remember. The anger that Ella could. The anger at the idiots who'd beaten her up and made her hit her head so hard that the whole thing was a blur.

"You haven't talked to him at all?" Ed interrupted her thoughts.

Gaia sighed and looked out across the nearly deserted park. People were hurrying through it, their scarves pulled up against the cold. She and Ed were two of only a very few psychos who had stopped to enjoy the frigidity.

"I went to his dorm, but I didn't go in," she said. She didn't go on to say she had stood outside the door of Sam's building for two hours, willing him to come down and find her but never finding the courage to find him.

Ed nodded and followed her gaze to the empty fountain at the center of the park. Suddenly everything looked gray. Everything felt even colder than it was. She wanted Ed to tell her that everything was going to be okay. That Sam would get in touch with her. That it would all work out.

But Ed seemed lost in his own thoughts. Maybe she had

really freaked him out for the last time. Maybe he had finally realized what kind of lunatic he was dealing with.

As they sat munching on their remaining doughnuts, the one thing that never happened, happened. Ed was silent.

TOM
MOORE

I've made my share of sacrifices. In my line of work, nothing is more important than the job at hand—and everything else, *everything,* must be expendable. I've watched
friends die. I've given up my identity. I've risked my life too
many times to name. That's how it has had to be.

At one time, my feelings for my family fit into that
mold. Undoubtedly, I loved them, but my work was the
ultimate priority in our lives. I stoically accepted the
months away from them, the stress it put on our lives,
the danger it brought into our home. But that was when I

had Katia. Looking back, I guess I never believed anything would actually happen to her.

But it did.

When I lost Katia—when *Gaia* and I lost Katia—I suddenly realized that there was something more important to me than doing the right thing for the world. That horrible night, I knew that I also wanted to do the right thing for my daughter. And the right thing for Gaia was for me to leave her. I still believe that.

So why do I stare at the phone at least once a day—agonizing over what it would be like just to hear her voice? Why do I write her letter after letter—knowing I can never mail them? Why do I keep coming up with a new, ridiculous plan to get back to New York and take her away with me?

And why, when I am halfway around the world on a mission that could save thousands of lives, do I only seem to care about one?

STILL NO CALL

OUT THERE SOMEWHERE, SMELLING PERFECT
AND LOOKING LIKE A GODDESS IN FADED CARGO
PANTS AND A RUMPLED SWEATSHIRT.

NOT HAVING GAIA

Sam Moon rolled over onto his back, kicked his flannel sheets away from his legs, and realized he was smiling. It felt *really* odd. He blinked open his eyes and looked around his room, confused in his half-asleep haze.

Sam never woke up smiling. He usually woke up gritting his teeth—something his dentist said was due to an excess amount of anxiety. Sam never felt stressed enough during his waking hours to grind down his teeth, but apparently the normally relaxing act of sleep made him tense up.

There was, however, a very good reason for this anomaly. And her name was Gaia Moore.

The grin widened just at the thought of her name. It grew almost painful when he remembered the kiss.

He couldn't believe he'd finally done it. Finally felt those perfect lips on his. She'd been so tentative. Careful. Almost as if she'd never been kissed before. But that wasn't possible. Not a girl like her. He only wished he might have stood out among the dozens of guys she'd probably had throwing themselves at her her entire life.

Stood out, that was, if she even happened to remember the kiss at all. When she'd passed out in his arms due to severe head trauma, the chances of her recalling the most important moment of his entire life seemed pretty slim.

Sam ran a hand over his wavy, brownish red hair and squeezed his eyes shut. He'd called the hospital to find out if Gaia was okay on Friday, and they'd told him she'd been released that afternoon. So she was fine. Living. Breathing. Out there somewhere, smelling perfect and looking like a goddess in faded cargo pants and a rumpled sweatshirt.

But did she remember that he'd said he loved her? Did she even care?

Sam's stomach clenched, and he turned over onto his side. All he wanted to do was contact Gaia and make her answer his questions. And a moment later all he wanted to do was avoid her for the rest of his life so that he could save that one perfect kiss in his heart. So that he wouldn't be open to rejection. Ridicule. Laughter. From the one girl he'd ever loved.

It was, after all, very possible that she'd only kissed him back *because* of the severe head trauma. She'd probably thought she was kissing Liam Hemsworth or something.

The self-deprecation train came to a grinding halt when a loud pounding sounded at Sam's dorm-room door. He sat up straight in bed, startled by the sudden noise.

"Yeah?" Sam said.

The door flew open, and Keon Walters, Sam's physics lab partner, came storming into the room, his arms overflowing with books.

"What the—"

"Glad you got your beauty rest, Moon," Keon said, dropping the books on the floor with an ominous thud. "Did you forget the mandatory review session we had this morning?"

Sam's stomach dropped. "Uh, kind of," he said.

Keon hovered over the bed, his arms crossed over his nylon jacket as he eyed Sam with barely veiled disdain. "You better thank your lucky ass that you've got me for a partner," he said. "I told Krause your mother was at Mount Sinai with a colon thing. I laid it on so thick, I think he's sending flowers."

Sam rubbed his forehead, still trying to fully wake up. "Thanks, man," he said, eyeing the strewn books and papers lying next to his bed. They didn't look fun. "What is all that stuff?"

They both stared at the pile for a moment as apprehension seeped into Sam's veins. He had a bad feeling about this. Finally Keon sighed and lowered himself onto the end of Sam's bed. He took off his little round glasses and rubbed at his eyes. "That, my friend, would be required reading for the final."

"Please tell me you're kidding," Sam said. There was no way he could absorb that much information on top of everything they'd already learned this semester. What was Krause thinking? He was an undergrad, not a Ph.D. candidate.

Keon leveled him with a glare. "Do I look like I'm kidding?" He crouched and started to neaten the load into two piles. "I figure if we split up the work and take notes, we *might* finish about five seconds before the exam."

Sam leaned back on his pillow, marveling at how one's outlook on life could shift so drastically in the space of about five minutes.

Gaia. Kiss. Love. Happiness.

Rejection. Loneliness. Regret. Misery.

Krause. Study. Death. Hell.

"Are you coming or what?" Keon said, picking up one of the stacks of books and raising his eyebrows at Sam. He was already halfway to the door.

"Where?" Sam asked, trying in vain to clear the soft Gaia images out of his head and replace them with velocity equations.

Keon clicked his tongue and rolled his eyes as if he were talking to a petulant five-year-old. "Library," he said, shifting his weight from one leg to the other. When Sam didn't move, Keon let out an exasperated breath. "Fine. If you're going to make me be the mommy here, I'll do it."

Sam rolled his eyes. "Keon—"

"Do you or do you not have to maintain a three-point-seven to keep your scholarship?" Keon interrupted. "Because if *I* had a full ride, and I had disappeared for two days before midterms and missed about ten classes for no apparent reason, I know I'd be scared shitless enough to handcuff myself to a reading-room cubicle."

Sam just blinked at Keon, a sudden pressure squeezing his chest. He hadn't missed those classes for no reason. He'd missed them for Gaia. And he'd disappeared before midterms because he was kidnapped, which also had something to do with Gaia, though he still didn't know what. Sam had been arrested for Gaia; he'd gotten his ass kicked for Gaia; he'd almost lost his girlfriend on several occasions.

He'd almost lost his life.

Sam dropped his head into his hands. God, he was pathetic. Physics was only the worst of a long list of problems. If he lost his scholarship, his future was toast. And for what? For a girl who might or might not know he loved her. Who might or might not care. This had to stop. Or at least be put on hold.

"Get your scrawny white ass out of bed and let's go," Keon said.

"Right behind you, man," Sam said, swinging his legs over the side of the bed. He eyed his designated workload and sighed. It wouldn't be *that* bad. And if he held off on seeing Gaia until it was all over, it would make the studying that much easier. It would give him a goal to work for. And some room to concentrate.

Right now he needed all the help he could get.

DISTRACTION

By the time the digital clock next to her bed switched from 6:59 to 7:00, Heather Gannis had been staring at the red numbers for three hours and twenty-three minutes. Her eyes were dry. Her stomach was empty. But she didn't want to get out of bed. Getting out of bed meant facing her parents. Her sisters. The world in general, and she just wasn't up to it.

The past two days had been bad enough. Waiting for Sam to call. Trying to look like she wasn't waiting for Sam to call. Inconspicuously picking up the phone five times an hour just to make sure the damn thing was still working. It always was.

But now it was morning again. Two whole days had come and gone.

Still no call, even though he'd broken her heart.

And walked out on her.

And told her he was obsessed with Gaia Moore.

After everything she'd been through—everything she'd tolerated and fought against and forgiven—this could really be the end. Of SamandHeather. HeatherandSam.

The end of everything.

Heather squeezed her eyes shut, telling herself to get a grip. Self-pity wasn't something she entertained very often. Hardly ever, actually. But it was hard to avoid this time. It was the holidays. The one time of year she wasn't supposed to have to *pretend* to be happy. The one time of year when it usually came naturally. But not now. Thanks to Sam.

The only thing keeping her going was that the words had never been said. No one had said "I think we should break up," or "It's over." Sam hadn't out-and-out dumped her for Gaia. And even though she'd told him she didn't want to see him, it wasn't too late to take it back. *She* had kicked *him* out. She could take him back.

There was still hope.

There was a tentative knock at her door, but Heather ignored it, rolling onto her other side so that the clock wouldn't be able to mock her anymore. She wasn't going to move from this bed until she heard the phone ring. Or until Sam showed up at her door with flowers and possibly jewelry. Until he . . .

"No," Heather said to herself suddenly, finally sitting up and pulling her covers away from her body.

She wasn't going to wallow. She refused. Heather knew from experience that there was only one way to deal with a situation like this.

Distraction. Forced activity. She'd get dressed. Go out. See people. Maybe even buy something if she could scrounge up enough cash.

And sooner or later he would call. He had to.

He always did.

Eventually.

ROMEO

There was something very satisfying about hearing them scream. He usually let them get out one good, loud one before he covered their mouths. No one ever responded to one quick scream. They wrote it off as playing. Or a spider sighting. Or crying wolf.

And he so loved the scream.

It made him feel alive. It pumped him up.

It made the sex so much better.

He sat down on his floor and pulled out his black lock box from beneath his bed, flying through the combination with a quick three flicks of the wrist. Inside was his prized possession. The only thing he'd ever had worth locking up.

His journal. His list. His conquests.

He pulled out the tattered book with its dog-eared pages and cloth cover that was just starting to pull away from the cardboard beneath. Soon it would be time for a new book. But it would be so hard to let this one go. It was like an old friend. It knew all his secrets. All his successes. All his triumphs.

Turning to the first blank page, he rolled the end of his pen around inside his mouth, carefully composing his opening. This wasn't just a place to brag. It was literature. One day, when he was long gone, people would read these pages and know him. Know everything he was.

They would be awed.

He uncapped the pen and started his entry.

Sunday, November 28th.

Thanksgiving holiday.

It certainly was a day for giving thanks. And Regina Farrell will thank me one day. When she finally admits to herself that she'll never have anyone better . . .

GAIA THE BRAVE

YES, SHE'D JUST COMMITTED HERSELF
TO AN ACTUAL SOCIAL FUNCTION.

BASIC GET-AWAY-FROM-ME
SIGNALS

Gaia stood on line in the cafeteria on Monday afternoon between two groups of people who couldn't possibly have been more irritating. The FOHs—short for Friends of Heather—and the turtleneck-wearing jock boys. If there was ever a time to cave in to modern technology and use an iPod, this was it. Words were being wasted all around her, and she would have given anything for a nice pair of earphones and a lot of guitar-type noise.

"Omigod!" one FOH squealed. "You totally should have been at Cafe Wha? last night. The hottest guy opened for Fearless. He was like a Lenny-Rob hybrid."

"Not possible," FOH number two said, sniffing a bowl of Jell-O in a perfect imitation of a rabbit and replacing the bowl on the counter. "God couldn't possibly have blessed anyone with genes like that."

"He's playing again in two weeks," said FOH number three, the one with the biggest hair ever to spring from a scalp. "Come and see for yourself."

"I am so there," FOH number two promised, placing her nearly empty tray in front of the register. "*I* was at the Melody last night, and you . . ."

FOH number two trailed off as she glanced in Gaia's

direction and noticed her not-staring. Her top lip actually curled up, and she huffed as she turned her back on Gaia, adjusting her tight leather jacket.

"Do you *see* what she's eating?" FOH number one sneered. All three FOHs turned to glare at Gaia's tray. Meatballs. Mashed-potato-like substance. Bowl of Jell-O not sniffed by FOH number two. Roll with tons of butter patties.

"Do you want some creamed corn, hon?" the lunch lady asked in a pleasant voice.

"Yeah," Gaia answered, mostly to disgust the FOHs. It worked. They all exchanged a very unoriginal look of grossed-outedness, paid for their food, and scurried away.

"There you go, hon," the big lady behind the counter said, heaping on the corn. She smiled at Gaia like she always did, and Gaia attempted smiling back. It didn't work, of course, but it was worth the try. Every student in this school might hate her, but at least she was universally loved by the lunch ladies. Gaia was pretty sure she was the only one who actually ate their food.

Gaia handed the woman at the register a crumpled ball of cash and automatically headed for the table she and Ed usually shared. Back corner, underneath the graph that broke down the four food groups. She was about to cut left when someone blocked her path.

This was so not the time for anyone to be starting up with her. Not on a Monday on which she'd woken up with a headache and the knowledge that Sam hadn't contacted her once all weekend.

Actually, maybe someone *should* start with her. She could use a scapegoat. "You're a brave girl," a slow, drawly voice said.

Gaia looked up into the deepest brown pair of eyes she'd ever seen. Spiky, messy hair. Sideburns. Expensive flannel. Not threatening. Definitely not asking for a beating.

"Are you going to move?" Gaia asked, shifting her tray slightly. Bad idea. Her plate of meatballs slid precariously close to the edge, taking everything with it. It was going over, and there was nothing she could do. More public spillage for the Spillage Queen.

"Careful," Sideburns said, righting the tray with lightning-quick reflexes. The kid in the chair next to them pulled himself a little closer to his table.

"Uh, thanks," Gaia told Sideburns. This was exactly the type of situation Gaia attempted to avoid at all costs. Was she supposed to try to converse with the guy, try to ignore him and look cool, try to . . . *flirt?* It was all too much for her socially impaired self to handle, so she attempted to move again. Unfortunately, he was still holding on to her tray.

"Aren't you going to ask me why I think you're so brave?" he asked, ducking his chin in an attempt to make eye contact. What was this guy's deal? Was he immune to basic get-away-from-me signals?

"No," Gaia said. Exasperation. There. He had to get that.

He released her tray, crossing his arms over his rather broad chest but not moving out of the way. Gaia turned around to head back in the other direction, but a complicated mélange of backpacks, chairs, and legs blocked her path. So much for the ignoring-and-looking-cool option.

When she turned around again, Sideburns was grinning. "It's just that in the three and a third years I've been here, I've never seen anyone eat Greta's meatballs."

Oh, how very original. "There's a first time for everything," Gaia said. She took a step toward him, hoping he wasn't going to force her to take him down with a quick flick of her foot to his shin. He seemed harmless enough, but if she didn't eat soon, this Monday was going to go from suckfest to hell pit in a matter of seconds.

"Okay, okay." Sideburns relented, turning sideways to let her pass. But as he did he flicked a little piece of pink paper out of his pocket and dropped it on Gaia's tray. It had black writing on it, and the only word she could make out without actually appearing to be interested was *music*.

"Having a little party tonight," he said, holding up his hands to give her more room. "You should show."

The irrational part of Gaia's brain couldn't believe that someone had just asked her to a party. Her. Public enemy number one. Other than Ed and Mary, no one had asked her to do anything at all since she'd arrived in New York. Except die, of course. The rational part of her brain formulated a sentence and sent it to her voice box.

"I'd rather sing 'Copacabana' in front of the entire school," she said, moving past him.

Sideburns laughed. "I'll rent a karaoke machine!" he called after her.

Gaia never smiled on Mondays. But if she did, the exchange might have been worthy of one.

SCREW HIM

As Gaia lowered herself into the chair across from Ed, he plucked a little piece of bright pink paper from her over-loaded tray.

"'Come one. Come all,'" Ed read aloud. "'Free beer. Free music. Free love.'" He chuckled and placed the tiny flyer on the table between them. "Going hippie on me, Gaia?"

She lifted one shoulder as she took a swig of her soda. "Some guy gave it to me," she said, jabbing a meatball with her fork. Ed's stomach turned over, and not just because she was actually consuming a cafeteria-made meat substance.

Another guy?

More guys?

Didn't he have enough to deal with?

"Who?" Ed asked, trying to keep the psychotic jealousy out of his voice. It was still there, but if she noticed, she didn't show a sign. She just chomped on another meatball as her eyes scanned the room.

"Him," she said finally, pointing with her fork across the large cafeteria at Tim Racenello. Abercrombie & Fitch boy. Skier. Former friend. Definitely charming. Damn.

"Are you going to go?" Ed asked, pushing his chicken noodle soup sans chicken—a cafeteria specialty—around with his spoon. *Please say you're not going to go. Please say you're not going to go.*

"Ed. Come on. No," she said.

Cool.

"I was kind of thinking about going to see Sam tonight," she said, actually sounding tentative. "You know, find out . . . if there's anything to find out."

Not cool.

"Well, I'll go if you'll go," Ed offered, putting down his spoon and laying his hands flat on the table. The action helped to keep him from sinking into the bottomless black pit that had opened beneath his chair at the sound of Sam's name. Amazing. It was just one little syllable. Sam. More like a grunt than a name.

Yet it held so much power.

"Go where?" Gaia asked, confused. Ed felt his delirious mind step off its rambling path and snap into the now. He wondered if she thought he was offering to go to Sam's with her. Not likely.

"The party," Ed said, forcing a smirk. "Focus, G."

Gaia froze with a forkful of mashed potatoes halfway into her mouth. It took her a couple of seconds to decide whether to eat or talk. She did both.

"You want to go to this thing," she said as soon as she'd swallowed. Statement. Disbelieving statement. When had he lost the moniker of Ed "Shred" Fargo, party animal? As if he really had to ask that question.

"Tim's pretty cool," Ed told her, hoping against hope she would go against every fiber of her being and agree to go with him. "We used to hang out before my hanging involved the chair."

Gaia's gaze flicked in Tim's direction. "He stopped hanging out with you after . . ." She let the sentence trail off, probably because she still didn't know how Ed had ended up without leg power.

"No," Ed answered the unfinished question. "I stopped hanging out with him. I stopped hanging out with a lot of people." He immediately felt his spirits start to wane. He was coming dangerously close to losing the nonchalant thing he'd gone to great lengths to develop. Clearing his throat, Ed pushed all melancholy thoughts aside. He'd rejoined the social world a long time ago. There was no need to dwell on the dark past. The now demanded his full attention.

"So are you going to go with me or not?" Ed asked, downing a spoonful of his now cold soup. Somehow it tasted better cold. Took the edge off.

"I don't know, Ed . . ."

She was thinking of Sam. He knew it. He could tell by the regretful little cloud in her eyes. Like she was thinking of him and ashamed of herself for thinking of him. There was only one way to make Gaia agree to party with him. The one way he could get Gaia to do almost anything. Get her angry. Or at least righteously indignant.

"Sam hasn't called, has he?" Ed asked, feeling like the soap scum wad in the corner of his shower. The one with the black mildew gathering on it.

Her eyes flashed. Score one for the soap scum. "No," she said flatly.

"Then why are you planning on going over there?" Ed asked casually, pushing his tray away. It hit Gaia's and moved it an inch over the lip of the table toward her.

"I'm not," she said, pushing her own tray back. Ed's went two and a half inches off the end. At least.

"Then go to the party," Ed said, pushing their trays back

so that they were centered evenly on the table. He laced his fingers together and rested his elbows on the arms of his wheelchair. "Screw him."

Gaia blinked. Ed could practically see the little consonants and vowels that made up his words sinking into her brain.

"Fine," she said. "Let's go."

FIRST EVER MONDAY SMILE

He was in her English class. How convenient. She'd never noticed him before, but there he was. Front row, window seat. Good view and a fast escape route. And he was eating a Hostess cupcake. That was comforting. At least he had good taste in food.

Gaia made her way across the room, her battered sneakers squeaking loudly on the linoleum floor. He didn't see her, and she didn't exactly have an opening line, so she dropped her bag on his desk with a half flop, half clatter.

If he was startled, he hid it well. He chewed, swallowed, and looked up. His eyebrows arched when he saw her, but he recovered quickly and leaned back in his chair, smiling up at her. He had chocolate stuck to his two front teeth.

"If it isn't Gaia the Brave," he said, running his tongue quickly along his bottom teeth to clear the sugary goo. It didn't help the top part of his mouth, but Gaia wasn't about to point that out.

"Got another one?" she asked, pushing a strand of hair behind her ear. It fell right back into place, and she didn't touch it. Pointless. As were all attempts at grooming in Gaia's book.

Sideburns Tim experienced momentary confusion marked by a quick squint. "Another what?"

"Cupcake," Gaia said, shifting her feet. That was when she noticed that Heather Gannis was sitting two rows behind Sideburns Tim, shooting Gaia a glare that was now so familiar to her, Gaia could probably have mimicked it in her sleep. She looked Heather directly in the eye and spoke to Tim. "If you give me a cupcake, I'll come to your little party."

Heather visibly paled. Even her normally lined lips were white. It was all Gaia could do to keep from breaking the no-smiling-on-Mondays rule. It was an odd Monday when that almost happened twice.

Sideburns Tim pulled a single wrapped cupcake out of his bag and tossed it at Gaia. She caught it in one hand without even blinking.

"I don't know if it's your lucky day or mine," he said with a smirk that displayed a small dimple just behind a very light layer of stubble. Probably sexy in some circles. In Heather's circle, from the look of pure horror on the girl's face.

"It's yours," Gaia said. His smirk deepened. She pocketed her cupcake and walked to the back of the room, allowing herself a brief moment of pride. It had been a long time since she'd come out with a comeback line she liked on the spot and not approximately three and a half hours later, when it was useless.

The fury was coming off Heather in waves. As Gaia took her seat, she wondered if Heather had spoken to Sam this weekend—if she knew what had happened between Gaia and her beloved boyfriend. If she did know, Gaia really wished the girl would clue her in. But somehow Gaia doubted that was going to happen.

In fact, since she hadn't received any idle death threats, Gaia figured Heather was thus far clueless. Maybe even more clueless than Gaia was. Gaia at least knew she'd been in Sam's room. Worn Sam's clothes. Even if there had been no touching of the lips, she was sure Heather would throw a Springer-worthy psycho tantrum if she knew what Gaia knew.

Leaning back in her chair, Gaia tore open the packaging on her cupcake and propped her knees up on the desk in front of her. Sure, Sam hadn't called. Yes, she'd just committed herself to an actual social function. And yes, she was living with a heinous woman who wore shitty clothes and bad perfume.

But the thought that she actually knew something about Sam that Heather didn't was the thing that brought the first ever full-on Monday smile to Gaia Moore's lips.

SICK OF EVERYTHING

Heather Gannis was having a very bad day, and trying to keep herself from screaming in the middle of English class wasn't making it any easier. Her boyfriend was avoiding her, her best friends had all gone out the night before without her and couldn't stop talking about it, and the only reason she hadn't gone was because she had fully expected said boyfriend to call her, which he, of course, hadn't.

What if he'd spent the weekend with Gaia? What if he'd left Heather's apartment and gone directly to wherever the reject holed herself up? After all this time and everything they'd been through, had Gaia finally won?

Heather traced the pink line down the side of her paper with her pen, pushing so hard, she tore a hole in the page. She was getting so sick of everything. Sick of Sam's avoidance-of-conflict policy. Sick of feeling unsure. Sick of friends who dropped money on cab rides and bars like they were a necessity. Sick, most of all, of Gaia Moore.

Mr. MacGregor sauntered into the room and immediately started passing out pop quiz papers. Lovely. What kind of person gave a quiz the day after Thanksgiving weekend? It was like the man lived to see students suffer. What next? Was her hair going to start falling out in clumps?

Heather adjusted the collar on her itchy wool sweater and pushed her thick brown mane back behind her shoulders. Whatever she did, she couldn't let her misery show. She needed to constantly keep the three Cs in high gear. Cool, calm, collected. Otherwise there would be questions from her legion of followers. And questions, at this point, were something she couldn't handle.

Missy Ryan handed the quiz papers back, and Heather

took one and passed the stack along. Nothing on the page looked remotely familiar. Her body temperature skyrocketed. Heather turned the paper over with a slap and took a long breath. She had to chill. Now.

She hazarded a glance over her shoulder at Gaia. She, of course, was busily scratching away at her paper, oblivious to the world around her. The girl practically looked happy. That never happened. Something in the cosmic balance of Heather's universe had shifted, and she didn't like it.

Tim asking Gaia to tonight's party was the last straw. Heather faced forward again and twisted a lock of hair around her finger violently, yanking at her scalp. The only thing that had kept Heather going this weekend was looking forward to tonight's little shindig. She'd talked it up to all her friends, making sure they would all be there. There was nothing better than a free party with free dancing and free alcohol, even when her boyfriend was freakishly AWOL.

But a party with Gaia Moore was another story.

A party with Gaia Moore was something to avoid at all costs.

FROM: smoon@alloymail.com
TO: gaia13@alloymail.com
TIME: 2:45 P.M.
RE: Thanksgiving

Gaia,
I still can't believe you were actually here. I can't stop
thinking about you and when I'm going to see you
again. I just
«Delete»

FROM: smoon@alloymail.com
TO: gaia13@alloymail.com
TIME: 2:46 P.M.
RE: Thanksgiving
Gaia,
I hope you're okay. The doctors said you would be, but
I hated to leave you, anyway. I haven't written before
because—
«Delete»

FROM: smoon@alloymail.com
TO: gaia13@alloymail.com
TIME: 2:47 P.M.
RE: Thanksgiving
Gaia,
Do you even remember what happened between us?
I remember every detail. Every smell. Every touch.
Everything. If you don't remember . . . I'll probably die,
actually.
«Delete»

FROM: smoon@alloymail.com
TO: gaia13@alloymail.com
TIME: 2:48 P.M.
RE: Thanksgiving
Gaia,
Thanks for an . . . interesting Thanksgiving. I'll never forget it. I want to see you, but I have finals right now and I really have to concentrate on that. Can I call you when I'm done?
Sam
«Send»

KIBBLE

Gaia really wanted a dog. As she stood outside the fence that surrounded the dog run in Washington Square Park, watching the little pink tongues and the little padded feet and the little twitching noses, she wanted nothing else more.

Imagine having something in your life that lived for nothing but you. Imagine unconditional love. Imagine a friend that could hide no secrets. A friend that couldn't hurt you, who would protect you at all costs, and all you had to do was throw him some kibble every once in a while. A friend who, yeah, smelled bad but hung out by the door every day just to see your face.

Gaia grinned. She could have just described Ed Fargo.

She gripped the fence with her frozen hands and watched a scruffy little mutt with a black body and brown ears chase a squirrel out through a hole in the other side of the fence.

Of course if she did get a dog, she'd probably figure out how to drive it away. She seemed to be very skilled at that. But maybe, just maybe, she only repelled humans.

With a huge sigh Gaia leaned back her head and watched the steam of her breath dance up into the air. After ten minutes of doing the go-in-don't-go-in boogie in front of Sam's dorm, she felt good to be momentarily still in the presence of the frenzied mayhem in front of her. For once she felt like the one sane being in a twenty-yard radius. Funny how she had to be in the company of a bunch of ankle-biting, loudly yelping animals that sniffed each other's butts in order to feel normal.

"Sadie! Sadie! Over here!" someone called, causing a little collie to look up from its dirt inhaling.

"Crystal!"

"Katie!"

"Buffy!"

"Aaaahhh! Get it off me! Get it off me!"

"Katie! Katie, no! Bad dog!"

Gaia smirked as she found Katie at the far side of the run, outside the fence. She was a beautiful golden retriever who had latched onto some suit's shoelace and was pulling back, her four feet planted firmly on the ground.

"Katie!"

"Gaia!"

"Katie! Stop it now!"

"Gaia?"

"*Gaia?*"

A hand landed on her shoulder, and Gaia spun around so fast, her hair whipped into her eyes and temporarily blinded her. She brought her hands to her face and shoved the hair away.

"Hey," a familiar voice said. "This is some exciting after-school entertainment."

Mary. Gaia felt a little stirring in her stomach at the memory of her last encounter with Mary Moss. And everything that had come after it. The cocaine, followed up by the cold, the beating, the theft, the explosion, the blood, and then all the stuff she couldn't quite remember.

"I can see how it doesn't live up to *your* standards of excitement," Gaia replied. She wanted to take back the words a moment later when she saw the hurt flash through Mary's eyes, but she didn't. Gaia was bad at relationships and even worse at apologies. She turned back to the dogs and focused on a patch of ground in front of her.

Mary stepped up beside her, shoving her hands in the pockets of her long wool coat. "Guess I deserved that," she said tentatively, seeming to stare at the same spot of dirt as if it could reveal Gaia's thoughts. "Did you get my letter?"

"Yeah," Gaia said. The letter had explained how Mary had a serious problem. How she wanted to get clean. How she wanted to get clean for Gaia. And Gaia was happy for Mary. She really was. But the whole doing-it-for-Gaia was just a little too much pressure, even if it was accompanied by a lot of chocolate. "I got it," she said finally.

"And?" Mary asked. She reached out and laced her pink-gloved fingers through the fence. Her fingers looked very small and very thin. Gaia looked into Mary's questioning, vulnerable eyes.

"And . . . I think it's . . . good that you want to, you know, quit," Gaia said. Damn, she was articulate. But she didn't know what she was supposed to do or say. And it seemed like one of those situations that called for exactly the right thing. Gaia was pretty sure she'd never said exactly the right thing in her life.

Mary took a deep breath, shifting her feet so that the gravel and silt crunched beneath her boots. "Well, I'm looking into some stuff, like NA and . . . stuff," she said, stumbling over her own words. "My parents are helping. I, uh . . . I told them everything; I figure I can't do this without them, and besides completely freaking out and crying and the whole deal, they're actually being really cool. But I need your help with a very important step in the clean-Mary plan."

"What's that?" Gaia asked. She noticed for the first time that her friend's pale skin was paler than normal, her unruly red hair oddly flat. The girl needed that unconditional love Gaia was longing for moments ago. She needed it maybe more than Gaia did.

"The good, clean fun part," Mary said with a smile that held just a trace of the Mary-mischief Gaia had learned to love.

"Good, clean fun, huh?" Gaia said with a smirk. Little did poor Mary know that Gaia wasn't exactly an expert on the subject of fun. She wasn't even a novice. Up until she met Mary, she'd been pretty sure she was, in fact, immune to fun. Still, she couldn't exactly let Mary down. It was time to throw the girl some kibble.

"I think I can handle that," Gaia said, pulling her jacket closer to her body and shivering slightly as a breeze fought its way past her collar and down her back. She looked Mary directly in the eye. "I just have one question," she said, causing the smile to disappear from Mary's face. "How do I know you're telling the truth? That you really want to do this."

Mary gripped the fence harder, and her face became

pale. For a moment Gaia thought her friend might faint, but she held her own. Seconds later, her features softened and a little color returned to her cheeks.

"Because," she said, her voice just slightly shaky. She cleared her throat and tossed back her hair. "Because I'm going to stay here with you and watch these stupid dogs." Mary's brow wrinkled slightly as she glanced around at the assembled owners with their steaming coffees and their leashes wrapped around their hands and wrists. "And you are going to explain to me what, exactly, is supposed to be interesting about this."

Okay, so maybe the girl was sincere. Gaia tilted her head toward the fence, inviting Mary to come closer. When their foreheads were practically touching the cold metal, Gaia brought her tingling cheek close to Mary's in conspiratorial spy fashion.

"See that dog right there?" Gaia asked, pointing out Katie, who was now terrorizing Sadie the collie by barking at her and chasing her every time she sat down. Mary nodded and smiled. "Keep an eye on that one," Gaia said. "I think you'll like her."

READY AND WILLING

"COME ON, GAIA," ELLA SAID, PLACING HER
NAPKIN ON THE TABLE. SHE WAS ALL GLEE.
"TELL GEORGE ABOUT YOUR LITTLE SAM."

The library was pretty. The books? Gorgeous. The leather chair felt like a little piece of cloud. But the people were all very uninteresting. Bland. Ugly, even.

None of them were Gaia Moore.

Sam was fully aware that at least three students in the East Asian Library were staring at him with a disturbed sort of curiosity. Why shouldn't they be? He was kicked back in a big green chair, his feet up on the table in front of him, about ten large textbooks piled around him—and he was smiling like an idiot. Like he was lying on a massage table on a white beach in the Caribbean.

It was almost finals week, and Sam Moon was summer-vacation giddy.

"What are you on, man?" whispered Sam's suite mate, Mike Suarez, leaning across the table. "And can I have some?"

"Shhh!" Keon refused to let anyone get out a sentence without scolding them. Sam and Mike both glanced at him, then smirked.

"Nope. Definitely not. None for you," Sam said, adjusting the physics book on his lap. Out of the corner of his eye he saw Keon shake his head in frustration, but the kid was just going to have to deal. Sam couldn't render himself mute for two weeks' worth of studying and exam taking.

Mike's whole forehead scrunched up, and he looked like he was suddenly reconsidering their living arrangements. "Well, at least cut the smiley face act. You're freaking people out, and we can't be driven from East Asia."

"Right," Sam said, attempting to force down the corners of his mouth. "No problem." For a split second he tried to concentrate on his book, but then he found himself looking around the room, Gaia thoughts flitting in and out of his mind. The East Asian room was the most comfortable, quiet study nook in the library, but only a select few people knew about it. Mike had found out about the cozy chairs and relatively private tables from one of his frat brothers and had let Sam and Keon in on the secret. Today they'd shown up early enough to stake a claim in the prime corner, right at the end of the stacks.

Sam had promised Keon he was ready to cram. Get down to business. Study like it was going out of style.

But he couldn't stop thinking about Gaia.

He could still feel her hands on his shoulders. Her tongue grazing his lips. Her—

"Is it Heather?" Mike whispered, causing Sam's little fantasy world to disappear in a poof of guilt-tinged smoke.

"Is what Heather?" Sam asked, glancing over his shoulder. Had she found him at the NYU library? Had she tracked him down? Somehow Sam wouldn't have been surprised to see her sauntering through the room, ready to grab his arm and force an in-depth analysis of the big blowout.

"The I-just-got-me-some look on your face," Mike said with a grin.

"Shhhhhh!" Keon exploded.

"Give me a break," Mike hissed. He looked back at Sam. "Did you and Heather get busy last night or what?"

Sam sighed in relief and righted himself in his chair. *Getting busy* wasn't exactly the phrase he would have used to describe what had gone on between him and Heather over Thanksgiving. Before he'd walked out on her. Before he'd gone back to his dorm. Before he'd found Gaia there. Waiting for him.

"Not exactly," he said, pushing himself back in his seat.

"Then what is it, Moon?" Mike asked, his brown eyes twinkling. "Some other girl?"

Sam cleared his throat. "I thought we were studying," he said, highlighting a random sentence on the glossy page of his physics text. He could feel that Mike was still staring at him, so he kept pretending to read until the kid gave up and flopped back in his chair, the cushions letting out a little hissing sound as air escaped through the seams.

Swallowing hard, Sam forced his eyes to the top of the page and started to read for real. The mention of Heather had brought him back down to earth, hard. Yes, they'd fought. She'd told him to leave. But he knew Heather, and he knew she said a lot of things she didn't mean. Which meant that she was still technically his girlfriend. Which meant that Thanksgiving night in his dorm, he'd cheated on her. With the one person she hated more than anyone else on the planet.

Sam had no clue what to do about Heather. He had even less of a clue how to proceed with Gaia. She wasn't a normal ask-her-out-on-a-date-and-don't-forget-to-bring-flowers type of girl. That had been proven many times over since the first time he'd met her.

With a deep breath, Sam pushed Heather and Gaia out of his mind and picked up his notebook, flipping it open to the first page of notes.

Suddenly he was glad to have something as important and all consuming as finals to command his attention.

ELLA'S SALVATION

One little e-mail message was all it took.

Even after Heather. Even after Marco. After David. After her father. After every deranged, psychotic, evil, slimy, grime-covered, bad-cologne-wearing midnight assailant.

Even after dealing with each and every one of these hateful beings, Gaia could quite honestly say she had never felt so much rage before in her life.

And from the look on Ella Niven's face, the woman was just smart enough to know that this rage was directed at her.

"You lied to me," Gaia said. There was no surprise in her voice. Only the rage. Ella's face went white for a moment underneath her layers of foundation and powder. She backed away from the foul-smelling sludge she was frying on the stove and crossed her arms over her chest. Gaia wondered if Ella was remembering when Gaia punched her. Remembering and fearing.

God, she hoped she was.

"I don't appreciate your tone, Gaia," she said, wiping her hands on her ruffled apron.

"I was with someone on Thanksgiving," Gaia said, trying desperately to ignore the burning, acrid stench that was assailing her nostrils and choking her airways. Her eyes were watering, and she suddenly registered the fact that Ella was actually cooking—or attempting an unreasonable facsimile thereof. She never cooked. Was the woman actually trying to kill her?

Ella took a deep breath—how she managed it, Gaia had no idea—and smoothed her blazing red hair back from her face. "And how, exactly, does that make me a liar?"

"You told me there was no one there, at the hospital,"

Gaia said, leaning onto the counter in front of her, her veins throbbing in her forehead. Ella had hated Gaia from the moment she'd first walked through the door. Gaia had picked up on it immediately and hated the woman right back. But why did Ella feel the need to take every single thing away from her? Gaia had never even met her before she came to Perry Street, but the woman was brimming with malice. Why?

Ella's amphibian green eyes narrowed into angry slits. "That's right," she said calmly. "There was no one with you at the hospital. God only knows what you did before then. I did tell you they found you outside some dorm, babbling about someone named Sam." She ran her fingernail along the side of her mouth, like a cat who'd just finished off the forbidden goldfish. "Is that who you're talking about?" she said with a light laugh. "Maybe he'd just kicked you out of his room."

There was a moment without air. No intake whatsoever. A moment when Gaia's heart felt like it was about to burst open from the pressure.

Her first inclination was to launch herself at Ella and make her take it back.

Her second inclination was to entertain the idea that the woman might be right.

That was the standard Gaia-as-masochist inclination.

But no. It wasn't possible. Sam's e-mail had said thanks.

He'd said he wanted to see her again. She was no relationship expert, but if he'd booted her, he wouldn't be saying
that. Right?

And he wouldn't have left her outside in the cold, bruised
and woozy and half comatose.

Not Sam.

Gaia rounded the counter and, in one long stride, got
within centimeters of Ella's pointy little face. She was quite
satisfied when Ella flinched.

"I swear to you, Ella, if you don't tell me the truth right
now—"

There was a door slam, and two pairs of eyes darted to
the kitchen entry.

"George," Ella whispered, sounding like she was utter-
ing the name of salvation.

"I'm home!" George shouted from the foyer. "What
smells so interesting?"

Gaia felt her muscles untighten, and she pulled away
reluctantly. The threats were going to have to wait for another
day unless she wanted to explain to George why she'd kicked
his wife's skinny ass as his homecoming present.

HEART-TO-HEART A LA GEORGE

"As soon as you're all washed up, come back down for dinner!" Ella called cheerily as Gaia slammed her way out of the kitchen and into the hallway, the heinous smell still clinging to her skin. George was shaking out his coat and hanging it up in the closet by the door. Gaia paused. He looked tired. Almost older.

"Hi, George," she said, going for the closet before he had a chance to close it. She pulled out her flimsy jacket and started to put it on, hoping he was so tired and jet-lagged, he wouldn't feel like starting up a conversation. She could talk to him about his trip later. She had to get out of this house, pronto.

Out of the corner of her eye she saw George's already wrinkled brow crease even deeper with concern. Damn. So close.

"Where are you going?" he asked, eyeing the arm that was half in, half out of the sleeve. "Aren't we about to eat? Ella told me this morning that she was going to give cooking a whirl."

He inhaled, and Gaia was gratified to see the tears spring to his eyes, not that he'd ever acknowledge them. "She was very excited," he said evenly.

"I'm not really hungry," Gaia said. She had been starving, but the stench, Sam's e-mail, and the almost fight took that right out of her.

George sighed and shook his head slowly. His eyes looked all heavy and apprehensive, like he was a doctor about to tell a couple he'd done everything he could, but he just couldn't save their kid.

"Gaia, Ella told me all about what happened while I was away. I know things are hard for you right now—"

The squirming started immediately. Exactly how much had Ella told the poor old guy? Gaia wasn't certain how much his creaky little ticker could take. And she'd hate to be a cause of stress to George. Any more than she already was, anyway.

"With your father gone and your mother . . ."

Gaia's eyes focused on a tiny spiderweb in the corner behind George's head. Heart-to-hearts weren't her thing.

"And after this whole Christmas . . . I mean—" He brought a hand to his forehead and laughed at himself. "Thanksgiving mess . . ."

Apparently George wasn't very good at them, either.

"Well, I just want you to know that if there's anything you ever need to talk about . . . whether it's boys—"

"Stop." The word was out of Gaia's mouth like a shot. George's face went from pink to crimson, and Gaia immediately felt guilty. "Sorry." She pulled on the hem of her baggy black sweater resolutely, inhaled, held back a choking cough, and looked him in the eye.

"Let's eat."

PATHETICALLY UNSORDID

There was a white blob, a reddish brown blob, and a pile of what looked like dried sticks. Gaia gulped her water as Ella related the fascinating details of her day of beauty at Aveda. George kept nodding as if he knew exactly what his wife was talking about, but Gaia wasn't even sure what exfoliaters and sloughing cream were—which just reminded her what a pathetic excuse for a female she was. This had to be over soon.

"So, Gaia," Ella said, spooning a heap of the white mush into her mouth as she finished a harrowing tale of an acid peel gone awry—a story that suddenly made Gaia feel *glad* she was a pathetic excuse for a female. Ella licked her lips daintily and touched a napkin to her mouth. She did this after every single bite she took. It was starting to drive Gaia insane.

"What?" Gaia said tersely.

"I don't suppose you would want to tell us how *your* day went, would you?" Ella asked, shooting George a look as if seeking affirmation that she'd now officially done her duty. She'd acted interested.

"Not really," Gaia answered, pushing at her pile of sticks with her fork. A few toppled over the rim of her plate onto the white linen tablecloth. Ella glared at them, but Gaia didn't make a move to clean it up. Fewer sticks for her stomach.

George shifted in his seat slightly, gearing up to talk. Gaia silently prayed he wouldn't bring up the whole boy topic again.

"Are you making friends at that school yet?" he asked, bravely taking a bite from the reddish brown blob. The flinch was almost indiscernible.

"Oh, she's making friends," Ella said, her eyes on her food as a little satisfied smile played about her lips. "Just not at that school."

Gaia felt an angry blush color her cheeks, and she shot Ella a glare that should have turned her to vapor. In a perfect world. In this world, Ella just smirked back at her.

"Really?" George looked intrigued. Gaia shrugged. Like she was really going to share. There was nothing *to* share.

Not yet. At least not with these people. Ella, after all, still quite possibly knew more than she did, a thought that did nothing for her already squirming stomach.

"Come on, Gaia," Ella said, placing her napkin on the table. She was all glee. "Tell George about your little Sam." The way she said the last three words made Gaia come unconscionably close to lifting her end of the table so that the entire meal slid into Ella's lap.

George smiled and looked from Ella to Gaia. The guy was definitely ready and willing. To hear what? That she might or might not have kissed the boyfriend of a girl she hated who also happened to be the most popular girl in school? That was sure to make George beam with pride. Not that Gaia cared.

"I have to go," Gaia said, standing up and letting her napkin slide from her lap onto the floor.

Ella's freshly waxed eyebrows arched. Gaia wondered if they colored those during her day of beauty, too, along with her fake red hair. "Don't tell me you have somewhere to be."

"Ella," George said in a tone that came close to a warning. Apparently he'd finally picked up on her ever sarcastic tone.

Gaia looked into Ella's eyes and paused. There wasn't just surprise and mockery there. There was something else. A guarded, defensive kind of look. Jealousy? Was that even possible?

"Party," she said, just to gauge the reaction. Ella blinked, and her expression went flat. Then she quickly looked away and picked up her water glass with one hand while fiddling with the gold pendant that always hung in her cleavage with the other. It *was* jealousy. Interesting.

"On a Monday?" George said. He looked at Ella as if he wasn't sure whether or not this was acceptable. Like Ella knew anything about propriety. Unfortunately, Ella was too preoccupied trying to look unfazed, and she didn't notice her own husband's stare for help. Gaia decided to put him out of his misery, if only so she could get out of here and put herself out of her own.

"I won't be late, George," she said, forcing a tight, hopefully reassuring, but probably just disturbing smile. She hoped he would just hurry up and tell her it was all right. If he didn't, she would sneak through the window, anyway, but it was much less trouble to go out through the front door.

"Okay," he said. "But you be careful out there. You never know—"

But Gaia was already down the hall and halfway up the steps to the relative privacy of her own room.

WHAT ED TRIED ON

One pair of corduroys
One pair of jeans
Two flannels
One V-necked shirt
A Hawaiian print button-down
Two baseball caps
One fisherman's cap
A pair of sunglasses
Two pairs of sneakers
One pair of in-line skates (for kicks)
Three T-shirts
One pocket watch
One fedora

WHAT HEATHER TRIED ON

Three pairs of jeans
Five of her sister's skirts
One skirt of her own
Three pairs of earrings
Her mother's pearls
One headband
Two barrettes
Three colors of lipstick, all in the brown family
One pair of ribbed tights
Four pairs of shoes—one clunky, one practical, two deadly
Two belts
Five blouses
One sweater
Two perfumes
Five bags
One choker

WHAT GAIA TRIED ON

One T-shirt
One hooded sweatshirt
One pair of cargo pants
One pair of sneakers
One blue sock
One black sock
One piece of Bubble Yum

SHOWTIME

Heather Gannis was not a stalker. She might have looked like one, hanging out in the shadows on the corner of Fifth Avenue and Tenth Street—across the street from Sam's dorm—intently staring past the traffic on Tenth to keep a constant watch on the door. But she definitely was not a stalker. She was a girl with a boyfriend who was ignoring her. And that merited certain covert action.

Okay, certain stalkerish covert action.

Heather rubbed her gloved hands together and cupped them in front of her mouth, blowing into her palms. Her toes were tingly in her sexy-yet-unprotective shoes, and goose bumps were fighting their way to existence even under her thick wool coat.

Where was he? Sam was generally a nice guy. Couldn't he cut a nonstalker some slack?

The glass door of the dorm swung open just as a stiff wind blew directly into Heather's eyes, stinging them painfully and blurring her vision. There was a tall person-blob making his way down Fifth toward her, bending into the wind with his books tucked under his arm. It had to be him. Heather couldn't see his face clearly, but she could feel it in her gut. And the butterflies surrounding her heart started to do a nervous little dance.

It was showtime.

She tossed her hair from her shoulders. Pressed her lips together. Straightened her posture. And started to search through her purse.

He had to see her first. That was key in the whole non-stalker plan.

Searching. Searching. He was coming across Tenth now. Searching. But there wasn't much more to search through. He was walking. Walking. He was right there. Her heart started to pound, and the search for nothing became more frantic. He was . . . He was . . . He was passing her by.

What?

"Sam?"

He stopped and turned around slowly, his whole body rigid. His face registered surprise, but the rest of him was pure discomfort.

Good.

"Heather," he said. He was probably expecting another fight. Or at least a reprimand for not having returned her e-mails and phone calls. He was in for a surprise.

"Hi!" she said brightly, walking up to him and giving him a quick kiss on the cheek. His stubbly face was still warm from inside, and as mad as she was at him, part of her just wanted to cuddle into him and not let go. Instead she pulled away quickly, pleased that he looked shocked. "Where are you going?" she asked.

It took him a moment to realize it was his turn to speak. "Library," he said. His gaze flicked over her outfit, and it was all Heather could do to keep from grinning. Now he would ask her where *she* was going, and she could say—

"I'd better get going," he said.

Wait. That wasn't his line.

"Uh . . ."

And that definitely wasn't hers.

Sam's face creased with regret, and he shoved his free hand into his pocket. "Listen," he said, backing away slightly.

"I know we have to talk, but finals are next week, and I just got slammed with all this work—"

"I'm going to a party," Heather heard herself say. At least she thought it was her who had spoken. Her voice had come out sounding more like a plastic doll's with a voice box and a string.

"Good," Sam said. He couldn't care less.

What was going on here? When had she lost control of the situation? And why did it suddenly seem like all of the bundled-up passersby on the sidewalk were mocking her? Laughing at her. Telling her to wake up and see that it was all over.

Sam was on the move again. Backing away to freedom. "Well, I really have to . . ."

And then Heather was struck with an idea. She knew how to get his attention. And maybe hurt him the way he'd already obliviously hurt her.

"Everyone's going to be there," she said nonchalantly. "Tim, Megan, Ed, Gaia."

He stopped, and Heather's heart tore free from the veins and arteries that kept it alive. She hadn't counted on more hurt for her.

"Gaia?" he said.

Somehow Heather smiled a beautiful, perfect smile. "Yeah!" she said, now backing away herself. "Tim Racenello invited her. You should have seen how psyched she was. I don't know, but I think there may be something there. You know?" She tucked her hair behind her ear and continued to beam as if she were talking about her best friend finding true love. "Well, have fun studying."

As if he was going to get any work done now. He was going to sit in the library, obsessing about this. Heather could tell by the stricken look on his face. Unreal. He didn't even try to hide it.

She turned and plunged onto Fifth Avenue without even looking up at the traffic light. Part of her truly hoped a nice downtown bus would come along and flatten her. It wasn't like it could do her much more damage.

FROM: gaia13@alloymail.com
TO: maryubuggin@alloymail.com
TIME: 8:07 P.M.
RE: tonight
Mary—
Forgot to tell you Ed talked me into going to this party tonight. When you stop laughing, you should stop by.
It's at 34th and 1st. Some big building with fountains in the lobby.
Show up and keep me company. I'm sure there will be plenty of mock-worthy people. Good, clean fun.
—Gaia

ROMEO

Normally, I don't go in with a plan. I never know who I'm going to want until I'm in the moment. I do have a special place in my heart for brunettes, though. They often think they're ordinary. Plain. Not-sexy. They act like they have something to prove. And that always makes things more interesting.

But I'm not averse to the occasional blond. Redhead. Asian, African American, Indian, Latina, etc., etc. I'm not averse to anything. Like I said, it depends on how I feel in the moment.

Tonight, however, I have a plan. Two, actually. One brunette. One blond. Maybe neither will resist. But hopefully at least one of them will.

It's the breaking-down process that makes for riveting reading.

INCONSPICUOUS

GAIA IMMEDIATELY WISHED SHE HAD WORN
SOMETHING A LITTLE LESS STREET RAT CHIC,
THEN IMMEDIATELY HATED HERSELF
FOR HAVING THE THOUGHT.

Gaia stood in the most inconspicuous corner of Sideburns Tim's apartment and watched the door, silently cursing Ed Fargo's name. Had they or had they not said they would be here at eight o'clock? She'd even swiped one of Ella's watches to make sure she'd be here on time. That was the last time Gaia would ever even consider being considerate.

There was something weird about this party. It was different from the last, and only, party she'd been to since she arrived in New York. The lights were dim. The music was low. Scented candles dotted the room, lending a heady aroma. Everyone seemed mellow. Comfortable. Cozy. It made Gaia want to crawl out of her skin. She gripped her water glass as if it were the only familiar object in the room.

"Gaia Moore?"

The grip on the glass tightened dangerously. It took Gaia about three seconds to recover from the surprise of someone actually saying her name. Of course, it was Megan Stein. Heather's right-hand snob, looking oh so fetching in some half-sweater thing over some half-shirt thing. She was standing there with another FOH, and each of them was sporting such overexaggerated expressions of shocked disgust, they could have just walked off a sitcom set.

"What are *you* doing here?" Megan asked, glancing at

her friend, who smiled and looked away. Like the remark was so clever, she could barely contain her laughter. Like she really cared about sparing Gaia's feelings.

"Having the time of my life," Gaia answered flatly.

Megan let out a short laugh. "It must be so fascinating to be so weird," she said, looking Gaia up and down. Gaia immediately wished she had worn something a little less street rat chic, then immediately hated herself for having the thought. She placed her drink down on the glass-topped table next to her. When her inner Gaias were having conversations among themselves, it was definitely time to bail.

"Leaving?" Megan asked, arching one eyebrow.

Gaia wasn't about to waste another syllable on the girl. She pushed by Megan and her silent partner. She could practically feel the cold outdoor air on her skin. The second she hit the street, she was going to find a pay phone, call Ed and ream him out, then call Mary and tell her not to bother leaving the house. What was she thinking coming here, anyway? Did she think she was going to have fun? At this point, it was pretty obvious that on top of being less one fear gene, Gaia was also missing the gene that allowed enjoyment of life.

"Aw, look," Megan said from somewhere behind her. "We scared her away."

Stopping in her tracks, Gaia felt her hands ball into fists.

Ignore her. Ignore her. Ignore her. Megan wasn't worth it. Heather, maybe, but not Heather Junior.

"Want me to kick her butt for you?"

Gaia glanced over her left shoulder. It was a guy. Tallish. Asian. Black hair almost hardened by gel. *GQ* handsome. Definitely Young Entrepreneurs of America. Definitely not the type of person who usually talked to Gaia of his own volition.

"What?" Gaia said, narrowing her eyes.

He walked over, brushing Gaia's arm with his own, and leaned one shoulder against the wall, crossing his arms over his chest. He studied Megan from across the room. "Because I think I could take her," he said. "I'm stronger than I look."

Flirting. Did everyone know how to do this but her? "I don't know," Gaia said flatly, pushing her hair behind her ears. "Girls like that have this habit of scratching. It's not pretty."

He laughed, and Gaia almost looked behind her to see who'd caused his mirth. But then she realized he was looking at her, his black eyes shining in the soft light. So he thought she was funny. Wittiness had slipped from her tongue.

"You should stay," he said, reaching past her to a bowl of peanuts on the counter. He grabbed a handful and cracked one open, letting the little shell shards pepper the plush burgundy carpet. He lifted his chin in Megan's direction. "She's a messy drunk. In about an hour I'm sure we could convince her to strip or chop off all her hair or something."

A short laugh bubbled out of Gaia's throat, and the guy

smiled. She felt her face turn bright red. Had she been partially possessed or something?

"What's your name?" he asked, munching on a peanut and holding out a handful to her.

Gaia took one and crushed it in her fist, adding her debris to his. "Gaia," she said.

He glanced at her peanut crumblings with an impressed smirk and held out his hand. "Charlie," he said. "You have no idea how nice it is to meet you."

THE UNATTAINABLE

The reflection was all blurry. Heather couldn't decide if she was drunk or if the Racenellos needed to remodel their bathroom. She turned on the faucet, stuck her hands under the water, and immediately pulled them away.

"Ow. Hot," she squealed, holding the side of her hand to her mouth and sucking on the reddened skin. Then she laughed. "Definitely buzzed," she told herself. She smiled contentedly. It was nice to be buzzed.

Heather was about to turn toward the door and go when she heard a faint pounding. She paused and squinted around. Where was that coming from? She padded across the large bathroom, looking at the ceiling, the tub, the tiled walls. Then suddenly the glass shelves rattled, and Heather jumped.

"Oh, Michael."

It was faint, but she heard it. Accompanied by another rattle of shelves. Heather laughed and covered her mouth with one hand.

"They're having *sex*," she whispered incredulously, her eyes wide. As if she didn't know half the bedrooms had already seen a ton of action tonight. She tiptoed over to the wall and put her ear to the cold tile. Somehow she could only hear less that way, so she pulled back again.

"Baby, you're so hot," Michael said. Heather almost gagged. How cheesy was that? Whoever that girl was, she should wake up and smell the bad cologne. The guy probably didn't even know her name if he was calling her baby.

That was when the moaning and intermittent yelping started, and Heather couldn't take it anymore. She lunged for the door and ducked out of the bathroom into the crowded hallway. A short guy who was definitely going to be balding in about three years was leading a giggling freshman down the hall toward Michael's Boudoir of Sex.

"Don't go in there," Heather warned as she shuffled by. "Give them, like, half a minute. He should be done by then." Then she cracked up at her own joke and kept walking, ignoring the couple's curious stares. Heather felt pretty good, especially considering her little encounter with Sam. She hadn't even thought about him once since she'd been here.

It probably helped that Gaia hadn't had the guts to show after all. If Heather had laid eyes on Gaia, she would have to be reminded of Sam. And how his eyes had finally focused at the mention of her name. And how the thought of Gaia going to a party had made him so jealous, his nostrils had actually flared.

Just as Heather hit the crowded living room, someone grabbed her arm and spun her around so fast, it took the rest of the room a few seconds to catch up with her. It all slid into focus and bounced to a stop like a ball on a roulette wheel.

"You're never going to believe who's slumming with Gaia Moore." It was Megan's voice. Her face wasn't all sharp yet, but it was definitely her voice.

"She's here?" Heather said, feeling the mixed drinks start to remix themselves in her stomach.

"Yeah. And she's talking to Charlie Salita," Megan answered, almost sounding pleased that she was the one who got to deliver this mind-bending news. Her little tendril curls bounced so crazily around her face, it made it all the more difficult for Heather to focus.

Heather turned, slowly this time, and scanned the fuzzy-figure-filled room. Sure enough, Gaia Moore was leaning against the far wall, looking like a homeless shelter reject, laughing it up with Charlie Salita, who was looking like he'd just stepped off a Milan runway. Charlie Salita. The unattainable. The only guy Heather had ever liked that she had never gotten to kiss.

Charlie laughed. Heather's stomach turned. It was either flee to the bathroom or the bar.

Heather chose the bar, although she was pretty sure she was done drinking for the night. She found a stool and plopped down next to one of Charlie's friends—a semicute jock named Scott Becker.

"Can I get you a drink?" Scott asked, leaning toward her and grinning.

"Uh, just a water. Thanks." Heather threw one last glance in Charlie's direction, but she was determined to at least *look* like she was having a good time. When she turned back around, Scott was still grinning and holding a beer in his left hand.

"Thought you might like a beer instead," he whispered, nudging her. Something in his smile put Heather on edge.

"Whatever." She shrugged, taking the beer and sliding off her stool. As she started making her way back toward

Megan, she looked over her shoulder toward Scott. He was scowling at her back as she walked away. What a creep, she thought to herself. Heather Gannis knew when a guy was trying to get her drunk. And Scott Becker had picked the wrong girl to take advantage of, she mused, as she took a sip of her beer.

ACTUAL LAUGHTER

Gaia watched as Charlie placed a peanut on the dining-room table and crouched down. He brought his eye level with the top of the table and studied the crowd as if he were lining up a cue with the ball. Then he reached up, pressed the tip of his thumb and forefinger together, and flicked. The peanut flew off the table and pelted some kid in a plaid shirt with a choppy haircut on the back of the neck.

He flinched, reached back to touch his wound, and turned around, glaring in Gaia and Charlie's direction. "What are you—"

"Duck!" Charlie whispered. Before Gaia could even

ask him why they should bother, he grabbed her wrist and tugged her to the floor. His face was inches away from hers as he laughed like a little kid who'd just found a dollar on the sidewalk. He had good teeth but onion-dip breath.

"Do you think he saw us?" Charlie asked, pressing one hand against the carpet to keep his balance.

Gaia rolled her eyes. "No. We're both invisible, actually."

"Your turn," Charlie said, pressing a few sweaty peanuts into her palm.

"I don't think so," Gaia said. "You've already taken out most of the room." She suddenly wished Mary *had* shown. Fun didn't get much cleaner than using Planters' Best as miniature weapons. And she had a feeling Mary would have perfect aim.

Charlie bit his lip and grinned. "Come on," he whispered. "There's gotta be someone you want to peanut pelt."

How about half the world's population? Gaia reached above her head and opened her fingers above the edge of the table, rolling the peanuts onto the thick surface. Then she pushed herself up on her knees so that just the top of her head was visible over the table. She scanned the room for her target, found her mercifully close by, and took aim.

Charlie popped up next to her just as the projectile nut hit Heather right on the cheek.

"Ow!" Heather protested, slapping at her face.

"Nice!" Charlie whisper-shouted.

Gaia cracked up laughing and rolled under the table. Charlie was practically crying from the effort to hold in his mirth.

"I didn't actually just do that," Gaia said, holding the heel of her hand to her forehead.

Charlie shrugged. "I'm buzzed—what's your excuse?"

Gaia had a slew of great excuses. She was obviously being controlled by an alien race. Or Ella had slipped some kind of upper into her water. Or she was asleep and dreaming. It had to be one of those because laughing wasn't something Gaia did in real life. Almost ever.

"Do you think it's safe to stand up?" Charlie said.

"Whatever," Gaia answered, pushing herself to her feet. She looked around, expecting the dagger glare, but Heather was off in the corner, flirting with some kid with an underdeveloped goatee. Interesting. Did this mean that Sam was a thing of Heather's past? The possibility brought yet another smile to Gaia's lips. Somebody should be writing this down. Recording it all for posterity.

Gaia Moore. Monday, November 30. Five-plus smiles. Actual laughter. Subject obviously acutely disturbed.

"You have an amazing smile," Charlie said, his voice so close, Gaia almost thought it was coming from inside her own head. She was surprised when it sent her heart racing. Her mind searched for something to say. She was sure there was a proper response for something like that, but it wasn't anywhere in Gaia's memory banks.

She just stopped smiling.

"Do you want to go somewhere?" he asked, looking out at the crowd as Gaia followed his gaze. The plaid shirt guy was still eyeing them suspiciously. "Somewhere where the natives aren't out for blood?"

Stuffing her hands under her arms, Gaia glanced at Charlie. His sparkly eyes had turned serious. He didn't want to get away from the natives. He just wanted to get her alone. Even someone as inexperienced in romance as Gaia could figure that one out. But being alone with him was out of the question. There was no telling, what she might manage to do wrong.

"I . . . uh . . ."

Yet another situation with no ready response. Gaia looked at the door, the hall, the window. At all places leading out. They each looked really far away.

Glancing at Charlie, Gaia was hit by the sudden urge not to hurt the feelings of the third person who'd been nice to her since she'd come to the city. Stranger still, she also realized some small part of her wanted him to continue wanting her. He was nice. Funny. Cute. Uncomplicated. And he seemed to like her. Gaia Moore. The freak with the huge shoulders and the even huger thighs.

Gaia racked her brain for a graceful bow out. She came

up blank. When was she going to wake up and start watching soap operas instead of *Scooby-Doo* reruns?

Somehow "Shaggy! Run!" didn't seem appropriate at the moment.

BLISS

About five seconds after entering Tim's apartment, Ed was convinced that the Tin Man from Oz didn't know how good he had it. Not having a heart seemed like a huge blessing.

Gaia was standing about ten feet away from him, and she was smiling. At Charlie Salita. Charlie every-girl-in-this-room-has-wanted-me-at-some-point-in-her-life Salita. The guy was wearing a brown chenille turtleneck and black pants with highly shined black shoes.

He made Ed look about as sophisticated as Elmo.

Ed was about to cut his losses and maneuver his chair around—no easy feat on carpeting that was about three inches thick—when he heard the most beautiful sound ever to float past his eardrums.

"Fargo!"

It was Gaia Moore, spitting out his name.

"Hey!" he said, looking up as Gaia stalked across the room toward him, leaving a baffled-looking Charlie in the dust.

Ed didn't care that Gaia looked like she was out for blood and that she could probably crush his fingers with a flick of her hand. He steeled himself for the onslaught of blame. He was over an hour late. He knew it. He was willing to accept his punishment as long as it kept Gaia away from Charlie the Suave for a few seconds.

"I know, hit me," Ed said when Gaia reached his side. "Let me have it. I know you hate me."

"Thank God you're here," Gaia whispered, glancing at Charlie over her shoulder. "Can we go now?"

"Hey! Gaia the Brave!" Tim Racenello sauntered up to Ed and Gaia and handed each of them a beer. "Hey, Shred," Tim greeted Ed, chucking his chin in his direction.

"Hey," Ed said, forcing a smile. Had it escaped Tim's attention that he'd just interrupted the nice little triumphant moment Ed had been having?

"So, Gaia," Tim said, shaking his hips comically and dancing right up to her. Ed almost cracked up at the unabashed look of irritation on Gaia's face. A look that Tim, of course, was oblivious to. "Want to dance?" Tim asked.

Gaia reached out, took Ed's beer, and placed it with her

own on top of the stereo console at the end of the hallway.

"We're leaving," she said, swinging around to face the door. Before Ed turned to follow her, he saw Tim's face fall so quickly, it defied the laws of physics.

And that was when Ed discovered what bliss felt like.

FROM: maryubuggin@alloymail.com
TO: gaia13@alloymail.com
TIME: 9:05 P.M.
RE: re: tonight
hey g!
i'm in! i'm in! but I can't get there till late. my dad has this business dinner thing and the client's bringing his son and my dad is just so incredibly sure that we'll hit it off he can barely keep the sadistic smile off his face. right. I mean, the man means well, but the last son of a millionaire had back hair and an excess of toe cheese. don't ask me how I got close enough to find that out. anyway, I won't be there till around 10:30–11. hope you're still there.
see ya!
mary

TIRED
HEATHER

THERE WAS KISSING. THAT MUCH
SHE REMEMBERED.

Heather leaned against the wall in Tim's hallway, staring at the white front door of the apartment. She wasn't sure why she was staring at it, but she'd been doing it for so long, she was sure there was a reason. If she could only remember . . .

"Heather?"

She moved her head too fast, and her eyes started to swim around in their sockets. Heather giggled. She felt like a fish in a very round bowl. She reached out and grabbed her friend Laura's arm, although she wasn't sure if it was Laura, or Megan, or someone else entirely who had said her name.

"Hey!" Heather said, rubbing the sleeve of Laura's sweater between her thumb and forefinger. "This is *really* nice."

"Are you okay?" Laura asked, pulling her arm away. Heather just stared at it.

"Yeah. Did the door, like, do something to offend you?" Megan asked, scrunching up her entire face so that she looked like a cartoon version of herself. "You looked like you wanted to kill it or something."

"I'm waiting for Sam," Heather said, blinking. At least she wished she was.

Megan's eyebrows shot up. "Sam's coming?"

"No."

"Oh."

Megan and Laura exchanged pitying looks that Heather wasn't about to stand for. These two were boring her, anyway. She had to find someone to talk to. Someone who wouldn't constantly remind her that she was supposed to have this perfect boyfriend as part of her supposed perfect life.

"I have to go," Heather said, walking along the wall away from them. She stumbled over her own feet and heard Laura and Megan giggle but ignored it. Like they were ones to talk. How many times had she walked them home, stopping every few feet so they could vomit in the sewers? She was allowed to get drunk every once in a while. Although she wasn't sure exactly how she'd gotten *this* drunk. She'd finished off the beer that Scott had given her and decided to call it a night, but somehow her head was now spinning out of control.

Where was Gaia? Where was the bitch hiding? Heather suddenly felt an intense need to tell the girl off. More intense than the usual, day-to-day, moment-to-moment need, anyway.

Heather took her hand away from the wall for a moment. Bad idea. Then someone walked into her shoulder, hard, and Heather decided that the wall was the safest place for her, at least until she found someone to talk to.

When had this party gotten so crowded? Everywhere

Heather looked, there was an unfamiliar face, and the place was starting to get unbearably hot. Probably because of the smells. All kinds of scents—perfume, colognes, alcoholic beverages, processed food, and smoke—were choking the oxygen out of the room. They seemed to make the place even warmer, combining to form a thick cloud that locked in the heat like the greenhouse effect.

Air. Air would be good.

"Hey, Heather."

She looked up to find Charlie hovering next to her, a semiconcerned smile on his lips.

"Where's Gaia?" Heather blurted out, forgetting momentarily that she was having breathing issues.

"I think she left," Charlie said, leaning one shoulder against the wall. He took a sip of his beer and grinned at her, his eyes sparkling. "Doesn't matter, anyway. I've been wanting to talk to you all night."

"Really."

It was a line. Even through her inebriation, she could spot that one from a good ten yards. But it didn't matter. Gaia had obviously pulled a Gaia and done something repelling to scare Charlie off. Why Sam was immune to her freakishness was beyond Heather.

Sam. What was going on between him and Gaia? It was something. She knew there was something on his side because he'd told her. Actually *told* her. But was there something actually *going on?* And if so, was it something big? Or something minuscule? Was it even real?

"Heather?"

No. It was real. It was in his eyes. Her eyes. Maybe Gaia had gone to find him. Maybe they were hanging out together right now. Kissing. Holding hands. Laughing at her.

Maybe they were in love.

"Heather?"

"Do you want to go somewhere?" Heather asked, her eyes truly focusing for the first time in over an hour.

Charlie's smile was practically blinding. He really was hot. Hotter than Sam, maybe. Certainly more wanted than Sam. Certainly more here than Sam.

"I have the perfect place." There was a flash of something in Charlie's eyes as he said it. Something disturbing enough to make Heather's heart skip a quick beat. But it was just a flash. And it was just Charlie. And Heather just wanted to get out of this room. He held out his arm, just like an old-fashioned gentleman, and Heather only stumbled a little as she took it.

FIFTEEN MINUTES

Gaia could have sworn she smelled the gas before she even heard the crash. She and Ed had just made it across Fifth Avenue when a moving truck skidded through a red light and fishtailed, taking two cabs and a VW Beetle with it. There was a huge cacophony of screeching metal, shattering glass, and earsplitting screams and then an odd sort of silence.

"Oh my God," Ed said, his voice sounding like it came through a black tunnel to reach her ears.

That was when she heard the baby wailing.

Ed grabbed at Gaia's fingers, probably predicting what she was about to do, but she twisted out of his grip easily. She busted through a group of onlookers, half of whom were gaping, the other half helpfully dialing 911 on their cell phones.

"Huge truck—"

"Fire starting—"

"Get an ambulance here as—"

A few words repeated themselves in Gaia's mind as she skidded toward the crumpled, flipped silver Beetle.

Gas. Fire. Baby. Mother. Explosion. Orphan.

Gaia hit the ground on her knees, ripping gaping holes in her pants. The grit and slimy grime of the street pressed their way into the wrinkly flesh around her knees, along with a few pieces of glass. Some part of her brain registered the fact that that was going to hurt later. All she could consciously deal with at the moment was the sight of a red-faced, screaming baby, relatively unharmed, hanging upside down in his car seat.

And the sight of a woman, knocked out, bleeding from the forehead, pressed at an impossible angle against the roof of the car, her arms flopped over her torso like a rag doll's.

"Lady!" someone yelled from the side of the street. "Get out of there! It's gonna blow." The voice sounded panicked. Gaia knew she was probably about to die, but it didn't hit her. Nothing ever hit her the way it was supposed to.

Gaia stuck her hand under the woman's nose, fully expecting to feel the cold absence of breath but instead feeling a little burst of warmth. She was still breathing. Good. But the baby had to come first. Gaia flipped over onto her back and shimmied her way through the smashed window of the car, sliding along the inside of the roof.

It was a close fit but she managed to cram her body under the screaming child. She held his stomach with one hand, and unhinged the tiny cloth belt on his seat with the other. Cradling the wailing baby against her chest, Gaia slowly squirmed her way back out the window.

Luckily there was a cop standing right over her, panting. His face was determined, but his skin was sallow.

"Give him to me and get the hell out of here," the tall, burly cop said.

Gaia handed him the baby and immediately crouched down to work on the mother.

"Girlie," the cop spat over the screams of the baby and the wail of too distant sirens. "There's gas. There's fire. How stupid are you?"

Stupid. Crazy. Fearless. It was amazing how the interpretations varied.

"So go," Gaia said, reaching into the car and grunting as she worked at the twisted mess. There was no more blood, which made Gaia feel a little better about her prospects, but the buckle seemed to be jammed.

"You're crazy," the cop said, before turning on his heel and fleeing. Gaia could smell the gas. She could hear the fire and feel its heat. Desperate yells and screams rang out from the side of the road, the loudest of which was Ed's. And the sirens grew louder and more persistent every minute, piercing her head with sharp slices of pain.

But she ignored all of it. She had to. It was the only way she could work.

Gaia jammed her thumb into the belt button with every ounce of strength one digit could contain, and it finally popped free. The woman slumped even farther. Gaia reached out a hand and cradled the woman's head.

She heard a popping sound and briefly wondered if that

meant the whole car was about to burst into flames. Would that be the last sound she ever heard?

The woman moaned, and Gaia grabbed her under the arms, pulling her free from the car. The woman's heel caught on a chip of glass. It pulled off her shoe, and a long gash opened in the flesh around her heel.

The woman didn't seem to feel it, so Gaia ignored it as she dragged the woman across the street at a run. As she got closer to the sidewalk, a large man in a business suit and overcoat came out and took the woman up in his arms.

"Inside," he told Gaia, nodding toward the Pier 1 Imports store, where a couple dozen people were ducked behind furniture, trying not to look at the wreck. Gaia saw Ed staring at her from behind the counter, his eyes full of fear, anger, and gratitude.

Gaia opened the door, the man ducked in with his burden, and the whole sky turned to flames.

There were more screams. A shower of glass. Still outside, Gaia felt the thrust of heat and turned to look at the road, watching as a puff of flame and smoke rose up from the Beetle in a cloud that extinguished itself as quickly as it had appeared.

It was actually kind of cool. Like a Fourth of July firework.

Before Gaia could even register how sick it was that these were her thoughts at a time like this, she was bombarded by more people than she ever wanted in her personal space.

"Are you insane?"

"How did you do that?"

"Do you want to go out sometime?"

"Hey! There's the news van! Over here!"

As Gaia wiped the itchy sweat from her brow, she caught a glimpse of a big blue van with a huge antenna screeching toward the scene of the accident. The Pier 1 crowd was gesturing wildly for the driver's attention, clamoring for their fifteen minutes and wanting to thrust Gaia's upon her.

There was a bright white light. A couple of flashes.

"Ed?" Gaia yelled, searching the crowd for him.

"I know," he said, right at her elbow. "Let's go."

ALMOST ABUSED

There were just way too many piles of clothing on Heather's bed. When she'd walked into her room after midnight on the night of the party, she didn't even have the energy to shove them all to the floor, so she lay down on top of them—face first. She felt like someone had hit her with a steamroller, backed up, and hit her again. Twice.

"Tired Heather," she croaked into her pillow. "Very tired."

Something was stabbing her in the stomach. Just a belt buckle. Or a hanger. Nothing compared to the overall ache that was crushing her into her center.

Her throat was incredibly dry, and her face felt like it had been rubbed down with sandpaper. Raw and itchy. Heather rolled over onto her back and felt like she was leaning on a small pillow. It took her a few seconds to realize it was her hair, tangled into a knotted ball at the top of her head. She gingerly touched her hand to it. That was going to hurt like hell to brush through. She tried to kick off her shoes, but her legs yelled out with pain, her thighs quivering like she'd just run a couple of miles.

"Don't move," she told herself. "Better not to move."

Better not to move so that she could think. Lie here and think and try to remember how, exactly, she'd ended up having sex with Charlie Salita.

There was kissing. That much she remembered. Lots of tongue and saliva. Groping. She'd even been quite helpful and popped open the ever-male-confounding front closure bra for him. He'd had a very smooth chest. Smooth and muscular and brown.

And there were a lot of pillows. Flowery ones with this ugly purple pattern that made it look like the Fruit of the Loom grape guy had barfed all over the bed.

Bed. Okay, she remembered that, too. Heather squinted at the stucco ceiling, her eyes playing games with the swirly patterns and making her whole body spin. She felt very nauseous. Very spent. Almost abused.

She'd had a crush on Charlie in the eighth grade, worshiped him from afar in the ninth grade, almost gotten him to kiss her in the tenth grade, and then been totally humiliated and heartbroken when he'd told her he just wanted to be friends. A teenage boy who refused to even kiss her and leave her. Hormones didn't even play a role. Very ego damaging.

It was a long, sordid history of daydreams, doodled hearts, and tears.

She was a senior now. She had a boyfriend.

Maybe.

She didn't care about Charlie anymore.

But she wouldn't have minded being able to remember the sex.

THE BIG TEN

This was supposed to be a party?

Mary Moss had never seen anything so pathetic in her life. A couple of kegs. A few tonsil hockey games. Bad music-store-compilation CD. It was no wonder Gaia thought this would be funny. These people must have learned how to party by watching reruns of *Friends*.

A dorky guy with a completely over-it Caesar haircut sidled up to her and held out a beer. "Night owl." His head bobbed up and down like it was hanging from a piece of elastic. "I like it," he said.

Mary took the beer, chugged half of it, and handed it back. "Do you know Gaia Moore?"

His eyes roamed up and down her body, and he leered a smile. "Of her," he said.

Suppressing an eye roll was almost painful. Mary's consistently small store of patience was nigh gone. "Is she here?"

"Saw her somewhere," he said with a little shrug. What she was actually there for obviously had no bearing. All he could see were the possibilities. Little did he know there were none. "Why don't you come sit down?"

"No, thanks," Mary said. "I wouldn't want to bother you. I can see you're really busy wasting space." His face registered no recognition of the insult, so Mary just snorted and walked away. This was a big apartment. There had to be someone here who had a line of coke or some real alcohol.

Wait, no. Not anymore. This was good, clean fun night. As much as she wanted drugs, as much as her body craved them, she was determined to follow through on her promise to herself.

It didn't matter, anyway, right? At this moment she'd settle for the stimulation of a lot of chocolate and a good game of Twister.

Mary made her way down a freshly painted hallway, pausing to listen at doors as she went. Nothing. Nothing. Moaning. Fighting. Nothing. Obviously Gaia hadn't gotten her message and had been intelligent enough to recognize lameness run amok when she saw it. Maybe it was time to go home and relax with Conan and a really big pillow.

Suddenly a burst of loud laughter made Mary jump, and a slow smile crept across her face. Finally. She fluffed her long, curly red hair, straightened the shoulders of her black leather jacket, and pushed through a large swinging door.

The kitchen was huge. White. Immaculate. There was a raucous group of testosterone-high guys standing in the corner, bent over the table. One of them seemed to be taking notes in a big, cloth-bound book. No one noticed her.

This was obviously some kind of meeting. She obviously wasn't supposed to be part of it. That obviously meant she was going to stay for as long as possible. Mary tiptoed past a sparkling butcher block and ducked behind a counter. Perfect view of the guys, but they couldn't see her unless they were looking for her. Or the dog food that, from the smell of it, she was hiding behind.

"What about you, Charlie?" the guy with the book asked, rolling his pencil end over end between his fingers. "Add to the grand total?"

"Only one tonight, gentlemen," the Charlie guy answered. He was one of those guys who was totally aware of how good-looking he was, thus making him entirely unattractive. There was a round of disappointed, jeering "ohs" from the crowd, and a bunch of the guys laughed. Charlie held up his hands and backed up a step, smiling the whole way. "Wait, wait, wait. She's a Big Ten."

The "ohs" turned to "ooos." Impressed glances all around.

"This I gotta hear," the note keeper said, leaning back in his seat and pushing up the sleeves of his off-white sweater. His beady little eyes were shining with interest, piquing Mary's own. Charlie was obviously a big manly man among the manly men.

Charlie looked around, as if checking to see if he had the full attention of his audience. Once satisfied, he opened his arms and gave a little bow. "Heather Gannis," he said with false modesty.

Mary knew Heather. If she was a big anything, it was a big bitch.

"No way!" some kid in a hideous lounge shirt shouted, thrusting his arm down like a kid who'd just been picked last for kickball.

Charlie grinned. "And boy, can that girl move." More laughter, catcalling, and applause from the crowd. Bad shirt guy shot an icy glare at Charlie from the other end of the table, never taking his eyes off the victor as he took a long swig from his bottle.

Mary felt her face go red as the reality of what these guys were discussing sank in. The disgust mixed with the pungent aroma of the dog food made her stomach crawl.

"You got a confirm on this?" Notebook Boy asked, his pencil now poised over the open page in front of him.

A short kid in the corner raised his long-neck bottle of beer. "I saw them go in, and she looked very happy when they came out."

"Five points for Charlie," Notebook Boy said, making a note in his tome with a flourish. "For bagging a Big Ten."

"To the Big Ten!" the short guy yelled. He was answered by a chorus of echoes, more applause, and another bow. That was when Mary couldn't take it anymore.

"Was it your total lack of decency that brought you guys together, or do you all just have really small penises?"

There was a brief, confused silence as Mary stepped out from her hiding place and into full view in the middle of the kitchen. A few jaws dropped and a few sets of eyes narrowed before anyone spoke. It was Charlie who finally processed what she'd said. Mary was surprised that he was the one with half a brain.

"Who the hell are you?" he asked, sounding like a B-movie cliché.

"Who cares who she is?" the note keeper said, standing up and squaring his shoulders, all menacing-like. "What matters is how much she heard."

Mary rolled her eyes. "About what?" she scoffed, tossing back her hair. "Your pathetic little sex ring? I heard enough to tell all your conquests about it."

The guys exchanged looks, clearly trying to figure out what to do about her and her threat. Mary's heart suddenly started to pound out of sync with its normal rate. There actually were a lot of big necks, large hands, and teeny-tiny intellects in the room. Plus they were a bunch of sex fiends. Not exactly an ideal place for an attractive girl like herself to be making challenges.

Charlie finally emerged from the group and started in her direction. Mary fought the urge to back up and raised her chin. She couldn't remember the last guy who had intimidated her. Or at least the last guy who had gotten any indication that he'd intimidated her.

Of course this was one damn big guy backed up by about fifteen others.

"I'm giving you five seconds to get out of here," Charlie

said when he was close enough for her to smell the Tic Tac–tinted beer stench on his breath.

Like that was supposed to scare her.

"And you won't be telling anyone anything," he added. "We're not afraid to hurt girls." He actually smiled as he said this, causing sweat to pop out in the center of Mary's palms with a maddening itch. "Got it?" he asked with a very serious edge in his voice.

"I got it," Mary said, surprised at the strength in her voice as she looked into a pair of very disturbed eyes. She glanced around the room, making sure to look at every single face so they would know that she wasn't, in fact, squirming.

The final look of disgust was saved for Charlie. She managed to hold it for a couple of seconds even though he was still glaring at her, and then she turned and went back the way she came, whacking open the door with a flourish.

It wasn't until the elevator doors had slid shut behind her that she let herself realize her knees were shaking.

ROMEO

I have my weaknesses. Things that make me lose my focus. Things that make me impossibly angry. Things that make me see red.

I only had the one tonight. Only the brunette. The blond slipped through my fingers. I don't know how, but she did.

That's one of the things that brings the fury, the not knowing. Being unable to pinpoint where I went wrong. What she saw or didn't see. Whether I said too much, too little, exactly what she didn't want to hear.

It's the not knowing that kills.

But I will have her. I will figure her out. None of them are that complex.

Not a one.

INDISPENSABLE

IT WOULDN'T BE ELLA'S FAULT IF SAM, SAY,
STEPPED IN FRONT OF A SPEEDING CAB,
WOULD IT? OR A SUBWAY TRAIN.

THE WORD

Ella stared out the plate glass window of the loft in Hell's Kitchen, watching steam billow out of a manhole in the middle of the street. The image left her feeling cold. Cold and angry. Ella hated the winter. Had ever since she was a girl. There was something suffocating about it. The thick clothes. The tight spaces. The holiday crowds.

It made her feel small.

"You know, I've had people shot for not listening to me."

Ella snapped to attention at the sound of the word *shot*. He would do it. She knew that. She wasn't as indispensable as some.

She turned from the window and faced Loki. His eyes, as always, were unmasked. Sinister. But there was laughter in them. He didn't really intend to kill her. At least not today.

"I'm sorry," Ella said, running the tip of her finger along the edge of the galvanized metal counter next to her. The one that held the plans. "I was distracted. It won't happen again."

Loki's mouth twisted into a smirk. "Daydreaming about the holidays, are we?" he asked. "Or are you just thinking about what will happen to you if I find out you're lying about our unfortunate friend, the doctor?"

They'd been over this already. Several times. And

although Ella had been frightened when Loki first confronted her about the doctor, the explosion, and what part she'd had to play in the whole fiasco, she was now getting a little bored. Of course Loki had found out about the events of the last few days. When it came to anything having to do with Gaia, Loki always found out. He knew about the explosion; he knew that Gaia had been at the station that night; he knew that a girl had been brutally slashed; and he knew of the doctor's unfortunate—and obviously more than coincidental—demise. He also knew that Gaia had ended up in the hospital.

The one thing Loki couldn't know for sure was what Ella's involvement had been. Loki was a master of information, but Ella had covered her tracks well, and she was a good liar. After all, she'd learned from the best. And although Loki was obviously still suspicious, Ella knew it was in his best interest to give her the benefit of the doubt for now. She *was* dispensable, but it would be very inconvenient to get rid of her. Besides, he could have no idea that Ella's hatred for Gaia went deeper than petty rivalry. He couldn't know that she wanted nothing more than to see Gaia dead. And his ignorance of that one simple fact was probably the only reason Ella was still alive.

Loki spread a blueprint out on the drafting table in front of him. Ella glanced at the corner of the page and noted the label New York Department of Public Works. It was amazing how Loki could get his hands on whatever he pleased.

"Sugarplums dancing," she said flatly.

"How is my Gaia?" Loki asked, studying the plans, oblivious to the fact that the mere mention of the name brought most of Ella's blood vessels dangerously close to bursting. "Is she excited about the holidays?"

Ella shrugged. "I don't know how she feels," she said, trying to keep the bite from her tone.

Suddenly Loki turned on her with the speed of a wildcat, his eyes crazed with anger as he thrust a crumpled-up newspaper into her face. "You don't even know what she's *doing,*" he growled, baring his teeth just slightly.

Ella's life stopped flashing in front of her eyes when she realized he wasn't, in fact, holding a weapon. Shaking, she gingerly took the newspaper from his hands and unfolded it. There was a large black-and-white photo of a twisted car wreck, accompanied by a headline that made the blood in her veins run cold.

MYSTERIOUS BLOND WONDER GIRL SAVES BABY, MOTHER

Finding her voice somewhere among the confusion her insides had been twisted into, Ella tried for an excuse. "We don't know that it was—"

"Of course we know it was her!" Loki spat, the rims around his eyes just a slightly darker shade of red than his skin. "Why didn't you report this?"

There was no way she could tell him she didn't know. No way she could tell him she was home, cleaning up the muck that passed for dinner in the pit that passed for a home where she lived a life that passed for a life with a man who could have been her father. And she was doing it all for him.

She couldn't tell him that.

"The girl is fine," Ella said slowly, realizing she was actually unable to recall whether or not she'd seen Gaia since she left the night before. "I didn't want you to worry unnecessarily."

He glared at her. "You're skating on thin ice, Ella."

Ella blushed, feeling like a small child who had just been reprimanded for skipping her homework. She hated being made to feel like this. Hated Gaia for being the cause.

Loki took a deep breath and let it out slowly, audibly, through his nose. "From now on I want to know everything," he said, his mouth turning into a sly grin. "I don't need your protection."

"Yes, sir," Ella said. And he turned back to his plans as if nothing had ever happened.

"What else has our Gaia been up to?" he asked, his gaze flicking over the numbers printed at the edges of the large page he was studying.

Our Gaia.

"She's going to parties," Ella said, lacing her fingers together behind her back to keep her hands from clenching into fists. "And she's been with that boy," she added, mostly to see if he'd react.

She wasn't disappointed.

Loki turned to her, one eyebrow raised. "Has she?" He seemed to be contemplating the news. Gaia getting too close to Sam could be risky for Loki. Ella knew this. It was only a minuscule risk, but still, Loki had gotten rid of people for less.

Ella was practically salivating. All he had to do was say the word, and she would gladly execute the job. In the most painful and messy way possible.

"Good," he said finally.

Ella almost choked. That wasn't the word she was looking for.

"I'm sorry?" she said, before she could think the better of it. But Loki was flipping through his plans, apparently willing to ignore the fact that she'd questioned him. His mood swings were completely unpredictable.

"If he makes her happy, good," Loki said, frowning as he leaned closer to the desk, tracing one of the hundreds of jumbled lines on the blueprint with his nail. "Maybe she'll stay out of trouble until I need her."

Need her. That stung. Ella was so sick of hearing it, she could scream. What could Gaia possibly do for him that she couldn't do? That she hadn't already proven she was willing to do time and time again?

"Ella!" he roared. Her heart hit her throat so fast, she coughed. Now his eyes were smoldering again. "Don't make me tell you a third time," he said. He thrust his finger at the plans. "There is work to be done."

Ella shoved images of Gaia and her little friend aside and joined Loki at the drafting table. She would have to deal with Gaia and Sam on her own, that was obvious. Loki might want Gaia to be happy, but it wouldn't be Ella's fault if Sam, say, stepped in front of a speeding cab, would it? Or a subway train.

But whatever she decided to do, the planning would have to be saved for another time.

If she wanted to live long enough to follow through with it.

STIRRING

Sam finished reviewing chapter seven of his physics book and tossed his mechanical pencil down on top of a pile of dog-eared notes. His eyes were dry, and he felt like he hadn't blinked in hours. Actually, it was quite possible that he hadn't. Physics was just that riveting.

Rubbing the heels of his hands into his eyes, Sam leaned back in his desk chair and sighed. He had about eight more chapters to go through, and his energy stores were sapped. If he looked at one more equation, he was going to snap and do something stupid. Like run through the hallway naked, singing Justin Bieber songs at the top of his lungs.

Some guy on his hall had done that during midterms. It wasn't pretty.

Sam knew from years of cramming experience that there were three options for restoring his brain to a functional level.

One: caffeine

Two: sugar

Three: exercise

And since exercise could translate into a walk, which could possibly lead to seeing Gaia, Sam opted for number three.

He pushed away from his desk, grabbed his worn wool coat, and was out on Fifth Avenue in thirty-five-point-three seconds, departure time hindered only by a slow elevator. Sam took a deep breath of the crisp afternoon air and turned his footsteps toward Washington Square Park.

With any luck, Gaia would have ducked out of lunch for a quick game with Zolov and he could get a dose of her.

Something to tide him over until finals were a thing of the past and he could see her again.

What a joke. Sam knew that if he saw her, it would only make things worse. It would only make it that much harder to work. He shoved his freezing, chapped hands into his coat pockets. He knew he should turn around and head home, but he didn't. Instead he walked directly through the arch at the top of the park and immediately started his search.

He knew it was bad for him, but he couldn't help it. He was a Gaia addict, and this might be the only place he could score a hit.

But it was possible to take Gaia in moderation. Sam nodded as this thought occurred to him, making him feel slightly better about his mission. He could just stand across the park and watch her as she anticipated her next move on the board. He could at least see for himself, with his own eyes, that she was okay. That would be enough.

Or would it?

Now that he'd felt what it was like to have Gaia in his arms, would anything less ever be enough?

He could talk to her, maybe. If he could get his voice box to work in her presence, which almost always seemed to be a problem.

As long as she didn't haul off and punch him, he could, in fact, kiss her.

Maybe that would help. If he did, maybe he'd see that it was just another kiss and not the mind-blowing, shiver-inducing, skin-tingling event he'd imagined it to be.

And then he saw her. And all the blood in his body raced into his heart. It was just the back of her head. The tangled blond hair. It had such an effect on him, he almost had to sit down.

This was bad. Very, very bad. If seeing the back of her head did this to him, what would seeing her face do? Her eyes. Her mouth. Hearing her voice. Sam suddenly knew for sure that if he went over to the table where she was sitting, probably lightening the wallet of the guy across from her, he would never be able to walk away.

It would be impossible. Gut-wrenching. If she gave him any indication that he could have her, he would flunk out of college before he could say "obsessed."

Still, of course, he found himself walking toward her, his eyes trained on the little space of her back and shoulders visible over the top of her chair. In moments he was right behind her. He could practically feel her concentration as she focused on the chessboard in front of her. The guy she was playing was so engrossed, he didn't look up as Sam stood there, hovering like some lunatic.

He opened his mouth to speak, but nothing came out. Probably because he had nothing to say that didn't sound ridiculous.

"Hey, Gaia. Did you know we kissed?"

"Hey, Gaia. How's that head wound?"

"Hey, Gaia. Will you marry me?"

His stomach suddenly wanted to exit through his lips.

Sam snapped his mouth shut, turned on his heel, and forced himself to walk away. It was the hardest thing he'd ever done in his life. But already he knew he'd be useless at his desk for at least a few hours.

He couldn't afford actual interaction. Even if he had left his heart on the ground under her chair.

NOT RAPE

There weren't many classes that were easy to handle in the midst of a monster hangover, but the worst was undoubtedly AP biology. Dissecting a fetal pig made Heather's stomach move in ways she'd never experienced before. She spent half the class period mentally calculating the distance between her lab table and the garbage can, wondering if her projectile vomit would make it that far.

Megan nudged Heather with her arm, and even the slight movement sent a stabbing pain through Heather's temple. It was two o'clock in the afternoon. Shouldn't she be over this by now?

"What?" Heather snapped as quietly as possible. More because saying anything louder would cause severe head trauma than from any concern over attracting her teacher's attention.

"Have you talked to Lucy today?" Megan asked, casting a glance in their friend's direction. She was sitting at her lab table, looking like three-day-old roadkill, watching blankly as her lab partner made the first incision.

"No, but it looks like she and her mirror had a little disagreement this morning," Heather said flatly. It was a sad day when she couldn't even glean any joy from her own creative insults.

"Come on," Megan said, pushing away from her table. "Crosby's not paying attention. Let's go talk to her."

Heather didn't see why they had to bother, but she wasn't in the state of mind to argue. She followed Megan over to Lucy's table and then trudged the extra steps to the window as Megan pulled Lucy to the wall. Heather slumped against the black counter that ran along the windowsill, hoping Lucy's tragedy, whatever it was, merited only a short story.

As Megan started the ritual poking and prodding, trying

to get the sordid details of why Lucy was makeupless and wrinkled, Heather zoned out. All day she'd been getting little flashes of her escapades the night before, and she was still trying to piece it together. Where Charlie had taken her. How she'd gotten there. And why. Only small snippets of the conversation reached her ears.

". . . thought he liked me . . ."

Typical.

". . . said I was beautiful . . ."

Shocker.

". . . said no, like, a hundred times . . ."

Wait a minute.

". . . I don't know if it was *rape*."

Heather's heart hit the floor, disturbing her already coiled stomach as it went.

"Lucy . . . *what?*" she said, finally focusing on her friend's gaunt face. A horrid pain stabbed at her temples, but she barely felt it.

Lucy seemed to shrink before her eyes, hugging herself so tightly, she could have been wearing a straitjacket. Megan turned to Heather, her eyes wide with disgust, disbelief, and fear over what Lucy had just told her.

"I said, I don't know if it was rape," Lucy repeated, sounding like a timid five-year-old being made to speak in front of the class.

Heather grabbed Lucy's tiny wrists and looked her in the

eye. "If you said no, it was rape," she said quietly but firmly. Lucy just blinked a few times, heavy tears filling her already puffy eyes. God, not Lucy. The girl couldn't have been more innocent if she'd grown up on a milk farm in Wisconsin instead of the Lower East Side. She still carried around a Hello Kitty pencil tin.

"Who was it?" Heather asked. Her skin felt like it was tightening over her bones, pulling her in.

Flashes of memory assaulted her brain like a strobe light. Charlie holding her down. Her bruised thighs. The rough, raw skin on her face and neck. His hand on her neck . . . covering her mouth . . .

Lucy just shook her head.

"Lucy—" There was an edge in Heather's voice that she didn't intentionally put there. She suddenly felt like pounding something, but at the same time it was as if her entire body had started to ache.

She remembered how she'd felt when she'd gotten home last night. Raw. Spent. Abused. What if—

"You don't have to tell us if you're not ready," Megan said, shooting Heather a warning glance as she ran her hand over Lucy's fine brown hair. Heather was shaking now. She reached out and grasped the edge of the windowsill, pressing her fingertips into the painted wood. She had to stay composed. She couldn't let them see the wall come down. And it was dangerously close to crumbling.

Charlie. The sweater. The bed. The bra. The pillows. The hands. The bruises.

What had happened between the living room and the bedroom?

She didn't remember saying no, but she didn't remember saying yes, either.

HEATHER

I have spent the past two years turning silence into an art form.

If you told my friends that, they'd laugh in your face. To them, I'm outspoken, opinionated, self-righteous, maybe even obnoxious. Loud in a number of ways. But what they don't know is that my being so vocal masks my silence. The more I say about things that don't matter, the less they know about the things that do.

I don't talk about the fact that my family has no money.

I don't talk about my sister hating school and whining about it all the time.

I don't talk about the hand-me-downs, the scholarship

applications, the sublet bedroom in my already tiny apartment.

I don't talk about my problems with Sam, Gaia related or other.

All I talk about is nothing. Lots and lots of nothing.

But this is one thing I don't think I can keep inside. Charlie may have raped me. But unlike Lucy, I really, *really* don't know for sure. I need to talk this through with someone. I need to figure out what to do.

Because this is one thing I can't be silent about.

A girl has to draw the line somewhere.

VULNERABLE

SHE USED TO SOUND LIKE THAT WITH HIM ALL
THE TIME. BUT THAT WAS BEFORE. WHEN THEY
WERE TOGETHER. WHEN THEY WERE IN LOVE
AND IT WAS SAFE TO BE VULNERABLE.

When it came to school day activities, it took more than a hallway catfight to surprise Ed Fargo. He'd seen a lot in his day. Danny Cicinia putting his fist through a plate glass door, Mr. Weitzman threatening to "toss" Jason Cirelli if he talked back one more time, Renee Barrow pulling the fire alarm just so she could get thrown out of school in time to make the bus out to the Meadowlands to see LMFAO.

Still, he was almost shocked into speechlessness when Heather Gannis walked right up to him in front of everyone who was anyone—at least to her—after eighth period.

"Can we talk?" she asked.

Ed would have really preferred not to. Lately, conversations with Heather either involved Gaia bashing or Sam gushing. Two topics Ed wasn't remotely interested in. Plus there was the whole pain-of-talking-to-an-ex thing. That never helped, either.

But one look at Heather's eyes told him not to turn away. She needed him. She had no right to, but that was a discussion for another time.

"Yeah," he said. "Do you want to meet me at Ozzie's later?"

She shook her head almost imperceptibly. "Now," she said.

Ed's brows knitted, and he automatically gripped the armrests on his chair. When Heather turned and headed into their history classroom, Ed followed without hesitation. Something was really wrong if Heather wanted to spend an extra two minutes in the school building after the freedom bell had rung.

As soon as he was through the door, Heather closed it behind him. She leaned back against the gray metal desk at the front of the room and regarded him for a moment, as if she was rethinking her decision to spill. Then, just when he thought she'd changed her mind, she spoke.

"I think Charlie Salita might have raped me," she said. At least that was what Ed thought she'd said. Part of him was now fairly sure he was hallucinating.

"What!"

"Don't make me say it again," Heather said, crossing her arms over her chest and looking away.

Ed knew all the color had drained out of his face and that every pore on his body was producing sweat at profuse levels. This was something no part of him was willing to believe. This couldn't happen. Not between people he knew. Not between people he was friends with. Once.

This couldn't happen to Heather.

"Are you going to say anything?" she asked. For the first time in recent memory, her voice sounded vulnerable. She used to sound like that with him all the time. But that was before. When they were together. When they were in love and it was safe to be vulnerable.

"Are you okay?" Ed asked, holding her gaze.

"I don't know," she said. She held herself a little tighter. "That's the problem—I don't know anything. I don't remember much."

Ed rubbed his hand through his hair, mostly to clear the sweat that had accumulated on his palm. "What do you remember?" he asked.

He would kill Charlie Salita. He would find a way to get up out of this chair if he needed to, but he would definitely kill the guy.

Heather sighed wearily and dropped into a chair next to him, causing a metallic scraping sound that echoed in the empty room. Ed could see the pores around her nose, smell the sweet trace of perfume that was left from her midday spritzing. It was the closest her face had been to his in years. His heart couldn't help responding with a strong hammering to his chest. He ignored it. This wasn't the time for that.

"More every time I think about it." She started to pick at her nails. They were all chipped and ripped and shredded. Was that from fighting back, or had she destroyed them in the trauma of the aftermath? "I remember him holding my arms down. I remember his hands on my neck. . . ."

As she spoke, Ed started to feel like he wanted to crawl

out of his skin. It was like his insides were clawing at him, but he couldn't tell her to stop. If she needed to talk about it, he needed to make himself listen.

"You don't want to hear this, do you?" she said, her tone flat.

Ed coughed. "I'm sorry. No. I'm fine. I just . . ."

"You want to know why I came to you," Heather said, staring straight ahead.

Ed said nothing.

She traced a tile on the floor with the toe of her boot, over and over again, getting faster each time. Ed watched, mesmerized, until she pressed her palm into her thigh, holding her leg in place.

"I didn't know what else to do," she said.

Ed's dark half wanted to tell her to go to Sam. That Sam was her choice. That she wasn't Ed's responsibility anymore. But the dark half's voice was weak and irrational. It wasn't who Ed was—most of the time.

"You have to tell someone," Ed said, fighting the urge to reach out and take her hand. If he touched her, she might shrink away. The emotions in the room were so raw, he wasn't sure if either one of them could take that. "I mean, someone other than me. Someone who can do something. The police or a guidance counselor or something."

"I don't want to," Heather said quietly. "At least not yet. Not until I'm sure."

Ed's heart clenched even tighter. She was broken. Charlie had broken her.

"How are you ever going to be sure?" Ed asked, trying to keep the rage and confusion he was feeling from coming through in his tone.

Heather rested her elbow on the desk in front of her and pushed her hand into her hair. "I don't know," she said, sounding a little desperate. "But you'll help me, right? Figure it out?"

He'd never seen so much trepidation in her expression. Not even right after the accident, when things had gotten intense in a bad way. It took more guts for Heather to be this openly confused than it ever took for Ed to surf the biggest wave in the ocean.

"I'll help you," he said, and before he could stop it, his hand reached out and covered hers. They both just looked at it for a moment. Ed marveled at how it hadn't changed—the look of her skin against his. It felt different, but it looked just like it always had.

"And you won't tell anyone?" she asked.

"I won't."

But Ed's other hand was hidden at the side of his chair, and his fingers were crossed. A childish gesture he hadn't used since the third grade, but then, a lot of things were happening today that hadn't happened in a long time.

Heather didn't want to involve the police until she was

sure, but Ed knew of only one way to find out. Get Charlie to confess.

And he knew of only one person who could do that. And it was the last person Heather would ever want knowing her secrets.

Gaia Moore.

SELF-EMPLOYED

Ella knew she was supposed to be working, but she consoled herself by remembering that Sam was part of all this. Loki might not think he was important right now, but Ella knew better. He was important. One day Loki would thank her. Commend her for her foresight.

When Sam left his dorm, Ella tailed him without much care for discreetness. He wasn't trained to spot her, so there was no reason to put in the effort. She knew where he was going, anyway. To the park, to look for Gaia.

How pathetic could he be?

Still, he was nice to look at. The way the late afternoon

sun highlighted his hair and the shape of his cheekbones. Ella wouldn't mind getting a piece of Sam Moon.

Which was exactly why Gaia wouldn't be.

Ella would make sure of that.

She followed him across Washington Square North and through the arch. He stopped to help a little girl who'd dropped her books pick them up and replace them in her bag. So he was chivalrous, too. Did the fun ever stop?

Ella kept walking, deciding to find a perch in the park where she could keep an eye on him while he kept an eye out for Gaia. Loki would have wanted Ella to be keeping an eye out for Gaia too. But right now that didn't matter. Right now, she was working for herself.

A THREAT

After school Gaia headed straight for the park as fast as her tattered sneakers would carry her. She felt the need to reimmerse herself in the world she loved. In the society of other social abnormalities like Zolov and Renny and Mr. Haq. Last night she'd come far too close to the normal high school experience for her own comfort. And this lunchtime's game with the Wall Street dork had done nothing to stimulate her brain cells.

It was time for a freezing-yet-challenging game of chess and some conversation with a little old Russian.

And if she bumped into Sam while he was on a study break, well, that wouldn't technically be her fault.

Gaia was just blowing by American Apparel when she could have sworn she heard someone call her name. The wind was definitely playing tricks with her. She kept walking.

"Gaia?" Jogging footsteps. "Hey! Wait up!"

She stopped and shoved her hands in the pockets of her sweatshirt jacket. As she turned, the wind blasted into her face, instantly watering up her eyes and practically tearing her hair out of her scalp as it whipped back.

"Are you crying?"

It was Charlie Salita. And he looked genuinely concerned. Go figure.

"No," Gaia said, touching her raw palms to her eyes. "Just the wind."

"Oh." He smiled. His smile really didn't suck. Gaia suddenly felt totally conspicuous, standing on the street corner with one of the Village School's elite. She was already getting sucked back into the social black hole. "Where are you headed?" Charlie asked.

Gaia pointed her thumb over her shoulder. "Park."

"Cool. Mind if I walk with you?"

He had to be kidding. Wasn't it illegal for him to be seen with her or something? Weren't there universally accepted rules about this type of inter-high-school-species fraternization? And she couldn't believe he hadn't been totally put off by her hasty retreat the night before. There was something very odd going on, and Gaia wasn't entirely sure what to do about it.

Avoidance seemed like a good plan, though.

"Do you want something?" she asked, starting off. He fell into step beside her as she crossed Washington Square West and headed into the park. He had a long stride and kept pace with her easily. Most people had to jog to keep up.

"No," Charlie said with a laugh. "Why do I have to want something?"

Gaia glanced at him out of the corner of her eye. "Most people do," she said.

"Okay, I do want something." He stopped and backed out of the walkway so that the other pedestrians could get by. Gaia hesitated for a moment, then backed off the path in the other direction. She faced him, but there was a steady stream of people bustling by between them, trying to get to their next destinations before their noses froze off.

"What is it?" Gaia semishouted.

"Can you come over here?" Charlie said, clearly amused.

"Whatever it is, you can ask me from there," Gaia said. She was bouncing up and down on the balls of her feet, trying incredibly hard not to scan the area for Sam.

"Fine. I was wondering if you would go out with me this weekend," Charlie shouted. A couple of younger kids going by on skateboards snickered and leered at her as they passed. As her face turned an extremely dark shade of confused red, Gaia had three simultaneous thoughts.

Charlie was brain damaged—which wasn't all that shocking.

She was flattered—which definitely threw her.

And there was no way she was ever going to say yes.

There was the whole interspecies thing. The whole date-awkwardness thing. The fact that the last guy she'd said yes to had turned out to be a serial killer.

And there was also Sam. Or at least the possibility of Sam.

"I don't think so," Gaia said, starting off toward the chessboards again. Thankfully, Charlie didn't follow this time. He didn't drop it, either.

"I don't give up that easily!" Charlie yelled after her. He sounded very happy about it. Like he'd just made the ultimate promise.

Unfortunately, to Gaia it sounded more like a threat. She was actually starting to like the kid a little. It would be a pain if he kept forcing her to say no.

A RIFT

The Asian boy laughed as he pulled on his leather gloves and strolled out of the park, right by Sam. Right by Sam, who had just narrowly missed the little shouted proposition. The flirtatious smiles. The flattered blush on Gaia's face.

Ella had to sit down.

Why did he have to stop for that little girl? That could have been such a satisfyingly awkward confrontation. It might not have caused a rift, but it could have caused a crack. A splinter. A little hairline fracture.

It would have been entertaining.

Ella glanced from Gaia's face back to Sam's. Each going off in an opposite direction. They'd missed each other.

At least that was something.

And it would have to be enough.

For now.

BEAUTIFUL CHOICE

Sam was very proud of himself. He'd managed to walk right through the park to the other side in a straight line without even glancing at the chess tables. He'd been very good. He definitely deserved a lollipop or something.

He walked down Broadway into the heart of Greenwich Village, finally allowing himself to glance around as he went—checking out the bizarre array of people milling all around him. A fake blond in a power suit walked by a guy playing a pair of metal garbage cans like drums on the sidewalk. Then a homeless woman hobbled past, yelling at him for making so much noise, and an obviously stoned college kid came to the drummer's defense, telling the woman she wouldn't know art if it bit her in the ass.

Sam chuckled and shook his head. *This* was a study break—people-watching in the Village. If anything could clear his mind of equations and formulas, it was this. When he got back to the dorm, he'd be refreshed and ready to focus.

"Watch it! Watch it! Out of the way!" Sam looked up just in time to jump out of the path of a messenger on a ten-speed doing mach twenty on the crowded sidewalk. He pressed his hand against a shop window to balance himself. There were laws against that these days, weren't there?

Suddenly there was an impossibly tiny Chinese woman

getting right in his face. "You get fingerprint all over window!" she snapped.

Flinching, Sam pulled his hand away. "Sorry," he said.

"Get out of here, or you be *very* sorry," the lady warned, scrunching up her face angrily.

Sam took off down the street, shoving his hands under his arms. Suddenly people-watching didn't seem very entertaining anymore. He ducked into the first shop he saw, just to get a breather from the bedlam outside.

Once he took a look around, he couldn't believe his luck. He'd fallen right into a specialty shop that sold board games. Lining one entire wall was a glass case filled with all kinds of chessboards, from the simple to the ridiculous. One pitted little metal American presidents against famous foreign leaders of the past. Another had intricately painted Disney characters dressed up as kings and queens and knights. Then there were marble sets and glass sets and ceramic sets. As Sam wandered along the case, he couldn't believe his eyes.

It was like Mecca for chess geeks. He wondered if Gaia knew about this place. He was sure she could spend hours in here.

Suddenly his eyes fell on a small wooden board on the bottom shelf. The squares were made out of dark cedar and light birch, and the pieces were carved down to the most minute detail. The whole thing had been shellacked and shined so that the shop lights bounced off the polished surfaces. It came in a small wooden carrying case that closed with a gold clasp.

The set was made for Gaia. It was beautiful, yet simple, and the girl who always seemed to be on the move could take it anywhere.

Sam rubbed his palms against the thighs of his cords and looked around. He hadn't even bought a Christmas present for his mother yet. Or for Heather. He never shopped until Christmas Eve, when all the salespeople seemed to want to gouge his eyes out just for walking into the store.

Was he nuts for thinking about buying Gaia a gift? He wasn't even totally sure how she felt about him. If he bought this for her, she'd probably think he was an overzealous, clingy freak.

But she would also love it. Of that he was sure. And it would be worth it just to see the look on her face when she held those tiny little pieces in her hand. Another reason to look forward to the end of finals.

A salesman in a maroon sweater vest with a bad comb-over practically tiptoed up to Sam. He placed his hands together and smiled. "Can I help you, sir?" he asked.

"I'd like the travel set," Sam said quickly.

"A beautiful choice," the man said so automatically, it was clear he recited those words about twenty times a day.

Still, Sam grinned as he reached for his wallet. It was a beautiful choice. For a beautiful girl.

THREESOME

When Gaia turned onto Perry Street on Tuesday night and smelled the smell again, she immediately turned around and started back up Hudson. Her taste buds had already been massacred once this week, and she was too smart to make that mistake twice. Her stomach wanted food tonight, not bark and slop. George was just going to have to suffer without her.

Now came the good part. Deciding among the many fine grease-slinging restaurants of New York City. If there was any pleasure in Gaia's life, most of it came from sampling every fried food and sugar-coated anything on the Lower West Side. She hadn't run out of dives yet but as soon as she did, she was going to branch out into other neighborhoods. Gaia hadn't seen Mary since she'd missed the party last night, so she'd yet to make good on her promise to help distract her friend. And the hunt for bad-for-you food was always distracting.

She would have called and told her to come down, but Mary had sent her a message this morning saying she was knee-deep in "family stuff" and would call when she could. She'd also included a cryptic p.s. saying that they needed to talk.

Gaia could guess what Mary wanted to talk about. The party had, admittedly, been relatively clean, but as far as "good" and "fun" went, there was no question it was a complete failure. Mary would be chomping at the bit to break the whole thing down into a play-by-play in which she'd find a way to make fun of every single person that was there. As far as "family stuff" went, Gaia already knew that probably meant "getting Mary clean" stuff like family counseling. Ick. Mary had described her program as being a cross between group therapy and Chinese water torture. When the poor girl finally came up for air, at least the party would be something for her and Gaia to laugh about.

Gaia gripped the strap on her messenger bag as she took the wind in the face. She ducked her head and watched the ground as she walked. Another of the many good things about winter. No one felt the need to make eye contact.

As she walked, Gaia passed by some of her standard favorites. Mama Buddha, where they sold the best wonton soup she'd found thus far. Franco's Gyro, where she knew better than to ask what was actually in the pitas. Before she knew it, she was headed up Sixth Avenue. When she passed by the colorful windows of Urban Outfitters, Gaia realized where her stomach was leading her.

Gray's Papaya. Home of the buck-fifty hot dog. Gaia had at least three dollars in her pocket. It was time to feast.

She mentally congratulated her belly on its choice as she swung open the door to the garishly lit eatery. But the congratulations ended when Gaia saw who was seated at the counter in front of the window along the right-hand wall. Charlie Who Didn't Give Up That Easily and Sideburns Tim.

Her stomach grumbled angrily as she turned to leave.

But it was too late.

"Gaia the Brave!"

"Buy you a hot dog?" Charlie asked gleefully. "I swear I won't consider it a date."

Gaia slowly faced them and rolled her eyes.

"Come on," Sideburns Tim said, holding up his orange paper cup. "We'll even throw in a drink."

Quickly Gaia weighed her options. Free hot dogs and annoying company or twigs and slop and even more annoying company.

Too bad there wasn't a curtain number three.

"Fine," Gaia said, plopping onto a stool. "Get me three, with everything. And a root beer."

Charlie and Tim exchanged half-amused, half-disgusted glances, and then Charlie got up to place the order. Sideburns Tim smiled at her as he took a sip of his soda. Gaia stared at her translucent reflection in the plate glass window. Her hair was a brilliant conglomeration of tangles and knots, and one side of her jacket collar was rolled under while the other stood straight up.

She was utterly hopeless.

"I like a girl who can eat," Tim said, wiping his hand across his mouth.

"Pardon me while I swoon," Gaia said, nonchalantly straightening her collar. Tim laughed, and she almost smiled. Another key comeback. She was getting better at this. It almost made up for her utter lack of hygiene.

"So did you ask her yet?" Charlie demanded when he returned a moment later, slapping a paper plate full of hot dogs and relish and every other condiment known to man in front of Gaia. Charlie's hair, on the other hand, was so ordered and flawless, he could have had a team of stylists in his back pocket. He straddled the stool between Gaia and Tim and looked back and forth at them.

Great. What were they going to ask for, a threesome?

"No. She was busy lampooning me," Tim said with a good-natured laugh.

Charlie rolled his eyes. "Fine, I guess I have to do everything myself." He swiveled on his stool so he was entirely facing Gaia and popped his feet up on the bottom rung. "We're having another party tomorrow night," he said. "My place this time. I'd love for you to come."

Gaia smirked. "You just want me there for my aim."

"Not my primary motivation," Charlie said.

There was something in the way he said it that made Gaia blush. God, she hated that. Couldn't she have been born without the blushing gene? "I don't think so," she said. Then, as an afterthought, she added, "Thanks."

"Why not?" Tim asked, popping his head up over

Charlie's shoulder like a parrot. "Didn't you have fun last night?"

Gaia shoved half a hot dog in her mouth, letting a blob of relish hit the floor. The word *ladylike* wasn't in Gaia's personal dictionary. She was kind of hoping her ickiness would drive them away, but they only looked more fascinated. "It's just not my thing," she said through a full mouth of food.

"Well," Charlie said, eyeing her plate. "We have three hot dogs' worth of time to convince you."

Gaia narrowed her eyes and shoved the other half of her hot dog into her mouth.

Charlie's brow knitted in concern. "You think you could eat a little slower?"

TO: gaia13@alloymail.com
FROM: shred@alloymail.com
TIME: 4:30 P.M.
RE: 911
Hey, G.—
I left a couple of messages with Ella, but somehow I get the feeling you'll never get them. I need to talk to you. It's kind of important. If you get this, meet me at Dojo's at seven o'clock. I wouldn't ask if it wasn't huge.
Thanks.
Shred

TO: gaia13@alloymail.com
FROM: shred@alloymail.com
TIME: 8:05 P.M.
RE: stood up
Hey, G.—
So I guess you didn't get the message. Call me when you get this. I really need to talk to you. I'm sure you can tell by the lack of bad jokes in this e-mail that I'm actually freaking.
Call me.
Shred

ROMEO

She's going to be a challenge. More so than any of the others. I can tell by the look in her eyes. She thinks she's strong, but she's not. She thinks taking a few classes at Crunch will make her invincible.

I can show her what invincible looks like.

I can show her a lot of things.

DAMN SCARY

"MIND YOUR OWN BUSINESS, SHRED,"
HE SAID THROUGH HIS TEETH. "OR THIS
CHAIR IS GOING TO SEEM LIKE A BLESSING
COMPARED TO WHERE YOU'LL END UP."

A LAUGH

Gaia bounded down the stairs on Wednesday morning, hair wet, clothes half buttoned, late for school as always. She cursed as she slammed her toe into a doorjamb on her way down the hall. It was then that she realized she'd forgotten to put on her shoes.

She came around the corner into the kitchen and stopped, skidding slightly on the freshly waxed linoleum floor. Ed was sitting at the kitchen table, nursing a steaming cup of coffee.

"Morning," Gaia said, walking by him on her way to the pantry. She was only moderately surprised to see him there. There were two amazing things about Ed Fargo. One was the fact that he was a morning person, and the other was that he seemed to think she was one, too.

"Morning," he replied. "George let me in on his way out." She could feel his eyes following her as she crossed the room. He was waiting for her to say something. As always, Gaia was clueless as to what he expected.

"I brought you a bagel," he said. "Tons of butter."

"Thanks," Gaia replied. "It'll save me the huge prep time for cold cereal." He didn't laugh. Odd. Gaia turned on her heel and trudged back to the table.

"You didn't call me last night," he said.

"Was I supposed to?" she asked, taking a bite of her bagel. The melted butter coated her tongue, and Gaia almost sighed. Heaven.

"I left you about fifty messages," Ed said with a sullen shrug. Gaia raised her eyebrows, and Ed immediately caved.

"Okay, *five* messages," he said, fiddling with the protective plastic top on his coffee.

Gaia glanced at the cordless phone on the wall next to the refrigerator. "The light wasn't blinking when I got home." Not that she'd actually looked.

"I talked to Ella," Ed said, almost apologetically.

Gaia snorted and picked at her front teeth with her thumbnail. "So this is my fault how?" she said.

"Okay, forget it," Ed said, shifting in his chair. Gaia really studied him for the first time—he was pale, and his eyes were rimmed with gray. He also hadn't cracked a joke or offhandedly complimented her once since she'd entered the room.

How insensitive could she be?

"Ed, what's wrong?" Gaia asked, forgetting about her breakfast.

He pushed his chair back slightly and maneuvered it so that he was facing the table straight on. Then he pulled himself up to the edge and leaned his elbows on the clean white surface. Gaia watched his preparations with growing concern. It never took this long for Ed to talk.

"There's a rapist at school," he said finally, his eyes almost wary as he waited for her reaction. Gaia felt all the muscles in her body recoil, tightening themselves as if she were getting ready to spring on someone.

"Who?" she asked.

Ed took a deep breath and held her gaze. "Charlie Salita."

Gaia blinked as her stomach contracted. "No way."

"I know it's hard to believe, but—"

"No," Gaia said, shifting in her seat. "I mean it. There's no way he's a rapist."

Ed's eyes widened slightly in surprise, and he studied her for a moment, obviously unsure of how to proceed. In that moment Gaia just wished he wouldn't proceed at all. She could actually see herself hanging out with Charlie, especially after last night, when a couple of hot dogs at Gray's had turned into a couple of hours at Gray's. There weren't many people who could keep her interest for that long. Besides Sam, of course. But most of the interesting stuff that happened between them happened in her imagination.

Gaia's mind flashed back to the night before, when Charlie had bought a few hot dogs and given them to a couple of homeless men outside. He was a good guy. She couldn't be wrong about this.

Not again.

"Gaia—," Ed began again.

"I'm telling you, Ed," she interrupted, her voice somewhere between pleading and demanding. "It's not possible."

A PAIN

Ed felt his face flush purple, and he pressed his lips together hard. He couldn't believe it. In every scenario he'd imagined for this conversation, he'd never thought Gaia wouldn't even let him talk.

"What do you mean, it's not possible?" Ed asked. "You spend five minutes at a party with the guy and you know him well enough to decide that?"

Gaia took a deep breath and leaned her forearms on the table. "I hung out with him last night, too," she said, causing a pain to sear through Ed, the likes of which he'd never felt before. "He's no rapist," Gaia added. "He's way too normal to have a secret like that." She paused and took a slow bite of her bagel. "He's also . . . nice."

Ed couldn't believe what he was hearing. Had she been

brainwashed? Gaia wasn't supposed to trust anyone, least of all a good-looking, spoiled, privileged jock like Charlie Salita.

"The person who told me wouldn't lie about something like this," Ed said, trying to remain on the logic tip.

Gaia ran a hand behind her slim neck and massaged the muscles there, shaking her head. "Okay," she said finally. "When did this girl say this happened?"

Now they were getting somewhere. "At the party," Ed answered firmly.

"He was with me at the party," Gaia reminded him. "For more than five minutes."

Ed's lips tightened. "What about after we left?"

"No way," Gaia said, tearing off a piece of bagel and popping it into her mouth. Suddenly Ed couldn't help thinking she was protesting a bit too much. Like maybe she was trying to convince herself. "He was happy-go-lucky boy that night," Gaia continued. "He wasn't even drunk." She paused and looked out the window, the sunlight slanting across her face and contorting her features. "If he was going to try it, he would have tried it on me."

Ed pushed his hands into the armrests on his chair and adjusted his position, mostly to give himself something to do as he tried to process Gaia's reaction. He'd always thought Gaia was the guilty-until-proven-innocent type. Charlie must have had a serious effect on her. The pain in Ed's chest cut even deeper.

"Why don't you want to hear this?" Ed asked finally.

Gaia's eyes flashed defiantly, as if she'd just received a huge challenge. "Fine," she said. "Tell me what this person said about Charlie. Exactly."

A sliver of doubt passed through Ed's heart. He knew what Heather had told him wasn't going to be very convincing coming from him. Gaia would have to see the pain and vulnerability firsthand. As if that was ever going to happen. Ed heaved a sigh.

"She said she was pretty sure Charlie raped her." Gaia sucked in air and was about to protest, but Ed cut her off. "But there was someone else raped that night. One of this girl's friends. There's more than one. I'm telling you—"

"This other girl said Charlie raped her, too?" Gaia asked.

Ed paused. "Well, no. Just that she was raped, so—"

"So maybe it wasn't Charlie at all," Gaia said, her brow knitted. "If this other girl was raped, she should press charges or something, but until there's something solid against Charlie, I—"

"I don't believe you," Ed said disdainfully.

"Well, what did you expect me to do?" Gaia said, sounding tired.

"Great, so you'll risk your own life to save random people from a car wreck, but you won't even bother to look into something that I'm telling you is real," Ed practically shouted, the veins standing out on his neck and forehead.

"Something that happened to someone I actually care about."

Ed's mouth snapped shut, and his face turned red so fast, his eyes started to water. He couldn't believe he'd just said that about Heather. It had been a long time since he'd allowed himself to acknowledge the fact that he cared for the girl.

There was a slight softening of Gaia's features when she saw his face. "Ed—"

"Forget it," Ed said, pushing himself away from the table. He angled his chair at the door. "I *thought* you would trust me," he said. "I thought we were friends."

As Ed made his way down the hall, a thought occurred to him that almost made him vomit on the spot. Heather *should* have gone to Sam. Gaia would have listened to Sam. She would do anything he asked.

Ed had never felt so useless in his life.

At the front door he realized she hadn't even bothered to follow him. From the sound of the silence in the kitchen, she hadn't even moved from her chair. She was probably sitting in there right now, munching happily on her bagel, totally unaffected.

While Heather was over at her apartment, unable to even think of food.

Ed pushed his way outside into the frost-filled air and took a good, long breath. It looked like he was just going to have to deal with this himself. He looked down at the wheels of his chair and sighed.

Somehow.

THE ACCUSATION

Ed waited until after study hall, when everyone else was getting out of gym, to make his move. He figured Charlie would be all winded and tired from working out for an hour, and Ed would at least hold the advantage of having his wits about him. Of course, there was also the possibility that working out would have Charlie pumped, adrenaline ready to explode.

Why didn't this occur to him until he was sitting outside the locker-room door? The class started to empty out, and every time the door was flung open, Ed's heart caught in his throat as he waited for Charlie to appear. Finally the flow lessened to a trickle and no Charlie. Just as Ed was about to give up, Tim Racenello walked out of the locker room, buttoning the top button of his shirt. "Shred!" he said with a grin. "What's up, man?"

Ed swallowed and pushed himself back so his butt was

hitting the back of his chair. "I'm looking for Charlie," he said.

"He's in that health section," Tim said, gesturing at the nearly empty hall. Ed rolled his eyes shut. What an idiot. Every quarter a section of the gym class had to take a class in teen health issues. That meant Charlie was somewhere across the school right now. So much for careful planning.

"Want me to give him a message?" Tim asked, his eyes flicking over Ed.

Suddenly Ed had an idea. Tim was Charlie's best friend, and they were nothing if not loudmouths. It was quite possible that Tim knew about everything that had happened between Charlie and Heather. It had happened, after all, in Tim's apartment. "Yeah," Ed said flatly, glancing over his shoulders to make sure no one was around. Empty. "You can tell him to stop raping people."

THE CHANGE

Ed knew he was being blunt. He knew he was going for shock value. But he never could have been prepared for the change that came over Tim's face when his words sank in. It looked like there was a string attached to his chin and someone was pulling down on it, drawing all of Tim's features closer together. His lips folded into a V, his eyebrows almost touched, his eyes were like slits, and his pupils shrank to the size of pinpricks. His chin even seemed longer.

It was pretty damn scary.

THE REAL THREAT

"You know Charlie," the new Tim-thing said in a voice that sounded oddly normal. "He wouldn't hurt a fly."

Ed pushed his chair back a few inches to alleviate the disconcerting feeling that Tim was hovering over him. "Look, Tim," he said. "All I know is that someone said—"

"Whoever this someone is," Tim said, crossing his arms over his chest and standing up straight, "she must have wanted it." His features seemed to return to normal as he said the last few words, as if the cliché was comforting to him.

"Tim, this girl is telling the truth," Ed said, feeling more comfortable now that Tim no longer looked like an angry bat. "She's not a liar."

"Heather Gannis not a liar? That's a laugh," Tim said, cracking himself up.

Ed felt suddenly dizzy. "I didn't tell you who I was talking about," he said.

This didn't even faze Tim. He gradually stopped laughing and smirked at Ed. "You didn't have to," he said. "Charlie told me all about it."

"So you knew," Ed said slowly. The ice in his heart was slowly moving to his extremities, freezing his fingers. He was sure it would have frozen his toes, too, if he could feel them.

"I knew they had sex," Tim said, adjusting his backpack and looking off down the hall as if he had better places to be. "And I knew she was all over him. He didn't rape her, Ed. Come to grips with the fact that your ex is a slut."

Ed had to hold on to the chair to keep from launching himself at Tim. He knew he'd just fall in a limp pile at the guy's feet, which definitely wouldn't get him anywhere. But letting him talk about Heather that way practically killed him. "You come to grips with the fact that there's some evil shit going on at those parties of yours," Ed blurted out, glaring up at Tim with a rage that could have flattened the entire school. "You have to put a stop to it, Tim. He might have done it to a lot of other girls. You never know—"

"And you never know when to shut up, do you?" Tim asked, leaning into Ed's chair. He gripped the armrests, placing his hands just behind Ed's, and brought his face within millimeters of Ed's. "Mind your own business, Shred," he said through his teeth. "Or this chair is going to seem like a blessing compared to where you'll end up."

The bell rang, but Ed barely even heard it over the blood rushing through his ears.

Tim straightened up, popped a piece of gum into his mouth, winked, and walked away.

Ed didn't even know what period it was anymore. He had no clue where he was supposed to be. All he knew was that he had to get to a bathroom. Fast.

LONER

Gaia walked into the cafeteria and quickly glanced over the crowd. She'd already decided she was ditching out on lunch today, but there was something she needed to get out of the way first.

She plunged into the seat-searching crowd and maneuvered her way over to the table by the window where Charlie and Tim were sitting with a bunch of their friends, some of whom had fallen victim to her projectile peanuts a couple of nights ago.

They were both surprised to see her, so she got to talk first.

"So, I'm in," she said, focusing on Charlie. The sweet if cocky face. The just slightly overlapped, yet ridiculously white teeth at the front of his smile. Not a rapist. Ed must have misheard. Misunderstood. She didn't care. She knew who she was dealing with.

"You're in," Tim repeated, glancing at the other guys around the table. A couple of them snickered and looked away. So juvenile.

"Tonight," Gaia said, pushing a strand of hair behind her ear. "I'll be there. Where's your place?"

Charlie finished chewing on a soggy-looking fry and pulled another little flyer out of his bag. This one was yellow with a cartoon of a little kissing couple.

"Oh, how sweet," Gaia said, stuffing the flyer in her back pocket. "Later." She turned and headed into the crowd again, ignoring Charlie as he called after her to join them. Screw Ed and his bogus accusations. His little speech that morning had reminded her of why she had sworn off friends in the first place. Too much pressure. It was like he thought he could use her as his own personal superhero. He got an idea in his head, and she was expected to follow through with it or what? He wouldn't talk to her for the rest of the day?

Gaia shot a look at their regular table and saw Ed immediately look away. Apparently that was the punishment.

What was the point?

Gaia took the steps in the stairwell three at a time and burst through the heavy metal door onto the street. Automatically her feet started to turn toward the park, but she stopped herself, reaching out to grip the wrought-iron fence that ran along the sidewalk in front of the school.

What was the point of going there? Another good question.

Sam wouldn't be there. Sam hadn't called. He hadn't written again after his original, blow-off e-mail. Hadn't called to clear up the mystery of what had or hadn't happened on Thanksgiving. Didn't even have the courtesy to let her know whether she was still Gaia the Unkissed. There was no reason to torture herself by going to the park. She was a sorry case for thinking about it. She'd already wasted enough of her life pining. Obsessing. Daydreaming.

Gaia started off in the other direction, sure she could find some distraction farther downtown.

She didn't need Ed. And she didn't need Sam. Gaia Moore was a loner. She did what she wanted when she wanted.

It was time she started to remember that.

THE BIG TEN

10. Christina Perraita
9. Tashana Rydell
8. Amy O'Neil
7. Caitlin Alesse
6. Michelle Sussman
5. Kim Goldberg
4. Jen Rinsler
3. Jen Malkin
2. Heather Gannis
1. Gaia Moore

THE ATTACK

THE GUY HOVERING ABOVE HER WAS TAKING OFF
HIS JACKET AND GOING FOR HIS ZIPPER.

FALLING APART

Mary quickened her steps as she turned off Barrow onto Hudson and started to walk uptown. She'd chosen a far too flimsy jacket, which she pulled more tightly around herself as the signal at the corner turned red. She'd lived in New York all her life, but it never ceased to amaze her how she could be perfectly comfortable on one street, turn a corner, and be freezing. The city was a climactic anomaly.

It was early, but she couldn't wait to get to the club and get all sweaty and gross on the dance floor. Mary much preferred hot to cold. She knew it was dangerous, going out with these friends to this place. She knew there would be temptations. But she could handle it. She could. All she had to do was think of Gaia. Think good, clean fun.

She'd yet to have any since she and Gaia had made their pact. Her first try had entailed staring at mutts while they tried to hump each other and getting threatened and the most nonpartyish party she'd ever come across. Mary was beginning to think "good, clean fun" was an oxymoron, but she would give it the old Mary Moss try. At least one more time. Mary took a deep breath and forced herself to smile. It was all good. She was going to be just fine without the coke. Perfectly, perfectly fine.

Making the left on Jane Street, Mary was suddenly

aware that the two guys walking behind her were the same two guys who were walking behind her back on Barrow. She hadn't gotten a good look at them, but they stood out because they were walking so close together and she hadn't yet heard them say a word. Her heart started to pound a little faster. She suddenly didn't like the feel of this.

She slowed her steps, hoping they were just a couple out for a walk and were just too in love for words. Maybe they would get frustrated at her pace and pass her by.

Which was exactly what they started to do. Big sigh. Mary stepped left to let them pass. And that was when she saw the masks.

The scream came out without her even willing it, but a large, gloved hand slapped over her mouth and practically twisted her head off as it pulled her back. Mary struggled, reaching her arms up over her head and scratching at his ski mask as the attacker pulled her down a set of darkened stairs.

She kicked out her legs, causing them both to stumble, and they crashed down into the little concrete cove in front of a basement apartment.

Mary had just enough time to register that the door was boarded up and the place was abandoned and that there would be no help before the masked guy backhanded her across the face. She tasted the blood before she even felt the pain pop behind her eye. Then he planted a fist in her gut.

Doubling over, Mary crumpled to the ground. She had to

cough, but her body wouldn't let her take in enough breath. Something sharp was cutting into her leg, and she could feel the blood spreading out over her skin, sticking to her tights. It was warm, and it brought her to her senses.

Enough to realize that the guy hovering above her was taking off his jacket and going for his zipper.

The terror that seized her heart was almost enough to kill her right there. But instead it seemed to take control of her body and tell it what to do. Mary quickly rolled over onto her back, lifted her bleeding leg, and delivered one hard kick to the masked guy's balls.

He let out a primal grunt and went over, falling right on top of her, his elbow grinding painfully into her chest. Mary struggled to get out from under him, which wasn't that hard this time since he was totally incapacitated. He fell over onto his side, holding his groin and sputtering a cough.

As Mary struggled to her feet, she scraped both knees against the concrete but barely felt it. She was too busy checking out guy number two through her throbbing eyes. He had his back to them, standing watch. Apparently he expected a loud struggle because the fight hadn't even caught his attention. But Mary running past him would certainly turn his eye.

How the hell was she going to get by him?

And what if she didn't? Was he going to rape her when his friend was done? Was that the plan? The thought sapped

Mary's strength, and her knees started to shake as hot tears blinded her vision. She was falling apart. And that scared Mary even more than the situation. She never fell apart.

Suddenly two arms grabbed her from behind, and Mary let out another scream. She reached back with her one free hand and scratched the guy's forearm as hard as she could. Her nails came back with skin and blood packed under them. He yelled out and dropped her. Mary immediately sprang to her feet, taking the steps two at a time.

The watchdog was just coming to the top of the stairs when she got there. He was big. Bigger than the attacker below, but Mary had two things going for her. Adrenaline and speed. She rammed into the guy's shoulder, sending him reeling backward in obvious surprise.

Then she ran, tears streaming down her face as she barreled by shoppers and theatergoers and drunks. Part of her wanted to go right home and hide under her covers, but the rational part of her brain kicked in and told her she was miles from home. She'd have to wait for the subway. They could follow and catch up to her, and who knew what they'd do to her now that they were pissed.

When she got to Perry Street, she hooked a left.

She just hoped Gaia was home.

PARALYZING

Gaia had yet to answer the doorbell at George and Ella's house, but there was a first time for everything, and she was sort of standing in front of it. Avoidance was almost impossible. But when she swung open the door, she immediately forgot about the novelty of it all.

Mary was standing there, looking like she'd just clawed her way out of the grave. There were cuts, bruises, blood, dirt, dried tears. A crushed cigarette butt hung from a tangle in her matted red hair. For a moment Gaia forgot where she was.

"Can I come in?" Mary asked. Her voice sounded like someone had rubbed her throat down with sandpaper. She pulled her hair back from her face, revealing more bruises, and shook the cigarette away, the effort almost bringing her to tears.

Gaia stood aside, holding the door open farther. As Mary entered the foyer, Gaia heard Ella stirring in the office.

"Can you get up the stairs?" Gaia asked, glancing toward the back of the house. Ella was closing drawers, putting things away. Any second she would walk out, and she would definitely want an explanation. She'd probably toss Mary out on the street before she'd risk getting blood on any of her "neocolonial" furniture.

"I think so," Mary croaked.

"Then let's go," Gaia said. She hustled Mary up the stairs, moving her faster than was probably comfortable for her. It was painfully, painfully slow to Gaia, but it was fast enough to get her friend out of Ella's sight in time.

"Gaia?" Ella called up after them. "Who was at the door?"

Normally Gaia just wouldn't bother answering, but she didn't want Ella coming upstairs and banging into her room again.

"Girl Scouts!" Gaia called back. "I put you down for a dozen boxes."

Mary stumbled into Gaia's bedroom and sat down hard on the floor, wincing in pain. Gaia slammed the door shut behind them and joined her friend, sitting Indian style on the hard wood.

"What happened?" Gaia asked, trying to keep from staring at Mary's wounds. There was a yellowish bruise forming around her left eye, and her lip was crusted with blood.

"Two guys just decided to use me for some recreational entertainment," Mary answered, gingerly touching a cut on her leg. Gaia reached up onto her bed, grabbed the white T-shirt that was balled up there, and handed it to Mary. Her friend looked at it quizzically.

"It's for your leg," Gaia said.

"It's brand-new," Mary said, holding it carefully away from all the blood.

"It's just a shirt," Gaia answered. She took it out of Mary's hands and held it to her friend's leg. A bright red splotch of blood seeped out across the stark white fabric. They both stared at it for a moment in silence. Gaia could tell by the steadying of her breaths that Mary was taking that moment to calm down. To come to grips with the fact that she was safe.

Gaia was just getting more and more angry.

"Did you get a good look at them?" Gaia asked finally, still staring at the blood. If Mary told her one was blond and one was brunette, Gaia would take out every Waspy guy in the city.

"No, but I took a chunk out of the one who used me as a punching bag." Mary held up her right hand. Three of her fingertips were covered in dried blood. Gaia was glad that Mary had gotten in one good blow.

"They were wearing masks," Mary continued, pressing her hands onto the floor and squeezing her eyes shut in pain as she adjusted her position. She pushed herself up so that her back was leaning against the side of the bed and let out a sigh. "But I know who they were."

Waiting for Mary to tell her was hard. It took away from precious ass-kicking time. But Gaia did wait. Mary needed to put forth obvious effort just to think.

"I went to that party the other night," Mary said finally, glancing at Gaia quickly. "You'd already left, I think."

Gaia felt like someone had just slammed a kick into her stomach. She suddenly had a suspicion about where this was going, and she didn't like it. Her self-flagellation mechanism immediately kicked in, telling her this was her fault. All hers. Somehow everything was her fault.

"I walked in on these guys . . . some kind of sex club or something. They were keeping score," Mary said. She looked down at her lap and picked at the little fuzzies on her sweater. The blood splotch continued to grow on her leg, but her sweater was cleaning up rapidly. "A couple of them threatened me."

"Names," Gaia said, clenching and unclenching her fist. "Did you get their names?"

"Only one," Mary said, looking Gaia in the face. Her eyes squinted, and she bit her bottom lip. "It was Charlie, I think. Yeah. Charlie. He didn't like me very much."

Gaia's vision blurred gray. Her head felt like it was going to explode. Her fist gripped so hard, her jagged, ripped nails cut into her palm. The anger was almost paralyzing. But it wasn't directed at Charlie now.

For the moment she was angry only at herself.

"Ed, where are we going?" Heather asked, sounding weary. She stuffed her hands under the arms of her black wool coat. Her collar was pushed up against the wind, and her hat was pulled down tightly over her ears. You'd think she was on an expedition in Antarctica.

"You asked me to help you, so I'm helping you," Ed said, bringing his chair to a stop in front of their destination. Bowlmor Lanes.

Heather looked up at the red banner with its big bowling pin and ball. Then she glanced inside at the neon lights and dingy tiled floor. Ed wasn't surprised by the grimace of disgust.

"Help me what?" she asked. "Immerse myself in cheese?"

"Cut the snob act, Heather," Ed said, rolling through the door and into the waiting elevator. He turned around and looked up at her. "You forget you're dealing with the one person who knows it's faked."

For a split second the mask fell, and Heather stepped into the elevator beside him, but by the time they got up to the lanes, it was back in full force. "Can you even play in that thing?" she asked, eyeing his chair as they approached the counter.

"I can do *lots* of things," Ed said in a little kid voice. Heather cracked half a smile and looked at the big Italian guy who was doling out the shoes.

"Size seven," she said. As he turned toward the wall of shoes, Heather almost grabbed for his arms, then obviously thought the better of it and pulled back. "Clean ones, if you have them," she said. Ed laughed out loud.

By the time Heather had picked out her ball—a purple one, of course—and strapped on her decidedly not clean shoes, Ed had already bowled four balls and hit one strike.

"I can't believe I'm doing this," Heather said, tiptoeing up to the line, ball in hand. "If anyone saw me—"

"If anyone saw you, they'd be here, too," Ed said, smiling cockily up at her. "So then they'd pretty much be in the same situation, wouldn't they?"

Heather gave him an oh-aren't-you-so-smart? look and held the ball up to shoulder level. Ed pushed himself back to give her room and watched her as she studied the lane. She could complain all she wanted, but Ed knew she loved to bowl. She got so competitive, you'd think she was on the Olympic team. If she wouldn't let him help her by going to the police, the least he could do was take her mind off things.

Especially after the way he'd crashed and burned with Gaia.

And crashed, burned, and almost been killed by Tim.

Heather took a few steps, pulled back her arm, and let fly. The ball careened down the lane and smashed into the middle pin, sending the entire set flying. The big dancing X appeared on the screen above their heads.

"Yes!" Heather shouted, throwing her arms in the air.

Ed laughed and automatically held out his hand to her. She slapped it as she strutted past.

"Beat that, Fargo," she said, plopping into an orange plastic chair and crossing her legs in front of her. The waitress came by, and Ed heard Heather order two turkey burgers and two sodas.

"Thanks," Ed said, grabbing his ball and placing it in his lap so he could maneuver to the top of the lane.

"For what?" Heather shouted over the loud music pumping from hidden speakers somewhere over their heads. "Loser's buying, so you'd better find your wallet."

Ed shook his head and pushed his chair forward.

It was nice to have the old Heather back in full force.

Kind of.

STUDY BREAK

"Sam Moon, prepare to die!"

Sam barely had time to duck under his desk before three of his so-called friends burst into his room and pelted him with water balloons. One splattered against his lower back, dripping ice-cold liquid down his pants and soaking his underwear.

"What the hell are you guys doing?" Sam shouted from the cramped space under his desk. Every part of his body was soaking and stinging except his head.

"Study break, man!" Mike shouted, flinging another balloon. This one bounced off Sam's back in one piece and rolled across the floor. Sam heard a scuffle as Mike and the rest of his friends started to go for it, but Sam was already on the floor, and he was just plain faster. He scurried out of his hiding place, grabbed the balloon, and flipped over into a sitting position, holding it back above his head. His friends all froze, eyeing him warily as they tried to figure out who he was going to decide to attack.

Sam moved the balloon to his left hand and slowly reached under his bed with his right.

"You forget who you're dealing with," he said matter-of-factly, then watched their eyes widen as he pulled out a brightly colored Super Soaker.

"Shit!" they all yelled in unison. They fell over each other as they clamored for the door, and Sam doused them all with one, solid pull of the trigger, chasing them out into the common room. He laughed evilly, drunk with power as they all ducked behind their torn, pizza-stained couch.

"Bow before my greatness," Sam shouted, following up with a cartoon-worthy cackle.

But there was no white flag. Moments later they all popped up again, each holding a balloon in each hand. Sam was toast. His heart actually dropped.

"Put the gun down and back away," Will said slowly.

"I'll never surrender," Sam said, taking a step back nevertheless.

"You will when you see the coolerful we have back here," Mike answered. The boy was very good at menacing. Sam turned and bolted back into his room, slamming the door behind him. He didn't have time to barricade it before they all crashed through. The enduring war was nothing if not disorganized. Everyone was soaking everyone, and Sam laughed harder than he remembered laughing in months. After stressing over finals and Gaia and Heather for the last few days, it felt extremely good to let loose, even if his room was suffering dire consequences.

At one point he finally dared to open his eyes to assess the damage and saw that Mike was about to step on Gaia's gift.

"Stop!" Sam yelled.

Miraculously, everyone froze. Probably because Sam sounded like a borderline psycho.

"Mike, don't move," Sam said, holding out his hand.

"What is it?" Mike asked nervously. "A rat?"

Sam quickly crawled over to where Mike was standing, the knees of his jeans squishing as he went, and gingerly pulled the box out from behind Mike's feet. It was undamaged. It wasn't even wet, which seemed completely impossible. But it was obvious to Sam that he had to get it out of here before the next study break brought an onslaught of food or something.

"Okay, guys, war's over," Sam told his friends as he held the box away from his sopping wet body. "I have someplace I gotta be."

GAIA

Generally, I'm not a person who plans things. I wouldn't be able to if I wanted to. Make big plans, I mean. I never know where I'm going to be from one month to the next. This time last year, if you'd told me I'd be living in New York, I would have told you to get fitted for a straitjacket.

But here I am.

And I've always been fine that way. Not planning. If you don't figure out exactly how you want everything to be, you can't be crushed when it all goes to hell. So not planning has always been fine.

Until now.

Yes, I can kick Charlie's ass. Yes, I can find out who his little sidekick was and kick his ass, too. I could probably take on their whole little club. But that's not enough. Not this time. I can admit that whatever I can do to them won't be nearly enough. Because with a pack mentality, there's no guarantee they won't just get back on the horse and keep doing what they're doing.

Bad metaphor.

The point is, this time I have to have a plan. These guys deserve real-world punishment. And Mary and I both know that with what she has right now, she can't prove anything. We have to catch him in the act.

That's where Gaia the decoy comes in. I'm the bait. Yippee.

But maybe I can get a confession out of him—who knows? I can, after all, be pretty persuasive when I want to be. That way, maybe none of us will have to go to court. Not me. Or Mary. Or Ed's friend, whoever she was. No one will have to relive it.

And at the very least, if the whole plan goes to hell. I'll still be there.

At least they'll still get their asses kicked.

MISS POPULARITY

NOT GAIA. SHE WAS GORGEOUS. NO MAKEUP.
DIRTY HAIR. SALVATION-ARMY-WORTHY
CLOTHES. AND SHE WAS GORGEOUS.
ELLA WANTED TO KILL HER.

IN CHARGE

Ella was sitting in the living room when she heard the door to Gaia's bedroom creak open. Her senses immediately went on high alert. It was her job, after all, to keep an eye on Gaia—to monitor her every move. It was also becoming her obsession.

The sound of footsteps on the stairs was followed by muffled whispers. There was someone with her. Ella pushed herself off the plush, peach-colored couch. If Gaia had smuggled Sam up to her room, there were going to be dire consequences. Ella would have to figure out what they were going to be, but she was confident she could devise some sort of punishment. The girl would have to listen to her at some point. Ella would make sure of that.

She got to the foyer just as Gaia was closing the door behind her visitor.

"Who was that?" Ella snapped, placing her hands on her rounded hips. She so wanted to go over to the window and check the streets, but she knew whoever it was would be far out of sight by now. And she didn't want to give Gaia the satisfaction.

"A friend," Gaia said, her voice very flat. Very low.

"A boyfriend?" Ella asked, frustrated by the high pitch her voice took on. She was jealous. She knew she was. Jealous that Gaia even had a shot at Sam Moon—that perfect specimen. The jealousy just frustrated her more.

Gaia snorted a laugh and walked by Ella. She ducked into the hall closet, rummaged through it, and pulled out a long, battered army coat. She shoved her arms into it, yanked down on the front of her gray sweatshirt, and checked her reflection in the gilt-framed mirror above the hall table.

Ella watched, almost mesmerized, as Gaia pushed her knotted hair behind her shoulders, licked her fingertip, and wiped a smudge of something from her cheek. If Ella had done that, she would have taken away a fingertip full of foundation and she'd have to start the whole grueling primping process all over again. Not Gaia. She was gorgeous. No makeup. Dirty hair. Salvation-Army-worthy clothes. And she was gorgeous.

Ella wanted to kill her.

"Where are you off to, Miss Popularity?" she asked, crossing her arms over her chest and leaning back against the wall. "You look good enough to go eat out of garbage cans in the park."

"Thanks," Gaia said, buttoning up the coat. "I would go join your friends at the cans, but I have a party to go to."

Ella narrowed her eyes, seeing red as Gaia swept past her, brushing her disgusting old coat against Ella's leg. The girl was so damned cocky. So damned cold and sure of herself. Ella could take that away in an instant. All she had to do was reach into the closet, just inches from where Gaia had grabbed her coat, and get her gun. What Ella wouldn't give to see Gaia's face.

Then Ella would be in charge. Then Gaia would get in line.

And then, of course, Ella's cover would be blown.

"Gaia, you can't just come and go as you please," Ella said, just barely staying in character.

"Watch me." Gaia slammed the door in Ella's face.

For one brief moment there was silence, and then Ella turned and swept the hall table clean, letting out a primal sort of scream. She picked up the largest piece of the now broken lamp and pulled back her arm, ready to hurl it at the mirror. Her reflection looked crazed—frightening—and it gave her pause. But all she had to do was imagine it was Gaia she was looking at, and she snapped all over again, flinging the lamp so hard that for a moment she thought her shoulder had pulled out of its socket.

She smiled happily as Gaia's reflection shattered into a hundred pieces and slipped with a delicious crash to the floor.

One day she would feel what it was like to crush the real thing.

And that day couldn't come soon enough.

Gaia walked into Charlie's brownstone and searched the slight crowd from just inside the door. She wasn't even remotely surprised when the lyrics of a familiar Fearless song crooned from nearby speakers.

Nobody's gonna hold you down. Nobody's gonna make you cry. Nobody's gonna break your heart if you don't let 'em say good-bye.

Gaia smirked at the cliché sentiments, rolled back her shoulders, and headed straight for the far end of the living room, where Charlie was already working his first victim. Some tiny little girl with tiny little arms and tiny little cheeks. Gaia practically shoved her out of the way.

"Hey!" Tiny Girl protested.

Gaia ignored her. The girl could thank her later.

"Hi," Gaia said to Charlie, somehow keeping the disgust out of her voice. He'd tried to rape her friend. Beaten the crap out of her just hours ago. And yet he could stand here in his designer sweater with his gelled hair and his stupid smile and act as if he was God's gift to the female population.

"Gaia," he said with an easy grin. "It's good to see you."

Gaia really wished she could say the same. She'd really liked the cocky bastard. Enough to go to two, count 'em, two high school parties.

"Can I get you anything?" Charlie asked, glancing

toward the makeshift bar at the front of the room.

"Yeah," Gaia said, unable to believe what she was about to say. "You."

Charlie's smile turned into a grin, and it was all Gaia could do to keep from laying him out right there. Instead she lowered her lashes and looked up at him through them, just like she'd seen Heather's flirtatious-by-habit friends do a million times.

"If you're still interested."

Charlie reached behind him and put his plastic cup down on the bookshelf just over his right shoulder.

"Oh, I'm interested." He reached out and took her hand, lacing his fingers through hers. He squeezed. She couldn't bring herself to squeeze back.

"My room's right down the hall," he said, eyeing her as if he was waiting for her to back out. He was in for a big surprise. Or two. Gaia stood up on her tiptoes and brought her mouth so close to his ear, she could smell where the cologne mixed with the gel.

"Let's go outside," she whispered, and almost vomited when she felt Charlie shiver. "I like to do it outdoors."

Not that she had any idea where she actually liked to do it.

But apparently Charlie agreed with her. Before Gaia could blink, they were halfway to the back door. Charlie, ever the gentleman, grabbed a chenille throw from the couch along the way.

SOMETHING OF HIM

Sam pushed his hand through his hair a few times, hoping he didn't look like a Santa Claus clone with red nose and cheeks from walking in the freezing cold. Gaia's gift, now wrapped with a card stuffed inside, was cradled under his arm. When he got to her house, he was just about ready to puke, but he took the steps two at a time, anyway.

He might as well at least look confident.

The bell played a little tune, but Sam was too distracted to even place it. He took a step back, watching the door as his heart pounded crazily. He heard noises inside and held his breath, hoping Gaia would be the one to answer the door. He wasn't sure if he could handle waiting all over again as someone went off to find her.

A few moments passed, and no one came. Weird. Sam was sure he'd heard noises. He reached forward and knocked. Total silence.

Sam had the sudden, odd feeling he was being watched. He looked up at empty windows. Was Gaia up there somewhere? Had she seen him and decided not to come out? Sam's heart plummeted at the thought. Well, he wasn't going to stand here looking like a moron.

He looked down at the gift in his hands and contemplated it for a moment. Before he could entirely think it through, he bent down and left it on the doorstep. If she wasn't in there laughing at him, maybe she'd get it and get in touch with him.

If she was in there laughing at him, she could have it. The pathetic part of Sam still wanted her to have it.

To have something of him.

NOT FAIR

Mary heard a footstep behind her and glanced over her shoulder for the tenth time in as many seconds. She mentally told her heart to just stay in her throat.

"Just go to the precinct, find a detective, and wait for her call," Mary repeated Gaia's instructions to herself, keeping her head bent against the wind. She watched her feet as they clicked quickly along the sidewalk. There were people everywhere, but Mary felt like she was entirely alone, walking in a spotlight. She was sure they were after her. Every garbage can she walked by hid a masked attacker. Every time she came to an alley, she quickened her pace.

She was starting to sweat under her jacket, and she swallowed hard. When she'd thought about getting hot and sweaty tonight, this wasn't exactly what she'd had in mind.

She hadn't thought that by the end of the night, she'd be afraid of her own city. The town she'd grown up in. The town she'd always loved as her home.

It just wasn't fair. Even less fair was the fact that she couldn't have anything to take the edge off.

"Just go to the precinct, find a detective, and wait for her call," Mary said again, ducking her head even more as frustrated tears burned at her eyes. "Just go to the precinct . . . wait for the call."

GAIA'S SECOND KISS

"Where do you want to go?" Charlie asked in what Gaia was sure was his best husky whisper. He sounded like a hoarse dog. Gaia pointed to a relatively clean corner in the tiny "yard" behind the brownstone. It consisted of a small patch of dirt and an even smaller patch of dead grass. There was a rusted-out barbecue against a splintering wooden fence.

"No one will come out here, right?" Gaia asked, trying to sound like an ingénue.

"Don't worry," Charlie said, leading her to the corner and spreading out the blanket. "I have a friend watching the door." He pulled his sweater off over his head, revealing a T-shirt beneath, and immediately shivered. Still, he tossed it into the corner and ran a hand over his hair. "A little cold out here, isn't it?"

Gaia just plopped down onto the blanket and looked up at him, trying to invite him along with her eyes. She was sure it wasn't coming across because the last thing in the world she wanted was this asshole touching her. She had to remind herself of Mary. This was for Mary and everyone else who hadn't been as lucky as her.

"I guess we'll just keep each other warm, huh?" Charlie said, dropping to his knees.

Gaia tried not to wince as Charlie placed one hand on either side of her body and leaned into her, bringing his lips down hard on hers. She really wished Sam would call and clear up the details of Thanksgiving.

Because she really didn't want this to be her first kiss.

MAKING IT BELIEVABLE

Charlie's lips traveled down her neck.

When should she tell him to stop?

He pulled off her sweatshirt, and his eyes hungrily took in the slight tank top underneath.

Did she have to really get him into it before he would lose it? Before he would be unable or unwilling to stop himself?

He pushed her down against the hard ground, holding her shoulders with his hands as he kissed her roughly.

Okay, that felt like the start of something.

His hand traveled down from her neck to her shoulder and hovered right over her breast.

Gaia pushed him back by the shoulders.

"Stop." Enough, after all, was enough.

THE BATTLE OF THE STUPIDS

"You're kidding me," Charlie said.

He was pulling away. Why the hell was he pulling away? Wasn't this where he was supposed to start with the violence?

"I'm—"

"God, Gaia," Charlie said, standing up and grabbing his sweater, which was now covered with dirt. "I never would have pegged you for a tease."

Gaia racked her brain for a response. He was taking no for an answer? This was definitely not part of the plan. She scrambled to her feet as he shook out his sweater. This didn't make any sense. He could grab a girl off the street and try to force her to have sex, but someone teased him into it and said no and he just stopped?

Was she just that bad at this?

The flash of a streetlight on Charlie's silver watch caught her eye, and Gaia instantly remembered Mary's words about the fight. The blood under her nails. Gaia quickly took in Charlie's forearms just before he pulled on his sweater. Not a scratch. He was innocent.

Gaia didn't know whether to be relieved or pissed.

"Charlie, I'm—"

"Save it," he said, grabbing the blanket and heading inside. "You can go home now."

Her eyes narrowed as he walked into the house, letting the door slam behind him. She was glad she didn't get the words out. He was still a big asshole. Gaia picked up her own sweatshirt desperately trying to come up with the appropriate next move. If it wasn't Charlie, who the hell was it?

It suddenly occurred to her that it could have very well been a random attack. The guys in this sex ring, while being beyond perverted, might not be rapists. Ed could still be wrong. Gaia was completely confused. It was time to grab Mary and regroup.

She was lifting her sweatshirt above her head when she heard the back door close again. Maybe Charlie had changed his mind and decided to jump her after all. Gaia started to turn but didn't even make it all the way around before a powerful punch to the side of her face sent her reeling in the other direction.

Gaia's whole body slammed into the fence, sending a shock wave of pain down her left side and stabbing splinters into her chin. She pressed her hands into the raw wood and started to push herself away, but she was grabbed from behind, spun around, and slammed back against the fence again.

The attacker wasn't that strong, and he was very sloppy. Gaia could have taken him down with any number of her favorite moves. But she wanted to find out who it was first.

His face snapped into focus just as he uttered his telltale greeting. "Gaia the Brave."

She couldn't believe the little runt had the balls.

"Sideburns Tim," she said calmly.

He blinked, obviously confused that she wasn't whimpering, writhing, screaming, and begging. He was probably even more confused when she pulled back and head-butted him so hard that the cracking sound was almost deafening.

Tim slammed into the ground hard and raised his hand to his forehead with a guttural moan. Gaia wouldn't have been surprised if he'd given in right then, but he didn't. Somehow he was on his feet within seconds.

"Gaia the Brave is also Gaia the Stupid," he said, spitting as he said the words.

"Not as stupid as most," Gaia answered. Another cloud of doubt passed over his face, but before it even cleared, Tim lunged at her, grabbing her wrist, twisting it behind her, and sweeping her legs out from under her in one seamless motion.

Gaia couldn't have been more surprised if he'd delivered an expert karate kick to her neck. She was on her face, and his knees were bearing into her back, and she was tasting dirt. Breathing it into her half-crushed nostrils.

"What was that about not being stupid?" Tim said, reaching up one hand to hold her face down. Between the pressure of the ground against her chest and her face full of filth, Gaia could barely take in a breath. And without breath she couldn't fight. She had to strain the muscles in her neck, but she managed to twist her head aside.

She could hear Tim struggling with his belt, the buckle clanging as he undid the closure.

He didn't waste any time, did he?

Gaia twisted her legs to the side and used all the power she had to flip herself over, knocking Tim aside from the force. He was on her again instantly, pushing down her arms.

His belt buckle was smacking against her knees, and Gaia realized he'd successfully pulled down his pants. She couldn't look. He must have had a lot of practice at this to do it that fast. The thought made her ill.

"You're it," he said, his face disgustingly close to hers. "You're the one I need."

For what, she didn't want to know. Somewhere in the recesses of her mind she recalled the fact that in order for it to be actual rape, she had to say no, stop, don't. Say something instead of just beating the guy to a pulp.

"You ready?" Tim asked.

"Don't even try it," Gaia said evenly. "I'm saying no."

Tim smiled gleefully. "That's exactly what I wanted to hear."

He released one of her hands for a split second and went to cover her mouth, but before he got anywhere near her face, Gaia delivered one swift hook to the right side of his jaw and followed it with an uppercut that sent him sprawling on his butt. Before he could get to his feet, she slammed her sneaker under his chin, holding down his neck.

Luckily Tim had never gotten his tighty whities off.

Tim coughed pathetically. She was crushing his windpipe.

"Get . . . off . . ." He tried to talk but couldn't get out the words. Keeping the pressure on his throat, Gaia bent at the waist and pulled up Tim's sleeves. There, practically glowing in the dim light, were three long, bloody scratches.

Gaia frowned with disgust. "We have a winner."

She pulled Mary's cell phone out of her pocket and dialed the local precinct. She only wished she could be there to see Mary's face when the call came through.

THE SEX RING

THEY WERE BIG, BUT PROBABLY SLOW.
SHE COULD DEAL, BUT THAT WOULD MEAN
PUTTING DOWN THE PHONE. AND JUST
WHEN THINGS WERE GETTING GOOD.

"Gaia, who the hell are you calling?" Tim asked, still pinned to the ground by her sneaker. The little diamond pattern on the sole was starting to make indentations in his neck. Gaia kind of liked it. Damn, she had a sick mind. "Can't we talk about—"

He wheezed to a stop when Gaia pressed harder into his throat. She thought she heard him mutter the word *bitch*. There was no reason to let up if he was going to keep talking like that. Too annoying. The line rang twice, and then a gruff female voice answered the phone.

"Fifteenth Precinct." She sounded beyond bored, and there was the distinct crackle of popping gum.

"I need to talk to whatever detective is in with Mary Moss," Gaia said quickly, shoving her free hand in her pocket. She pulled out a wrapped peppermint. Something to get the Charlie taste out of her mouth.

"Oh, you do, do you?" the woman said, the grogginess leaving her voice as it was replaced by an edge of amusement. Gaia's request was apparently a good source of entertainment. "Detective Rodriguez is a very busy man. What makes you think you can just—"

"I have his perp or his collar or whatever," Gaia said, rolling her eyes. She looked down at Tim as if she just couldn't believe the incompetents at the police department. Tim lifted his head slightly and glared at her. He squirmed, but she didn't budge, so he cursed in defeat and slapped his head back onto the ground. Gaia unwrapped the mint and popped it into her mouth.

The woman on the other end of the line cleared her throat and then audibly shuffled through some papers. "Are you Gaia Moore?" she asked finally, sounding a bit chagrined.

"That's me," Gaia answered, rolling the candy around on her tongue.

There was a brief pause. A sigh. "He's expecting your call. I'll patch you through."

Gaia smiled slightly. It was kind of nice, being important among the incompetents. She looked up at the black sky while she waited on hold. Tim started to struggle a little, so she pushed down again, causing a strangled hacking sound to gurgle from his throat.

"Gaia?"

It was Charlie, along with a couple of friends, barreling out the back door. The wooden steps groaned like they wanted to buckle under the combined weight. Gaia checked them over to assess whether or not she could take them if they decided to defend their friend. They were big, but probably slow. She could deal, but that would mean putting down the phone. And just when things were getting good.

"What do you think you're doing?" Charlie spat, his

black eyes glimmering in the semidarkness. His raw-from-the-cold hands were clenched into fists.

"Charlie, thank Go—"

Gaia slammed her foot down again. She really had to pay more attention to keeping the captive silent.

The three guys lined up in front of her, holding their arms out slightly at their sides like a bunch of linebackers. Gaia could see their breath as it steamed from their mouths and noses in quick, short bursts. She could only hope they didn't know about Tim and his escapades. Maybe, just maybe, they'd be disgusted enough not to interfere.

"Sideburns Tim tried to rape me," Gaia said in a matter-of-fact tone. She held the phone out about an inch from her ear. "I'm in the process of turning him in."

A cloud of confusion settled onto Charlie's features, and he looked at his prone friend. His fists relaxed. "What?" he said, his brow a mass of wrinkles. "You . . . you tried to rape—"

In the middle of his sentence one of Charlie's sidekicks took off at a sprint, ripping open the back door so fast, he nearly took it off its hinges. Gaia heard a girl inside shout indignantly as he careened through the living room.

"Who was that?" she asked Charlie, raising her chin toward the back of the house.

"Chris Parker," Charlie answered, his face still drawn with shock.

"Detective Rodriguez," a voice snapped from the other end of the line.

"Yeah," Gaia said. "I have a rapist here by the name of Tim Racenello. And his accomplice is running up Horatio right now. His name's Chris Parker, and he has a really uneven buzz cut."

SAFE

Mary grinned when Detective Rodriguez picked up the phone and a surprised and indignant expression fell over his face like a curtain. He was definitely talking to Gaia. She was the only person in the world who inspired that exact reaction.

"Yes," the detective said, glancing at Mary from under his bushy eyebrows. "She's right here." He paused to listen and then turned in his chair so that one big, beefy shoulder was staring Mary in the face. She looked down at his gun in his leather shoulder holster, just below the ugly patch of sweat under his arm. She had a clear shot at the pistol. Not that she cared. But she wouldn't mind seeing his face if she stuck the barrel in it. He'd just spent fifteen minutes grilling her like she was the one who'd just kicked the shit out of someone for no reason.

"Yes, she told me the whole story," Rodriguez stage-whispered, his back hunching.

Not that he'd believed it.

"You have the perp there?" he asked, sitting back in his chair now. It creaked loudly in protest. Mary figured he'd decided there was no longer any point in keeping the truth from her. That her story was confirmed. That he was going to have to eat all his doubts with a shovel.

"We'll send someone over to pick him up," the detective said, making a few notes on a big yellow legal pad that was stained with old coffee rings. "Yes," he said, looking at Mary again. He almost looked like he wanted to hurt her. Some people just couldn't deal with being proven wrong. "Yes, I'll tell her." He paused and wiped a pudgy hand over his brow. "Thank you, Miss Moore."

He hung up the phone and let out a wet-sounding sigh, staring at the address he'd scrawled in front of him as he wiped his palms on his thighs.

"That's Ms.," Mary said with a cocky smile, tossing her curly red hair back from her face. The motion sent a pain through her skull, but she refused to wince.

"Huh?" Rodriguez asked.

"*Ms.* Moore," Mary repeated, crossing her arms over her chest and kicking out her legs. "You said Miss."

His face turned bright red, and for a second Mary thought he was going to reach out and strangle her, but a moment later he composed himself and ripped the page from his pad.

"Callahan!" he shouted, prompting a skinny little rookie in a pressed blue uniform to appear at his side like a hungry puppy. Rodriguez snapped the paper in the kid's face. "Take Robinson and go get this Racenello guy. He's at this address under the supervision of a Gaia Moore."

"Yes, sir," Callahan said, almost smiling as he took the paper and scurried off in search of his partner. Apparently, this was a big thing for him. Mary hoped Gaia didn't give him any grief.

But it wasn't her problem. Her problem right now was that sometime in the next hour or so, she'd have to face the guy who attacked her. At least see him as he was dragged in. A big part of her didn't want to see his face. She didn't want to match a person with the animal that had attacked her. She didn't want to look into those eyes.

Mary leaned back in her uncomfortable chair, every bit of her body aching. Still, somehow she couldn't help smiling. Under the supervision of Gaia Moore.

She liked the sound of that.

Even after spending the last hour in the police station, it was the first moment she'd felt safe since the attack.

NEVER SHOULD HAVE STARTED

Gaia watched, feeling detached, as the young officer pushed Tim's head down and half shoved him into the backseat of the squad car. It was the first real interaction she'd had with the police since the night Heather was slashed. The night everything about her was brought into question. The flashing red-and-blue lights should have signaled something good tonight. She'd caught the bad guy. Hopefully he'd be brought to justice.

Instead they just reminded her of what a general screwup she was. And she immediately thought of Sam.

He'd hated her after what happened to Heather.

Had anything really changed since then? Was she ever going to know?

"Gaia?"

She glanced at the ground to her left and saw Charlie's scuffed-yet-expensive brown loafers next to her sneakers. Her stomach responded with an angry twist. She pulled her hands up inside the sleeves of her sweater and blew into the wool, warming her fingers as the car pulled away.

"What?" she asked finally, when she realized he wasn't going to speak again without being prompted. Like she felt like putting in the effort right now.

"I just wanted you to know I had no idea what was going on with him," Charlie said, shoving his hands into the back pockets of his jeans. "I swear I would never—"

"What you did was just as bad," Gaia said coldly, staring across the street at a decaying garbage can. She was totally disgusted with him, but she was sure that if she looked into his pleading eyes, she'd be even more sick. She couldn't believe she'd actually thought this guy could be a friend. That she took up for him to Ed.

Ed. Gaia squeezed her eyes shut. God, she was such an idiot. She'd defended a sex fiend to her one and only friend and practically called Ed a liar. She had some serious explaining to do. Pronto.

"What do you mean?" Charlie said now, sliding over so he was standing in front of her. He tilted his head down to catch her eye, making her look at him. He looked just like a puppy dog sitting under the table, begging for scraps. Gaia wanted nothing more than to kick him in the face. She would have, too, if the police weren't still milling around, asking questions. "I didn't try to force you. You know that."

"I know," Gaia said, a cold edge in her voice. She lifted her chin slightly and stared him down. "But you would have taken points for me."

The surprise in his face was highlighted by the sheer embarrassment. He took a step back, studying her warily as if she might be a witch or a psychic or something. "Who told you?" he asked.

"It doesn't matter," she said, pulling her jacket more tightly around her body. "I have somebody I have to see." She bowed her head and started up the street, steeling herself against the cold breeze.

"Gaia," he called after her.

"We're done talking, Charlie," she said, just loudly enough for him to hear. "We never should have started in the first place."

A WINE-WORTHY VICTORY

Ella waited a good five minutes until she was sure Sam was gone. She'd never passed a more frustrating five minutes in her life. Every fiber of her being wanted to open the door, pull him inside, and seduce him as she so easily could.

But now wasn't the time. Not when she looked like a crazed lunatic and had just trashed her own house. Not her most attractive moment. Ella knew her limits.

Slowly she reached for the doorknob and pulled open the door. A little red box fell at her feet. Aw. A gift for Gaia. Ella almost puked from the sweetness of it all. She squatted with difficulty in her tight skirt and picked it up. When she shook it, it rattled noisily. Something with lots of pieces. Not jewelry. Sam obviously wasn't practiced in the art of wooing a girl. But then again, jewelry would be lost on Gaia. Almost everything of any importance was lost on Gaia.

Turning around, Ella whipped open the closet door and shoved the present way into the back. Behind her bagged furs and boxed hats. Behind all the stuff she'd never worn but absolutely had to have. She wasn't sure, at that moment, why she didn't just burn it. Destroy the evidence completely.

But knowing it was there was somehow comforting. It'd be a silent reminder of the day she first triumphed over Gaia.

Something she would undoubtedly do many more times to come.

Ella laughed quietly as she closed the door with a click. Her stiletto heel ground into a piece of broken glass, and she surveyed her earlier damage with an amused glance. She could deal with that another time. She strolled into the office and sat down at the computer, hacking quickly into the e-mail account George had set up for Gaia.

Within five seconds she'd found an e-mail from Sam. One saying thanks for an interesting Thanksgiving. So that was how Gaia had found out. Well, things were about to get interesting in a whole new way.

Ella clicked the reply button and typed a quick e-mail. She snickered at her own creativity. But then, Gaia was so awkward, writing like her was easy.

It was almost too easy.

FROM: gaia13@alloymail.com
TO: smoon@alloymail.com
TIME: 9:05 P.M.
RE: re: Thanksgiving
Sam—
Thanks for the gift. You should know I have a boyfriend. From before. It's not going to happen between you and me. Sorry I didn't tell you before.
—Gaia

When she was finished, Ella clicked send, then erased the e-mail from the list of sent mails so that Gaia wouldn't find it. Then she stood up and rubbed her hands together, feeling ever so much calmer than she had just fifteen minutes earlier.

This little victory definitely merited a glass of wine. Maybe even a large piece of cake.

Hell, she might even be nice to Gaia later.

In an alternate universe.

FORGIVENESS

Without the wind, the cold wasn't so bad. It was almost refreshing. It gave Gaia a chance to think. At first when she'd left Charlie's, she'd been determined to go see Sam. She'd even made it as far as the south end of the park. But when she'd looked out at the shadows, looked ahead to the arch, she'd realized there was something else she needed to do first.

Now, standing outside the apartment building, Gaia felt almost calm. Almost at peace. She knew she was where she was supposed to be. There was only one person in this damn city who really cared about her. Who'd put her in front of everyone else. A friend who would hang out by the door every day just to see her face.

That is, if she hadn't totally destroyed the whole thing.

"Hey."

Gaia turned and looked into Ed's guarded brown eyes.

"I just came to say you were right, almost," Gaia said quickly. "And I'm sorry."

The other amazing thing about Ed was it took him only seconds to forgive her.

TO: studentbody@villageschool.edu
EXCLUDE: all males
FROM: shred@alloymail.com
TIME: 9:05 P.M.
RE: payback
To whom it may concern:
There's a group of guys in our midst who have been
taking advantage of many members of our female
population. If you feel used, angry, even mildly
dissatisfied with this randy group of partyers, meet us
at the front office tomorrow morning at 8:30 sharp.
We'll help you get your revenge.
Rock on.
Shred

OPERATION EXPOSURE

"MY POINT IS, LADIES," HE SAID, NARROWING
HIS EYES AND LOOKING THEM OVER AS IF HE
WERE SIZING UP HIS PLATOON, "MAKE YOUR
COMMENTS BRIEF, AND MAKE THEM STING."

GOAT CHEESE

"First of all, I'd like to thank everyone for coming," Ed said, maneuvering his chair in front of the group of five girls who had responded to his semicryptic schoolwide e-mail. He glanced up at Gaia, who stood as inconspicuously as possible with the others, and flashed her a smile. "I've managed to lie my way into approved use of the PA system for a few minutes this morning, but once the administration figures out what we're doing, you can bet they'll be banging down that door before you can say Operation Exposure."

He earned a few small laughs and giggles, so he paused to bask in the approval. Until Gaia grunted at him, eyeing the clock.

"My point is, ladies," he said, narrowing his eyes and looking them over as if he were sizing up his platoon, "make your comments brief, and make them sting."

He nodded at Gaia, who walked over to the door of the small auxiliary office and stood in front of it like a bouncer at a bar on Canal Street. For now they had the room to themselves, but Gaia was their only line of defense should Principal Hickey decide to come barging in. She wasn't going to beat him up or anything, but she did have some delay tactics in mind. Ones she wouldn't share with Ed, of course.

"Who's up first?" Ed asked, glancing at each of five wary

faces. Chrissy Margolis bit her lip and glanced at the others, then stood, pulling down on her batik print skirt.

"I'll go," she said, her face disturbingly pale.

Ed smiled reassuringly, picked up the PA mike, and flipped the switch. The clock read 8:42 A.M. Just about the entire student body should be milling around the halls right now, exchanging last minute homework and gabbing about last night's *Modern Family* plot. It was perfect timing.

"Can I have your attention, please?" Ed recited into the microphone. "My name is Ed Fargo, and I'm here to talk to you about a very insidious plague that's running rampant in our school. It calls itself the Stud Club, if you can believe it, and the guys who hold memberships think they're pretty damn suave." He glanced over at Gaia, who rolled her eyes but was obviously concentrating to keep from smiling. "But I have some women here who would like to set the record straight," Ed finished.

Looking up at Chrissy's face, Ed had a sudden logic flash. "You'll understand in a moment why I choose to withhold their names."

As he handed the microphone up to Chrissy, her expression was all about relief. She lifted her chin, tossed back her curly hair, and cleared her throat.

"I'd just like everyone to know that Josh Talbot loses more saliva when he kisses than my dog produces in a year."

The girls behind her laughed, and she handed the microphone off to Gina Waters, who suddenly looked like she had attitude to spare. Ed wouldn't want to be on the receiving end of this one. Gina grasped the microphone as if it were a relay race baton, her knuckles turning white as she brought the mike to her mouth.

"My message is for Charlie Salita. Charlie, my friend, you last about as long as a biscuit in a dog kennel."

She bowed to the applause from the peanut gallery and gave the mike to a scrawny little girl who couldn't have been more than a freshman. It made Ed's stomach twist in a hundred directions to think someone had taken advantage of a girl so frail.

She cleared her throat demurely before speaking. "Charlie Salita . . . ," she said, smirking slightly and looking up at Gina, "wouldn't know what to do with his tongue if it came with an instruction manual."

Gina let out a cheer of approval and high-fived the girl, who was giggling crazily at her own audacity. Gaia even cracked a smile, and Ed couldn't help thinking that it looked like Gaia was agreeing with the frosh. So she *had* kissed Charlie. Ick. Ed's life couldn't possibly get more unfair.

The freshman held the microphone out at the same instant the doorknob started to rattle. Ed's heart jumped and started racing at a pace that couldn't possibly be healthy. He shot Gaia a questioning look.

"Keep going," Gaia said, glancing at the lock. "They definitely have a key."

"When Chris Parker isn't sucking in, he has a gut that small children could use as a trampoline," the next girl said quickly, her eyes flashing with triumph as she passed on the mike.

Ed could hear the jangling of an overstuffed key ring outside the office door. His heart was in his throat. At this point lifelong detention was a given—he just wanted all of the girls to get in their insults before they got busted.

Mara Trauth grabbed the microphone, watching the door from the corner of her eye. It started to open, and Gaia grabbed the knob, slamming it closed again and using all her weight to pull against it. "Come on," Gaia urged through clenched teeth.

"That's your delay tactic?" Ed hissed, glaring at her.

"Now you understand why I didn't want to share it," Gaia deadpanned.

Ed turned his attention to Mara, who didn't seem to be breathing. "Um . . . uh . . ."

He hit full panic mode when he realized she was shaking and her hands were sweating profusely. She looked at him wide-eyed, like she was asking for help, but Ed had no idea what he could do for her.

"It's okay," he said, going for the calming-guidance-counselor tone. "Just say whatever comes to your mind."

Swallowing hard, Mara took in a shaky breath. "Dan Swarski smells like year-old goat cheese."

Her brow knitted, and she looked at Ed. "Was that okay?"

Ed nodded with a grin just as the door flew open and Principal Hickey burst in with his army of Village School rent-a-cops. The man looked like he'd just eaten a plateful of red-hot chili peppers.

"My office," he said with a growl. "Now."

They were big-time busted, but as Ed looked around at the gratified faces of the women around him, he knew it was worth it.

He only wished Heather had joined in on the fun.

WAITING FOR ED

Heather licked the tip of her pinky and smoothed the end of her left eyebrow, leaning in close to the scratched-up mirror in the school bathroom. As always, her exterior was calm and flawless, but inside, her heart was pounding like a dance club bass beat.

And for the first time in ages, it was because she was waiting for Ed.

She had something she needed to say to him, and just thinking about what he'd done that morning—what he'd done for her—made her pulse do strange things. So here she was, hovering in the deserted bathroom across the way from the detention hall, waiting for Ed without looking like she was waiting for him.

When she heard his wheelchair in the hall, her breath caught momentarily, and she shook her head at her reflection. There was definitely something wrong with her. Something deep-seated and possibly pathological. But there was no use analyzing it. Right now, she had a mission.

Shaking her hair back from her face, Heather swung open the door and walked out into the hallway just before Ed turned his chair into the detention hall. What a coincidence.

"Heather," Ed said. She was sure there was a hint of excitement in his voice, just a tad.

"Ed," she said, totally surprised to see him. "What's up?" She smoothed down the front of her white button-down shirt and half smiled.

"Nothing," Ed said, glancing into the classroom. He moved down the hall slightly, out of sight of anyone inside, and Heather followed. "How are you?" Ed asked.

"I'm okay," Heather said nonchalantly. "Listen, I've been

meaning to thank you for what you did this morning," she said in a whisper.

Ed grinned. "Charlie really got the brunt of it, didn't he?" he said, completely satisfied with himself.

Heather smirked and crossed her arms over her chest. "Yeah, he did." Her heart was still racing, and it brought a blush to her face. She was heading into dangerous territory. If he noticed anything was different about her, there would be no going back. "So, anyway," she said. "Thanks. For everything."

"You're welcome." Ed said seriously, lacing his fingers together in front of him. "I didn't do it for you, you know," he said, a flash of mischief in his eyes.

Heather smiled back. "Yeah, I know," she said with a laugh. "I'll see ya," she said, and turning on her heel, she started off down the hall, her head holding itself high for the first time all week.

She knew exactly why Ed had done what he did. Why he'd gone to all that trouble to round up those girls and give them a chance to skewer the assholes who had used them. The assholes who had used *her*. He'd done it because he was a good person. And he had a good heart.

And because he still cared about her.

A LITTLE RED BOX

Gaia had actually left school feeling pretty damn good about herself. Not only had she helped Ed expose the Stud Club boys that morning, but she'd not had one evil thought about Heather all day, and she'd spent the entire time in detention thinking solely in Russian. All in all, in Gaia terms, it was a perfect school day.

But by the time she walked up the steps at George and Ella's that evening, Gaia was back on self-deprecation mode. And it was all Sam Moon's fault.

Okay, so she wasn't exactly experienced in this stuff, but she hadn't stopped obsessing about Thanksgiving once since he'd e-mailed her. Well, except for those brief moments of focused hatred on Charlie and Tim and beating the crap out of people.

Gaia sighed as she closed the heavy wooden door behind her. She leaned back against its cool surface and stared at the foyer. Didn't he know that a person couldn't send a cryptic e-mail like that and not follow up on it? Didn't he know what he was putting her through?

"You're being a whiny girl, Gaia," she told herself, pushing away from the door. "You're annoying me."

After all, she hadn't contacted him, either. Yeah, she'd skulked around the park, staked out his dorm, triple checked her e-mail, but she hadn't called him or written to him or buzzed his room. This was an equal opportunity non-relationship.

Gaia pulled her messenger bag off over her head and dropped it on the floor under the now conspicuously empty hall table. She briefly wondered what Ella had done with all her hideous knickknacks but then decided not to waste brain space on it. She should just count herself lucky they were gone and hope they weren't replaced by something even more ceramic-y and pink.

Opening the door to the closet, Gaia automatically reached for the empty hanger she always left behind, but her hand hit a nylon jacket instead. She looked at the rack and groaned. Someone had taken her hanger. She opened the door wider and started to search, pushing aside a few of Ella's musty fur coats until she found a bent and abused wire hanger.

As she fought to pull it out, her eyes fell on a little red box stuffed onto a shelf between a hatbox and a stack of old magazines. Gaia just looked at it for a moment, wondering if it was some Christmas gift for George from Ella. She could just imagine the kind of present Ella would buy for her husband. Probably a copy of *Eight-Minute Abs* or one of those spray-on hair kits.

Gaia rolled her eyes, slung her jacket over the hanger, and slammed the closet door.

She was sure she wouldn't be getting anything for Christmas this year, at least not from her dad or her uncle or anyone who mattered. But as she grabbed her bag and trudged up the stairs, she realized she didn't really want gifts, anyway.

As pathetic as it was, all she wanted was for Sam to call.

SAM'S CALL

The phone was ringing when she walked into her bedroom, and she dropped her things onto her bed, diving for the receiver.

"Hello?" she said, breathless after climbing about a million stairs. She sprawled out on her stomach across her comforter.

"Hey."

Her heart skipped crazily, and she rolled over onto her back, a slow smile spreading across her face.

"I was wondering if I'd ever hear from you," she said.

"I know," he said slowly. "I'm sorry it's been a while. You don't know how sorry."

"That's okay," Heather said, grinning for real. "I'm just happy to hear your voice."

WANT MORE?
HERE'S A PEEK AT
THE NEXT FEARLESS BOOK:

REBEL

BY FRANCINE PASCAL

GAIA

Honesty is a funny thing. People always tell you that they want you to be honest with them. But they're lying. Nobody wants that. Honesty sucks. That's why the word *honesty* is always preceded by other words, like *brutal* and *painful*.

I keep all of my secrets for just that reason. They'd hurt too much if anybody knew. And I don't mean they would just hurt the people I told. I mean they would hurt me, too.

So I keep them to myself. And it's not all that hard. After all, dishonesty kind of runs in my family.

Just look at my father. He ditched me without ever telling me where he was going or why—and he did it on the worst night of my life. And my uncle has apparently been watching over me my entire life, but he never even bothered to introduce himself. He only shows up when I'm about to get shot in the head or stabbed by some crazed serial killer. Great, thanks. But can I take care of myself.

Come to think of it, everybody I know seems to hide the truth somehow. Sam. Ella. Even Mary. In fact, the only person I can think of who *doesn't* hide the truth is Ed Fargo. He's honest about everything.

But as far as keeping secrets goes, I have to admit, I really take first prize. I've never told Sam how I feel about him. And that's just scratching the surface. I've never told him or anyone else about my total inability to feel fear. Or why I'm trained to kick almost anyone's ass in about three seconds flat. Or why I'm stuck with George and Ella.

And here's the biggest one of all. I've never told anyone about my dad or about my mother's death. But I have a good reason. If I were totally honest with my friends about my past . . . well, I'd put their lives in danger. I already have. More than once.

Maybe everyone has a reason for hiding the truth. After all, honesty seems to create more problems than it solves. It can hurt. It can even kill. I guess that's why people are afraid of the truth.

But I wouldn't know about that. I'm not afraid of anything.

HER KIND
OF GAME

HIS BODY WENT LIMP. HE WOULDN'T TRY
TO MOVE. SHE KNEW IT. HE'D TASTED
AN EXCRUCIATING PAIN. . . .

THE THREE WISE MEN

Skeletons.

That's exactly what the trees in Washington Square Park looked like at this time of night: spindly, grotesque skeletons. At least that was how they looked to Gaia Moore. It was amazing how a place could feel like an amusement park one month and a cemetery the next. But that was New York City. It was constantly changing, and often not for the better. That could be said of a lot of things, actually—Gaia's life included.

"Why does this park totally die right before Christmas?" Mary suddenly asked of nobody in particular.

Gaia smirked. One of the coolest things about Mary Moss was that she had an uncanny knack for saying exactly what Gaia was thinking. She also shared the same intolerance for bullshit.

"Because there's no action down here," Ed said. His breath made little white clouds in the frigid December air. "The real action is in Midtown. I say we buy some little red suits and pom-pom hats, then go volunteer to be elves outside some big megastore, like Macy's."

"I'm too tall to be an elf," Gaia replied.

"Me too," Mary added.

Ed shrugged. Dead leaves crunched under his wheelchair. "Then we'll get some fake beards for you guys. Instead of being elves we'll be the three wise men."

Gaia had to laugh. The three wise men. That was funny. A wheelchair-bound ex–skate rat, a female ex–coke addict, and . . . *her.* Whatever Gaia was. She probably *could* pass for a man. Easily. She wasn't beautiful and skinny like Mary. Nope. Forget a wise man; Gaia had the body of a prize-fighter. She didn't even need the beard. All she needed was a little five o'clock shadow. Now that she thought about it, the only remotely feminine aspect of her appearance was her unkempt mane of blond hair. But there was probably a direct correlation between one's freakish looks and the swirling mess inside one's head, wasn't there?

"I guess it's too cold for any Christmas pageantry, any-way," Ed mumbled.

Ed was right. It was too cold for anything. Even chess. Gaia had never seen the park this quiet or deserted. Usually *some* die-hard chess fanatic was out at the tables, trying to hustle a game, no matter what the weather. Like Mr. Haq. Or her old friend Zolov. But Gaia hadn't seen a whole lot of Zolov since he'd been slashed by those neo-Nazi idiots who used to hang around the miniature Arc de Triomphe on the north side.

She almost *wished* a few skinheads were around just so the place would feel more like home. In fact, she wouldn't mind at all if one of them jumped out of the shadows and tried to attack her. She'd walked this park many times for that exact reason. But seeking combat wasn't a group activity. It was something she did on her own. In secrecy. Besides, at this moment she wasn't really craving a good fight. No, what she really missed right now were the sounds and smells of months past: the gurgling of the fountain, the laughter of the NYU students, the sweet odor of roasted peanuts. . . .

Mary abruptly stopped in her tracks.

"You know what? We *should* do something to liven things up." She adjusted her black wool cap and brushed a few wayward red curls out of her eyes. "It's winter break. We're free. I say we create a little excitement of our own."

Gaia met Mary's gaze. She knew that gleam in Mary's green eyes all too well. It whispered: *Let's do something crazy.* And in a way, Gaia could empathize. After all, courting danger was one of her favorite pastimes, too. But Mary's reckless tendencies led down a much more self-destructive path than Gaia's own.

Then again, some people might argue that deliberately looking for fights was a hell of a lot worse than snorting a big fat line of white powder up your nose. But Gaia had never paid any attention to other people's opinions. Ever.

"Why don't I like the sound of that at all?" Ed muttered.

Mary laughed. "Come on, you guys. We're here in New York City. By the looks of things, we basically have the place to ourselves." She waved her hands at the empty benches and frozen pavement. "I mean, everyone else is holed up in their apartments or vacationing in the Hamptons or doing whatever it is that normal people do."

"Your point being?" Ed asked.

"That I'm bored!" Mary cried. "I don't do drugs anymore, so I have to find *something* to do, right?" She laughed.

Gaia kept quiet. Unfortunately, the joke wasn't very funny. Mary had only been off cocaine since Thanksgiving, and Gaia knew enough about drugs to know that a lot of addicts relapsed in those first precarious weeks of clean living. Especially when they were bored.

"I don't know," Ed said quietly. He fidgeted in his wheelchair, tapping his gloved fingers on the armrests. "If you ask me, a little boredom is a good thing. Anyway, aren't we supposed to be going to Gaia's house right now?"

Ed was right. They *were* on their way to the Nivens' house (Gaia never thought of it as her own, and she never would), but there was really nothing to do there. Gaia shook her head. Poor Ed. Part of her agreed with him. Ever since he'd met Gaia, Ed's life had been a little too exciting. Kidnappings. Serial killers. Random acts of violence. Part of her wanted to protect him—to shield him from the danger that surrounded her at all times.

But the other part of her—she couldn't ignore—was just as bored as Mary. Besides, if Mary was looking for a way to keep her mind off drugs, Gaia was all for it. After all, Mary had appointed her to help out with getting involved in "good, clean fun." Whatever that was.

"What do you have in mind?" Gaia asked Mary.

Mary raised her eyebrows. "A little game," she said. She smiled down at Ed, then back at Gaia. "What do you guys think about truth or dare?"

Ed snickered. "Ooh. That sounds *really* exciting. Can we play spin the bottle next?"

Mary ignored him. "Gaia?" she prompted. "What do you say?"

"Sure," Gaia said. It actually *did* sound exciting—at least to her. The fact of the matter was that she had never played truth or dare before. *Or* spin the bottle. Or any other games that normal kids would have played, the ones who didn't have twisted secret agents for fathers.

But that was the great thing about hanging out with Mary. She introduced Gaia to all kinds of normal experiences. And always in a very abnormal way.

WOOF, WOOF

Ed Fargo's biggest problem wasn't what most people might think: namely, that his legs would never work again. No. He'd learned to deal with that. Or at least *accept* it. It was just another part of his life now. An unpleasant part, sure—like suffering through history class, or seeing his ex-girlfriend Heather Gannis every single day, or forcing himself to smile back at all the phony bastards who pretended to take pity on him. But it wasn't *torture*. No, Ed Fargo's biggest problem was that he couldn't say no to Gaia Moore.

That was torture.

Even more torturous (or pathetic) was that he was completely, utterly, one hundred percent in love with her. And she had absolutely no clue.

On more than one occasion he'd almost mustered the courage to tell her. He'd even gone so far as to compose a few e-mails and letters, but he always tore them up or deleted them at the last minute. A voice inside inevitably reminded him that it was better to live with delusional hope than crushing rejection.

God. One of these days he was really going to have to shut that voice up.

But for now, it looked like he was resigned to following Gaia around like a dog and catering to her every whim.

Unfortunately, this frequently involved getting into fights, or ducking bullets, or discovering secrets that were probably best left buried.

As every lame-ass soap opera was quick to point out, love sucked.

"So what do you say we get started?" Mary asked.

"Can we at least play at Gaia's house?" Ed groaned. His teeth started chattering. It wasn't from cold, either. The park didn't exactly fill him with a sense of safety and well-being. He'd almost been *murdered* here. He peered into the shadowy tangle of barren tree limbs that lined the path on either side. "We're all freezing our butts off, in case you forgot."

Mary shook her head. "I say we start here. Gaia?"

"No better time than the present," Gaia agreed.

It figured neither of them would listen to him. And he wasn't about to leave without them, either. He really *was* a dog. Woof, woof.

"So who goes first?" he grumbled.

"We'll shoot for it," Mary said. "Rock, scissors, paper." She stuck her hand behind her back. "On three . . ."

Great, Ed thought. He hated rock, scissors, paper almost as much as truth or dare. With his luck, he'd probably lose— and they would dare him to strip naked and streak up Fifth Avenue in his wheelchair.

Mary smiled. "One . . . two . . . three . . ."

Ed extended a fist: rock. It always seemed safest,

although somebody smarter—like Gaia—might disagree. His eyes flashed to Gaia's hand. *Ha!* Scissors. He glanced at Mary. Rock, too. Unbelievable.

Gaia Moore had actually lost.

It was probably the first time he'd seen Gaia lose at anything. He couldn't help but smile. Maybe this wouldn't be so bad after all. It would be nice to see her do something ridiculous, wouldn't it?

"Oh, Jesus." Gaia moaned.

"Now, don't be a sore loser," Mary teased, winking at Ed.

"So which is it?" Ed asked gleefully. "Truth or dare?"

Gaia pursed her lips. "Dare. And you don't have to ask me again. It's dare for the duration of the game."

Mary clapped. "Perfect."

She turned back toward the arch. A solitary figure was sitting on one of the benches, wrapped in a scarf with a hat pulled low over his eyes—a skinny and grizzled older man Ed had never seen before. Ed's excitement began to fade. He could see where this was going. He should have known Gaia would never pick truth. He also should have known Mary would dare Gaia to take some inane, meaningless risk. Why did the two of them have to *create* trouble? Why did they have to pluck it out of thin air? He held his breath as Mary raised her hand and pointed at the figure.

"I dare you to go kiss that guy," she said.

THE GOOD THING
ABOUT RATS

Truth or dare was right up Gaia's alley. She could tell right away that she would be able to add it to that short list of loves that made her life tolerable. Everything else on the list was food related. Well, she loved a good chess match. And Sam. But there was no point in dwelling on *that*.

What she really loved were diversions.

She loved anything that distracted her from the dismal specifics of her existence. And kissing some random stranger in the park certainly qualified as a diversion, didn't it?

She walked toward him on the darkened path, waiting for him to look up and notice her. But he didn't move. He was slumped on the bench. His legs were spread in front of him, his skeletal chest rising and falling in the even rhythm of sleep. Icy puffs of breath drifted away from his open mouth. Gaia's nose wrinkled. *Yuck*. Maybe he was drunk. Or *something*. She'd be sure to ask him if she could just kiss him on the forehead—

Wait a second.

He wasn't asleep. He was just pretending.

Only someone with Gaia's acute awareness in sizing up a potential opponent could detect the subtle clues of consciousness: the exaggerated way he exhaled, the concen-

A shocked whimper escaped his lips. His hold on her instantly loosened. Quick as a flash, she clasped his right hand against her left forearm. His eyes bulged. With a single deft maneuver she flipped him off the bench to the ground at her feet—flat on his back.

"What the hell?" he gasped.

He tried to wriggle free, but Gaia held his hand fast. She bent it back slightly.

"Ow!" he screamed.

His body went limp. He wouldn't try to move. She knew it. He'd tasted an excruciating pain. That was the beauty of this particular grip. She could snap his wrist in a second, but there was no need to injure him. It was the essence of true kung fu and one of the first lessons her father had taught her: the art of intimidation—the art of threatening torture without actually having to inflict it more than once.

"Now, you aren't going to try this with anyone else, are you?" Gaia asked calmly.

He didn't answer. He gazed up at her, wild-eyed. His breath came quickly. Even though the temperature was below freezing, she could see beads of sweat forming on his bulbous nose.

"Are you?" she persisted.

"No!" he grunted, cringing. "Come on! Lemme go! Lemme go, you bitch!"

Gaia frowned. "What did you call me?"

"Nothing." His eyes squeezed shut. "Just lemme go," he pleaded. "I'm sorry. . . ."

"That's better," she said. "Now I'll let you go. Just as soon as you promise me you won't try to grab some other girl who—"

"Gaia!" Ed's voice sliced through the night air.

Oh, brother. Once again her self-appointed Superman was swooping in to save the day. Why did Ed always try to get involved? He was undeniably brave and undeniably sweet, but he must have had a short-term memory problem. He'd seen her kick a dozen scumbags' asses, and *this* situation was certainly under control—yet he was still racing down the path as fast as the chair would carry him, with Mary close on his heels. They made quite a rescue party. She almost smiled.

"Come on," the guy at her feet murmured one last time.

Gaia glanced back down at him. "Fine," she said in a soft voice. "But if I ever see you in this park again, I'll think twice about letting you get off so easy." Her tone was very matter-of-fact, as if she were explaining the rules of chess. "Got it?"

He nodded. His face was etched with what Gaia knew, intellectually, was fear. She let go of his hands, then leaned over and lifted him by the lapels of his coat. Jesus. He even was heavier than he looked. She shoved him out on the path and watched as he scurried away.

A rat, she realized. That's exactly what he looked like. A big, fat rat.

trated stillness of his eyelids. So he was lying in wait. Setting a trap. The asshole was waiting to attack her.

A familiar electric energy shot through Gaia's body—the jolt that always came in place of fear. This was going to be even more fun than she had expected. How come she'd never thought of playing this game before? It was tailor-made for somebody with Gaia's unique condition: somebody who felt only a sublime emptiness in the face of any threat.

Let's see what you can do, she silently taunted as she stepped in front of him.

She placed her feet squarely between his own. A smile played on her lips. Yes, she could see the tension building in his arms as they lay at his sides. His breathing quickened—just a little. He was getting ready to make his move. To take her by surprise.

Gaia glanced back at Mary and Ed. They were a good thirty yards away, silhouetted against the leafless trees. Their expressions were unreadable in the darkness. She gave them a quick thumbs-up. Then she caught a whiff of bourbon and winced. Disgusting. But she had to get it over with. Otherwise she would lose—and losing was something she was not prepared to do. Fearlessness had to serve *some* purpose, even if it was for a game. And besides, this jerk needed to be taught a lesson. Gaia *lived* for teaching bullies lessons. She was committed.

"Excuse me, sir?" Gaia bent over to look into his eyes.

Two hands clasped around her wrists.

"Gotcha!" the man cried.

She almost laughed. "Give me a break," she mumbled disappointedly. It figured he would grab her by the arms. It was the most obvious and idiotic form of attack. But she'd let him enjoy the illusion of control for a second or two. His thick fingers dug through the fibers of her coat.

"Now what do you think you're doing?" he asked.

She didn't answer. Instead she just gazed into his haggard face. Talk about disgusting. His skin looked like an oil field. He must have been fifty years old. His beady black eyes were rheumy with alcohol.

"You wanna play with me?" he hissed, laughing. He gave her arms a sudden yank, pulling her closer. "Well, it's your lucky night, sugar. I'm gonna warm you up. I'm gonna give you something you'll never forget."

Gaia rolled her eyes. She only had to remember creeps like Charlie Salita and his rapist friend, Sideburns Tim, to feel a surge of anger. But this guy was just too pathetic for any kind of major confrontation. And even though she wanted to prolong this encounter—just for the sake of excitement—the stink of this guy's breath and body were enough to make her puke. Too bad. Sighing, she stamped the heel off her combat boot on the man's toes.

"What the—"

But one who'd learned never to proposition another teenage girl again.

Yes. The good thing about rats was that they could be easily trained. All they needed was a little negative reinforcement.

"Gaia?" Ed gasped breathlessly, skidding to a halt. "Are you all right?"

She turned around. "I think I'll live," she said, trying not to smile.

"Holy shit!" Mary cried delightedly. She doubled over beside Ed. Her lungs were heaving. "That was *awesome*. What did he try to do to you, anyway?"

Gaia shrugged. "He told me he'd give me something I'd never forget," she replied. But as she spoke the words, a wave of exhaustion swept over her.

Without thinking, she slumped down on the park bench.

Her face twisted in a scowl. It was ridiculous: Even after a fight as pathetic as *that* one, she still felt completely drained. She supposed she should learn to expect it. Her body was like a balloon. In combat it would fill up with adrenaline and strength— and then *pop!*—it would deflate. Instantly. For a few minutes she would be unable to move. And somehow this peculiar handicap always managed to slip her mind when she was fighting someone. Maybe because she'd never understood it.

"Are you *sure* you're all right?" Ed asked, peering at her closely.

"Fine," she whispered. She shook her head.

After a few seconds her strength began to return. It flowed slowly into her arms and legs, filling them like a thick potion.

She dusted off her hands and stood.

She found herself smiling again.

In spite of the stench, kissing that guy had been a lot of fun. In a very weird way. It had been very diverting, too. She hadn't thought about Sam or her father or any other stupid crap at all during those precious few moments. Truth or dare was *definitely* her kind of game. It helped her to forget. And forgetting was a very, very good thing.

"So," she said, glancing at Ed and Mary. "Whose turn is it now?"

ABOUT THE AUTHOR

New York Times bestselling author Francine Pascal is one of the most popular fiction writers for teenagers today and the creator of numerous bestselling series, including Fearless and Sweet Valley High, which was also made into a television series. She has written several YA novels, including *My First Love and Other Disasters*, *My Mother Was Never a Kid*, and *Love & Betrayal & Hold the Mayo*. Her latest novel is *Sweet Valley Confidential: Ten Years Later*. She lives in New York City and France.

SECRETS. REVENGE.
BUT BEST OF ALL, BLOOD.

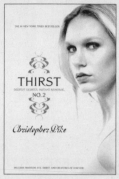

#1 *NEW YORK TIMES* BESTSELLING AUTHOR
CHRISTOPHER PIKE

FROM SIMON PULSE | PUBLISHED BY SIMON & SCHUSTER
TEEN.SIMONANDSCHUSTER.COM

SIMONTEEN

Simon & Schuster's **Simon Teen**
e-newsletter delivers current updates on
the hottest titles, exciting sweepstakes, and
exclusive content from your favorite authors.

Visit **TEEN.SimonandSchuster.com** to
sign up, post your thoughts, and find out what
every avid reader is talking about!

ATHENEUM FICTION

Margaret K. McElderry Books

SIMON & SCHUSTER BFYR

SIMON PULSE